THE REAL FAKE FIANCÉ

A SWEET, SMALL TOWN ROMANTIC COMEDY

LOVE IN MIRROR VALLEY
BOOK 3

SARA JANE WOODLEY

Dee & Noah art by
VECTORSMARKET

 ELEVENTH AVENUE
PUBLISHING

1

DEE

Go on a date with that hot plant guy, they said. It'll be fun, they said.

Well, *they* were categorically *wrong.*

And even worse—*they* are not responding whatsoever to my glaringly obvious, previously-agreed-upon signal to get me the fudge out of here.

Once again, I scratch the tip of my nose. I must surely look like Rudolf by now. The fact that Oliver (he introduced himself as "Ollie", but I've started to mentally refer to him by what I assume to be his full name) hasn't noticed should be a sign that this date is not going well. He hasn't moved his gaze from the screen above my head in the past ten minutes. Which *would* have given me ample time to escape, had any of my so-called "protective detail"—also known as my community volleyball team—dared glance my way.

I scratch my nose again, delicately, this time, as my skin is going raw. I can only imagine the jokes Noah would be making if he were here right now to witness this...

Christmas coming in July this year, Dee-bug?

About time we get you tied up to the sleigh for the North

Pole.

Can you ask Santa if I'm on the naughty or nice list?

Forget the sunscreen again?

Okay, so that last one has nothing to do with the world's most famous (fictional) Arctic dweller, but rather refers to the *one* time in high school that I forgot to wear sunscreen to a springtime volleyball game (when the sun was at its highest and brightest) and I lobster-ed the heck out of myself. Sadly, I'm not blessed with the easily-tanned complexion of my older sister Daisy. Nor do I have the seemingly sunburn-proof skin that belongs to our dad.

Nope. We have one distant family member from Ireland, and I managed to inherit that fair skin that immediately burns bright red in the sun.

My skin was on fire for less than a week, but Noah still finds a way to slip that little memory into conversation on a bi-monthly basis. As if it wasn't bad enough that he was made to sunscreen my shoulders and upper back every single day for the rest of that season—a truly humiliating experience to have to go through in front of your brand-new varsity volleyball team when you're 14 and on the brink of womanhood.

But Noah's mom simply would not let me step foot into the sunlight again without proper coverage, and I simply would not let anyone else touch me. I mean, my team was made up entirely of prepubescent boys poised somewhere between the "girls have cooties" and "ohmygoodness bra straps" phases, and the thought of any of them rubbing my shoulders gave me the heebie jeebies.

That left Noah. My best friend, prank buddy, and sunscreen-applier forevermore.

"So, Oliv—Ollie," I correct myself, taking a chip loaded with cheese, bell peppers, meat and sauce from the plate, and sticking a non-loaded chip on top. Noah calls this a nacho sandwich, and it's delicious. There's a light sheen on the surface of the sour cream from the amount of time we've been stuck on this date: approximately fifteen years. "You moved here for a work contract?"

Oliver drags his light green eyes to land on me. He really does have nice eyes. They're covered by round, golden framed glasses perched above an adorably small nose. He scratches his jawline, which is peppered with a light blond scruff, like he's seriously considering my question. My inner pessimist says that he's trying to remember what I asked. "Yup, at the greenhouses in Summer Lakes. It's a little far, but the rental I found here in Mirror Valley was too good to pass up."

I nod. Finally, some common ground. If there's anything I can relate to, it's the importance of having a good home base. There are so many things that are impossible to control in life, but the place you choose for yourself? You can always rely on that. "That's great that you found somewhere nice to stay."

"Well, that... and the rent's cheap. Like *dirt* cheap." He chuckles, his eyes never wavering from the game on the tv screen as he bites into another chicken wing. I wonder, if I was to start hopping around the bar whilst singing "Cotton-Eyed Joe", whether he'd acknowledge me then. "I mean, I make good money. Could probably afford to buy a place out here on my bonus alone if I wanted to." Then, he quickly adds, "Probably won't, though. Money is one of those things... you can never have too much!"

He lets out a surprisingly loud honk of a laugh and I smile thinly in return. I appreciate fiscal responsibility as much as the next person, but I can only imagine what Noah would have to say to that.

Granted, the man has no need to worry about finances and is, generally speaking, the least responsible person I know. But Noah tends to have a "give what you have" approach when it comes to his money.

Speaking of Noah, he would be picking up what I'm putting down in a second. I would even forgive the Rudolf jokes. He's on our volleyball team as well, but he had to miss tonight's viewing of the game (and a front row seat to my nose-scratching party) because of his own date. With Yanica from Longhaven, a town a few miles from here. Noah's had to start fishing outside the pond given that he's dated basically every eligible woman in Mirror Valley.

Though he's been on a couple of dates with Yanica now. I'll have to tease him about things getting serious.

"Well, cheap rent is... nice," I say to Oliver unenthusiastically.

"I know, right?"—*munch, munch*—"I put my place in Chicago on a new house-sharing platform"—*munch*—"you would hardly believe the amount of money I'm making. I can show you my portfolio later if you want some tips on how to get into the real estate game."

"Great," is all I can muster.

Meanwhile, all I can think about is what Daisy always says: *"You've got to get out there, Dee. Date. See what you like and don't like. Make lists."* I can conclusively say that Oliver is *not* going to be on my list.

But that was *her* strategy when she was single. Mine has always been to just... not.

Not date, not be in relationships. Just a no to all of it.

It's not that I don't believe in love, or think that relationships are doomed, or take the defeatist "50% of marriages end in divorce, so what's the point anyway?" stance. I'm not that cynical. It's more that I never felt the urge to date. I grew up with boys, and I've never seen the appeal in pairing myself up with one for the next seventy years. I like my life, just as it is. Working hard (as a software developer), playing hard (at volleyball), and spending free evenings on my living room couch watching movies with Noah and Bruce (my cat), or at his place gorging ourselves on extra-cheesy pizzas and extra-stuffed California rolls.

I should specify that by "free evenings", I mean *Noah's* free evenings. The guy doesn't get a lot of them, what with all of his dating. Though he usually calls me after a date or comes over unannounced to watch the end of a movie with me.

Daisy says this is weird. I've never thought anything of it. It's just what we do.

At that moment, Amir—our team's libero and (hopefully) my saving grace—glances in my direction.

It's a quick action, barely a side-eye.

But I jump on it like an overexcited pug jumps onto a turkey sandwich that fell on the floor.

My hand whips up, fingers aloft in prime nose-scratching position...

And I whack myself in the face.

"Oof!" I exclaim, shocked at what just happened. In the corner of my eye, Amir snorts and hits Jarrod in the arm, pointing my way and whispering. They both burst into cackles.

Yeah, laugh it up, guys. No damsel in distress over here or anything.

Here I was, thinking I was being smart inviting the team out with me tonight on this "protecto-date", as I'm calling it. Oliver has no idea that I'm being accompanied by four brawny men, but that would defeat the purpose, right? You just never know who you might meet online—Tinder Swindlers, Craigslist cannibals and the like.

Hence why Amir, Jarrod, Parker and Finn are all here to rescue me if needed.

Something they are sorely failing at, by the way. Oliver

is clearly not a serial killer nor Craigslist cannibal. But it's the thought that counts, you know?

And sadly, my protective detail are as invested in the game tonight as Oliver is (I am too, mind you, though I've basically given up on watching at this point).

Right on cue, Oliver lets out a booming cheer while the rest of the bar boos at whatever happened on the tv screen above my head. And just like that, I've lost Amir and Jarrod to mutters and grumbles over a loss that I wish I got to see.

I wince, both from the pain and embarrassment of hitting myself in the face, but also because I'm currently sitting across from the only person in the entire bar who is loudly and shamelessly cheering for the *other team*.

Noah really got me good tonight.

"Can I get you guys anything else?" Tony, McGarry's bar manager and one of the grumpiest people I've ever met, is suddenly by our side. His scowling face is a godsend right now.

I grasp at his t-shirt sleeve (dramatic, I know, but can you blame me?) "Yes. Please. Can you—?"

"We're good!" Oliver says with a casual wave of his hand, not even sparing Tony a glance.

Tony looks appropriately miffed with Oliver's flippant response, but I say firmly (okay, order, more like). "Hang on, Tony. Would you be able to tell that group of four guys over there that they are disrupting our viewing experience?"

I wave towards my failure of a protective detail, all four of their faces riveted on the game on the screen. Maybe, if Tony gives them a talking to, they'll pay attention.

Tony must take pity on me because he responds with a gruff, "I'll see what I can do. My job isn't to solve your problems. I just serve drinks."

Which, honestly, is quite a nice response from him. They don't call him Grumpy Tony for nothing.

He shuffles off and I turn back towards Oliver, pursing my lips and cursing the day I agreed to give my sister a honeymoon present.

See, it all started when I made the mistake of telling Luke, Daisy's now husband, a few months ago that I was potentially interested in getting to know someone *romantically*. And because I stupidly told the guy who stupidly loves my sister, Daisy hasn't been able to contain her excitement about my newfound, very potential, very vague interest in dating.

So they pitched that the perfect honeymoon present (still not convinced this is a thing) would be for me to let them set me up. Just once. Daisy was staring at me pleadingly, making those doe eyes that turn most peoples' "no's" into automatic "yes's".

Being her sister, I'm immune. Noah, however, is not.

Or more likely, Noah figured this was a prime opportunity for a prank (spoiler alert: he was right).

I love my sister, love her dearly with all my heart and soul... But I had little faith in the man she'd pick for me on RightMatch. Given my non-existent dating history, it's not like she had anything to go off of: it would just be her gut instinct and innate matchmaking abilities.

Apparently, Noah had his doubts too, because he was more than happy to accept the date on my behalf with a mischievous twinkle in his eye. At that point, it was me against Noah and Daisy (and Luke, by extension) and I simply didn't have the time, energy, or will to argue. No one in their right mind would try, unless they had several energy bars on hand and a few hours to kill.

Don't get me wrong, I *wanted* to like whoever she picked for me. And to Daisy's credit, she did a good job— picked a guy that I might have actually picked for myself. On paper, Oliver is male-Dee incarnate—dedicated to his job (as a botanist), owns his own house (in Chicago), and loves sports. He, too, plays in a community sports league. And he, too, has a pet cat.

The issue? He's just so... *blah*.

He invited me to meet at McGarry's Pub for dinner, which I thought at the time was a smart, low-key, no-pressure kind of move. McGarry's might be a bar, but they have delicious food and their baked potato nights are legendary.

However, our date is coinciding with the *highly* anticipated Rockies vs. Brewers MLB game, and McGarry's is currently packed with Colorado Rockies fans (and Oliver, who is cheering for the Brewers). It's very much a "crowd around the TVs, perched at the standing tables while repping your team sweatshirts" kinda night. Instead, Oliver and I are having a sit-down meal at a table in the corner—a table I eventually realized he chose because there's a tiny TV broadcasting the baseball game right above my head.

Oliver then proceeded to half-listen to our—admittedly also blah—conversation about Powerpoint presentations (why?) before giving up on the pretense altogether and fully tuning into the game. He's got his hands deep in his basket of chicken wings, and I'm scratching my nose like a desperate raccoon, wishing the guys would pick up on the signal already.

I can sense the tension in the bar right now. Feel it ripple across my skin in waves.

What I wouldn't do to take a little peek... just a small, tiny look at the TV...

I do a subtle stretch and lean forward, twisting my head around and feeling not unlike a pelican on the lookout for its prey. Which is very attractive, as I'm sure you can imagine.

"What do you do for work?" Oliver suddenly asks. Clearly, my inner pelican was the key to his attention.

I whip back around, and remembering Daisy's coaching right before this date, I offer what I hope is a cute, sweet smile and not my "trademark dry smile". Whatever that means. "I'm a developer at RightMatch, actually."

"Wow. Never been on a date with someone who basically created the dating app we met on." Oliver swipes another wing from the basket. I refrain from telling him that I didn't actually *create* the app, I just write the code for it. The fact that he's paying any sort of attention right now is a miracle. "Been on lots of these dates, then? Any memorable men?"

My cheeks flush the slightest bit. That feels like an intrusive question. Is that an intrusive question? I decide to be honest. "This is the first. I don't date a lot."

"You don't say." Oliver's eyes flick up to the screen again. "Well, I consider myself honored to be your first date after a drought."

Drought? More like: long period of content singledom where the most effort I had to put into my appearance on a Saturday night was having to wear my cleanest sweatpants while the others were in the wash.

I push the little pot of sour cream around my basket. "Right. Well, despite not dating much myself, I love my job. It's been a... turbulent few months. We were bought out by a big tech company that have a ton of online dating services, and a lot of people from RightMatch have either been let go, quit, or moved around within the company. It's making me nervous."

I stop myself from talking, but realize that Oliver isn't listening anyway. Maybe that's what spurs me to go on. Fill the silence. Pass the time. Make this date come to an end already. "Actually, my new boss is coming to Mirror Valley next week. As I'm the lead dev at RightMatch, he figures it's time we meet in person. Put a face to the name and all that."

"Hm."

"I can't help but feel like I've got something to prove. I want to show how valuable I am to the company, and how valuable the app is itself. After all, it *does* work for some people."

Not for me and Oliver, of course.

But it worked for Daisy and Luke. Kind of.

I tap my fingers against my can of cherry cola. "I've been with RightMatch almost since the beginning, was one of the first developers they hired and even dabbled in management for a bit before realizing I'm a dev at heart. I put years of blood, sweat and tears into it, making it the best it can possibly be." I give a snort. "In a way, it kind of feels like my baby. Is that weird?"

Oliver's head snaps down and he stares at me with wide, terrified eyes. "You have a baby?!"

Sigh.

Good to know where the guy's head is at, at least.

"No, uh... Never mind."

Oliver swipes the back of his hand across his forehead in a *phew* type of motion and lets out another honk laugh before turning his attention back to the screen.

Double sigh.

I still can't believe that Lachlan Chase is coming to Mirror Valley. He's not my new boss so much as he is my new boss's boss's boss. The mere thought of meeting him in person makes my stomach turn over on itself and twist into a big knot all at once. I've video-chatted with Lachlan. He has a loud, sharp voice, a distinct lack of laugh lines, and a jaw that seems perma-clenched. He's your cookie cutter Wall-Street-businessman type, and I have no doubt that, should he decide I'm not an asset, he'll axe me without a second's thought.

And if I lose my job, well...

I can't think like that right now.

Oliver lets out another cheer, smacking the table so one of his chicken wings flops out of the basket. Beside me, there's another round of boos. Guess the game is going about as well for the Rockies as this date is going for me.

"Anyway, Oliv—*Ollie*!" I correct myself again. "I'd be interested to hear more about what you do. You must have quite the green thumb, huh?"

Oliver looks at me, but instead of answering my really very simple question, he levels one back with an annoyed twinge of his brow. "Why do you keep calling me Olive?"

I flush a little. Guess he *was* listening. "Sorry. I defaulted to calling you by your full name in my head."

"I haven't told you my full name."

"Oliver, right? Shortened to Ollie?"

"It's Olaf."

He turns back to the screen. I turn his name over in my head.

Olaf, like the former goalie for the Capitals. Olaf, as in the snowman in *Frozen*.

But if his name is Olaf, and my name is Diandra...

Daisy *clearly* didn't know his full name either. Because Daisy's celebrity couple name rule thing clearly states that our name would be "Diandr-af".

Dandruff?!

At that moment, there's another round of boos, cut with Ollie's booming cheer. I'm feeling pretty much completely over this and am itching to see what's happening with the Rockies, so I put down my can of cola. "Be right back, Oliv—Olaf—*Ollie*!"

With that, I skitter off to the bar, ready to give my alleged "bodyguards" a *very* stern talking to.

2

NOAH

Dee: Dud.

I smirk as I read those three simple letters, my heart doing something totally uncalled for in my chest.

Dee's date tonight was a dud.

"Noah, are you listening?"

Yanica's melodic voice brings me back to the present, where we're strolling along Main Street in Mirror Valley. We're at the end of our third date, which consisted of a horseback ride in the fields close to the mountains. I brought us a picnic, she brought her guitar, and we had a great day in the sunshine. There was something so peaceful about being out there with the reins in my hand and the sun on my face...

Granted, my blue jeans have now seen better days, and Yanica and I have bits of straw peppering our clothes from when we returned the horses to the barn. Plus, the cowboy boots I found in a bag of stuff from my parents' old house are reminding me how much I love sneakers, and I'm wishing I brought another pair of shoes like Yanica did...

But all in all, it was a fun date.

If only my mind hadn't been somewhere else.

"Sorry, Yan," I say, and I mean it. "Didn't mean to zone out again. What were you saying?"

"Silly." She giggles. "Don't you know it's rude to check your phone on a date?"

I give her a charming smile. "I was checking the clock. Can't believe how fast the time went today."

"Well, you know what they say about time passing and having fun," she says flirtily, swatting my arm gently.

But she has a point—it *is* rude to check your phone when someone's talking to you. "Nah, I really am sorry about that. My focus is now totally on you."

"As it should be."

She drags the tip of her index fingernail along my forearm. It's flirty and cute... but it's also hitting that ticklish sweet spot right near my elbow that Dee often uses against me because it makes me jitter like I've just rubbed up against an electric fence. Before I can start wiggling or spontaneously laughing or something, I pull my arm out of her grasp and scratch the itch, pretending to be stretching.

"Are your arms sore?" she asks, gathering her thick brown hair over one shoulder.

"Yeah, had a football game a couple days ago. We won against a team out of Boulder."

"My muscles are *always* worse two days after a workout. Massages are key. Let me know if you want one, I know an amazing masseur in Longhaven." She takes my arm again. "Or if you play your cards right, *I* can give you one."

I smile at her politely. "Thanks, Yan, I'll let you know."

She sighs happily, gripping my arm tighter as we continue walking. "It's just so, *so* cool that I'm on a date right now with the most famous pair of legs in the country." She winks one perfectly mascara-ed eye. "Usually, *I'm* the one with the good legs."

My smile falters a little.

Right. The leg thing...

"About that." I give her a sheepish look. "Dylan was joking, the other day. I'm not the poster boy for those Running Store ads."

Yanica blinks up at me in confusion. Frick. I need to tell Dylan to stop messing with people. "So you *aren't* a leg model then?" She places her hands on her hips. "What on earth do you do?"

"He was right in that I don't have to work, but I've never been a leg model."

Yanica continues to stare at me blankly.

"My legs are just... normal, run-of-the-mill legs."

"So where'd you get your money from?" she demands.

I play off her question with a joke. "If I tell you that, I'd have to kill you. And you're much too interesting for that."

Yanica stares at me for a long moment, lips pursed and eyes narrowed. Then, apparently deciding that my unremarkable legs aren't a dealbreaker for her, she lets out a high, tinkling laugh. "Well, model or not, you're living the dream, No-no," she coos.

I keep my smile firmly in place through the unfortunate nickname. I can't remember when Yanica started up with the "No-no" business, but I can confirm that it isn't my favorite. Dee would have a field day with that one. "Am I."

It's not a question, but Yanica answers anyway. "'Course you are. Not having to work? Having a ton of disposable income while putting in absolutely *no* effort? You're a lucky guy. And here you are, just playing ball games all day."

She giggles again, but now, I can't stop the grimace that twists my lips.

Yup. Yanica sure captured that well.

Thing is, I might not *need* to work, but that doesn't mean I don't *want* to work. Make a difference. Do something meaningful. I've been trying to find that thing, that passion, for awhile now. I've worked a ton of different jobs in a ton of different industries. But nothing's... clicked.

Maybe it's just my quarter-life crisis talking. Dee says I'm too old for a quarter-life crisis, to which I say that I'm actually right on track if I live to be 108.

"You'll have to invite me to one of your games," Yanica continues. "I'd love to meet your friends."

My phone vibrates in my pocket again. I resist the urge to check the message. Instead, I turn my ball cap to face frontwards. "Race you to get ice cream?"

All of a sudden, Yanica's twirling to a stop right in front of me. Her sultry-sweet perfume bathes my senses and I move my gaze from her twinkling hazel eyes to the piece of straw clinging to the shoulder of her dress. For a minute, I think she might rise up on her tiptoes and kiss me. I take a subconscious step back. Don't get me wrong, Yanica's beautiful. I just... can't bring myself to go there right now.

But instead, she grabs the brim of my ball cap and turns it so it's facing backwards again. She smiles coyly, eyes wide and unblinking. "Race? In these heels? I think not."

I let out a chuckle and we start walking again, Yanica interlacing her fingers with mine. I don't drop her hand, but I also recognize that this might be getting out of hand. I'm usually good about telling women where I stand—early on so that no one is led on. Yanica is pretty much any guy's dream girl. She's kind, and she has this witty banter that speaks to her intelligence. Plus, she's a certified ten, as you would expect from a former Haybale Beauty Queen.

The fact that I'm only half here right now has absolutely nothing to do with her and everything to do with me.

Because what kind of idiot would rather be in a hot, crowded bar that smells of potatoes, sweat and beer, half-cheering for his favorite baseball team while also half-checking in on his best friend as she goes on her first date in years?

The most dire of idiots.

Or that's what Dee would say if she knew how much that insistent part of me wanted to ditch this otherwise perfect evening. The sun is setting and the sky is all kinds of crazy colors right now, for crying out loud. If we were in one of Dee's guilty-pleasure romcoms, this would be the part that I take Yanica aside and kiss her.

If I was any other guy, after a day like this, I would. I'd be sweeping this girl off her feet STAT.

Problem is, I'm not good at the part *after* the sweeping. The whole "serious, committed relationship" part.

I've been in relationships, of course. Been a good boyfriend for stints of three to six months. The issue was always just past that, when things started to get serious. Because when things got serious, Dee would always, always come up in conversation.

And Dee was never someone I was willing to lose.

My phone vibrates in my pocket again, and this time, I can't stop myself from checking it.

Dee: SOS. The guys aren't responding to my signal.

I stop dead on the sidewalk.

Noah: Is everything okay? Did the guy try something??

Dee: Goodness, no. I could take him anyway.

My heart restarts again. Through the blood pumping in my ears, I hear Yanica asking what I'm doing and why I've stopped.

"A friend of mine is on a date tonight, her first date in years," I explain to her. "I thought she was in trouble."

Yanica's right eyebrow pops a little when I say "she". "Is this the same friend that you spoke about last time? The one who eats her nachos weird?"

Uh oh. I hear the edge in her voice and decide to tread carefully. "Yup, that's Dee. We basically grew up together, so I'm a little protective of her."

Yanica's shoulders relax. "Oh. So you're like siblings."

I cringe internally at the label.

Yeah. I guess, according to Dee, that's correct.

Right before I pocket my phone again, I scan the rest of Dee's texts.

Dee: The date's blah. I'd rather be watching the game. And the worst part is...

Dee: He's a BREWERS FAN!!!!

I snort a little, and cover it with a cough. Dee's never been into dating, but here she is tonight, on her first date in literal years and it's with someone who backs the team we're playing against.

But I am being terrible right now, and I don't want to be rude or disrespectful. So I push Dee to the back of my mind and focus... for real, this time. "So what's your favorite kind of ice cream? And don't say Birthday Cake because I might have to walk away right now."

Yanica laughs again. "Lucky for you, I'm more of a Rocky Road kinda girl."

"You don't say. I'm a Rocky Road kinda guy."

"We clearly have tons in common already."

I give Yanica a nod. "Guess we do."

And it would be so nice, so easy to lean down and kiss her right now. Sweep her off her feet, and tell all my friends about her, and bring her home to meet my parents and brothers for some family vacation down the road.

If only I wasn't totally and completely in love with my best friend.

3

DEE

There are a few things of which I'm completely certain:

1. Programming is my favorite, most useful and most used creative outlet. (And yes, I do think writing code is creative. I even like to do it in my spare time. Party of one, over here).
2. My life would not be the same without my big sister Daisy, my cat Bruce, and my best friend Noah. But obviously don't tell any of them that. Don't want Noah's head getting too big. Or Bruce's, for that matter.
3. Sticking to batting averages when making a bet on the MLB against the volleyball boys has never once failed me. Though I'd never tell them that.

"Cough it up!" I cackle as I hold out my palm and make a gimme motion.

"Dang it, Dee. It's the bottom of the line-up, how'd you know he'd hit that one?" Amir whines, gathering the last of his precious Corn Nuts. "Seriously, I wanna know."

I shrug angelically. "C'mon, where's the fun in that?"

"I was hoping my fun would come from eating your portion of my favorite snacks all night," he grumbles.

"And now, that will be *my* fun."

With pursed lips and glinting eyes, Amir hands over the last of his Corn Nuts, but before I can pile them into my mouth, Jarrod wraps an arm around my shoulders and pulls me into a headlock. He does this on occasion and it annoys the pants off me, but I'm powerless to stop it. Jarrod's our middle blocker for a reason—he's by far the tallest, biggest player on our volleyball team. Might even be the biggest guy in town. His shoulders alone are so broad, they basically require one of those "Wide Load" signs.

"Hey, don't mess up her hair," Finn chastises Jarrod, placing a warning hand on his shoulder. Finn might be lean and trim, built more like a long distance runner to Jarrod's linebacker, but he's as tough as the rest of 'em. "The girl's on a date. How would you like it if Isobel showed up with her hair all mussed?"

Jarrod waggles his eyebrows, eyes dancing. "I don't mind when she *leaves* our dates that way."

I give Jarrod a swift punch in his sizeable arm while the rest of the guys snicker. "He has a point, though." I peek between Amir and Finn's shoulders. "I've been here too long. Probably should get back to Olaf."

Parker makes a salute motion. "Good luck with the Brewers fan."

"Are you guys actually going to look over this time? I almost scratched my nose off earlier trying to get your attention."

Amir runs a hand through his hair, looking sheepish. He's shorter than the other guys and this expression makes him seem adorably innocent. "Sorry, Dee, that was my bad. I should've come over when I saw you making the signal.

You're not about to get online-date-murdered on our watch."

Jarrod nods. "We can't lose you. You're the best outside hitter around."

"Aside from yours truly." Parker winks with a smirk that makes him look even more like a leprechaun than normal. "Plus, none of us want to go up against Noah if something happened to you while we were supposed to be watching you."

"Gee, thanks, guys. Feeling the love all around."

"You know we're here for you," Finn says with a genuine smile, nodding towards McGarry's dining section. Which is empty relative to the bar area full of eagle-eyed fans crowded in front of the big-screens. "We'll be watching."

"Me? Or the game?"

"We can multitask," Amir replies.

I roll my eyes, take a deep breath, and make my way back to Ollie. "Uh, sorry. I ran into some friends by the bar. Didn't mean to ditch you."

Ollie doesn't look at me. "No problem, I was pretty invested in the game anyway. I see your team's getting it together."

"Guess so."

"Finally. I love a fiery game, and it hasn't been going that way 'til now."

I press my lips together as I take a slow, slightly reluctant seat. How do people *do* this? The awkward and forced small talk, the "does he like me, do I like *him*?", the kinda-woozy date jitters that don't feel unlike shooting six espressos. "So you follow the Brewers, huh?" I ask haphazardly.

Ollie's eyes drop to meet mine for a second and he smirks in such a way that he looks exactly like *Home Alone*-era Macaulay Culkin after making one of the bad guys fall down the stairs. "No, I'm a Dodgers fan. But I heard how crazy this town is for the Rockies and figured I'd mix things up a little tonight. Cheer for the other team."

These words make me bristle a little. Being a true fan—even if the team is a competitor—is something I can understand. But loudly cheering for the other team just to get a rise out of people? Kind of obnoxious.

Then, he continues, "Plus, I figured this would be a fun date for us. Spark some friendly competition, you know?"

I pause, my words evaporating on my tongue. Yeah, I get it—*competitive* is my middle name. It had to be, given the team sports I played growing up. Not to mention the hours upon hours that I spent with Noah and his rowdy brothers.

My heart thaws towards Ollie. Maybe I was too quick in judging him. He clearly *did* do some planning before this date. Intentionally wanted us to come here for this MLB game. The guy's new in town—maybe he didn't realize that the McGarry's game night atmosphere wouldn't exactly scream "date friendly". Maybe he didn't know that getting-to-know-you conversations would be heavily stilted.

"Oh. That makes sense." I give a small smile, leaning forward and trying to give him a real chance. "I *was* really looking forward to this game, and it seems like you—?"

"NO! Idiot!!" Ollie shouts so suddenly that I jump back in my seat. Cheers around the bar signal that the Rockies finally did something right. He shakes his head, clucking like an old hen. "What an idiot."

"The most dire of idiots," I murmur automatically, thinking of Noah and our stupid inside joke.

All of a sudden, a chair just behind me scrapes up to our table.

"Dee! Long time no see." Amir settles into the chair. "Mind if we join you?"

Before I can say anything, Jarrod's plopped into a seat on my other side. "Who's your friend?"

Parker speaks next, from behind my right shoulder. "Looks like he's cheering for the Brewers."

Olaf is now officially paying attention in a way that he hasn't all night. His gaze darts from Jarrod and Finn on my left side, to Parker and Amir on my right. His eyes narrow the slightest bit, his shoulders straightening. "I am," he says. "It's probably dangerous to say in a place like this."

"Not at all," Finn responds with a smile. He's the most friendly of the bunch on first meeting. "We Mirrorites are Rockies superfans, but we wouldn't turn you away just 'cuz you back a sub-par team." He winks and holds out a hand. "I'm Finn. And this is Parker, Amir, and Jarrod."

Olaf smiles warily. Which is fair. The four men crowded around me are the sweetest guys at their cores, but they're all athletes—strong and muscular to varying degrees. "I'm Olaf." He sets his jaw. "Dee and I are on a date. So... can we help you with something?"

"Olaf?" Jarrod asks, ignoring his question. "Like the snowman?"

I hit him in the shoulder, rolling my eyes. "Olaf's a very common name, Jarrod."

"After the *Frozen* baby boom, yeah."

"Anyway." Amir picks up the pot with my sour cream remnants and runs his finger around the sides. "Haven't seen you around here before. What's your deal?"

"From Chicago," Olaf replies. "In Colorado for work."

"The windy city!" Parker chimes in. "Always wanted to go. Are sundresses a thing there?"

I whip around and whack him straight in the arm. Parker recoils. "What was that for?!" His eyes widen a touch. "No! Because I heard it gets cold there... even colder than here... sometimes."

22

I raise my brow skeptically.

"Don't be a turd, Parker." Jarrod turns back to Olaf. "You're clearly a baseball fan. Into anything else? Football, hockey, volleyball?"

And so, for the first time all evening, surrounded by the best men I know (minus Noah), Olaf manages to keep his eyes off the TV screen long enough to hold an entire conversation. Soon enough, the guys are all heckling each other and joking around like they're old friends.

"Gonna get a drink," I announce when there's a pause in the conversation. The Rockies are making a strong comeback, so it's time I order a celebratory light beer before the bar goes crazy.

I make my way through the crowd, squeezing past people until I find an unoccupied pocket of space by the water station. I lean my elbows on the cool countertop. Tug at the hem of my shirt.

Believe it or not, I had no idea what to wear on this date. And while Daisy insisted on putting me into a denim skirt with a trendy, oversized sweater and tall black boots ("the *peak* of June-time date attire", she'd said), I staunchly refused to wear anything but my dark blue jeans and Converse. I did compromise on the shirt—a white blouse that's a little too cinched around the waist for my liking—and I let her add some "beachy curls" to my hair, purely because she wouldn't shut up until I handed her the curler.

She tried to dress me up with jewelry but I stood my ground. I've only ever worn one piece of jewelry at one time in my life, and that was in high school, when Noah brought me a silver trinket ring with the cutest volleyball insignia on it after he went away to volleyball camp for three weeks.

That little ring was the light in the midst of a very dark summer. I wore it like it was a lifeline, until a few years

23

later, when Noah and I went for a swim in a lake on a hot summer day, and somehow, the ring slid off my finger.

I still think of it sometimes, wondering where it ended up. Hoping it's coexisting peacefully with the lake life.

In any case, despite Daisy's best efforts to transform me into "date material" tonight, it's come to nothing as there is *no way* I'll be going out with Olaf again anytime soon.

The same might not be said for the guys, though.

I glance over my shoulder and glimpse them laughing together loudly. The bar's packed, and I'm happy enough standing here for the moment, directly in front of the lone fan above the bar. It might be a crisp, early summer night outside, but you wouldn't know it being in McGarry's. How is it *so hot* in here?

I look around quickly, ensure that no one's paying attention, and then duck my head and do a subtle inhale.

Mostly fresh linen. Good, good.

"I saw that, Dee-bug."

Before I can register what's happening, a pair of arms wind around my waist and I'm being hoisted into the air. I let out a screech as I topple unevenly onto a set of strong, muscular shoulders, landing with my head down near one of the most famous backsides in town.

"NOAH!" I yelp. "Put me down!"

But my best friend only cackles, patting me on the butt as he swings me around. The crowd gives us a wide berth, thankfully, seeing as I'm unable to do anything but flail around helplessly. Noah's hands finally lock around my waist again and he pulls me off of him. I slide down the front of his body, feeling like I've just gone upside down and topsy-turvy in a roller coaster.

He smirks, removing his white ball cap from his head and placing it on me. "Glad to see you survived your catfisher."

"No thanks to you."

"*All* thanks to me. I messaged the guys telling them to get their crap together and help you out."

"Look at you, exacting your power as team captain from afar," I say dryly, pressing my fingers into the back of my neck where it twinged a little during my upside-down journey. "You sure know how to make an entrance."

He waggles his eyebrows. "Hear that a lot."

I gag. Noah laughs.

He's right, though—people notice when Noah Jackson walks into a room.

My best friend is what you would call "Hollywood Gorgeous". Or "Top Athlete Gorgeous", if that's more your standard. He's too pretty for his own good; is basically the lovechild of a young Tom Brady and Kris Bryant. Noah has perfectly symmetrical features and a charming, boyish smile that makes it impossible not to fall for him when he directs it your way. He's tall, lean, and unbelievably toned, because of course he is. His brown eyes, ringed with thick, dark lashes, are the exact color of roasted chestnuts, but with a sprinkling of gold flecks that are only visible when you're up close.

Plus, his lips. They're a full Cupid's bow that any woman would die to have for herself, but the little crease down the middle of his bottom lip gives him this sweet innocence that's totally disarming.

Long story short—Noah looks like anyone's picture-perfect romcom movie hero. Minus the movie star arrogance and haughtiness. The only "imperfections" in his beautiful features are the crescent-shaped scar next to his right eye, and his slightly chipped incisor (I was there for both incidents that brought those about, by the way).

Even now, standing at the bar with him, I can see women glancing over their shoulders, noticing him.

Noticing *us*. I can understand why their brows furrow in confusion: where Noah looks like he belongs in one of those smiley dental ads featuring unreasonably hot people, I look reasonably ordinary. I *am* reasonably ordinary. And I like it this way. Being ordinary gives you a free pass to get away with stuff. If people aren't noticing you in the first place, it's easy to fly under the radar. I'm never pulled into random conversations (my nightmare), and I'm never invited to places or parties with lots of people and not enough pets (also my nightmare).

And yet, while everyone's staring at him, Noah's giving *me* a once-over. "I barely recognized you. Nice shirt."

I punch him in the arm. "Shut up. It's Daisy's."

"Hey, I'm being serious. You clean up good, even when you're sniffing your pits."

I hold back from punching him again. Because I'm a lady. "How was your date with Yanica?"

Noah shrugs in answer, and I finally register what he's wearing: a white T-shirt that sets off his bronzed skin, along with blue jeans.

Dirty, dirty blue jeans.

I snort. "What did you guys do? Roll around in dirt?"

"Something like that." Noah waggles his eyebrows in that outrageously flirty way that could ensnare any woman within five feet of him. He plucks a piece of hay off his shirt and I suddenly wonder whether he and Yanica really *did* roll around together... I bite the inside of my cheek, pushing that thought far away. "Nah, we went horseback riding."

"You? On a horse? And it actually carried you?"

Noah presses his fingers to his chest in mock-hurt. "Dee-bug, are you calling me fat?"

I roll my eyes with a very, very tired sigh. Any sane person with two eyes and their optic nerves intact can see that Noah is very clearly not fat. "No. I'm just surprised

26

that you didn't get impatient and run off without the horse at some point."

"That is something I would do." He glances around the bar. "So, where's the dud?"

I nod towards the dining section, but my view of our table is now obscured by the crowd returning to their positions for the next inning. "Over there with the guys. And he seems fine, just a little distracted. He's not for me."

"So you think there *is* someone for you?"

Noah's voice is teasing, but there's an intensity beneath it that I'm not sure I'm imagining. Plus, he's peering at me with this intense curiosity in his eyes. I stumble a little on the maybe-tone-change in the conversation. "I mean... I don't know. I haven't thought about it much." I give a shrug to play it off. "Onto the next, I guess."

He pauses, then breaks into an abrupt, very bright smile. "Well, let's go meet this man not-of-your-dreams, shall we?"

Before I can respond, his big hand wraps around mine and he drags me through the crowd.

4
———

NOAH

I can't tell you the exact moment I fell in love with Dee.

We were friends before I even knew what a friend was. Our moms met while practicing breathing strategies in their Lamaze class—my mom was eager, breathing too quickly, and her mom was distracted, one eye on her pager, so they were paired together in an effort to balance each other out. Which is a pretty accurate assessment not only of each of our moms, but also of Dee and me.

I may not know much, but I do know that we strike a good balance. Dee is the salt to my pepper, the Diane to my Sam, the ML to my B…

You get the picture.

What I *can* tell you is the moment that I *realized* I was in love with Dee.

We were 14 and experiencing all the joys, glories, trials and tribulations of high school. Dee grew up as a part of the Jackson clan, and that meant that she was fiercely competitive, hungry for a challenge, and determined to prove herself. My brothers and I never pushed Dee to do anything she didn't want to do, obviously, but she went headfirst into our games and competitions anyway. She didn't shy away when things got intense, and was sometimes the instigator of the rowdiness herself. We corralled around her, adopted her, and were all protective of her. Would never let anything happen to her.

This all meant that, when she joined the varsity girls' volleyball team in our freshman year, Dee was out of her depths. Ahead of her depths, actually. It was a shame as the girls who had just graduated had been as competitive and determined as she was. But by some stroke of bad luck, the team that year were more interested in the style of their uniforms and in the football players who worked out next to the courts during their practices.

By the spring, Dee was sporting a nonstop sour expression, especially when she came to the boys' volleyball practices and matches. I couldn't blame her. Dee was a talented player, she would've been an asset to any team.

And that's exactly what she—and I—told the boys' coach. It was a bittersweet moment when Alec Hudson injured his knee in an early season match that we were very much losing. Dee stepped up as an alternate, the team all backed her, so Coach put her in to finish the set.

She finished the set. Finished the entire match.

We won.

But even with the joy around that unexpected win, even with the cheering and the excitement (except on Alec's part, obviously), it didn't happen until later that night. We'd eaten our body weight in nachos, wings, and ice cream with the team, and then Dee and I decided to run home. Which was a wildly stupid idea. We were bent over with horrible cramps within minutes, and then limped the entire five miles back to our houses. It was not a pretty sight.

Right before she went into her house, we hugged good-bye, as we always did. It was totally normal for us, except that our skin was tacky with dried sweat, and her hair was matted, and my belly was so full, I still felt nauseous.

But when we hugged goodbye, something clicked and I just... knew. Felt it in my heart in that totally inexplicable way that makes absolutely no sense and that you think you can easily brush off as a fluke. Endorphins. Whatever.

Only I couldn't brush it off. Couldn't explain what had changed, but just that *something* had changed, because now, I knew that I was in love with Dee.

I spent the rest of the year trying to grapple with this realization while simultaneously having to apply sunscreen to her bare, smooth shoulders every time we had practice. Torture, by the way, when you're trying to hide feelings you shouldn't be having.

My solution? To date other people. A *lot* of other people.

After all, if I could feel those sparks with my best friend at the end of a sweaty volleyball match, surely I could feel them with the beautiful head cheerleader?

And there were sparks with Eliza. And with Megan. And with every other girl I dated through high school. But they didn't give me that feeling—that heart-feeling that I only had with Dee.

I wish I could say that feeling faded, but it hasn't. I had it again tonight, when I walked into McGarry's and saw a pretty girl standing alone at the bar. I saw the white blouse first, followed by the soft curls in her caramel blonde hair. It wasn't until I spotted the jeans and Converse that I realized it was Dee. And I had confirmation of that when she oh-so-subtly sniffed her pits.

For a minute there, I thought I might be feeling something for someone else.

Nope. The woman's totally and completely ruined me. Without even knowing, without even trying.

Which is why I let Yanica down tonight after our ice cream. Told her that she's wonderful and I had a great time with her, but I couldn't see a future with us. To my surprise, she didn't seem surprised. Said that she suspected my heart was somewhere else. We parted ways on a good note, which is maybe more than I deserve.

"Why so glum, chum?" Dee asks loudly, knocking into my shoulder. She's had one and a half beers since I arrived at McGarry's an hour ago and she's getting to that shouty level she gets to on the rare occasion that she drinks. Not that I blame her after the Rockies' comeback—you could get drunk off the atmosphere in McGarry's, *alone*.

"Me? Glum?" I chirp. "You must have me confused with someone else, dude."

"Dude. Dud. Same thing." Dee waves a hand. Like that made any sense at all.

The dud is fully out of the picture now, by the way—as soon as the Brewers lost, he stormed out of McGarry's.

Sore loser, that one. But I am not one to judge.

"Speaking of, what terrible manners I have. How was your date with Yanica?" Dee turns to me, her already huge steel-gray eyes wide and earnest. The color of her irises is my favorite color in the world—sparkling and bright and complex all at once. Like a kaleidoscope every time you look at them. "You gettin' serious about her or something?"

She snorts with laughter, like she's just told the world's funniest joke. To her credit, Amir and Jarrod cackle alongside her.

Dee doesn't laugh often, but when she does, it's this glorious, uninhibited sound. There's a small gap between her front teeth that she hates, but I couldn't love more. Her cheeks turn into rosy pink apples, and her eyes clench shut so her light eyelashes brush her cheek. When she laughs like this, she tilts her head back slightly, showing off the delicate stretch of her neck.

Friends, Noah. Nothing more...

"The real measure of serious-ity is if he'd tell her the truth about how he makes his money." Amir hiccups gleefully. "What was it this time? That you're a real estate tycoon? That you invented the slow cooker? That you discovered a pacific island that Elon Musk then bought off you?"

I shake my head with a chuckle. "Leg modeling for those Running Store ads. We ran into Dylan on our second date and the guy had that one locked and loaded."

"Leg modeling!" Dee cackles anew, clutching her stomach as she laughs. "That's a good one!"

"You don't think I could be a leg model, Dee?"

"No, you've got great legs. The best legs in all the lands!"

She and the guys continue laughing and I have to roll my eyes. These guys (and Dee) are some of the only people who know where my money actually came from. I wouldn't say I'm rolling in riches by any stretch, but I live comfortably. Making up these odd little stories has become a sort of tradition for our group (and Dylan, apparently).

The truth is, unfortunately, much less glamorous than discovering a Pacific island. You try telling people that you accidentally invented a new type of scent-absorbing sole for running shoes. Yup, smelly shoes are my game.

It was a total fluke that one of the top athletic brands in the country picked up the soles, and I've been getting money for them ever since.

"You're all being drunken hooligans," I announce. "I'm getting water for the table."

"Spoilsport!" Parker hoots.

"Talk to me when you're DD," I shoot back, standing up.

Jarrod hauls himself after me. "I'll come with."

We walk together across the bar. It's a little quieter now, but not by much. The celebrations are alive and well, as you'd expect after white-knuckling it through a game. I hear Dee's laugh from the across the bar and smile—I could never get tired of that sound.

I'm grabbing a canteen of water and a couple glasses when Jarrod says, "So how'd the date go tonight, for real?"

"It was good."

"But?"

"But nothing."

"That's what she said."

I snort. "Don't be stupid."

"Whatever. Are you gonna see her again?"

I press on a smirk. "You interested? I can introduce you."

Jarrod lets out one of his rare, genuine, sweet smiles. "You know I'm all in with Isobel." Then, he gives his head a shake. "The guy was a no-go, by the way. He seemed decent once he actually started paying attention, but he's not good enough for our Dee."

The subtext is there, clear as day. You'd be hard-pressed to find someone who could win over our pack of guys quite like Dee has.

Dee just has a *thing* about her. She's rough around the edges, tough as nails in so many ways. She plays everything close to the chest and doesn't often let down her walls, but at the same time, she inspires a vulnerability in you. It comes out of nowhere until, all of a sudden, you find your-self on the edge of your seat, seconds away from divulging your darkest secrets. And when you're at that point, you just know that she won't let you down.

She's got your back. Like you've got hers.

Maybe it has to do with her childhood—with everything that went down with her parents, and the way she and Daisy found their chosen families with me and my brothers, and with the Brooks, respectively.

In any case, I've never met anyone like Dee. And while some might be put off by her prickliness, I love her for it. Love her for all her quirks and layers.

Jarrod raises a brow. "You gonna talk to her?"

"I talk to Dee all the time."

"Now you're being stupid."

I know I am. I'm stalling.

It didn't take long for the guys on the team to pick up on my feelings for Dee. I've never been the best at hiding what I'm feeling except from the one person who's inspiring those feelings. I can't tell if that's a good or a bad thing.

My brothers used to give me a hard time about it when we were younger—I guess I wasn't exactly subtle when my younger brother Sam asked Dee out in our senior year. She said no, which just proves that dating has never been her thing because I knew she had a crush on him.

In any case, eventually, it was just easier to tell the volleyball boys that yes, I did have feelings for her, and no, those feelings wouldn't go anywhere because Dee doesn't date.

This was our status quo: Dee not dating anyone, me dating everyone.

Until tonight.

"Come on, man," Jarrod prods. "Things are changing. Dee's dating now."

"So I heard." I chuckle dryly. "I don't know what to say, dude. Dee didn't date for so long. That line was drawn and set—she was never into relationships, and that was fine. But now that she's getting out there..." I shake my head. "I thought going out with Yanica tonight would distract me, but all I could think about was her and how her date was going."

"I think you should say something. All the guys do. Dee hasn't been on the market before, but apparently, she is now."

He gestures towards our table, where Finn and Parker are arm wrestling while Dee and Amir both heckle and cheer them on. As we watch, Dee drapes her caramel hair over one shoulder. She looks amazing tonight.

How naive I was pushing her to go on tonight's "pro-tecto-date", as she calls it. At the time, I thought it'd be an opportunity for us to share a laugh over the guy Daisy found for her. Until Dee made it clear that she very much *is* intending to get back on the dating scene.

I wasn't laughing then.

"How would I even start that conversation?" I ask Jarrod as my eyes linger on her. "Tell her that I've loved her basically our entire friendship and I'd rather become a Brewers fan than see her with another man?"

Jarrod grimaces so that funky little dimple of his pops. "You could start by asking if she'd want to go on a date before hopping to the whole 'I wanna have your babies' part."

"Might be a bit much, huh?"

"Yeah. I mean, who knows if she even wants babies in the first place."

My mouth twists at the thought. I can't wrap my head around the thought of her kissing someone else, let alone *having babies* with them.

"Excuse me."

The woman's voice comes from just behind my left shoulder and I step aside to clear a path to the water. "Sorry," I say, shooting her a smile.

She smiles back at me, clearly not here for the water. "Are you Noah, by chance?"

I glance at Jarrod and he smirks. I turn back to her. "I am."

"Thought I recognized you." She giggles. "My name's Crystal. I'm Kimber's cousin."

Ah, Kimber. We dated a couple years back. Great girl, but again, she wasn't for me. Mainly because she wasn't Dee.

"I wanted to come up and introduce myself. Kimber mentioned you a couple times while you were together. Did you know that she's married now? Who woulda thought; the girl never seemed to want to settle down. I heard you guys didn't date for very long either, hm?"

"Just a couple months. She's great."

Crystal does this long, slow blink of her eyelashes. Her eyes are a clear, ocean blue, almost the same color as Dee's older sister Daisy's. "She had nothing but good things to say about you, too. Made me want to meet you myself."

Jarrod clears his throat, and I give her another smile. "Looks like you came to the right place. But we should get back to our friends. It was nice to meet you, Crystal, maybe I'll see you around sometime."

And with that, I stride back to our table with Jarrod in tow. He keeps up with me, coming in close. "See? Even *Kimber* is settling down and getting married."

I look at him with an eyebrow popped. "Do you even remember Kimber?"

"Was she before or after Jayme?"

I grimace. "After."

Jarrod shakes his head. "Look, man. You should talk to her. Be honest. You never know what might happen."

"I don't think Crystal cares for my honesty."

"No, not—"

"I know, I know." I chuckle. "I've thought about it. Thought about telling Dee how I feel now that she's looking for something real. I'd be stupid and/or a coward not to."

"This is the time, dude," Jarrod says all too reasonably. "You miss 100% of the shots you don't take."

The Gretzky line is pretty appropriate for this moment and I have to acknowledge that my all too reasonable friend has a point. "I'll see what I can do. We should get going, though. Last I saw, Parker was half-asleep in Dee's nacho basket."

5

DEE

It took fifteen minutes, six half-hearted attempts, a promise to get the burgers after next practice, and some Tetris-style moves for us all to fit into Noah's truck. It's a big vehicle, but for five muscular guys and one relatively tall girl, it's a squeeze. I end up squished between Jarrod and Noah on the front bench seat.

"I feel like a sardine," I say regretfully.

"Smell like one, too," Parker cackles from the backseat, quickly followed by an "ouch!" as someone—probably Amir —whacks him on my behalf. "What? It was too easy!"

"Now I *know* that isn't true," I retort. "I sniffed myself earlier, as did Noah. And we all know he'd tell me the truth."

Jarrod suddenly chokes on something, and I peer up at him from the corner of my eye. In a very sardine type of way, actually. "Too many Corn Nuts, Jar? They're coming back on you."

"I have no regrets."

While the guys fall into beer-induced laughter and chatter, I look up at Noah next. He's got a funny little smirk —a telltale sign that he's lost in thought. I want to ask him what's on his mind, but this is neither the time nor the place. As is evidenced all too clearly when Amir belches loudly. It might be the one-and-three-quarter glasses of light beer talking, but I'm very aware of where my thigh meets Noah's, the way his leg feels so warm and firm and sturdy against mine.

Warm and firm and sturdy, just like he is.

"Hey," I say quietly. "Thanks for coming tonight. I know you had the date with Yanica, but I appreciate you being DD."

"Anything for you, Dee-bug," Noah says easily, off-the-cuff in that way of his that instantly puts me at ease. "How're you feeling about that lock person coming next week?"

I frown, my mind half on Olaf and the way I didn't feel anything *close* to ease when I was with him. The only thing I felt was a mild desire to build a friendly snowman. "Lock person?"

"Your boss."

"Oh." I snicker, then go serious again as the sobering thought hits home. "The opposite of excited."

"He's gonna love you."

"He's gonna love firing me."

"He'd have to be an idiot to fire you."

"The most dire of idiots." We say this together, in tandem, like we always do when someone says the word "idiot" even on a breath. It's an inside joke from junior high when our gym teacher, Mr. Wilhelm, covered for our English class and spent the entire hour grumbling about the idiots in Shakespeare.

Needless to say, Mr. Wilhelm did not return to sub for that class.

"I've got my office on Main Street mostly set up for him." I shift on the seat. "I'm just so nervous. There have been so many changes since the acquisition. What if he wants to move me within the company? What if he doesn't want me working from Mirror Valley anymore? What *if* he lets me go, Noah?"

The thought makes my stomach shrivel up to the size of a pea. I've worked at RightMatch for so long, it feels like a part of me. Over the years, I've sacrificed so much for this app. My work has always been my everything.

"Well, if that's the case, we've already established that he's dumb. But also, you'll find another job, Dee. Any tech company would be lucky to have you. Any *company* would be lucky to have you. You could work for a soap maker and they'd be thrilled."

I let out a giggle. "What kinda soap maker needs a developer?"

Noah raises a shoulder in a shrug, and his bare upper arm presses against my bicep. Warm and firm and sturdy. "Everyone and their dog needs a dev these days, Dee. Maybe you can inspire their next range of soaps. Python and Mint hand wash. C++ and Turmeric toilet spray."

"Well as long as there's a nice-smelling toilet spray in the mix."

Soon enough, the guys in the back are whining to know what we're talking about. As my friends, my team, my "protective detail" talk all around me, surrounding me with laughter and stupid jokes and the vague smell of Corn Nuts, all I can think is that I don't want to lose *this*. Don't want to lose these moments.

Dev jobs are few and far between in a small town like Mirror Valley, and it took careful negotiating, painstaking research on remote working, and a manager that trusted me blindly to get the work life I have now. Most companies require at least *some* time in the office on a weekly or monthly basis, which would mean having to move from

Mirror Valley. Leave this place that I've always called home. The family that I've always chosen to be mine.

I can't imagine leaving these guys, leaving Bruce or my adorable house. Don't even get me started on the thought of not seeing Daisy for weeks at a time.

And leaving Noah? Impossible to even consider.

We drop off Parker and Finn first, followed by Amir, and then Jarrod. I live the furthest away, in the bungalow that was mine and Daisy's childhood home.

Noah, meanwhile, rents an apartment in town. He has more than enough money to buy his own place, but he hasn't. A quiet, annoying little voice in me asks whether he hasn't bought because he plans to leave someday.

I shove the voice aside as I shift into the spot on the bench seat that Jarrod just vacated.

"Finally, I can breathe again," I say, throwing my arms out.

Noah snorts and sits back, spreading his legs. "Your breathing isn't nearly as important as my ability to manspread."

"You're right. My priorities are *way* off."

"What'd I tell you, Dee. I'm always right."

"Well, that's a stretch."

"No," Noah says slowly. There's a slight twitch in the corner of his lips. "*This* is a stretch."

He opens his arms wide, and then, before I can say or do anything, he wraps one arm around my waist and drags me to his side of the seat. I let out a yelp, laughing as I literally smoosh into him. He lets go, and I notice the automatic scan he does of my face. He knows I'm not a touchy-feely kind of person, but he's an exception to that. Maybe because we grew up together. It's just so easy to be comfortable around him, to feel like his arms and legs are an extension of mine.

Doubt anyone would believe I'm a leg model, though. I'll leave that to Noah.

"You got me," I say with a laugh, scooting a little, but not the full way, back to the passenger side of the truck.

Noah gives me his special little smirk—the one reserved just for me—then puts the truck in gear and we get on the road towards my house. "I'll tell you who doesn't get you: that Olaf character."

My lips twist into a grimace as I check his glove compartment. *Bingo!* Secret stash of candy corn. And better yet, these are the (only slightly stale) special edition Easter candy corn with the cute colors!

I take the clip off the bag and dive in, going for the pink and blue ones. "I was wondering when you were going to bring up the snowman."

Noah smirks as I hand him a couple of yellow and green candy corn. "Seriously though, did you like the guy? Maybe the whole 'getting you' thing can be learned."

I frown at the road. The street lights blink into the truck, giving me flashbacks to the strobe lights at a bachelorette party I went to at McGarry's a couple years ago. "I don't think I'll see him again, but it felt... kind of nice to be on a date."

"Really?"

"Yeah. I mean, you know I've never really been into dating."

"So what changed?"

For some reason, I feel an urge to look at him. He doesn't see me looking, so I scan his side profile for a minute. Register his strong nose, the way his thick, dark hair curls out below his white ball cap, the stubble on his jawline that's grown out after a day of not shaving. How does he still look so groomed after horseback riding and "maybe" rolling around in dirt?

I bite my bottom lip, unsure how to answer his question. This is new territory for Noah and me, which is saying something. We have no problem talking about anything and everything, and we've seen each other through every high-light and lowlight of our lives—from tedious high school things, to my parents splitting up and leaving Mirror Valley, to Noah's family moving away. He's seen me ugly cry with frustration when parts of RightMatch's code weren't work-ing, and he's held my hair back when I've had nasty bouts of food poisoning.

I thought "new territory" didn't exist for us.

Then again, me dating, as a general concept, is new territory.

It would be nice to use *his* dating as our roadmap, our rulebook of where the boundaries are in our friendship, but we don't actually talk about his dates much past the surface stuff. All I really know about Noah's romantic life is that he dates often and almost exclusively gorgeous women with at least one other enviable quality: Intelligence. Kindness. Baking ability. Access to dogs (she was a vet).

"I don't know if something necessarily 'changed' so much as I figured it was time I tried something new." I frown. "I've watched all these couples get together over the past couple years—Daisy and Luke, Val and Ethan, Ivy and James. Maybe I want to see if I can find something like that for myself. I work for a dating app; my job is to make romance happen. I kind of want to see what the fuss is about."

I shift in my seat to hear my own words come back to me. For so many years, I convinced myself that I didn't need any of that, didn't need to fall in love to be happy. And it was true, I didn't. I was happy, just as I was. I buried myself in my work, convinced myself that RightMatch's mission was bigger and better than anything in my personal life.

But maybe my priorities are shifting.

"I get it. You know I'm all about trying new things to find the right fit." A smile touches Noah's lips, and he takes the brim of his ball cap and switches it frontwards—something I know he does when he's unsure of himself. Probably considering the multiples and multiples of jobs he's tried over the years. "Have you thought about what you want in a guy?"

"What is this, 20 questions?" I joke as my gut reaction kicks in to protect, defend, keep those walls up. But my laughter sounds nervous and pitchy to my own ears and I know that Noah, of all people, won't let me get away with it. "Uhm. I don't have a list, like Daisy would. But I have a general idea of what I want. I'm a data scientist at heart, you know, so I have my criteria."

"Which are?" Noah prods, and now, I have to look at him in confusion. He shoots me a look back. "Maybe I know a guy. I could set you up."

I chuckle, although the thought of Noah setting me up on a date makes me intensely uncomfortable for some reason. "I know everyone you know, dude."

"Not everyone. You don't know Spence from football camp."

"Spence... like the guy who ate too many corn dogs and yarfed all over the field?"

"That was *years* ago, back when we were in high school. He's a good guy, Dee, just give him a chance." Noah blinks innocently. "Last I heard, he's working in sales at a Tesla dealership in Denver."

My nose crinkles as I question my best friend's instincts. "So he's one of those overly peppy people whose entire job is to charm you? You are hereby banned from setting me up."

Noah chuckles. "But seriously, what is it you're looking for?"

"I don't know... I'd like for us to have lots in common. He has to love sports, but especially baseball and volleyball. I *guess* I can make an exception that he cheers for a rival team so long as he isn't obnoxious about it. And he has to be smart. And genuinely kind. And attractive. And he has to love nacho sandwiches as much as I do."

Noah shoots me an amused glance. "Is that all?"

"Maybe my standards are too high."

"Your standards are just fine. You know, a lot of people say that your spouse should be your best friend. My mom jokes that that's the main reason she's still married to my dad—no one has ever supported her and made her laugh like he does."

"Really?" My response sounds far away to my own ears. Something in Noah's words is tripping me up.

"Absolutely." Noah looks at me for a moment. "A good friendship is key to any good relationship."

I'm not sure how to answer that and there's a pause, a hesitation. Of course, the song's changing as well, so the silence feels extra loud.

I'm sure Noah didn't mean anything by those words, but I suddenly have a bad feeling churning in my stomach. And then, I realize why.

If our spouses are meant to be our best friends... well, that means that *we* won't be best friends after he gets married to someone else. So where would that leave us?

I breathe through it. "Your parents do have an enviable marriage, so that checks out. But honestly, I can't imagine having a better friend than you, Noah."

I want to look at him but I'm worried what my expression might show right now. Truth is, I can't picture my life without Noah in it. Don't think I could bear it if we weren't as close as we are now.

Noah's silent and I almost wonder if I said the words out loud. But when he speaks, I hear the smile in his voice. "I can't imagine not being your friend either, Dee. And besides, not seeing Bruce on a daily basis is simply not an option for me."

I finally venture a look at him to meet his gaze, and he smiles, but there's something peculiar about the smile. Almost a weariness that I can't recognize. But the next minute, he looks forward again and I realize it was just a trick of the flashing strobe road lights.

That bad feeling is still gnawing at me, but I push it away. Open the bag of candy corn and take out another handful, picking out the pink and blue ones. Pure sugar and corn syrup cures everything, right?

"So tell me about the carpentry job," I ask to change the subject. "Is this it? Have you finally found *your calling*?"

Noah shoots me a teasing wink, and relief fills me as things return to normal. "Feels closer to my calling than accounting, I'll tell you that much."

I snort. Noah's by far the least serious, buttoned-up person I know. He might not *have* to work with the money he gets from NoSmellSoles, but I know that finding a job he enjoys, a job that brings him meaning, is important to him. He's tried working at cafes and restaurants, at the garage, at the town hall.

The months he spent interning at Luke's accounting firm were perhaps the most bizarre of all the jobs he's had, but it also shows just how desperate things were getting.

Then, Noah heard that our town's carpenter, Raymond Hall, needed help at his shop. Noah's been working with him for the past couple weeks, and while I can't confirm this, it seems like he might be enjoying this job more than the others.

"Yeah, I still have nightmares of you grilling me about taxes," I say through another mouthful of candy corn. "Luke, on the other hand..."

"The guy was born in a suit. He was the OG Boss Baby."

"My thoughts exactly."

Noah opens his mouth and I take aim, throwing him a green candy corn. He catches it on his tongue. "I'm enjoying the carpenter thing, though. Crafting things with my hands, creating something beautiful from nothing—"

"Working with your shirt off, sawing wood all intense and manly-like."

"That's right." Noah presses his lips together. "That's really all I'm doing at work—sawing, cutting, being shirtless. The ladies go nuts."

I laugh, relaxing into my seat as the bad feeling from earlier finally tapers off. Whatever it was, it's passed, and it's not even worth worrying about. This is Noah and me. Me and Noah. Best friends.

And I wouldn't change us for anything.

6

DEE

"HOW'D IT GO?!"

I wince and wrench the dial down on the speakers as Daisy's voice blasts through the car. "Eek. Too loud, Dais. I forgot to turn down the volume the last time I was driving."

"That sounds like a you problem, sister of mine," she chortles. "Listening to the whales again?"

"What? It's grounding. I always listen to the whales before practice. They get me in the zone." It's an odd little habit, but I swear it works. I've never lost a volleyball match after a ten-minute whale session.

"Uh huh. And how was practice?"

"It was okay." I smirk. "The boys spent more time arguing over who won at arm wrestling on Saturday night than actually playing volleyball. So the whale sounds weren't really needed, anyway."

"You have to be the only person I've ever known who listens to whale sounds to get themselves pumped. And I used to work at a gym; I've heard it *all*."

"Don't knock it 'til you try it."

Daisy laughs and I have to laugh with her. My sister and I are polar opposites on practically everything. I'm a certified tomboy who can be found sitting inside coding, or playing hard at volleyball. Daisy is a ray of sunshine who lives for the outdoors and is totally in touch with her feminine side. But I rely on her in ways she doesn't even realize.

Growing up, our mom and dad weren't super present in our lives, and with Daisy and I being normal teen girls, we didn't always get along. I spent most of my time with the Jacksons, and Daisy was often with her best friend Ivy Brooks and her family. Eventually, the Jacksons left Mirror Valley to settle in different cities around the country, so Daisy and I reconnected.

She's now my best friend (after Noah), and I love her dearly.

"I'll get Luke to listen with me the next time we go for a run," Daisy says. "Now, I know it's been a few days, but I want to hear about your date with Ollie. And spare no details!"

"It was fine," I say, unsure exactly what details Daisy might want to hear. I'm not usually on this side of the "date dishing", as Daisy used to call it. "We had a good time, but I don't think we'll see each other again."

"Why not? Wasn't he cute?"

"He was."

"And wasn't he smart?"

"Definitely."

"So what's the problem?"

I shrug, flipping on my turn signal to get off Main Street. The Thursday market is on this evening and the roads are a mess. I don't know what I was thinking taking this route. Plus, it's baking hot outside, and the A/C in my car recently conked out. It's yet another expense that I'm putting off until I know, for sure, that I still have a job. "He just wasn't my type. For one thing, he's a Brewers fan."

"And that's a bad thing because..."

"They're a rival team."

She lets out a sigh so forceful that I almost feel her exhale blow through the car. "This is just like that astrology thing where some people won't date a person because their star signs aren't compatible. Dee, you can't get the full scope of someone based solely on their choice of sports team."

I let out a laugh. "I know, Dais, it's just an excuse. Ollie wasn't it for me. He didn't give me the, you know…"

I grasp for a term. Some word, preferably a highly analytical and scientific word, to describe what I'm looking for. I'm a head over heart girl at every turn, and I do have my criteria, as I told Noah.

And yet, the only thing I can come up with is: "The sparkly feeling."

"Sparkly feeling?"

"Like in movies." My cheeks start to warm. I don't advertise my love of romcoms, but I am a religious romantic comedy movie watcher, and this is the only point of reference I have to help describe what I mean. "When the couple is about to get together, the music gets all dreamy and there's, like, the sparkly feeling."

"Okay… And have you ever had that with anyone?"

I bite my lower lip. I think I had it once, way back in high school. But I'm not about to tell Daisy that. It was probably a fluke anyway. "I'll know it when I see it."

"Alright, goof, whatever works for you. Have you been going through the app? Finding any potentials? You know what they say when something doesn't work out, you gotta get back to it. Get back on that horse. So to speak."

"Horses aren't my thing."

"Just humor me, will ya?"

I roll my eyes. "I've been looking, but no one's really standing out."

"*Yet*," Daisy adds with gusto. "You'll find someone who interests you."

"I guess so," I reply blandly. I truly can't muster any more enthusiasm than that. Sure, I've seen some attractive men on RightMatch, have started talking to a couple guys who enjoy sports, but the whole process exhausts me. I find myself caught up in the actual operation of the app and how I could improve the UX versus actually trying to make a connection with someone.

Daisy must assume (correctly) that I'm losing interest in the date chat because she goes on to say, "Wasn't there a big game you were looking forward to the same night as the date? How'd that go? Were there a lot of homers and people at bats?"

Bless her heart, my sister knows nothing about baseball. I appreciate the effort, though.

Now on much more comfortable ground, I tell her about the game. "The Rockies made a crazy comeback towards the end. You should've seen how excited everyone was at the bar. Even Grumpy Tony was smiling." My own lips tip up at the memory. I'm still stuck in traffic and I pull up the emergency brake to give my foot a rest while waiting for the crosswalk to clear. "It was lucky that Noah was DD; the rest of the guys definitely had a beer too many."

"Noah was there?" I hear the frown in Daisy's voice. "Didn't he have a date that night, too?"

"He came by afterwards."

"What a surprise."

I ignore her sarcasm. And maybe it's the heat of the evening, or the relentless traffic, or my anxiety about Lachlan's arrival tomorrow, or the fact that my stomach's been a little off ever since that drive home with Noah on Saturday night, but I then say, "We had a weird conversation on the way home, though."

"Oh?"

"We were talking about my starting to date and he said that he'd want his spouse to be his best friend." The bad feeling is churning again. Maybe Daisy will have some insight.

"Why is that weird?"

"I don't know." My frown deepens. "Noah and I are best friends. I guess I'm worried about losing him."

Daisy's silent for a long moment. Too long. I remember the days when she used to insist that Noah and I should be together. But we'd never date. It simply wouldn't happen. Noah is firmly in my friend zone, just like I'm in his. That's the way it's always been and the way it will always be. But I hold my breath, expecting Daisy to say something along those lines again—*why don't you just date him already? What's keeping you two from being together?*

Yadda yadda yadda.

Instead, she says, "Didn't you think that this might happen someday?"

I frown. "What might happen?"

"That Noah would want to settle down. Get married. Be in a real, long-term, committed relationship."

I swallow thickly as the bad feeling intensifies, now heavy and itching as it washes over my skin. I rub my arms, wishing I could so easily brush it away. "He never has before. His relationships only ever lasted a few months and then they'd break up. Jayme was his most serious girlfriend and they were together six months."

"You guys are getting older now. Things change. Maybe Noah wants something more serious than he's had before. Maybe he wants kids someday."

Kids? Noah? The heavy feeling is sliced with an odd, not unpleasant warmth deep in my belly at the thought of baby Noahs running around.

Dang, he'd have some cute kids. But with who?

His wife, I guess.

Goodness, I can't imagine Noah having a *wife*.

There's a pressure on my chest. It feels like someone's punched me in the gut and I'm trying to catch my breath, though I'm still just sitting here. In traffic. Staring at the big, stupid balloon cowboy hat that some high school kid strung up above the town hall. "What does that have to do with anything?"

"Well, Dee..." Daisy's voice is gentle, and I have a vivid flashback to the time I went over to Noah's house when I was twelve and Mrs. Jackson kindly let me know that I had a training bra static-clung to my back. Daisy can't see me, but does she know what this is doing to me? "It means that you and Noah will always be best friends, but maybe Noah's looking for that special *other* best friend."

Oof. There it is.

I feel like I've taken a fall in beach volleyball, scraping bare skin against the cement beneath the sand. I cannot handle whatever's happening in my body right now.

Beeeeep!

I leap in my seat and bump my head on the roof of my car.

Peek out the side mirror to see none other than Grumpy Tony waving at me to get going. The road ahead is clear and the light's about to turn yellow.

"Fudgsicles," I mutter as I put the car in gear. Press on the gas.

Go nowhere because the emergency brake's up.

"Sorry, Tony!" I holler out the window when I finally speed off. In the rearview mirror, the guy's shaking his head, gray mustache twitching angrily.

"Dee, you okay?!" Daisy's asking in a panic. "What happened?"

"Sorry, sorry. I was stopped at a green light and Tony was very politely letting me know."

"Patience of a bear, that one," Daisy tuts.

"I'll say. Listen, I'll be at Fran's soon, so I gotta go."

"Why are you at Fran's?"

"She borrowed my duffel bag for a trip to Denver with Raymond. I usually keep all my work stuff in there for when I move between the Main Street office and home. I want to get it back before the boss arrives tomorrow."

"So soon. Are you nervous?"

"You have no idea."

"Come over tonight. Luke and I will make you dinner."

"That's okay, I just ate my bodyweight in burgers at the diner. And Noah's coming by later."

"'Course he is."

Daisy and I say our goodbyes right as I'm pulling up to Fran's house, but after I park the car, I sit for a moment. Catch my breath. Recover from the Grumpy Tony green light situation, but also from the conversation with Daisy. And what it might mean for my future with Noah.

There's some irony in the fact that I'm having these thought spirals while sitting outside of Fran's house. Fran Bellamy is brilliant, charismatic, and deeply kind, but she's also a bit of a nut. Last year, she set up a fortune teller tent at an event that Daisy and Luke had organized, and when Noah and I went in to get our fortunes read…

She predicted that Noah and I would be married.

Which is bizarre. And weird.

I couldn't get out of there fast enough, and since then, I have simply never thought about it again.

Because seriously, weird.

But if Daisy's right and Noah *is* looking for someone who will, one day, be his wife—someone who's not me, of course—as his best friend, I should do what's best for him, right? Which probably means giving him space and time for another best friend.

Logically, that would be the kindest, best thing to do.

Honestly, I'd rather never watch baseball again than give up my time with Noah. But this isn't about me.

I give my head a shake, open the car door, and head towards Fran's multi-colored townhouse. Ring the doorbell, and wait barely three seconds before the door wrenches open.

"Hello, Dee!" Raymond Hall booms, smiling wide. The guy is wearing khakis and a sensible forest green button-up shirt beneath a bright purple apron that clearly belongs to Fran. "Come in, Franny said you'd be dropping by this afternoon."

I step into the house and am immediately hit with the smells of warm apples, caramel, and cinnamon. My mouth waters. "What is *that*?"

"We're baking pies with apples we got from the market this evening," Raymond explains. "Want a slice?"

I pat my stomach regretfully. "I just filled up on burgers with the guys after volleyball practice. But I'd love to take a couple slices home for Noah and me, if that's okay."

"Of course, my dear." Raymond steps back and gestures for me to go first towards the kitchen, where I find Fran standing at the stove with a wooden spoon held to her mouth as she tastes the pie filling.

She drops the spoon with a wide smile as soon as I walk in. "So good to see you, my girl!"

Fran's usually a hugger, but she knows I'm not touchy feely, so I appreciate the way she instead simply pulls out a chair at the kitchen table for me. She gestures for me to sit, and I do, folding my hands in my lap.

"How are you two doing?" I ask, looking between the two seniors.

55

We spend a few minutes catching up, with Fran and Raymond telling me about their trip to Denver for a butterfly convention, of all things. They have me in stitches while describing what happened when Fran's motorbike got a flat tire as they were leaving a gas station. It took a few concerned attendants, a couple phone calls to a dealership that unfortunately didn't carry the right tires, and a kindly biker gang to help them out.

As they speak, I can't help but notice how comfortable they are with each other. Their conversation is so fun and light, and they laugh easily, sharing inside jokes I don't understand. The two have been friends for years, and Fran insists that that is all they are to each other—good friends. Nothing more.

Just like Noah and me.

Good friends, and nothing more.

7

NOAH

The guys and I are still sitting around our booth at Mountainview Diner when I get a text from Dee. I pick my phone up off the table, unable to move much more than that. We are in full, shameless manspread position after stuffing ourselves with burgers stacked to half the lengths of our forearms. I don't know how Dee managed to roll herself out of this booth, let alone drive all the way to Fran's house in Thursday night traffic.

I skim her text about Fran and Raymond. The pair are such opposites and probably shouldn't even be friends, and yet, they just... work.

I'm smiling at my phone, mid-reply, when a fry hits me in the face.

My friends let out a chorus of "ohhhh"s.

"Sorry, cap," Parker says sheepishly. "I was aiming for your phone."

"What're you smiling at anyway?" Amir asks, scraping up the last of the ketchup on his plate with a miniscule piece of potato. "Funny message from that Yanica chick?"

"It's just Dee." I set down my phone. "Yanica and I aren't a thing."

Finn and Parker both loll their heads from side to side on the back of their booth. Jarrod, of course, doesn't seem the least bit surprised.

"Dude, you've got it so bad," Amir tuts.

Jarrod crosses his arms so his massive biceps pop. "That's what I told him."

"It's not a big deal." I switch my ball cap so it faces backwards. "Look, I spoke to Dee. I know where I stand."

This gets their attention. Parker and Amir both sit up straight, while Jarrod leans forward, eyes wide. "You spoke to Dee?! When?"

"The night of the Rockies game. After we dropped you off."

"And?! Come on, don't hold out on us now."

I shake my head. Everyone knows about the prolific Mirror Valley rumor mill, but what people don't know is that the twenty-something-year-old athletes are just as involved and invested in it as are the "town gossips". But I trust that they won't go around spilling what I have to say. "Nothing much. She just confirmed what I already know: I'm comfortably in the friend zone."

Frustrated grunts and grumbles sound around the table. So much so that Alice, our waitress, looks over with an eyebrow raised. I shoot her a reassuring smile to say that the noises have nothing to do with the food and everything to do with the fact that my friends are basically cavemen.

"So she said she only sees you as a friend?" Finn clarifies. "Even after you told her how you feel?"

"Maybe she didn't believe you," Amir adds, earning him mutters around the table. "What?! Noah has a bit of a rep, you know."

Jarrod and Finn both shoot him a look but I sit up in my seat. "No, no, he's right. I've obviously dated a lot over the years, but this is different."

"So what happened when you told her?" Jarrod asks.

I clasp my glass of soda. The condensation is cool against my fingertips. "Well, we... didn't get to that part."

"What do you mean?"

"Dee started talking about how we're best friends, and she can't imagine not having me in her life. And I realized that that's all she sees for us. She's happy with our relationship, as it is." I take a breath and hold it, remembering the fall in my chest when she spoke those words. "I got to thinking that, if I told Dee how I feel and she doesn't feel the same way, what would happen then? I don't want things to become awkward with us, or make her uncomfortable."

"That all made sense when Dee wasn't dating or looking for anything," Finn says. "But now that she is..."

The guys are frowning, looking very unlike their normally happy-go-lucky selves. Actually, they're all making the exact expression I made when I got home that night and wondered if I'd done the right thing by not telling her.

"Correct me if I'm wrong..." Amir points another tiny potato my way. "But Dee hasn't even *tried* to see you as something other than a friend. It's not that she rejected you or won't take you seriously, but she just hasn't made that leap." A smirk grows on his lips. A dangerous, dangerous smirk. "Boys, we all know what that means."

Smiles grow around the table, one by one, as my friends clue in.

"What?" I ask.

"You, my friend, have to woo her."

"*Woo* her?" I snort. "What is this, the 1800s?"

Amir ignores me. "You have to *show* her that you two could have something more than friendship. 'Cuz you're not imagining it, dude, you guys are flirty. You joke and tease each other in a way that she doesn't do with anyone else."

"Plus, Dee's *so* not touchy feely, except around you," Parker adds. "There's something there. You just have to show her what it is."

"So... you want me to sweep her off her feet."

"Exactly."

"Isn't that a bit sneaky? Manipulative? I don't like going behind Dee's back."

"It's not going behind her back. If anything, it's showing her something that's *directly* in front of her *face*," Amir says passionately.

"Sometimes people can't see what's right in front of them," Finn adds sagely. "You tried telling her and that clearly didn't work out, so this is your chance to try a different angle. It's not like you have to do anything drastic, but just little things, here and there."

"Little things." I repeat the words like I have any clue what these guys are going on about.

Jarrod picks up on my unasked question. "Like, being sweet with her and giving her compliments. Helping her out with things that she needs or wants but would never ask for. Bringing her favorite food and drinks when you see her. Doing her favors, and bonus points for doing them shirt-less." He winks.

"Brush her hair back from her face and look deep, deep into her eyes..." Parker volunteers next, blinking comically wide a few times.

"Have you heard of the love languages?" Jarrod asks.

"Love languages," I repeat again. I swear I'm not usually this dense, especially when it comes to women. But these guys might as well be speaking a foreign language.

"Ooh, good one!" Finn tells Jarrod. "He should look into those."

"Isobel made me find mine." Jarrod harrumphs, crossing his broad arms over his broad chest so his biceps pop. But his eyes are absolutely gleeful. "I'm quality time and acts of service."

"No way. I'm—"

"Guys." I hold up my hands. "Should I be taking notes or something?"

"Well, duh," Parker replies helpfully.

Amir rolls his eyes. "You, of all people, don't need to take notes, Noah. Just charm her. It's not like you've never done it before. You definitely don't need us to tell you how."

He's right. This is crazy. I've done my fair share of "wooing" over the years. I have a pretty good idea of what women like; know how to flirt and touch and listen. Above all, listen. And make them laugh.

But something about trying it all with Dee makes me feel like I'm an awkward fourteen-year-old all over again. Like I'm starting from scratch. I've never felt so uncertain in my life. Maybe because I've never liked a girl like I like Dee. The stakes are so high. "Love languages aside, I can't just walk up to Dee and brush her hair back from her face while staring into her eyes. She'd think I was losing it."

"Well, you'd have to work up to that," Parker agrees. "Start small, little brushes and flirty comments and... love language stuff. Then get to the sparks and hand-holding, until finally, you get the big, cheesy movie kiss."

He puckers his lips stupidly and the guys crack up. But the air officially leaves my lungs at the thought of kissing Dee.

Wrapping her in my arms.

Claiming her lips with mine...

Way to take 1000 steps ahead of yourself. "Well, I kinda failed at telling her, so I guess the whole 'showing her' thing is worth a shot."

"Might want to tone down the enthusiasm," Amir says.

"Well, I don't want to make Dee uncomfortable."

61

"So don't." Jarrod loops an arm over my shoulders. "And trust me, you won't."

I roll my eyes. "Alright, I'll do it. And if she's not receptive, I'll back off and return to the friend zone."

"*Oh*, she'll be receptive," Parker says in a tone of voice that earns him a swift punch in the shoulder, which he then returns. In her corner of the diner, Alice peers over again, looking at once deeply exhausted and annoyed.

The boys and I shoot her beaming smiles until she turns away.

As they all move onto the next topic of conversation, I drum my fingers against my glass, lost in thought. I still don't know how to begin addressing these boundaries with Dee. And even if I *did* start trying this with her, would she actually consider it?

8

DEE

I never thought I'd see the day when the whales aren't enough.

But it's here. On a *Friday*, no less.

I pace around my office on Main Street once more, a rowdy, claw-filled game of cat and mouse taking place in my stomach. Anxiety, nerves, foreboding, and a *skosh* too much caffeine are not a good mix. I don't know what I was thinking taking an extra shot of espresso in my Americano this morning.

New standing desk and office chair ready to go? *Check.*

Floor vacuumed and office tidied? *Check.*

Mini fridge stocked with all the energy drinks, sodas, and water you could ever need? *Check check.*

Pillows on my silly, totally out-of-place red couch plumped to perfection?

I frown. *Not plump enough!*

I return to the couch and pick up a pillow, beating it aggressively. Maybe too aggressively. My entire body is vibrating, every single one of my muscles clenched into a tight ball. I'm like a cat ready to pounce. But not in a sexy, jungle leopard kind of way. More like a deranged tabby.

When Ria knocked on my door earlier, I almost leaped out of my skin. Apparently, the sounds coming from my office above her hair salon were frightening her customers. Once I apologized and explained that they were whale sounds, she seemed relieved.

Which did make me wonder what on earth she thought was happening up here...

Anyway. No time for that. Not when I'm mere moments away from meeting the man who holds my entire career—and therefore, my future—in his big, Wall Street-y hands.

I check my watch once more and brush down the front of my shirt. I wish I could say that I hadn't spent literal hours trying to decide what to wear today, but then I'd be lying. And I never lie except in dire circumstances.

I spent three hours picking out my current outfit—dark jeans, my nice white Converse, and a pressed, royal blue polo with the sleeves rolled up. I brushed my hair back into a low ponytail, and even put on a bit of makeup.

See, the problem with these cool tech companies and their laidback culture is that you have *no idea* how "business-like" you should be when your new boss comes to town. There aren't any guidelines for this sort of thing. I don't want to appear too formal, in case Lachlan—Mr. Chase?—is dressed casually, and I don't want to be too casual for fear of conveying a lack of respect. My parents were self-proclaimed workaholics when I was growing up, and their motto was to "always put your best foot forward".

I don't think they ever considered what to do if your feet are absolutely free to wear whatever the heck they want to wear.

Can you tell I didn't sleep last night?

"Is there a Dee-bug in here?"

The voice—so deep and honeyed and familiar—shocks

my poor, over-caffeinated heart and sends a jolt of adrenaline rocketing through my system. I yelp and my legs spring into action, launching me onto the couch so that I end up squishing the newly plumped pillows.

"Noah!" I shriek. "Can't you knock?!"

He cackles as he jogs up the stairs, and then raises a dark brow when he spots me cowering on the couch with a hand at my chest like I'm a swooning Scarlet O'Hara. "I did knock. You didn't hear?"

"Not over my heartbeat." I grimace. "I had too much coffee this morning."

Noah flashes those gorgeous pearly whites at me. Seriously, the guy has such perfect teeth for an athlete. He's somehow managed to avoid losing or chipping any teeth aside from that one incisor. "Rookie mistake when you've got something big coming up. Here." He steps forward, holding out his steel canteen. "Drink some water. It'll mellow you out."

My eyes narrow to slits. "Please promise me this is only water. I could *not* handle anything else right now."

Noah laughs hard—too hard—at the reminder of the day he filled my water bottle with buttermilk during a sweaty beach volleyball game in the height of summer. It did not go down well, let me tell you.

But at the sound of his laughter, my heart calms a little. Regains a somewhat steady rhythm.

"Top 10 best pranks. But I wouldn't do a repeat, that's just lazy. Besides, you got me back good, and I have no interest in repeating *that* experience."

I smirk. "You got off easy. With your lactose intolerance, filling your ball cap with buttermilk was a small price to pay."

Small price for Noah. Big payoff for me.

I will always delight in the memory of watching him

unknowingly flip the baseball cap onto his head while flirting with a woman he liked. Watching the thick, creamy substance absolutely soak his face, hair and shoulders was a delicious moment. Lauren—the flirtee—looked positively horrified...

Until Noah took off his shirt and used it to wipe himself down.

Lauren had no complaints after that.

On my end, I got to see someone's eyes physically turn into cartoon hearts and pop out of their head. Not that I could blame her. Noah's physique could serve as a model for the muscular cartoon characters that inspire such a reaction.

Yeah, I looked, not that I needed to. I know the landscape of Noah's upper body extremely well—the triangles of muscle between his neck and shoulders, his perfectly symmetrical pectorals, the actual washboard of his abdominals, the curves and swells of his biceps...

Hm. If everything goes down the drain at RightMatch, I might have a future in physiology.

I take a few glugs of water, and the liquid soothes my body even further. I hand Noah his canteen and stand from the couch. "Thanks. So aside from giving me unfortunate buttermilk flashbacks, what're you doing here?"

Noah places the canteen on the desk, then removes his ball cap, tossing his fingers through his hair a couple times. I know he prefers to keep it short, but I love his wayward curls. Something to grab onto if he's being annoying or overly pranky. "I wanted to see you before the boss arrives. Feeling better about it than you were last night?"

My lips tilt downwards. After I got home from Fran's yesterday, Noah came over and we had some of Fran and Ray's delicious apple pie (seriously, Ray might be a carpenter by trade, but he could easily moonlight as a pastry chef). And instead of talking about my nerves, I asked him to distract me. Something he does very effectively, I might add. We spent the evening playing a board game, followed by watching *He's Just Not That Into You*. Which isn't really your classic romcom, but it made me feel a tiny bit better about the fact that I'm not desperately and terribly in love with someone I could never have.

I suppose my subconscious might have chosen the movie because of what's happening at work and the current "love of my life" being this stupid dating app that I've spent years of hard work developing. But let's not go there.

"I feel fine. I feel..." I frown. "I feel like I might laugh, throw up and start crying all at the same time."

"Sounds about right." He grabs hold of the tangled, frayed threads on his wrist—the friendship bracelet I made for him at summer camp the year after he gave me the volleyball signet ring. The thing is ancient and ratty now, but Noah has never taken it off. I sometimes wonder why, but honestly, the little thing makes him seem somehow *more* charming and disarming. So, it's probably for dating reasons.

"Anyway," I say. "I feel like all we've talked about lately is me. How're *you* doing? How's work for you?"

Noah gives a lopsided little smirk. He's looking at me like I'm a highly unusual specimen that is amusing him. "Dee, it's okay to talk about how you're feeling. I want to hear about what's stressing you out."

"I'm not stressed, see?" I give him what I hope is a calm, breezy smile.

Noah practically leaps back. "Good grief. Don't do that again."

I glare at him.

He leans on the desk, kicking his legs out so his eyes are level with mine. "Seriously, though. It'll be okay. I know it's been a rough go with RightMatch lately and you don't know where you stand or where you *will* stand, but I'm always here for you. I will always support you, in any way that you need to be supported."

I smile at him. Normally, this time. "Thanks, Noah."

He raises a shoulder in that charming way of his. "I'd do anything for you, Dee."

The words reverberate through my body—from the top of my head to the tips of my toes, soothing every part of me that is worried and tense. My muscles relax, my heart finally slows to a normal pace, and I can take full breaths again.

I fall forward and loop my arms tight around him. Let him fold me against him like I'm the cheese in his burrito. I feel so much better here, in the endless comfort of his firm chest and even firmer arms. Noah might be built like a marble statue, but he's still tender and warm. And he smells like laundry soap and something uniquely *him*, mixed with a faint hint of sawdust from his job.

Anyone else might expect a guy like Noah to smell spicy and musky, effusing cologne on top of pheromones. But his scent is my favorite in the world—the Noah smell. If I could bottle it up and ship it out, it would surely ease the anxieties of people the world over. Stop wars, bring peace, make cranky kids smile.

After a few more moments wrapped in his arms, I look up at him. "Can I ask you a question?"

"Shoot," he replies, his expression open and curious.

"Are you... I mean, do you... Do you want to get married someday?"

Noah blinks. "What?"

"Like, have a wife. Stop the casual dating and short-term relationships, and actually marry someone."

A flash of something I can't recognize passes over his

face. His expression closes up the slightest bit. I regret asking the question almost as much as I feel gnawing curiosity for his answer.

He doesn't give it to me right away. Instead, his eyes scan my face slowly. "Yeah, I would like to get married one day."

My heart does a strange little squeeze at the confirmation, and I hug him again, pressing my cheek to his chest. I can't say I'm sad, exactly—that wouldn't be fair to him and his future happiness—but I suppose I'm already anticipating the days when I'll miss him.

"I don't know what I'll do without you," I whisper, because I don't trust my voice.

After a moment, I look up to see that he's smiling, but it doesn't touch his eyes. Eyes which have taken on a new intensity, are focused in a way I've rarely seen them before. His brows are slightly furrowed, like he's working something out. When he speaks though, his voice has his usual joking, light-hearted quality to it. "As if you'd ever be without me, Dee-bug. I'd get you a body pillow with my face on it rather than leave you alone."

I lean into his joke. "It better smell like you, too."

"I can put a t-shirt on it."

"I'm a little worried about what ideas you're cooking up right now." I note the small twist in his lips. I almost hear the gears turning in his brain, generating future pranks.

He lowers his mouth close to my ear, dropping his voice. "You won't see it coming."

His breath on the bare, sensitive skin of my neck triggers a wave of goosebumps all across my body, and I'm suddenly intensely aware of how close we are—his hands locked behind my back, my palms pressed to his firm chest...

I don't hate it. This the safest place in the world for me.

Then, Noah does the strangest thing.

Or maybe, it's not that the action is strange, but my own reaction.

He brings his left hand from behind my back to my face, sweeping a couple stray hairs from where they hang in front of my eyes. His fingers lightly trace along my temple, leaving cool fire against my skin. He wrinkles his brow, his eyes on my hair like he's intensely concentrated on the task.

And something deep inside me switches. Warmth gathers in my stomach before extending out through my extremities. I feel light. A little fizzy. Like after having a glass of champagne.

The world feels almost...

Sparkly.

Noah's eyes return to mine. "Sorry. Wanted to fix that before the boss arrives."

I can't respond. Words, sentences, the entire English language are caught in my throat.

Our gazes lock for one long, lingering minute. Two.

Wait. Is this—?

Knock knock!

Noah and I bound apart so quickly, I almost fall back onto the couch. And unfortunately, my stress levels bound, too—right back to where they were moments ago. Noah's my only effective stress-release apparently, and now that we're disconnected, it's all racing back.

"Ohmygosh, that's him." I wring my hands. "He's here."

Noah picks up his cap, places it on his head, and busies himself putting his canteen in his bag. When his eyes meet mine again, he smiles confidently. Easily. "You got this. Show him who's boss."

I steel myself and head downstairs with Noah on my heels. And when I open the door, I come face to face with a man I've only ever met through video calls, but even so, could tell that he was larger than life.

I was right. At an easy 6'5" and built like a tank, Lachlan Chase *is* larger than life.

He holds out a hand the size of a brick, his eyes glancing over Noah before returning to mine. "You must be Diandra."

A Greek god.

That's Lachlan Chase. But not just any Greek god—he would be Zeus. Exacting his power from above while gazing upon us mere mortals like we're cockroaches he could zap at any moment with his thunderbolt.

Lachlan Chase might be the most formidable, intimidating, terrifying person I've ever seen in my life. He looks like he stepped off the set of a Superman movie and squeezed himself into a suit that strains across his shoulders and broad chest as it tries to contain him. Like at any moment, he might Hulk out and burst his buttons if you so much as look at him wrong.

I'm mixing metaphors. I'm a mess.

It doesn't help that we're not seated in my lovely and established office space (with perfectly plumped pillows, I might add), but in Morning Bell cafe. And as you would expect if Zeus/Superman/the Hulk strolled into your small town, everyone is *looking*. Staring. Mouths open like they're codfish, but Superman and I are the ones stuck in the aquarium.

I'm living someone's fever dream, I swear.

"Doesn't this town have any oat milk?" Lachlan tsks as he scowls at the menu in what I can only describe as blatant disapproval. Meanwhile, I'm frozen in my seat, fingers clenched in my lap. I'm counting the pain points, knowing that my knuckles are white, but unable to relax.

Is this a rhetorical question?

I'll answer. Just in case.

"You can find oat milk at Mirror Grocery, and in the bulk supermarket close to Summer Lakes." My voice sounds robotic. I could make a pretty convincing Siri, if I do say so myself. "Of course, you'd need a car to get all the way out there, and the rental car market is insane right now. Especially if you're renting on a Friday. My friend Val is—"

"Found it." Lachlan cuts me off. Blessedly.

After we order our drinks—coffee with a sprinkle of oat milk for him, a calming chamomile tea for me—Lachlan leans back in his chair. It's comically small beneath him. I'm half-expecting the metal to let out a desperate cry for help before folding in on itself. I'll have to compliment Ethan, the cafe owner, for his furniture choices later.

Unfortunately, now that our drinks are on the way, Lachlan's attention can return to me. And does it ever. His eyes—a blue so light and frosty that they almost glow—rest on my face. His lips are pressed into a firm line that makes me wonder if he's ever so much as smiled. Something in his very presence is tuned towards me in a completely absorbed, intense kind of way.

Yeah. Lachlan Chase is *intense*.

It occurs to me that many women are probably drawn to this energy. Like moths to a flame. Like fish to turquoise, crocodile-infested waters.

Plus, the guy's gorgeous. All chiseled angles and sharp edges. But while he and Noah share the whole "carved of marble" thing, I can already tell that Lachlan doesn't have an iota of warmth to him. Where Noah's edges meet with tenderness, Lachlan's seem harsh and jagged. I've never hugged the guy, but I already know that he wouldn't have the Noah smell. Wouldn't have the Noah comfort and safety.

And speaking of Noah...

What on earth was happening in my office before? That felt like... something.

"So, Diandra," Lachlan says. His voice somehow sounds like pouring cement. "It's great to meet you in person."

I shift in my seat slightly. Try to unclench my hands, but I can't. I've never felt so out of sorts in my entire life. And instead of getting *into* sorts, my stupid brain keeps jumping back to that moment in Noah's arms. "You can call me Dee. And yes, it's meet nicing you, too." My eyes widen a fraction. "*Nice meeting* you. Sorry, I'm nervous."

Ugh. Why did I say that?

Lachlan's lips barely twitch. "No need to be nervous. Consider this a casual introduction. A meet and greet. You're the lead dev at RightMatch, so I want to see what you're working on. And *how* you're working all the way over here, so far from the rest of the team. "

I give an easy one-shoulder shrug. Cool, calm and collected, that's me. "I have no complaints. Working alone suits me perfectly, and I try to keep lines of communication with the rest of the dev team open at all times."

"Yes, but there's been a lot of turnover lately. I just want to be sure that RightMatch is getting its best chance at success with the acquisition. That's all."

He might intend for this statement to sound encouraging, intend for it to seem like he believes in RightMatch. Instead, it sounds like a vague threat of what would happen in the case of failure. I bob my head a few times. "I understand."

"Good. Over the next week, I want to be fully briefed on everything you have going on. All of your projects." Lachlan then goes on to list what he expects of me and details exactly what the next week will look like, along with the rest of today.

It's a lot. I don't expect to see the light of day until he leaves next Friday.

And this is summer. The days are *long*.

I clasp my fingers around my empty mug—I finally managed to unclench my hands, and the mug is my new victim—as Lachlan sips the last of his coffee. "Why *did* you choose to come to Mirror Valley on a Friday, anyway?" I ask. Boldly, if I do say so myself. "Wouldn't it have made more sense to start fresh on Monday?"

It's the first time I've really spoken up. The first time I've asked a question of *him* instead of the other way around. Lachlan raises a brow at me. Part of me wants to shrink back and cower, but I stay strong. Meet his gaze with firm resolve. If I've learned anything from my years living and breathing and studying and working in this male-dominated industry, it's that I have to make myself known. Create space for myself and use my voice. Not only for me, but for other women who love this career as much as I do.

"I wanted to see what the work environment is like here," Lachlan responds slowly, like he's choosing his words. "You are the only RightMatch employee who is completely remote so I figured I'd join you. Give you some company for once. Plus, I needed a break from the city."

He waves Ethan down to pay the bill using one of those obnoxious hand scribbles I've only ever seen in movies. Ethan's a teddy bear of a person, but even *he* seems perplexed by the gesture.

I'm about to stand, eager for us to return to my office so I can focus on our afternoon tasks instead of Lachlan's scary face.

Instead, he leans back in his chair again, and this time, the metal squeaks in protest. The corners of Lachlan's lips have turned down and he's staring at me quizzically. I perch in my awkward half-stand for a full minute before placing my butt back in my chair.

"You seem like an intelligent, go-getting, no-nonsense type of person, Diandra. So can I speak frankly?"

The knot in my stomach tightens at the tone of his voice. "Yes."

"Myself and the board of directors have doubts. We've looked at the effectiveness of RightMatch in comparison to the other dating apps within our portfolio and, if you'll pardon the expression, it doesn't quite match up. Frankly, we have concerns…"

And just like that, Lachlan's voicing all of the statements I was up all night worried I'd hear.

"We're not sure what the future looks like for RightMatch."

"The market's not picking this up at the moment. There are too many competitors."

"We're trying to figure out where RightMatch fits within our broader business."

Yadda yadda yadda.

I only really hear snippets of what he says over the high-pitched ringing in my ears. I'm in full panic mode, my fingers clenched back around my mug so tight, I'm surprised it doesn't shatter.

This app that I've put endless hours working on to grow from scratch. This thing that truly does feel like my own baby, my pride and joy, the fruit of all that labor…

Let's just say that the thought of it all coming to nothing feels not unlike having a meteor hit me square in the face.

Not to be dramatic.

But somehow, I'm bobbing my head at Lachlan, trying to remind myself to keep breathing. Somehow, I hear a voice within myself that sounds a whole lot like Daisy.

Stay present. Deep breaths. Listen.

There's got to be a way to fix this.

Daisy is the optimistic one of the two of us. I'm the real-ist. "Prepare for the worst, hope for the best" is my motto. But the worst is happening right now, and though I've been stressing for weeks about this meeting, nothing could've prepared me for this emotional impact.

So maybe I need to change tack. Take a page out of Daisy's way-too-smiley book for once (with the knowledge that I can slam the book shut if and when I need to).

Through the cotton balls in my ears, I strain to listen to Lachlan's next words. "We understand that RightMatch is fairly new on the market, and it only fully released last year, but unless we see results—"

"What kinds of results?" I manage to ask.

Lachlan's brows draw together, creating a shade over his eyes. I can't tell whether he's deep in thought or surprised that I asked another question. Or upset that I cut him off.

Probably the latter.

"We want stats," he says. "A better scope of the usage. Success stories. That kind of thing."

Success stories?

Ding ding ding!

"I have a success story!" I practically shout. Over Lach-lan's shoulder, Ethan raises a brow at me as if to say "pipe down, dude".

Lachlan is staring at me warily, his nose wrinkled. He might be questioning my sanity, but this is hardly the time and place for tact. Not when my app-baby is on the line.

"And is this a success story with tangible, long-term results?" he asks, his words heavy with skepticism. "I won't stand for a three or four month fling."

Oh, he's going to *love* this. Daisy and Luke got together because of RightMatch. Sure, they already knew each other well given that Luke is Daisy's best friend Ivy's big brother, and they used to see each other at the gym all the time. But they fell in love (in part) thanks to the app.

I nod proudly. "The story ends with a happily-ever-after."

Somehow, despite this, Lachlan seems even *more* doubtful. His right eyebrow is all the way up near his hairline, defeating any argument that his lack of laugh lines are from botox usage. "And this is an *actual* story involving people you *know*. I don't care about a friend of a friend's hairdresser in another town far, far away."

I pause for a beat, noting Lachlan's skeptical expression, his words dripping with disbelief. And I come to a very sobering observation: Lachlan Chase has no interest in maybes, potentials, or probabilities. He cares about facts. Black and white. Yes or no. There is no middle ground with him. Whatever I say, it needs to convince him once and for all, straight away. Needs to be exactly what he wants to hear, exactly what he wants to see.

He needs the facts, right in front of him.

Because if I hit that gray area, I doubt he'll give me a chance to try again.

So as I watch my one lifeline start to slip away, I make a snap decision. And before I can give myself time to think it through, the words are already spilling from my mouth. "The story is near and dear... because it happened to me."

Lachlan's left eyebrow joins his right all the way up his forehead. He seems almost as taken aback as I am by my words.

Remember how I said I never lie?

Well, if there was ever a dire circumstance...

"You're married?" His voice is filled with so much disbelief, I'm a little offended.

"Engaged," I clarify. Uselessly. Because what on earth am I even doing right now?

Apparently, I'm co-opting Luke and Daisy's story. And while they might be married, the lone voice of reason in this chaos is telling me that Lachlan will never believe that I myself am married. He's surely seen my employee file, might be tipped off by the fact that I didn't mention a husband during our morning together.

An engagement is simply more believable. "More" being the operative word.

"For how long?" Lachlan asks cooly.

Keep it vague. "A few months."

He continues to assess me. His eyes drop to my left hand. "I don't see a ring."

"It's being resized."

Where is this coming from?! Am I the Tom Brady of lying under pressure?

Honestly, I'm a little stung by his disbelief. Sure, I'm brand spanking new on the dating scene and haven't even considered if I want to get married someday, but surely me being someone's fiancée isn't *that* absurd?

And yet, Lachlan's eyes are light blue, frosty slits. "Right. And the lucky guy is..."

He trails off, and finally, his brow clears. *Finally*, he seems a touch less doubtful.

"The man in your office this morning," he finishes.

I blink.

Oh, boy. Noah's gonna *love* this.

"So how'd it happen?" Lachlan asks before I can either confirm or deny, crossing his arms over his massive chest.

My brain scrambles and short-circuits for a moment as I try to keep up with my own deception.

Sorry, Daisy!

And so, I launch into telling Daisy and Luke's love

story... but with Noah and me as the protagonists. I explain that I'd been looking for my soulmate for years when I decided to give RightMatch a go. I tell him that Noah signed up for the app a year after getting out of a broken engagement. We matched, not knowing that the other was a good friend in real life, and after an app glitch gone right, things began to escalate and our relationship kicked off. A relationship that culminated in a proposal.

A success story, through and through.

For Noah and me. Yup.

When I've finished, Lachlan's gaze doesn't waver from my face. I don't have extensive experience lying, but I've been told I have a good poker face. I hope it's carrying me through.

"That's quite the story," he says, giving nothing away. "It almost sounds made up."

I set my jaw. This, at least, is not a lie. "It's not."

Lachlan bobs his head once. Slowly. "Well, if that's the case, I'll put you in touch with our communications team. They're going to go nuts over a story like that."

It takes every muscle within me to keep from collapsing with relief. He believed me. My job is safe, at least for now. If nothing else, I've bought myself time, and I don't intend to waste it. I keep my expression steady, poker face firmly in place. "Absolutely."

"I hope to see your fiancé over the next week. Hear his side of the story." He does a funny flip of his wrist to check a watch that likely costs more than my car. "For now, let's get back to the office, we have a lot of work to do. I'll use the restroom and we can go."

Lachlan strides towards the back of the cafe and it's like my world opens up again. My vision expands. I see the way several heads turn to follow Lachlan's path to the bathroom, some squinting curiously, others still blatantly staring.

But one thing is clearer than ever: every single person in Morning Bell cafe heard my lie—from the tables of seniors having lunch, to Mrs. Perez at the cafe counter, to Ethan behind the display case.

Cool fingers of dread trail down my spine as I run up to the counter on shaky legs. "So, you all heard?"

Ethan nods as Mrs. Perez tuts. "Sure did. You know it's wrong to lie, dear."

"I know. I was stuck. It just... happened."

"Lying to your boss about being engaged to Noah, *and* using Daisy and Luke's love story, 'just happened'?" Ethan asks, his brow popped. He's grown out his beard and looks very mountain-manly these days—a look which I'm sure his wife Val appreciates, but is making it very hard for me to gauge his expression right now.

"He seemed so skeptical, the lie just came out." I wring my hands. "I don't know what to do. I can't lose this job. I can't leave Mirror Valley."

Mrs. Perez's expression softens slightly before she frowns. "I'm going to go ahead and assume that being caught in a lie could also cost you your job."

"Absolutely. If Lachlan finds out before he leaves next Friday, he'll surely let me go."

My sentence gets caught on something resembling a sob. I can't believe the hole I've dug myself. Excuse me, the *grave*. I've dug my very own career-grave, with a headstone that reads: "Herein lies Diandra Griffith's promising career as an app developer. Instead, she spent the remainder of her days crocheting sweaters for her cat, Bruce."

"If that's the case," Mrs. Perez muses. "There's only one thing we can do..."

She stands from the counter and claps once. The entire cafe goes silent as everyone's attention shifts our way. Mrs. Perez is in full retired-English-teacher mode, her chin lifting slightly and her voice ringing clear. "Everyone, please. You all heard Dee's story just now. I'm going to need you all to spread the word. For all intents and purposes, Noah and Dee are engaged to be married until next Friday."

Several of the cafe customers bob their heads in agreement.

And the most miraculous thing happens: I watch as the infamous town rumor mill starts up.

Phones come out, people start whispering, and like a tsunami of words, news of our fake engagement sweeps around the cafe and out the door.

I'm powerless to stop it. It simply can't be stopped.

I turn back to Ethan and Mrs. Perez. "What do I do now?"

"Well, my dear," Mrs. Perez replies. "*You* are going to act like a woman in love with your best friend."

9

NOAH

I lift the boards onto the worktable and line them up carefully. I hand-picked each and every one of these as they are the deepest, richest, most vibrant shades of brown. I can already envision the table in my head, picture how these boards will fit together like a perfect game of Tetris.

This walnut dining table is my side project at Raymond's workshop. He's letting me use the tools and space when all my work tasks are done. It's been a slow week, so I've had time to make progress on the table. It feels good to see, and feels even better to imagine giving the finished product to Rosie—a kind, feisty lady at the senior center who first said that I'd make a good carpenter, and then jokingly suggested that I should make her a table.

So, I'm making her a table. I'm a man of my word.

And while I'm not yet sold on the whole carpenter thing, I'm optimistic. Working with Ray over the past month (and building this table from scratch with my bare hands) has given me so much satisfaction. More than I would've thought possible.

The early summer sun is warm on my bare back, and I

whistle as I play around with the order of the boards. Ray has one worktable outside, and this is by far my favorite spot. Limited, though, as all the electrical tools are inside the garage-turned-workshop out back of the office. There's nothing like working outside with the breeze, and the sun, and the smell of fresh flowers instead of sawdust.

After a few minutes of fiddling, it's clear that my initial setup was the best, so it's time to get ready for gluing. I head into the garage, put on an apron, and get to work.

But my mind keeps flitting back to the place I've been trying (and failing) to avoid all morning: that moment in Dee's office when she was in "Dee-stress" (the name I've given to her anxious moments; the stupid pun usually pulls a reluctant smile out of her, at least) and I had her wrapped in my arms...

I love being this person for her. Love being the one who supports her, literally holds her up when she's down. Dee is one of the strongest, fiercest people I know. She could knock a guy out with a single punch, could dominate an argument with a single look. And there is something so meaningful about being the one person with whom she lets herself go. I love her for letting me be this person for her. Love her for trusting me like she does.

When she fell into my arms earlier, I had that heart-feeling again and I almost spilled my guts right there. Almost told her that, now that she's dating again, I want to be the first and only one in line.

But I stopped. Tried the whole "staring into her eyes while moving her hair out of her face" thing instead. That old chestnut. Problem is, I'm a coward and couldn't actually *meet* her eyes, so instead, I stared at the top of her head like I was inspecting for lice or something.

Hot.

Whatever. It's a step.

Step one of many to woo my best friend.

I can't just ask Dee out, I can't come right out and romance her. But my friends are right—I have to do *something*. If this morning showed me anything, it's that I can't keep my feelings tamped down forever. Something's gotta give.

That question she asked about whether I wanted to get married someday... It was the sort of thing I'd normally laugh off or make a joke about. Instead, I answered her seriously. I want to show her that I'm looking for something different, so that, if it ever came up, she'd believe I'm serious about her, too.

But for now, I'm gonna take it slow, take it easy. *Show* her how great we can be. The sparks between us feel so strong sometimes, I can hardly believe she doesn't feel them, too. There's never been any indication that she senses the chemistry between us that everyone else seems to see.

Baby steps. That's all it takes. I'm playing the long game, baby, and just like with sport, it'll take patience, diligence, and dedication.

I'm gluing the final boards together when my back twinges a little. I stretch and check the clock back in the workshop.

Holy. I've been at this for over an hour without a break. No wonder my back's hurting.

I grab my canteen and head into the shade of the garage, dropping down on a relatively non-sawdusty patch of floor. I take a long swig of water before grabbing my phone to check my messages. Dylan (of Leg Model fame) wanted to practice his baseball pitching tonight, so I should—

The first message on the screen shocks me so much that I inhale a mouthful of water.

Once I've recovered from almost drowning myself, I

place the canteen on the floor and rise to a stand. Pacing, I scroll through to the second message. The third. The fourth...

Fifty-nine.

I have fifty-nine text messages and ten missed calls. All relaying more or less the same thing.

Noah! You're engaged?? Since when?

Happy engagement, bro! I had no idea things were so serious.

I thought you'd never settle down. But with Dee, I can see it.

You and Dee? That's amazing, man. So happy for you.

I skim through message after message, the words not computing. I must be asleep and am having an epically vivid dream. Or maybe I hit my head on something and am in a coma. Or I inhaled too much of that toxic glue and am having the most wildly intense hallucination of my life.

Yes. To one and/or all of the above.

There has to be a logical explanation for the fact that, according to basically everyone I know, Dee and I are engaged.

The whole notion is so ridiculous, so out there and at odds with my "baby steps", that I start laughing. Actual, full-belly, keeled-over laughing.

Clearly, I am losing my mind.

At that moment, my phone screen lights up again with a phone call from my brother Sam, of all people. I love my family and all my brothers equally, but Sam is the one I'm closest to. Maybe because we're both middle children. He also lives physically closest to me: in Seattle, with his now-wife Karina and their brand new nutrition business.

And so, because this is clearly a dream or a coma, and therefore has no real-world consequences, I answer the call.

"Did ya hear the news?" I say chirpily. "Your big bro's getting married."

"Yeah, dude! I could hardly believe it when I heard," Sam exclaims. "What on earth is happening over there? I didn't know that you and Dee have taken things to the next level. Way to keep me in the loop."

"Sorry, man, you know how it is when you're in love. Things move quickly." I laugh again, deciding that I might as well lean into this.

Funny, I always thought that my coma-dream would have me on a baseball field, hitting a World Series winning home run and then bringing Dee up from the crowd to kiss her.

This is fine, too.

"How'd it happen? *When* did it happen? I don't really get..."

The door at the front of the garage/workshop opens and Sam's voice fades out when I see Dee walking towards me.

This is more like it. My coma has officially, properly kicked in.

"Gotta go, call you later." I hang up the phone and smile at Dee, opening my arms for a hug. In real, non-coma life, I only saw her this morning, but I'm blown away again by how beautiful she looks. How she takes my breath away, even in her work clothes.

"Hey," I murmur. If none of this is real, can I tell her how crazy I am about her? "I'm so glad you're here. I have something to tell..."

I trail off when I register her expression. She doesn't look nearly as happy and excited as I would expect for my coma-fiancée.

No, she looks... sheepish. Guilty.

"What's wrong?"

"Oh." Dee bites the inside of her cheek. "So you haven't heard."

Yeah. Something is *very* wrong here. Dee looks anxious and worried, which would certainly not be the case in my coma dream. My own face falls as I wonder how to approach this. *Let her do the talking.*

"Heard what?" I ask.

Dee lets out a sigh and points to a chair. "I've got something to run by you. Put your shirt on."

Still confused as to what's going on—and now wondering if this really *is* a dream, because if so, it sucks—I pull on my t-shirt and tug it down my body. For a moment, I could swear that Dee's eyes linger on my bare chest, but I know better. I've learned time and time again that Dee is totally unaffected by my shirtlessness.

I pull up a chair across from hers, bringing it close so that our knees almost touch. Dee's hands are clasped in her lap, her fingers crashing against each other in a way that must be painful.

"What's on your mind?"

Dee's silent for a long, long moment, staring down at her hands so strands of caramel hair that have fallen out of her ponytail hang in front of her face. Her shoulders are tense, her posture straight as a knife. It takes every morsel of strength I have not to reach out and take her wrists. Release her grip, wrap her hands in mine, and soothe the places where her fingers dig in.

Then, Dee barks out the scariest laugh I've ever heard in my life. It's like a dry, desperate, humorless cackle. She finally releases her hands to slap them against her knees violently. "You... You are going to *laugh*."

I raise a brow. "Am I?"

"Yes. Because I beat you. Yup."

"Beat me..." I scan her face, trying to catch up. Trying to

understand what she could be talking about right now. "Beat me how?"

Dee lets out another of those scary laughs, and I idly wonder if I should draw her a bubble bath and not let her leave the bathroom until she's got her head back on straight. "I just pulled the biggest prank of my entire pranking career."

I give one very slow nod. "Uh huh. You pranked me..."

Then, something starts to come together. Those texts and phone calls earlier...

Dee is nodding in a big way, and I almost wonder if I said the words out loud. "Yup. See, uhm, I kinda made a boo-boo."

She's got this frenzied, lopsided grin I've never seen on her before. Usually I'm the one sporting that grin when I've done something bad. Real bad. "What kind of boo-boo?" I ask carefully.

"I kind of... lied to my boss."

My eyes widen, though I tell myself to keep neutral. If she's being the Noah in this conversation, I need to be the calm, level-headed Dee. "You lied to your boss about what?"

"Aboutbeingengaged."

The words are unintelligible for how quickly they come out of her mouth, but I'm well-versed in all Dee languages, so I know what she said. And now, I can't stop my mouth from dropping open. "You told your boss that you're *engaged?!*"

"Yes. To you."

Ah. It's not a coma dream.

Just the strangest shade of reality I've ever experienced.

I sit back in my chair, processing her words. Processing what it means that Dee—the girl I'm *actually* crazy about— told her boss that we're engaged. It isn't until she leans forward, placing a small hand on my knee and meeting my eyes, that I realize I haven't said anything for several minutes.

"I didn't know what else to do, what else to say," she says on a quick breath. "He was going on about how Right-Match is basically useless to his company and I panicked. Hard."

"But you never lie."

"I'm surprised I pulled it off." Dee says this morosely, shaking her head like she regrets getting away with it. "I shouldn't have done it. I freaked out."

I push a hand through my hair. It's too long these days, and I hate the way it hangs low in front of my eyes. It's a small comfort to know that Dee prefers it this way. "So now, your boss thinks that we're…"

"Together. Engaged to be married."

"Wow. That's quite the freakout, Dee."

"He was asking for success stories on the app, and he just looked *so* skeptical of every word coming out of my mouth, and…" I'm only half-listening as Dee explains what happened during her discussion with her boss. The fact that Daisy and Luke's love story is now *our* love story.

Is it weird that all I can think is that I wish we had a chance to actually *have* our own love story?

"He's here until next Friday," Dee finishes. "So to make this work, we'd have to pretend 'til then. But you're my best friend, Noah, and you come first, so just say the word and I'll tell him… I… lied to him."

Dee's entire face slips into an expression way too close to despair for my liking. And now, I do take her hands and hold them in mine. It's the perfect reminder of us, of this friendship that I treasure so much. I hold her gaze and say with full sincerity, "I've always said I'd do anything for you, and I mean it. So, okay. I'll be your fake fian—"

Dee smashes a finger to my lips before I can finish, and I

89

jerk back in shock. Her eyes are wide and tender, but a little frenzied and wild... not unlike Bruce when he has the zoomies.

She stands from her chair and kneels on the sawdust covered floor.

"What're you doing?" I ask.

She pops up a knee.

"Oh, no," I say, jumping to a stand. "No. No way."

"Noah Jackson," she starts. "Will you do me the honor of being my fake fiancé—"

"You're a nut."

"—to have and to hold until next Friday—"

"Dee, seriously. You don't have to do this."

"—at which time we can return to our best friendship, never to speak of this again?"

My lips purse as I look down at her. This is the exact opposite of how I thought an engagement between us would go. The wrinkle of concern between her eyebrows highlights the sweet vulnerability behind her question, and her beautiful gray eyes are so full of hope and guilt and embarrassment and that same mildly insane glimmer...

How can I possibly say no to this woman? Even if this is fake. Even if she has no idea that I wish this could be real.

I let out a sigh and get down on my knees in front of her. I still tower over her, but at least we're on semi-equal ground now. Her lips twitch and I know for a fact that I could never let her down. I couldn't live with myself.

"Alright, Dee-bug. You win this one. I'll be your fake fiancé."

Before I can say anything more, Dee bounds forward, wrapping her arms around me in a hug so forceful that I lose my balance and fall back onto the floor. Sawdust and plane shavings break my fall, and I land on a cloud with Dee on top of me, my arms locked around her.

"Thank you, thank you, thank you!" she's wailing against my chest. Then, she climbs up my body so we're eye to eye. "You have no idea how much I need this. I only have a week to prove that RightMatch is worth keeping, and this is going to be a *huge* help."

I chuckle, a little breathless at having her *this* close to my face, every inch of her body pressed against mine. "Should be fun."

"I'll make it fun. *And* you get full prank benefits for the next three months, how does that sound?"

"Make it six," I manage, though I truly couldn't care less. I just want to keep this conversation going because having Dee this close feels right in ways I can't even describe.

There's a slam of a door at the front of the shop, followed by footsteps.

"Hey there, lovebirds," a deep voice announces.

"Oh!" Dee springs right off me. "Sorry, Ray."

I take a moment to catch my breath, reminding myself that Dee *doesn't* fit so perfectly against me. That having her in my arms *doesn't* feel just right. Nope. None of that.

Friends and nothing more, Noah.

I get to a stand and brush down my shirt before facing Ray, who has his hands on his hips as he looks between Dee and me. "Well, kids, I heard the happy news, but this is a place of business. I will *not* stand for any hanky-panky in here, understood?"

I blink in confusion as to how Ray, of all people, knows what's going on. But Dee speaks up immediately. "It won't happen again."

He gives a firm nod even as his eyes twinkle, and he returns to his office. Meanwhile, I turn to Dee with my brow raised. She gives another sheepish smile. "I was at Morning Bell when I told Lachlan about our engagement. Mrs. Perez is spreading the word so the town knows and won't mention anything to him."

That explains the text messages and phone calls. "So can I tell anyone the truth?" I ask.

"Of course, tell whoever you want. I just don't want it to get back to Lachlan." Dee pauses for a moment. "And, you know, if you have dates lined up this week with Yanica or someone, feel free to go ahead. Don't let this stop you."

My lips quirk up. "Dee, you know I'm a one-woman kinda man."

"Well, I'm just saying... Don't feel you can't date because of this stupid lie."

"I've been meaning to take a break from the casual dating anyway."

I swear I see a flicker cross Dee's face, but then, it—and whatever it could have meant—is gone. Dee steps forward and wraps her arms around me. "Thank you, Noah. I'll make this as painless as possible for you, I promise. And in the meantime, we should probably come up with some ground rules in case we see Lachlan around town. You know, stuff we can do to make this, uhm, engagement thing convincing. But we can talk about that later. No rush."

I nod against Dee's hair. She smells like vanilla and cinnamon spice. Our hugs always end too quickly, in my opinion, but I'd never linger because Dee and I are friends. Nothing more.

Until this fake engagement.

My heart does a flip.

Wait a minute. *Ground rules.* Things we can do to make our relationship—our engagement—look convincing...

Did I just get free rein to be romantic and try to "woo" Dee under the guise of being engaged to her?

I can hardly believe this twist of luck. Fate. Whatever. It's like the stars are aligning for me. For *us*.

Here's hoping that Lachlan's around a lot this week, because I intend to do everything I can to spark the sparks with Dee.

I have one week to show my best friend that we are meant to be, and I'm not going to waste it.

10

DEE

I remember every second of the experience in Fran's fortune teller tent last winter.

It was a cold and blustery day, as you would expect for the Winter Carnival, but the minute I stepped through the heavy curtain draping over the door to the maroon tent, a wall of warmth hit me. The tent smelled of incense and perfume; so strong, at first, that I almost sneezed. Quiet, calm, gong-laden music played from hidden speakers. I quickly grew warm and took off my jacket, while Noah stripped down to just a t-shirt.

The thick fabric blocked any light from outside, so the inside of the tent was serene and moody, lit only by candles and standing lamps with funky shades. With the Winter Carnival happening on the grounds of our town's community center, I spent too much time wondering how on earth Fran had managed such a thing without, you know, electrical outlets. I voiced these thoughts to Noah and he said something stupid about the woman having magic powers.

Once my eyes adjusted to the low light, Noah and I took our seats at the round table at the center of the tent. Atop the table was—you guessed it—a crystal ball.

It was all very cute and kitschy.

It took awhile for Fran to come greet us—probably adding to the mystique or something. When she did appear, it was as dramatic as you'd expect: she materialized from the back of the tent in a cloud of smoke, and she welcomed us with this grand accent—not unlike the accent she used when she was into boudoir photography and went by the name "Madame Françoise" (that's a story for another day).

The next few minutes featured a mix of tarot card readings, palm readings, and all other kinds of readings. I remember feeling hungry and kicking myself for not getting a snack before Noah had pulled me into the tent.

And then, Fran's conclusion. Her announcement as to what the future held for Noah and me...

"The stars tell no lies," she'd said, and paused a moment too long. "You two are destined for marriage."

Destined for marriage?!

The very proposition was too much for me to handle. And I left.

If only that Past Dee could see me now. If only she could see what Present Dee is dealing with.

Destined for a fake *marriage,* is what "the stars" must've said.

I snap out of the memory. Notice that my fingers are resting on my keyboard.

Don't mind me, just zoning out. Again.

"Get it together, Dee," I chastise myself, grabbing my mug and drinking the cold remnants of my coffee. On his little shelf above my head, Bruce lets out an angry meow. I reach up and give him a pat. "Sorry for waking you, buddy."

He snuffles and shifts in his cat bed before falling back asleep and paying me not one more second of attention. The shelf above my work desk at home is Bruce's favorite place to hang out. Noah built it a couple years back when

Bruce started shoving himself into the small space between my computer and the wall to sleep. What is it about cats that they like to be at the center of everything, but heaven forbid you treat them like it?

I putter around my room for a moment, stretching my legs and moving my body. I have my office on Main Street, but the cramped work desk and one file cabinet in my bedroom also come in handy in the case of work emergencies. Which do happen at a dating app, believe it or not.

Case in point: when a tiny little app glitch sends a user's "want to go out with me?" message to basically all their matches, effectively setting up twenty dates for the same night.

This may or may not be based on a true story.

In any case, I've thought of moving my stuff over to Daisy's old bedroom and creating a proper home office, but I haven't gotten around to it yet. And with the way things went with Lachlan yesterday, it's probably best to put my home office planning on hold with everything else.

That conversation at Morning Bell is also why I'm working today, on a Saturday. I want to get on top of things for Monday. One week is not a lot of time to save my app-baby.

I head down to the kitchen to brew some more coffee. Daisy moved out the week that she and Luke got married, so I have the bungalow to myself now. I don't miss the hazardous cacti garden in the living room, the dishes left in the sink from when she was working a hundred jobs at once, the music she'd blast in the evenings when she thought I was done working. But there's a lot I *do* miss. Daisy has this calming, happy presence. Having her around is a breath of fresh air, and I miss the sound of her footsteps, her off-key shower singing.

The house sometimes feels too quiet. Too empty. Too

clean. Which might be why I love it so much when Noah comes around.

I grab my fresh mug of coffee and head back to my room, determined to actually get some work done this time.

But the moment my butt hits my work chair, the front door downstairs bursts open.

Even without seeing him, even without hearing him, I know that's Noah. The guy *never* knocks. Doors only slow him down.

And right on cue: "Where's my incredibly awesome fake fiancée?!"

I pad to the top of the stairs. "You mean Bruce?" I quip. "He's been waiting for you for *hours*. He's all stretched out on his cat bed, the shameless minx."

Noah takes the stairs two at a time and comes to a stop directly in front of me. He's not even out of breath. His dark eyes twinkle, and I gaze up at him with my hands on my hips, mouth twisted in a smirk. I get a sudden, insistent urge for him to hug me. Have his arms wrapped around me like they were after I jumped on him at the workshop yesterday.

I can almost taste it, feel the residual warmth on my skin where our bodies were pressed together.

Weird.

"What's up, smoogy-tush?" he asks.

My smirk flattens to a glare. "Nope. Absolutely not."

"But, butterlips," he whines, causing me to turn on my heel and march back into my room.

"This has to stop."

"What? You don't like being called my snoogums?"

I shoot him the dirtiest look over my shoulder. "*Snoogums?*"

Noah smiles back, all sweet and disarming. "What would you prefer? Babycakes? Snufflelump? Honey, baby, sweetie, darling?"

"First of all, I think Snufflelump is the thing from *Winnie the Pooh*. And second of all, do we *have* to do nicknames?"

"Do you want Lachlan to believe us?"

I give him my best squinty eyes, but of course, he's right. "Okay. I think I can make my peace with 'honey'. And what would you like me to call you?"

Noah raises a finger to his chin, stroking his jawline. He shaved today. I bet he smells like that nice, mellow after-shave he uses. I almost stand on my tiptoes to get a whiff of it before firmly reminding myself that sniffing Noah's face out of the blue might be a weird move. We have other priorities right now.

He shoots me a sudden smirk, lips drawn up at one corner. "How about you call me by my name, but say it like you do when you're happy or excited to see me."

"How do I say it?"

"I dunno. Whenever I've done something that makes you happy or that surprises you, you say my name real nice."

I nod slowly. Remember how I felt when he came in the door just moments ago and summon that feeling. "Like... *Noah*?"

He beams. It's a sight to behold. "Just like that."

I laugh. "Done."

He glances around my room, and I notice the furrow in his brow, the slight clenching of his jaw as he registers my computer screensaver, the steaming mug of coffee, the chair pushed out from my desk. "You're working today? Dee, it's the weekend."

"I know." I sigh. Noah's respectful of the fact that I sometimes work long hours and would never say anything, but I can tell he worries. "It's just this Lachlan thing. I want to make sure I'm ready for next week. And we have a match tomorrow so I only have today."

"Hope I'm not interrupting."

"You're not. I was kinda taking a break anyway."

"Good." He lounges across my bed, making himself right at home. It's not a small bed by any stretch, but Noah's so tall that it seems tiny beneath him. "Who is this guy that's got you all wound up, anyway? I mean, I get that he's a little scary looking on first meeting, but you're used to being surrounded by tall, athletic, good-looking guys like myself."

He jokingly raises an arm and presses a kiss to his own bicep. I gag again to make him laugh before my tone goes serious. "You'll meet him properly at some point, don't you worry. He wants to see us together. Hear 'your side of the story'."

Noah's expression immediately changes. He knows how sensitive I am about this kinda thing. "Your side wasn't enough for him?"

"Guess not." I shrug. Lachlan is a stern, grouchy, cynical type of person, but he doesn't seem overtly misogynistic. Hard to tell, I suppose.

Noah's lips press into a line. I love how much he cares about the things I care about. How much he cares about the things that affect me, no matter how seemingly small or insignificant or completely removed from his experience. Noah just... *cares*. "Now I really can't wait to meet him," he says.

I collapse into my chair, blowing out a breath. "On that, we should probably come up with those ground rules. Figure out exactly what we're doing."

Noah leans back on his hands so the veins pop in his muscular forearms and his navy t-shirt falls flat on his toned stomach. He's wearing his white ball cap, and his curls stick out above his ears in a way that just *begs* you to take off the cap and run your fingers through his hair...

I notice these things, then abruptly snap myself out of noticing them.

Is it weird that I'm noticing them?

Now that I'm dating again (and I use that term *very* loosely, as my one and only date so far has been with Ollie, and I haven't gotten to the meet-in-person part with any of the guys I've been speaking to on RightMatch), I feel like I'm picking up on things that I've never registered before.

On men who aren't Noah too, of course.

It's not just Noah.

"So what're you thinking?" he asks casually. He's so comfortable with all this, so unaffected by the fact that we have to make it seem like we're *engaged to be married.*

Meanwhile, I feel totally affected. I don't even know how to start approaching the concept of Noah and I acting like a couple. Would Lachlan believe it? Aside from the fact that Noah is an objective ten and I'm a comfortable seven (I know where I stand and I'm fine with it), my new boss seems so completely on guard. He filters through every single word out of my mouth with such fervor, he might as well be panning for gold.

I have a feeling that, to win him over, Noah and I will have to *work* to sell this thing. *Show* him that we are a real couple that do couple-y things...

A warmth rises from my chest, up my neck, to my cheeks as I consider how to broach this topic with my best friend. I'm never embarrassed in front of Noah (he's seen me at my worst too many times for me to feel embarrassed about anything) but this is something else. Something adjacent to embarrassment that I can't put my finger on.

"First, we need to have our stories straight."

"I'm Luke, you're Daisy, right?" Noah's brows flatten

and his lips form a line. "I'm a super serious, frowny accountant who hates smiling and loves ABBA."

I snort. "Nailed it."

"I very reluctantly downloaded a dating app—what's it called, FightMatch?—to find the love of my life after my fiancée ended things."

"Yup. And I was just a girl, looking for a guy, turning to a dating app, and falling for my best friend's older brother."

"Classic story."

"I figure Lachlan won't care very much about the actual details of our relationship—the guy seems like he'd rather have his toenails pulled than do lovey-dovey chats. I think if we can sell the story of how we got together, he won't actually care about the rest of it." I shift in my seat. Swallow thickly. "But that brings us to the next part... The, uh, *look* of it all."

I can't bring myself to meet Noah's eyes. That almost-embarrassment feeling is taking over my body. I remind myself that this is basically just business—a proposal to help save my job, a trade giving him full pranking benefits for six months. Easy peasy.

With that in mind, I set my jaw. "We need to act like we're together. Like, physically." My eyes go wide. "I mean, not *physically* physically! Uh..."

"Don't worry." Noah's lips quirk. "We don't have to be a PDA-heavy couple."

I let out a whoosh of relief. "Thank goodness." Hear the words and correct myself again. "I mean, thank goodness you understood! Not thank goodness about the PDA stuff. Listen, I bet you're great at PDA and an awesome kisser and all, but—"

Noah bursts into abrupt laughter, cutting me off. "Geez, Dee, it's fine. Let's just stick with what you're comfortable with."

My entire body is on fire with the heat of many suns. "Okay. Yes. Comfortable. I'm thinking that we should keep things basic and act like we normally do, but with a tiny bit *more*. Hugs are fine, kisses on the cheek, hand-holding if the situation is appropriate and it's not too hot out. And no terrible nicknames. You get it?"

Noah nods. His face is red, but I think it's from holding back laughter. "Got it."

"And I think, uhm..."

Ohmygoodness. I can't believe I'm bringing this up, but I have to. One of us has to. We're two adults in an apparent long-term relationship.

"I think we should do our best to avoid any, you know... lip kissing."

"Romantic."

"Shut up."

Noah chuckles. "Alright, Dee. We don't have to *lip kiss.*"

"Okay, good. Just because I don't want to blur anything. Not that I think lip kissing would blur anything, but..." I trail off uselessly. I can't remember the last time I felt *this* awkward around Noah.

And yet, he's still nodding, as if my sentence made any sense or required an answer. Finally, he exhales loudly, his chest collapsing so that I realize he's been holding his breath. "Phew. Now that that's over, can I give you a hug—a friend hug—and go do the thing I came over to do?"

Oh! So he actually had a purpose in coming over aside from listening to me blabber on about *lip kissing* for ten minutes. "Of course! What did you come over to do?"

His familiar teasing smile is back and it makes me feel a hundred times better. "Your fence is broken on the far right side and I've been meaning to fix it since I saw it a couple weeks ago. Would hate if Bruce caught himself on a piece of wood or an old nail or something. My tools are downstairs, I just have to repair it and you'll be good to go."

I blink. "I hadn't even noticed. Thank you, Noah."

He stands and gives a shrug. "What're fake fiancés for?"

I get up from my chair and wrap my arms around him. The Noah smell washes over me and I close my eyes happily. His heartbeat is firm and steady next to my ear and I hold on extra tight for a minute or two longer than I normally would.

Bruce meows loudly, and that's what pulls us apart. Noah gives me a peace sign and walks out the door, bounding back down the stairs and whistling as he goes outside. I watch him walk down the fence to a part hidden behind a big, unruly bush. It looks like he's still whistling. Looks like nothing's changed and this is an ordinary day that he's doing me, his oldest friend, a favor by fixing my fence.

Imagine what he'd do for his *real* fiancée one day. His real wife.

She'll be a lucky, lucky girl.

The thought of this future person fills me with regret. Noah told me that he wants to get married someday, wants to have a wife. His other best friend. What a spectacular failure on my part that I not only glued myself to him physically at the workshop just hours after having that very conversation, but on top of that, we are now effectively engaged to be married.

And furthermore, he told me that he's been wanting to take a break from casual dating. Probably to find this person sooner rather than later.

Wow. I don't think I've failed at something quite so successfully in my entire life. I should write a book about it.

But at least it's only for a week. One week.

So I make another resolution: Noah's sacrificing his

time, energy, and dating life to make *my* dream come true, so as soon as Lachlan leaves, I'll give Noah the space and encouragement he needs for *his* dreams to come true.

Somehow, despite any residual awkwardness from my *lip kissing* discussion with Noah (along with Bruce's random meows, purrs, and protests), I manage to get some work done.

And by "work", I mean compiling an entire glossary of items for the next week of work. An itemized list, if you will.

Okay, fine. It's really just a shuffling and ordering of my Desktop and work folders. I want us to start off on the right foot come Monday morning, and having everything meticulously organized—down to all files and spreadsheets—can only help.

Because compartmentalizing is my forté, and in this, I *thrive*.

You can't build something strong if you don't have a solid base, am I right?

And now that everything is properly sorted and demarcated, I'd say it's time for a treat. Because yes, I have Pavlov-dog-trained myself to get a reward every time I accomplish something. Anything, really. But it might not be ideal that I've started treating myself for even folding the laundry that's been slung across my chair for over a week...

Hey, I'm only human.

A human with a healthy, if mildly obsessive, love of candy corn.

Look, it might be a Halloween candy, but I am an absolute fiend when it comes to candy corn. Regular, Easter, whatever. In fact, last fall, I heard about a line of chocolate "Harvest" candy corn coming to Mirror Valley Grocery, and well... I won't say that I camped outside the store the night before the delivery, but I also won't say that I didn't.

I begged Noah to join me so it wasn't weird.

I skip down the stairs with Bruce hot on my heels. The gray furball thinks he's getting a treat with my treat, and he's not wrong. I don't like to eat alone.

After giving Bruce a couple of his favorite salmon-flavored cat biscuits, I grab a stool and pull it in front of the tallest cupboard in my kitchen—the one with the broken door that I keep wanting to get fixed but never have. It's one of a few things that are falling apart in this house that I haven't gotten around to fixing yet.

I have plans for a big renovation someday—want to transform this little bungalow into a cozy, functional, modern-ish home base. I can see it now: the hearthstone stove in the living room, the gorgeous wood paneling, the big windows overlooking the mountains out back...

And of course, the thing that needs the most attention: the *kitchen*.

But those plans are also on hold until I know that I still have a job.

I avoid grasping the handle of the broken cupboard as I climb onto the stool and reach for The Promised Bag (okay, a little dramatic, but you get it). Noah stashed this extra-large bag of (regular) candy corn here awhile ago for emergencies. Which loosely translates to: if I'm all out, and am in "Dee-stress", and the grocery store is closed, and he isn't around. But I ran out of my own stash yesterday, and am too lazy to go to the store right now... so this has to count as an emergency, right?

I collect the bag and get off the stool, unfortunately brushing up against the cupboard on the way down. The door falls right off, clattering noisily to the ground, and I freeze, watching the entryway in case Noah chooses this precise moment to come back inside. He would so grill me for stealing from the emergency stash. Noah might play fast and loose with most of his responsibilities, but he can be surprisingly strict when it comes to candy corn consumption.

Thankfully, there's no movement and I manage to grab a couple handfuls of the candy.

"Nailed it," I mutter as the sugar melts on my tongue.

Speaking of, I wonder how things are going with the fence. When I looked out the window earlier, I could only see a small slice of Noah's bare upper back behind the bush. It's a hot day—it makes sense that he would work shirtless. He's probably all sweaty, the sun glinting off his muscles with every movement. I imagine his shoulders working over-time, the taut muscles in his back forming a line down his spine...

I should get that bush trimmed. Maybe remove it all together.

Not because it's obstructing my view of Noah or anything, but because it would keep the garden looking neat. Like my Desktop is now.

I brush over my strange new fixation on Noah's upper body, and pour a big glass of water. I drizzle in some lemon juice, and add a few ice cubes before grabbing my sunglasses and walking outside.

I follow the fence all the way to the obstructo-bush, where Noah's hard at work.

Or hardly working, I tack on lightly when I make out a couple of voices from behind the bush. One is very clearly Noah's, and the other belongs to a man, but I can't work out who he is.

"Diandra told me how you two got together."

I freeze.

Lachlan Chase is here, outside my house? Talking to Noah without me?!

Suddenly, I'm very much *not* frozen and my legs spring forward. I bound around the obstructo-bush, spilling water all over my hand.

"Lachlan!" I say a little too loudly. "You're here!"

He understandably looks taken aback. Though for someone with a face about as expressive as a block of concrete, he must be truly shocked to see me. Beside him, Noah stares at me with a forced smile as if to say "where did you come from, you stalker?!"

Lachlan regains his usual flat expression. "That's very observant, Diandra."

I paste on a smile, but the slight twitch in Noah's lips tells me I look mildly insane, so I drop it. "Sorry. Just surprised to see you here. Outside my house. For some reason."

Lachlan nods, his ice blue eyes fixed on me. Why on earth does he look skeptical about even *that* statement? "Not that I need to explain myself, but I was out for my afternoon run and recognized your boyfriend from the other morning..."

Lachlan gestures at Noah, trailing off for an introduction that Noah is all too happy to provide. "Noah Jackson. The *fiancé*. Pleased to meet you."

My eyes dart to Noah's and he gives a slight smile, seeming as cool, calm and collected as ever. But the reality sets in: we're off to the races now. No turning back. Noah is going along with my lie, which means that I have to go along with it, too. Here's hoping my poker face holds up this week.

"Yes. I noticed Noah fixing the fence," Lachlan says, oblivious to our silent conversation. He steps back and assesses my little mint green bungalow. "Can I assume this is your... house?"

Hm. Gotta love that hesitation.

"Yes, this is Dee's place," Noah replies easily, his gaze on me. "I'm planning on moving in just as soon as we're married."

My face heats up and I hope that, somehow, my sunglasses are hiding my blush.

"Do you need a hand?" Lachlan says to Noah, pointing to the fence. I'm surprised by the offer, and judging from the jump in Noah's brow, he is, too.

"Thanks, man, I've got it covered. I'm training as a carpenter, so this is good practice for me."

"I see." Lachlan bends to inspect his work. "So how did you..."

Noah and Lachlan then begin to chat about fences and wood and nails and whatever else guys talk about when they're standing all together looking at something that needs fixing.

And while they talk, I gape. Shamelessly.

Because I cannot tear my eyes away from Noah.

He looks exactly as I expected he would look, exactly as he always looks, but somehow... different. I almost can't believe the sheer amount of *him* that I'm seeing right now. He's only wearing his ball cap, his sneakers, and the gray running shorts that go to his mid-thigh. Which isn't an unusual clothing combo for Noah, but it shocks me all the same.

Now, I can't help but notice the way his shorts sit low on his hips, showing off the flat planes of his stomach and the V that dips below his waistband. In the sunlight, his skin glistens with a sheen of sweat, making him sparkle. Almost like that vampire from the *Twilight* movies, but much, much better.

As I watch, he plucks his sunglasses off his head and puts them on his face. The entire bicep-popping, strong-hand-wielding action seems to happen in slow motion, just like in those cheesy ads that make me cringe. But I get it now. His sunglasses aren't quite Aviators but they're in that style (actual Aviators make him look even more like a freaking celebrity than normal), but with these, he looks like my Noah.

He gestures casually as he speaks and my eyes travel from his blinking abs, over his pecs, and up to the muscles at his neck. I wonder, if I was to run my hands across his shoulders, what they would feel like. Taut and muscular and firm. I bet he smells good—the Noah smell mixed with sweat and sunscreen.

And it's crazy that I'm having these thoughts because I *know* what Noah feels and smells like. I've hugged him countless times when his shirt was off after volleyball. I've put my arm around his shoulders, clapped him on the back. And yet, I don't think I've ever taken the time to properly appreciate any of it.

My cheeks are hot again, and I snap myself out of it. I zoned out for only a moment or two, but it feels like longer, and the guys are now silent. I'm suddenly very thankful for my sunglasses, which hopefully hid my lingering eyes. I'm also thankful for the glass of water in my hand, which now gives me something to do.

"Here." I shove the glass towards Noah so fast that water splashes onto the grass. Between this and my leaping around the obstructo-bush like some kind of anxiety-stricken cricket, the glass is mostly empty.

Noah's dark brows pucker as he reaches for it. "Thanks? I finished the last of my water, so this might *just* quench my thirst."

I ignore his teasing tone. Offer a grin that feels almost shy. "I put lemon in it."

His smile turns genuine. "So thoughtful. Thanks, Dee."

His praise makes me feel like a child who's just been given a gold star by her teacher. Since when do I care if Noah praises what I do? I love to make him happy, of course, but I don't think I've ever felt this glow to hear his appreciation.

"Anyway." I clear my throat and turn back to Lachlan. I almost forgot he was there. "You're out for a run? Would you like some water as well?"

"No need. I've got a bottle right here."

He removes a high-tech squeeze bottle thing from his running belt. His Adam's apple bobs as he drinks, and it's only then that I notice his loose-fitting white shirt that leaves little to the imagination. And though I see his biceps as he drinks the water, along with his chiseled upper body and muscular legs—the guy has to be a gym junkie—the reaction I have towards him is nothing like I had towards Noah.

My eyes don't linger, my face doesn't get warm.

He's just... an attractive man out for a run.

I look back at Noah, and while I can't see his eyes behind his sunglasses, I have the uncanny feeling that he's watching me closely. Maybe looking at the way I'm looking at Lachlan? Maybe wondering if I'm noticing how fit the guy is?

He doesn't look particularly happy about it. And that gives me a thrill I can't really identify or understand.

Lachlan smacks his lips and replaces his bottle on his belt. "I'm happy I ran into you two. As you know, Diandra, I was hoping to meet your fiancé sooner rather than later."

"Well, here he is." I gesture towards Noah grandly like I'm showing off a brand new luxury car at an auto show.

This gorgeous model hasn't been seen yet in ANY show-rooms... It's the Fake-Fiancé 1000! "He's been meaning to get to the fence all week, haven't you, sweetcakes?"

Noah's eyes flash with mischievous delight, and I realize what I've done: by not sticking with our agreed-upon nick-names, I've just given him de facto permission to call me whatever the heck he wants.

Noah literally bounds over the fence and comes to my side, wrapping an arm around my waist and pulling me up against him. I'm so shocked and distracted by the Noah smell suddenly permeating my senses and his firm side pressed against mine that I have to fight to hear what he says next.

"Anything for my honeypants. I couldn't bear the thought of this fence bringing even a moment of unhappi-ness to my dewdrop."

Then, to my absolute horror, he boops my nose.

Thankfully—or not thankfully—Lachlan also looks horrified, but probably more so by the gesture of PDA, which just goes to confirm my assumption. *Not* the lovey-dovey type.

Noah keeps right on smiling, apparently oblivious to the hiccup in our conversation. I, however, am anything but oblivious to having him this close to me. I'm wearing a tank top and black athletic shorts, and I'm blisteringly aware of all the places where our skin meets. So many places—legs, arms, shoulders. His big hand is wrapped around my waist, his palm on a sliver of bare skin above the band of my shorts.

It's all making me a little dizzy and breathless. Like the culmination of all these points of contact are going straight to my head.

"Lachlan, did you know that our girl plays volleyball?" Noah asks conversationally. Like this is all *totally normal and not weird.*

Lachlan's brows rise all the way up on his forehead, and suddenly, I'm not thinking of Noah or the weirdness so much as the fact that Lachlan's surprised. Yet again.

What did the man think of me on first meeting?

"I had no idea," he replies.

"She's the best outside hitter in the county. Maybe even the state. She's an absolute firecracker."

Lachlan nods, brows drawn in his characteristic scowl, and I sense Noah peeking down at me. Almost like he has something up his sleeve...

He gives me a small smile as if to say, *trust me.*

And it's Noah. So I do.

"We have a match tomorrow," he says lightly. "You should come."

My body stiffens. Noah shoots me a wink.

Meanwhile, Lachlan looks placid as always. "A volleyball match? Haven't been to one of those in awhile. Or ever."

"You won't want to miss this one. Besides, you're only in town for a week—might be a nice way to see what Mirror Valley gets up to on a Sunday."

Now, I stare at Noah with full surprise. No one ever comes to our matches. Most Mirrorites go to the mountains or have picnics around town on summer weekends. What is he playing at?!

Then again, there's no way a guy like Lachlan would want to see a small town volleyball game. I'm sure he has stocks to watch, buzzword-heavy podcasts to listen to, women on his speed dial to chat with. He wouldn't care less about a tiny volleyball game in a random town in which he doesn't even live... Shoot, the suggestion alone probably bores him.

As expected and to my relief, Lachlan shakes his head. "I've got a few things to get done tomorrow."

"Really? You can't take a short break?" Noah presses, earning himself an elbow to the ribcage that clearly doesn't phase him in the least. "An hour, tops. It'll be a fun one, against a rival team from a town nearby."

Lachlan screws up his face in thought.

Oh, no.

And then, he says: "I'd be happy to stop by."

Oh, NO!

Noah smiles brightly and my heart skips fifteen beats before grinding to a halt. He gives Lachlan the details while keeping his arm loosely around my midsection, effectively locking me in because my traitor body doesn't want to move.

It's an unfortunate preview of what's to come tomorrow. If Lachlan's around, that means that Noah and I will have to play our parts. Be like... *this*. And given that Noah's proximity right now is distracting me to no end and making my knees feel like two goopy jellyfish, I can't imagine how gameplay's going to go.

I'm so caught up in my thoughts, I barely notice when Lachlan continues on his merry way. Once he's run around the corner and out of view, Noah releases me and stands in front of me.

"Dee, you okay?" he asks with a funny little smile. "You went quiet there."

I clear my throat, but I can't meet his eyes. I walk to the fence instead, pretending to check out his work. "I'm fine. Just thinking about tomorrow."

"Yeah, I hope that was okay. The guy seems like he has a stick right up—"

"Hey." I warn.

"Up where the sun don't shine." He blinks angelically. "Figured I'd invite the guy out, show him some of that small town hospitality everyone goes on about." His jaw clenches a little. "But then, he had that look on his face. Like he didn't believe that you're a solid hitter or that volleyball could be worth watching or something. It triggered my competitive instincts."

"See?!" I burst out. "There's something about him that, like, challenges you."

"I get it. It's probably why he's such a bigshot VP or whatever—he makes you want to work hard, even just to prove him wrong. I would've said anything to convince him." He smirks. "Well, not *anything*. A fake engagement is pretty out there."

I laugh, happy that Noah understands. Happy that he validated my feelings and helped (kind of) justify my insane lie.

But then, his expression softens into one I recognize.

"Alright." I sigh. "Let me have it."

"Have what?" Noah asks innocently. Too innocently.

"You clearly have an opinion on what just happened. You have something to say. So let's hear it." I puff out my chest. "I'm ready for a Noah truth bomb."

He looks highly amused. "Can I trademark that?"

"First, I want to hear what you think of Lachlan and that whole conversation."

"Okay, but you asked for it." He places his hands on his hips, and I have to work to keep my eyes on his face and not drop down to his glistening torso so close to mine. "Look, Lachlan's clearly a tough nut to crack. He's probably dealt with some stuff in his past that makes him come across so cynical. But I don't think it's that he doesn't believe *you* or trust *you*... I don't actually think it's about you."

I nod. It stings a little to hear the words, to consider that I might've taken something personally that had nothing to do with me at all. But I appreciate Noah being honest with me, bringing me back to reality. "You're probably right. I just automatically go there."

"You've had reasons to go there with some of the stuff you've been through with guys like him. And maybe I'm wrong. But Dee, you know you don't have to prove anything, right? You don't owe that guy anything. And you have so much to offer, so much to be proud of, just as you are."

He gives me that special smile of his, and I physically feel my shoulders relax.

"How do you do that?" I ask him.

"What?"

"Call me out and keep me grounded while also validating me."

"That, my friend, is what people call the 'Noah magic'. And I'll be trademarking that also." He smirks, throwing an arm over my shoulders. "Let's go inside for a minute. I need water and a break from the sun."

"Sure thing." I'm about to turn us back towards the house when I pause. "Uhm, would you mind putting your shirt back on? Can't have people stopping by all day to see the hot shirtless guy. You're gonna give me a bad rep."

Noah laughs but lets me go to tug on his shirt, hiding at least some of his most distracting assets.

As we climb the steps to my bungalow, chatting easily, Noah suddenly stops, opens the front door, and lets me walk through first. It's sweet. Gentlemanly. The kind of thing heroes do in romcoms. But again, I'm not sure if this is something Noah always does, or if I'm only just waking up to it.

I grab a jug of water as Noah settles into his spot on my couch with Bruce curling into a ball on his lap. To anyone else, this would look like a totally normal weekend day for Noah and me.

As if I hadn't started to notice certain things about my best friend that I don't think I should be noticing.

11

NOAH

I hang out on Dee's couch with her until the sun starts to set and she starts vibrating next to me, eager to get back to work. I promise to finish the fence tomorrow, and she promises to bring her A-game for our volleyball match.

But right before I leave, I stop at the front door.

And before I can lose my nerve, I turn back to face Dee. "Hang on. There was one other thing I came over to do today..."

I feel around in the pocket of my shorts. I meant to give this to her earlier, but I got a little distracted by the whole *lip kissing* conversation.

Meanwhile, Dee leans against the wall, arms crossed over her chest. I love how she looks today; her "Dee at home" look. This Dee doesn't wear any makeup, has her hair gathered up in a messy bun with baby hairs flying out in every direction, and is dressed down. She's changed out of her athletic shorts and is now wearing her favorite oversized sweatpants—the ones that she has to roll over at the waist a couple times, but even still, the bottoms graze the floor so much that they're a little ragged.

And Dee's not short. If anything, *she* could be the leg model.

"Looking for gold in there?" she jokes after a couple more moments of me patting at my pockets like a fool.

"Not quite as good as gold." I smirk, playing it off. Playing it like I'm not so nervous, I'm grateful for the dark shirt I'm wearing.

Finally, I find what I'm looking for in my toolbox: a small, sheer bag.

Dee raises a brow as she opens the bag and shakes a silver object out onto her palm. She frowns at it for so long that I start to realize I've made a terrible mistake.

This was dumb. And meaningless.

She won't get it. Or will want something else entirely.

Then, her mouth pops open and her gaze flickers up to me. "Is that...?"

I grin, instantly relieved. "You remember?"

"'Course I do." Her throat is tight. I can't tell if it's a good thing. "The volleyball ring. I thought I lost it at the bottom of that lake."

I shrug, my heart pounding. This is so *not* a big deal, and yet... it feels like it is. Because I'm offering my best friend a ring. Sure, it's a stupid ring from a volleyball summer camp I went to years ago, but a ring all the same. "I went back and found it," I say, almost embarrassed. "It took a little while, but hey, I live for a challenge."

That obviously wasn't the *real* reason I went back. But she doesn't know that.

"You swam back into the lake," she repeats slowly. "And *found* my tiny silver ring."

Embarrassment gives way to pure awkwardness and I shift on my feet, feeling like a kid who just asked his crush to prom or something. I am giving myself away here, aren't I? Surely, she's going to sense the hours upon hours that I spent diving below the surface of the water, searching, coming up empty-handed, and going under again. All to find a stupid trinket that's worth less than ten dollars.

But the look on her face when she lost it that day...

I couldn't let it go. And when I went back the next day and *did* finally find the ring perched on a rock underwater not too far from the beach, I couldn't wait to show it to her. I never did, though. When push came to shove, I was too nervous. Telling her that I went back to the lake to dive for her ring would've given me away and I wasn't ready for that back then. I promised myself that if Dee ever brought it up, I would give it back to her.

And now, I am.

Dee's eyes dart between me and the ring, and I suddenly wonder if I've overthought this. If I should've just kept the stupid trinket ring and given her a proper one.

"You don't have to wear it," I say quickly. "I'll get you something else. A ring Lachlan will actually believe is an engagement ring—"

"Don't you dare," Dee cuts me off, running her fingers along the metal like it really *is* as good as gold. It's such a small gesture, but the way Dee's eyes are misting right now, I feel weirdly validated. This means something to her, too. "This is perfect."

I take her left hand in mine. Her fingers are cool and soft as I gently fit the ring on her finger.

Then, she holds up her hand, pressing the other to her cheek. "My goodness, Mr. Jackson," she says with a thick Southern accent. "I never thought I'd see the day."

I laugh and tug her towards me for another hug, inhaling the mild cinnamon scent of her hair and loving the way her body curls up against mine. I linger there with her for a little longer than usual—can you blame me?—before

Dee steps back, waving a hand at me. "Now, off with you. Some of us have work to do."

She gives me a peace sign as I head out, closing the door behind me.

I'm halfway back to my truck when I pull out my phone and dial a number.

"Hullo?" Sam answers on the third ring.

"Can you talk?"

"Sleeping." He yawns. "Three minutes."

"Three minutes to talk, or call back in three minutes?" The sun's only just set here, and while Washington State is an hour behind, Sam is an early-to-bed, early-to-rise kinda guy. Which checks out given he gets up to go to the gym every day at like 5am.

"Talk."

"I'm just leaving Dee's house."

"Okay." There's a shuffle on Sam's end like he's rolling over in bed. "That's not exactly breaking news. You basically live there."

"No, but I think something happened today."

"Let me guess: Dee fake proposed to you to avoid pissing off her scary boss, so now, you two are pretending to be engaged." Sam pauses. "Hang on, that already happened once this month."

"Ha, ha." I roll my eyes. Sam thinks he's hilarious. He's not.

The day that Dee and I agreed on the fake engagement, I gave Sam a call back, called my entire family actually (because yes, Mirror Valley gossip still somehow reaches my brothers and parents in Atlanta and New Orleans and New York City), and let them all know that the engagement news was a lie. Pretend. Made up so that Dee could save her job, and so that I could get six months of prank benefits.

"This is something different. Something real." I look

over my shoulder one last time and spot the top of Dee's messy bun in her window upstairs.

"What do you mean?"

"Dee was looking at me funny." And she was, wasn't she? When Lachlan, Dee and I were standing together in the garden earlier, I could swear that her eyes lingered on me. And yes, she was wearing sunglasses, but ones that didn't completely hide her eyes. I don't think I was imagining that her gaze did a long, slow journey up my body...

Almost like she was checking me out.

"Well, she *is* supposed to be your fiancée. Maybe the girl's a great actress."

I smirk. "Remember when we did *Romeo and Juliet* our sophomore year? Yeah, I've never seen Dee so out of her element as when she was Lady Montague. She got recast as a background tree, and she was much happier with that, let me tell you."

"Maybe she was just uncomfortable with the thought of being your mom, *Romeo*."

He snickers for a moment. I do not. "You're lucky Karina thinks you're funny, Sammy."

"Most of the time I do!"

Of course. Why wouldn't I be on speakerphone?

"Hey, Karina," I say flatly.

"Hi, Noah. I'll let you two talk. Sounds like some absolutely groundbreaking stuff."

I snort. I can appreciate my sister-in-law's humor a whole lot more than my brother's.

Sam and Karina chat about something related to their business for a moment, and I get into my truck, closing the door but opening the passenger side window to let in some fresh air without risking Dee overhearing our conversation.

I know Dee so well, better than she probably realizes. I can read her micro-expressions, understand the meaning behind the slightest purse or pucker or blink. And I swear that something shifted today. For real.

After I caught Dee looking at me, I tried to see if she did the same with Lachlan. I'll admit, the thought made my stomach harden. The guy's handsome; I wouldn't have been surprised if Dee was checking him out, but that doesn't mean I'd be okay with it. And unfortunately, Dee started speaking before I could get my answer.

Is Dee the type of person who would date her boss? I don't think so, but I have no idea who Dee *would* date because this is all new. For both of us.

"Let's just say that Dee *was* looking at you differently today," Sam finally comes back on the line. "What would you do about it?"

I frown. "That's the tough part. It's one thing if she's, like, attracted to me. It's another thing if she's into me like I'm into her." I blow out a breath. "I think I should try talking to her again. Telling her how I feel about her."

"You sure this is the right time?"

"Well, no. But does a 'right time' even exist?"

Sam doesn't respond right away. "You said you're doing this whole engagement thing for Dee's boss, right? Have you met him?"

"This afternoon when I was fixing her fence. The guy's rough around the edges but he seems to have a good head on his shoulders." I smirk. "He'd probably be a great addition to our community baseball team. He'd kick everyone's butts into gear, for sure."

"I still don't understand why he would care if you two are engaged."

I throw my ball cap to the side and run my fingers through my hair a couple times. I might not agree with Dee's lie and am still not convinced that it was totally necessary, but I can see *why* she did it. Ever since she was a kid,

Dee has come up against men who speak over her and speak for her. She's been underestimated and undermined and spoken down to so many times. She's had to work harder than anyone I know just to prove that she deserves her spot at the table.

It just so happens that Dee shines in areas that are usually more male dominated. Dee often has to go above and beyond to achieve the same results and validation as her male counterparts. So I understand why her gut reaction now is to prove. To push. To win.

It doesn't feel like my place to say this though, so I just answer with, "It's a long story. But promise me that you and Karina will keep hiring and elevating women in your company."

"Oh, we're all about it, don't you worry," Sam says with a wheeze of a laugh. "Karina's part of a women's leadership group here in Seattle, and we are both committed to equality in the workplace." He yawns before continuing ruefully, "Please at least tell me that you guys set parameters for this whole thing. Like, what's allowed and what's not. It's not just a Wild West situation."

"Well, we don't have guns and cowboy hats and tumbleweed, if that's what you mean."

"Obviously not that."

I chuckle. "It's Dee, so we set ground rules. It's not a free for all."

"Good. That might help keep things in check." He pauses. "I'm just looking out for you, man. It was hard to watch you go through it in high school."

"Well at the time, she had a crush on *someone else*."

Sam snorts. "I may not know much, but I do know that girl did *not* have a crush on me. I thought seeing her turn me down would show you that. It was so obvious."

Agree to disagree, I tell him. In my head. Back then, Dee

made it clear that she liked him, but to this day, Sam insists she didn't. I always figured that Dee turned him down because she couldn't be bothered dating anyone.

"Look, man, I don't want to rain on your parade, but be careful." Sam's voice is gentle but resigned. "Just don't get ahead of yourself. Dee probably isn't taking any of this seriously."

The thought hits me like a bucket of ice water to the face. A sobering reminder of exactly what we're doing and why.

"No, I guess she wouldn't be," I say.

And I'm suddenly very grateful for our "no lip kissing" rule. Because I don't know if I could handle it if I was to kiss Dee only to find out that was fake, too.

12

DEE

It's game day and I am a mess.

But not because of the game. Nope, not at all.

I'm a mess because today, I'll have to kick butt at volleyball, while also pretending to be engaged to Noah, while also ignoring the weird "notice-isms" I'm having about him. Honestly, I'm most afraid of him showing up in those gray shorts again, because I really don't know what I might do. My brain fell out of my head yesterday when I saw him working on the fence. I can't imagine that happening again today, when I'm meant to be focused on the match.

I pull up to the community center with my whale sounds *blasting*. We have all of our Sunday afternoon matches here, in the newly renovated and totally gorgeous gymnasium. But, Daisy messaged this morning to say that the town choir is using the space for an emergency rehearsal before they perform in Denver, so we'll have to relocate.

Unsure what could possibly constitute an "emergency" for a choir practice, but that's a question for another day.

In any case, Daisy, as the head of the community center, let me know that she created a makeshift court on the baseball diamond behind the center instead. She assured me that it's all "up to code" in that breezy, smiley voice she always uses when she's trying too hard to be positive.

Needless to say, I'm skeptical.

But then again, this might work in my favor. It's cloudy and overcast today, and the cool air could be my saving grace. It'll be much easier to keep my head in the game if Noah isn't shirtless and sweaty like he was yesterday.

It takes me awhile to find a parking spot. Shockingly, the lot is packed full. My heart sinks when I realize what that might mean, and when I get to the diamond out back, my suspicions are confirmed.

"What the..." I trail off, mouth hanging open as I gaze around the bleachers.

Very, very full bleachers.

I've never seen so many people at one of our matches. It's like the entire town has shown up for this random mid-season volleyball game. And we're playing Summer Lakes today—it's not like it's an important, exciting game, by any stretch. In fact, I'd argue that our Summer Lakes matches are the most casual—more about the social beer at the end than the game itself. Plus, it's not like it's a nice day to be sitting outside...

So why on earth is practically the whole town in attendance?

At that moment, I spot Fran looking directly at me. She gives an enthusiastic thumbs-up while mouthing, "Good luck!"

I shoot her a wary smile before jogging over to Finn, Parker and Jarrod. "This is insane. What's everyone doing here?"

"They came to see us play," Jarrod replies. "Aren't you pumped?"

"Pumped is not the word I would use," I mutter as my nerves amp up ten-fold. Acting in front of Lachlan is one thing, but acting in front of Lachlan plus an entire population who *know* I'm acting?

This is going to be a disaster.

Over Jarrod's shoulder, I then spot the makings of my future nightmares. Daisy is sitting in the bleachers with Luke, a huge bag of popcorn balanced between them. When I meet her gaze, she smirks and begins to obnoxiously point at the seat in front of her.

A seat which is currently occupied by Lachlan.

He's not wearing a suit or athletic gear today, but a crisp white polo, chinos, and brown suede loafers. He's also got a pair of Wayfarers perched on his nose and one of those fancy snapback ball caps, despite the gray weather. He looks way too city for a small town sports game.

Before I can turn away, Daisy mouths, "He's hot!"

Luckily, Lachlan is staring down at his phone and therefore isn't being subjected to the ridiculousness that is my sister. I shoot her a scowl in response, already dreading what she'll be saying later:

Who cares if he's your boss? You should date him once this fake fiancé shindig is over.

Big city guy meets small town girl is the start of many great romcoms!

I've only just dipped a toe into the dating pool; I'm not going to go and *date my boss*. I'm still grappling with the fact that I'm having mildly non-friendly thoughts towards my best friend.

Who I'm pretending to be engaged to.

What is my life?

"Hey, team!"

Speak of the devil.

The guys and I turn to see Noah and Amir jogging towards us from across the diamond, both sporting beaming grins. Amir stops when he reaches the rest of the guys, but

Noah comes right up to me and lays an arm across my shoulders. Against my better judgment, I lean into his side, my knees melting a little.

But the moment Noah and I touch, people in the bleachers erupt into loud cheers and wolf-whistles. I'm not kidding. The crowd is so wild, we might as well have just scored the game-winning point.

Is *this* why it's so busy today?

It's not about watching our volleyball match, but to watch Noah and me play a happily engaged couple?!

"Woohooo, Noah and Dee!" shouts a woman who sounds suspiciously like my sister's best friend, Ivy. "Looking great, you two!"

"Nice ring!" a British-accented voice calls. That has to be Ivy's husband, James.

"You two are so cute!" someone else shouts, and the crowd goes wild again.

"Does this count as heckling?" I grumble. "I think we can kick people out for heckling."

Noah laughs. "Don't worry about it, Dee-bug. They're here to help us sell this thing. And to support our team. It's been awhile since this many people came to one of our matches, let's enjoy it." Then, his body goes a bit rigid next to mine. "Is this okay, by the way? Having my arm here?"

Of course it's okay, I want to say. In fact, it feels right in a way that I can't explain or have ever noticed before. But I can't say any of that, so I go with a very put-together, blasé, "You do you, dude."

Noah gives me a funny look and I clear my throat, turning towards the rest of the guys. "Okay, what's the plan?"

We take a few minutes with the Summer Lakes team to make sure that the so-called "court" (which is really just a flimsy net and a chalk square drawn over the red dirt of the baseball diamond) is properly set up. And soon enough, we're playing our first set.

The game starts off well—surprisingly well, on my part. I manage to keep focused, and it probably helps that Summer Lakes is feeling the pressure from the crowd because they're bringing their A-game. In fact, I can't remember the last time our teams played this hard against each other. It feels good.

Everything's going well until I take up my place behind Noah. My eyes linger on him and I watch the way he moves —gracefully, but with so much power. He's a born athlete, and it's never been clearer than it is today, when he jumps for the ball or executes a perfect dive. He moves with such care and precision. So much confidence.

It's incredible to watch someone play a sport they have mastered completely.

It makes me wonder what else he's mastered...

I know we agreed on the no lip kissing thing, but I've caught myself thinking about it over the last day, wondering what it might be like to kiss him. From a purely objective standpoint, of course. With my track record of no dating, I've only kissed one man and it was at a party when I was in college. I was curious what it would feel like, but after doing it—and having the guy's sweaty hair, awkward hands, and beer-soaked breath in my personal space—I've never again ventured into that territory.

I have a feeling that Noah would be a much better kisser than Beer Breath. I'm sure he has loads of experience. Plus, he's got such nice lips—

"Head's up, Dee!"

Amir's shout shocks me out of my daydream. The ball is coming my way, fast.

I launch forward a second too late and I mess up my dive, landing badly on my knee. I let out a yelp as my kneecap hits the red dirt, pain exploding all the way up my leg. I cradle my hands over my knee, curling into a ball with my eyes clenched shut.

It hurts so much, I can feel it in my teeth.

A pair of large hands suddenly land on mine and I'm aware of a body coming to sit in front of me. "Dee, are you okay?! Where does it hurt? Let me see."

Noah asks me question after question, but all I can do is clench my jaw, rocking back and forth.

"My knee," I finally manage. To my horror, a single tear escapes my eye.

At that moment, something warm presses against my forehead. I flinch, opening my eyes to see that Noah's placed his forehead against mine. It's surprisingly grounding, and all my attention shoots to that singular spot rather than the pain radiating through my leg.

As my focus changes, the ache ebbs a little.

I keep my concentration on Noah and any other points of contact. His arms wrapped loosely around me, creating a little cocoon. His right leg pressed against my non-injured one. One of his hands placed firmly on my back, keeping me still. Supporting me.

Despite my injury, I could stay here all day, wrapped in his arms with our foreheads pressed together. I'm also very aware of how close our faces are. A simple tilt of my head could answer the very question that distracted me and led to this injury in the first place...

Noah sits back. "Can I see it?"

I remove my hands. Noah swears under his breath and I can see why. My knee looks *bad*, all scraped up and bleeding beneath a dusting of red dirt.

Noah's brows draw together, his mouth pressed in a grim line as he turns away. Only then do I realize that the rest of the guys are huddled tight around us with similar concern in their eyes.

"Jarrod, can you grab the first aid kit?" Noah asks. "We have to take care of these cuts."

Jarrod takes off towards the bleachers. The crowd is quiet and I spot Daisy with her face pressed against the chain-link fence, clearly panicked. I give her a little nod of reassurance and relief floods her expression.

"You okay, Dee?" Amir asks.

Parker shakes his head. "That looked painful."

"It was no picnic, I'll tell you that for free," I reply. "But it's starting to feel a little better now."

"You sure?" Finn says. "I think I saw Nurse Fletcher in the crowd. I can go get him."

At that moment, Jarrod returns with the first aid kit and Noah hijacks any attempt on my part to take it. He lays out supplies, biting his bottom lip as he assesses my leg.

"I can do it," I say, reaching for the alcohol pads.

"Absolutely not. I'm pulling rank, Dee. Now get ready, this is gonna hurt."

I wince as he carefully (painfully) cleans the cuts on my knee and places bandages over them. They aren't very deep, won't even leave a scar. It's really just a case of road rash. But holy fudgsicles, it *hurt*.

"It's going to bruise, but it doesn't look like you broke anything," Noah says once he's done. "You might have pulled or torn something, though. How does it feel now?"

I try to straighten my leg. It aches a little, but nothing like a few minutes ago before Noah's mysterious forehead-pressing magic. "Better. A lot better."

His face fills with relief, and the guys relax. Finn says, "that's our girl."

"Do you want to finish the set?" Amir asks. "I think Summer Lakes would be fine cutting it short."

The team are gathered by the nets, peering our way while they talk amongst themselves. I grit my teeth and get to a stand with Noah's help, his arm looped around my waist to help support my weight. I lean onto my injured leg, and am happy to feel that the pain has dulled. Nothing ice packs and more bandages won't be able to fix later tonight. "I'm fine. Let's finish this."

Noah doesn't let go of my waist. "Dee, we should stop."

He looks so concerned that my heart squeezes. "I'm okay. Let's keep playing."

"You don't have to do this."

"I know I don't have to, but I want to. And I promise I'll be careful. I'll tap out if it's too much."

Noah's making his best Lachlan impression—as in, he looks skeptical as can be. After a long moment of silence, he grumbles, "If I see even a *single* wince, I am putting you over my shoulder and carrying you off the court. Do you understand me?"

Deal! I think all too eagerly before promptly telling my brain to shut up. Out loud, I say, "Sir, yes, sir."

Jarrod whoops and holds up a hand, which I high-five.

The crowd catches onto my recovery and starts cheering and whistling. At first, I think it's because the game will go on, but then I hear it...

"Kiss, kiss, kiss!"

The chant is relentless, unstoppable, circling around the bleachers like a wave. Noah still has his arm looped around my waist, and ever the performer, he brings me close and presses a sweet, chaste, way-too-short kiss on my cheek. My face flares red and I glance up at him, but he's looking at the crowd and smiling easily.

Totally and completely unaffected.

But the chant continues. Someone shouts, "Give her a real kiss!" and "Come on, kiss the girl!"

Noah shakes his head and laughs. And all my stupid brain can think is, *yeah, kiss the girl!*

Then, my eyes land on Lachlan. He's not looking at his phone anymore. In fact, he's taken off his sunglasses and is staring straight at us—straight at me—with those ice blue eyes. He isn't cheering, isn't chanting, he's just looking with that single eyebrow raised. I can almost sense what he's thinking: *"Well, what're you waiting for? You're engaged but you won't kiss?"*

I peek up at Noah right as he looks down at me. He must see something on my face because his smile fades.

I take a breath. "If I do something, will you play along?"

He frowns, but gives a single nod.

And so I rise on my tiptoes, throw my arms around his shoulders, and press my lips to his.

13

NOAH

Vanilla, mint and a hint of candy corn.

That's what Dee tastes like. Like sugar and happiness and *home*.

The moment her mouth meets mine, the world stops. Time stops. My heart stops.

And then, my body takes over.

My arm around Dee's waist moves her so she's standing in front of me. My other hand rises to her cheek, caressing her face. Softly, tentatively, just like I'd so often dreamed of doing. Just as I'd so often done before with women who weren't Dee, but this time is different. This time, it's *her*.

There's a moment of hesitation on her side, a pause of surprise, before she leans in, too.

Leans in *a lot*.

She grasps the collar of my shirt and drags me even deeper into the kiss.

My heart's beating again, stronger than ever, and my skin sparks everywhere we touch. I lock my arm behind her back and her fingers race along the bare skin of my arms, up my neck and tangle into my hair. She's grabbing on tight, but she isn't pulling me away, she's bringing me closer. Her cinnamon spice smell overwhelms me, makes me feel light-headed in the best way possible. My thoughts aren't coherent, aren't even English.

All I know at this moment is Dee. And all I can feel is that this is so easy, so *right*. Like water breaking free from a dam and flowing downstream towards the ocean.

I suddenly know in my gut that *this* is what we were meant to be doing all along.

I'm lost in this moment. I don't ever want to be found.

But then... I am.

A forceful tap on my shoulder, followed by Jarrod's hesitant voice, propel me straight back down to earth. "Uhh, guys? I think you've sold it."

I release Dee's lips. Only then do I realize that I'm wrapped around her, one arm behind her back, the other hand resting lightly on her cheek. She's up on her tiptoes so I'm supporting most of her weight, and her fingers are in my hair. At some point, she must've knocked off my ball cap. Her cheeks are rosy pink and she's slightly breathless. My own breaths are coming in short spurts.

Around us, the world has gone quiet.

And I suddenly hate everything about this moment. Hate how my heart is racing, and my body feels lit from within. I hate how gorgeous she looks, her lips slightly parted.

I hate it all, because none of it was for me, for us. It was all for show. For freaking Lachlan.

And the realization of what we've done—what *I've* done —feels like an electric shock to the spine.

I drop my hands, and take a big step away from Jarrod and Dee. I need a moment, need to be free of her cinnamon smell, the taste of her on my lips. I need to process what just happened.

Because I kissed Dee Griffiths. I let myself get swept

away, let myself believe for a second that this was something we both want. For a second, I almost convinced myself that she wasn't acting, that she wasn't in it just to "sell it".

I'm an idiot.

Around us, the crowd is cheering again, whistling again. It occurs to me that we probably only kissed for a minute or two, though it feels like much longer. Feels like it lasted forever, and yet not nearly long enough. Because something tectonic has shifted within me.

I kissed my best friend. And I don't think I can ever go back to the way things were.

14

DEE

The rest of the match goes by in a blurry haze. I can't bring myself to look at Noah, to talk to him. Half of me is still there, locked in his arms, experiencing something so intense, I doubt I'll ever fully recover.

Is there such a thing as a kiss hangover? Because I have it.

Somehow, we win. Somehow, we shake hands and congratulate Summer Lakes on playing so well. Somehow, I huddle together with the team and stand next to Noah, feeling with startling clarity the empty space between our arms, how our hands could brush at any moment.

I'm racked by emotions I've never felt before. It's like Noah's lips unlocked a new dimension of reality for me. I'm still consumed, completely shocked, at just how *good* the kiss was. My theory was correct—Noah has *definitely* mastered that skill. He kissed me with such tenderness, carefully and slowly and patiently... until it wasn't slow anymore. He was so confident, so firm and direct in the way he kissed me. Like he knew something I didn't.

Wow. It left me breathless.

I followed his lead, because what else could I do but melt into him? Melt into that moment and the toe-curling way his lips felt against mine?

But the high of that kiss clashes strongly with the regret I felt immediately afterwards. I'll never forget the look on Noah's face when Jarrod interrupted us. We stood for a moment, frozen together, and he looked aghast. Almost... disgusted?

There are no words to describe the wave of shame that rolled through my body. I'm kind of amazed that I'm still standing, honestly. My legs went through a lot in the span of a few minutes: a physical injury, to turning to jelly when he kissed me, to almost collapsing beneath the weight of guilt and mortification.

Noah's right, I took it all too personally again. Did it to prove something to Lachlan and wipe that skeptical look off his face.

But was it really for Lachlan? asks a tiny voice.

If I'm being honest, I don't think it was... completely about him. Because a part of me *did* want to do it for myself. See what it would feel like to kiss Noah Jackson.

Now I know, and I almost wish I didn't. The kiss was better than I could've dreamed or imagined. Better than ones I've seen in romcom movies. I can't imagine any kiss ever measuring up.

I'm now essentially ruined for kissing anyone else.

Serves me right.

The bleachers are mostly empty now—the crowd filed out after the kiss, which just goes to confirm that our town is full of busybodies who are watching us like we're on some sort of Netflix reality show.

Noah fist-bumps the guys, and he doesn't meet my eyes when his fist knocks against mine. Now, I can't *not* notice the sparks that travel out through that point of contact, all the way up my arm. It's like the kiss triggered something, unleashed something. I don't know yet if it's a good or bad thing.

He turns to walk away and my stomach twists sickeningly at the knowledge that I upset him. And as he strides across the makeshift court, I jog after him.

"Noah, wait! I—"

At that moment, Lachlan steps out onto the diamond, stopping Noah in his tracks and cutting me off.

"That was quite the game, you two," he says, his muscular arms crossed. Is it possible that his chest has become *even more* broad overnight? This guy constantly seems about two seconds away from Hulking out.

I've caught up to Noah now so I can see the way his jaw is set, his face carefully neutral. I can't read him, can't tell what he's thinking, and that scares me more than anything. I definitely took things too far. Overstepped his boundaries and the boundaries of our friendship. And what's worse is that I *enjoyed* it. For a moment, I convinced myself that Noah was into the kiss too.

How could I forget that Noah has ample more practice with this than I do. He *knows* how to sell a kiss, how to make it look real.

I'm the most dire of idiots.

Lachlan is clearly waiting for one of us to say something, and as much as I'd like to respond, I have a very sudden, very potent feeling that if I open my mouth, I'll spill out my apology to Noah for kissing him.

But as per usual, Noah's on it. "Summer Lakes are a good team. Thanks for coming out."

"It was better than hanging around my rental all afternoon, that's for sure." He looks around the court-née-baseball diamond, his Wayfarers back on his face. Still can't fathom why he's wearing sunglasses on such a gray day, but to each their own. "This town... there are some characters here."

To my surprise, Lachlan's lips tilt up at one corner.

Is he... smiling?

"Mirror Valley's a funny little place. Lots of well-meaning and quirky folk," I manage to say, but I don't risk a smile myself. It would probably come out looking more like a Pennywise grimace right now.

"I'll say," Lachlan agrees and his response feels weirdly layered. "You're a good player, Diandra. It's a real shame you aren't working in our LA office. We could really use you at our monthly company beach volleyball tournaments."

"Thanks, but I'm pretty happy here."

Lachlan checks his watch. "Well, I should get back. I have some work I'd like to wrap up before we get started tomorrow. I want us to hit the ground running, bright and early."

"Sounds great." I wonder if he hears how distracted I am right now. All I want is to talk to Noah.

"I intend to have a good, long conversation with the two of you. I have a feeling your story can help us optimize RightMatch, maybe give us a different angle on the app. Let's do dinner tomorrow night."

Noah shifts his bag. "I coach baseball on Monday nights."

"Yes, surely we can do this without Noah? He doesn't need to be involved, does he?" I ask eagerly. This, at least, is one thing I can do. I promised this whole charade would be painless for him, and I need to start holding up my end of the bargain.

But before Lachlan can answer, Noah says, "I can do Tuesday night."

"Tuesday, it is. And I do think that having both of your

perspectives will be helpful. I'll work out the details and get those over to you, Diandra."

With that, Lachlan strides away, typing on his phone.

Noah makes to walk forward again, but I grab his arm. Have a vivid flashback to the way he locked my body against his with this very same arm just a little while ago. "Wait, Noah, hang on. Please?"

I hate the desperate note in my voice, but I need to make sure that he's alright and we're alright. Luckily, he does stop. Lets out a sigh that sounds resigned. "What is it, Dee-bug?"

His use of my nickname fills me with so much relief that I almost keel over. "I shouldn't have done that." The words rush out of me like air leaving a balloon. "I crossed a line. I'm so sorry."

He smiles, but it doesn't reach his eyes. "We said we wouldn't do it, Dee."

The kiss really *did* bother him, and of course it did. Noah would never do anything like that to me—he's so respectful of me and my boundaries at all times. I may have been the one to propose our "no lip kissing" rule, but I'm also the one who broke it.

"It was a mistake. I'm so sorry. Please forgive me?"

Noah takes a deep inhale and holds his breath. His mouth is twisted, those perfect lips that kissed me so well all pinched up. I hold my breath, too.

Finally: "'Course I forgive you." His lips tilt in a real, genuine grin. "Everyone's allowed one slip, right?"

I let out a breathless laugh. "You're too good to me. I'll get you out of dinner on Tuesday."

"Don't worry about it. A guy can't say no to a free meal, can he?"

I match his smile and he gives me a peace sign before

continuing on his way towards the parking lot, leaving me alone with the clean-up crew.

He doesn't look back.

15

DEE

By the time Tuesday afternoon rolls around, I am one large ball of flaming Dee-stress.

Flaming, because all I've eaten in the past 32 hours is Flaming Cheetos.

As promised, Lachlan got us started bright and early on Monday morning and I've barely had time to breathe, let alone sleep through the night or eat a balanced meal. The guy is a veritable powerhouse, managing to keep one eye on his phone and the other on his laptop (and if possible, a third eye on me and my computer screen). I don't understand how one person can be quite so efficient. I think I'd be impressed if I had a moment to think about something other than work.

We've been cooped up in my office on Main Street for the entirety of the past two days. Lachlan's already there working when I arrive in the morning, and he stays on after I leave at night, locking up with the spare set of keys I gave him.

I assume. His perfectly pressed suit pants suggest that he surely can't be sleeping on my big red couch.

The good news is that Lachlan is more or less

completely up to date with everything he needs to know about RightMatch. The way the guy has familiarized himself with the app, the scripts, everything, must set some sort of record.

And over the last couple days, I've come to the conclusion that, while Lachlan gives off this cynical first impression, he's a pretty fair boss. He seems genuinely interested in seeing RightMatch succeed within his company's broader portfolio. Having him in my corner while knowing the board of directors has doubts feels like having Gandalf on my side against an army of Orcs (Did I mention that I went over to Daisy and Luke's house last night for my first proper meal in days and they insisted on watching the first *Lord Of The Rings* movie? Extended cut. With commentary).

Needless to say (and compared with extended scenes featuring freaky looking orcs), Lachlan isn't actually *that* scary.

Which means that Noah was right. Go figure.

At the thought of Noah, my fingers slip on my zipper, slicing my skin.

"Ouch!" I suck the tip of my index.

"You okay in there?" Daisy's sing-song voice is followed by the crunch of a chip. I wonder how many of my life-giving Cheetos she's consumed since I've been in the bathroom getting into this ridiculous WonderBra of a dress.

"The zipper's stuck." Frustration colors my voice, and I throw my hands up. "I give up. I don't see why I have to wear this stupid thing anyway."

"Becauuuuuse..." To my horror, the bathroom door bursts open to reveal Daisy leaning against the frame. I let out a yelp, covering myself, though the dress is already (mostly) on and covering (mostly) everything that needs to be covered. "I'm older than you, and because I said so."

"That's ageist."

"Pretty sure it's not. And being your wise older sister, you should believe me."

I heave a very, very tired sigh.

Daisy laughs. "Look. If you hate it, you don't have to wear it."

"I hate it," I say without even looking in the mirror. The only reason I agreed to try on the freaking thing in the first place was to make Daisy stop eating my Cheetos, and clearly, that's come to nothing. "It's too tight. And too... I dunno, sundressy."

"Well, it's summer. *And* you're going to Mirror Valley's most bougie restaurant tonight. Don't you want to look nice?"

"I don't think that The Brookrose Inn's dining room counts as bougie, Dais."

"Try telling Ivy that. She worked hard to get that star rating, you know." She steps forward. "Can I just try the zipper? When I saw this dress, I knew you had to have it. Please. Indulge me?"

"You are basically one massive, constant indulgence to me already," I grumble. "I don't know why I do it."

"Because you love me."

She smiles sweetly and I bite back my retort.

Of course I love her. Dang it.

I turn around, muttering beneath my breath. "I don't see the point. I'm going to be taking this thing off in a second..."

Daisy doesn't respond and is likely ignoring my very valid point. Instead, she places a hand on my waist and tugs the zipper up my back. It zips easily, of course, breaking through the seam of thick fabric where it caught for me.

I'll grudgingly admit that the dress fits well, snug like a

glove but with enough stretch to allow for any food babies. Assuming I can stomach that much during dinner.

Tonight's the first time I'll be seeing or talking to Noah since our stupid kiss. I've been too busy at work the last couple days to text him much. Part of me has been waiting for him to cancel on our dinner with Lachlan tonight, but he messaged earlier to say that he'd pick me up so we can arrive at the Brookrose together. For Lachlan's sake.

Daisy fluffs out my hair across my shoulders. "There. Take a look."

I roll my eyes heavily before turning to the mirror...

My breath catches.

I never wear dresses. I am a pants and leggings girl all the way. The most I'll ever do is a skort. *Maybe* a romper, if it's a special occasion. Dresses simply don't suit me, don't fit me. They don't make me feel comfortable, and I place comfort above most things when choosing my clothes.

But this dress is something else. The fabric is a rich teal blue with small white and darker blue polka dots that, upon closer inspection, I realize are actually flowers. The waist is tapered, but not tight, showing off my form without being *too much*, and the skirt flares out all the way to my knees.

The top of the dress is padded in the chest area, which is why it fits like a WonderBra, but I can understand why you wouldn't want to wear a bra with this. The off-the-shoulder sleeves and sweetheart neckline manage to high-light my *assets* without showing them off to a level of discomfort.

It's a sundress that manages to be classy. Elegant, but not too girly.

It's somehow just right.

And I hate being wrong.

"See?" Daisy says smugly. "Do I have good taste, or do I have good taste?"

I meet her gaze in the mirror and notice the color on my cheeks. Notice how the teal blue somehow makes the gray in my eyes shine bright. "It's not so bad," I say softly.

"Town councilor by day, stylist by night." Daisy giggles with a flick of her wrist.

Then, with no warning, she scoops up my hair and starts playing with it. Piling it on top of my head, tugging it down around my shoulders, doing a strange half-up, half-down hairstyle that makes me look like a balding elf. Meanwhile, I'm scowling at both of our reflections in the mirror.

Finally, she grasps for a few bobby pins on the bathroom counter and gathers my hair into a little chignon at the back of my head. After securing it in place, she steps back to admire her work with a satisfied sigh.

"Noah is going to lose his *mind* when he sees you tonight."

In the mirror, I see the color rising to my cheeks again and I abruptly stand up, busying myself uselessly. "No..." I say noncommittally, though the thought of Noah having *any* sort of reaction to my appearance makes my heart race.

I walk off towards my bedroom and Daisy follows, plopping herself down on my bed. "Now that we have your outfit out of the way, are we going to talk about that kiss?"

"I was wondering when you were going to bring that up."

"It's all the town's been talking about the last couple days. *Phee-ew*! I think everyone was hoping for a kiss, but that was..." She fans her face. "*Hot*."

My blush amps up a few notches and I turn to the closet now, scouring for a pair of shoes while conveniently hiding my face. "Was not."

"Was too. Dee, that was a *kiss*. A proper kiss."

"Well, it may have cost my friendship with Noah."

"May have *enhanced* your friendship with Noah, you

mean." Daisy says this with a knowing smirk and a waggle of her eyebrows. "Tell me you guys are planning on doing that again."

I shake my head firmly. "We are not and will never be doing that again. This is fake, remember? We're only pretending to be engaged so that I don't lose my job. And so he can have prank benefits for six months. I never should've kissed him in the first place."

"Are you insane? That's not the kind of thing you want to take back."

"But I do. You should've seen the look on his face, Dais. He looked... disgusted or something. I think the kiss offended him."

"You did not *offend* Noah. He seemed just as into it as you did."

This makes me pause for a beat. "He's a better actor than I am. The guy has a ton of experience. He knows how to make a kiss look passionate."

"Dee," she says, her annoying big sister voice coming out in full force. "Noah may be unreasonably good at many things, but he is *not* that good an actor."

Oh, how I want to believe her. Something warm and hopeful is threatening to bloom in my chest, but I quickly tamp it down. "No. Noah is my *best friend*. He wouldn't go there. *I* can't go there."

Daisy's mouth pinches and she seems extremely hesitant. Her face turns red, little by little, until she explodes. "I know you said never to bring this up, but I have to. Dee, *why not*? You're already friends, and clearly, there's some sort of chemical attraction there. What on earth is the big deal?"

Fear is clawing at my throat, making it close. I've explained this to her so many times, but now...

Well, now I've had the best kiss of my life and it's making my brain all foggy.

"Dais. Even on the *very* off-chance that he feels something for me, I can't lose him."

"What makes you think you're going to lose him?" she asks impatiently.

I take a seat on my bed. "You know all the important people in my life: you and Noah. That's it." I stare at my hands. "That's part of the reason I've never left and never want to leave Mirror Valley. You guys are my home. If I lose Noah, or if I lose you, I genuinely don't know what I'll do. You two are my anchors."

"What about Val? What about your coworkers, and everyone in this town?"

"Yes, they're my *community*, but they're not vital to me the way you are. The way Noah is." I shake my head, wishing I could explain myself better. The fact of the matter is, I simply can't picture my life without these people in it. I have this funny picture in my head of me as a balloon, bobbing around in the atmosphere, totally lost. Which may or may not be based on a fever dream I once had, but hey, the image speaks for itself. "Let's say we give it a shot and it doesn't work out and we end badly... I'll lose him."

"I don't think you're giving yourself enough credit. Or Noah, for that matter."

"Well, it's too big a risk. He's too important to me to shake things up and mess with our status quo."

"What about what we talked about before?" she asks. "What if he finds someone else?"

I swallow, biting the inside of my cheek. "I'll... cross that bridge when we come to it. I just need to make sure that bridge stays standing until then. And if I try to kiss him again, based on his reaction, it won't be."

Daisy looks like she might argue that point, so I stand up and start puttering around my room. I can't talk about this anymore. It's too much, too close to a hope that I shouldn't have in the first place.

Instead, she just says, "Okay. I just want what's best for you, you know that. Because you're my baby sister and I love you dearly."

My lips quirk into a smile. "I know."

Daisy leans back on her elbows. "Now onto the next topic of conversation, how're things going with the hot boss man?"

"Uhm, I'll take *any other topic* for 500, Alex."

"Request denied. You and your boss's gorgeous little self are just too important."

"Have you even seen his face?"

She shrugs. "I saw the back of his head at the volleyball game, but you can tell a lot by the back of someone's head. Trust me. I spent a *ton* of time staring at various angles of Luke before we got together: his nose, those veins in his forearms, his calves, his—"

"Got it, Dais."

Then, thankfully—surprisingly—she lets it go. Doesn't bug me about trying to date Lachlan once my little fake engagement comes to an end. "But seriously, Dee, how's it all going with him? I know you were stressed about him coming to town. You seemed so preoccupied during our *LOTR* dinner last night."

I don't tell her that my pre-occupation had more to do with my lack of interest in anything involving elves or talking trees or adventurous hobbits or magical rings.

Aside from the volleyball ring on my finger, of course.

"Things with Lachlan are going well, actually. I mean, he's super intense and I'm pretty sure he's sleeping at the office given that he seems to take *no* breaks, but I feel like he's on my side. Like he isn't just going to give up on Right-

Match." I have a real smile now. "I think there might still be a chance."

"I'm so happy to hear that, Dee. You deserve to have a boss who will fight for this as hard as you've fought over the years. And besides, there will always be a special place in my heart for RightMatch."

Her eyes get a bit misty and dreamy, and I bite my tongue. Far as I know, the only information that leaked from the town rumor mill the day I lied to Lachlan was that Noah and I are engaged. The actual *how* of it all didn't even factor in. So Daisy doesn't know that I basically stole her love story with Luke for the purpose of appeasing my boss.

I battle within myself for a moment, wondering if I should tell her. But before I can make any decisions, she speaks again.

"Here's hoping you can stay in Mirror Valley, because I actually have some news..." She pauses, mouth twitching. "I think I might be pregnant."

"What?!"

She laughs as I bound towards her and jump on the bed, attacking her with a hug. "Okay, okay! I haven't even told Luke yet, but I'm officially a week late. I'm going to take a test first thing tomorrow."

"I can't believe this," I say, arms locked tight around my sister. "I'm so happy for you. I can't believe you let me go on and on about Lachlan and my stupid kiss with Noah."

"You come first to me, Dee. Well, you and Luke and maybe-baby and Ivy... You guys are vital to *me*."

We're still mid-hug when there's a sudden, very loud *thump* on the front door downstairs, followed by a muffled swear.

I look towards the stairs, bewildered.

"I locked the door." Daisy gives a sheepish shrug. "Now that I'm not living here anymore, someone had to do it."

A quick knock sounds, and I chuckle ruefully. "Definitely Noah. Wish me luck tonight."

"Luck."

I nod at her. "Luck to you."

I grab a pair of dark blue flats and my favorite black purse (which Daisy yanks out of my hands and practically throws against the wall while handing me a comically tiny white clutch instead). Then, she takes my hand and we head down the stairs.

When I unlock the door, my stomach goes from clenched into a tight, nervous ball to launching into free-fall...

Noah's wearing light slacks and a dark blue work shirt—the color is almost the same as the polka dots on my dress—with the top button undone. He's cut his hair since Sunday, but it isn't too short, just groomed. Neat. Nicely styled. He's not wearing his ball cap, and his curls make him look like some sort of a dashing hero. Plus, he shaved and even from here, I smell that aftershave I love.

He looks like a million dollars, and my stomach does a series of flips before he even steps forward to present the red rose in his hand. "Thought the door would be unlocked." He smiles, and this time, my heart does the flip. "This is for you, *honey*."

I can't move, can't speak. The man has literally rendered me speechless.

"That's great, Noah!" Daisy says for me, plucking the flower from his hand. "Dee's very grateful."

I clear my throat. "Yes. Sorry. Thank you. I just... wasn't expecting you to show up looking like... that."

Noah winks teasingly, and his eyes drop down my body. "At least we're both kind of dressed up. You look great, by the way."

I blush, fiddling with the skirt. "This old thing?"

"That means 'thanks'," Daisy translates, and then very rudely shoves me out the door so that I topple into Noah's arms. "Now, get going you two. Don't want to hold up the boss man."

As soon as I'm upright again, Noah holds out an arm for me. "Shall we?"

And as he looks down at me, his eyes so warm and soulful and wonderfully *Noah*, those newfound sparks gather in my abdomen and send a blissful glow out through my extremities. Maybe just for tonight, I can pretend. Maybe just for tonight, I can act like this could actually happen, like this could be real.

Pretend we're not pretending.

I loop my arm through his. "We shall."

"Have fun, kids," Daisy calls as we walk to his truck. "Don't do anything I wouldn't do!"

I stick my tongue out at her over my shoulder before pulling myself closer to Noah. As if this could be real, as if we could actually be this couple without risking it all.

"Look at that. My beta couple has arrived."

Lachlan stands from the table and shakes my hand. Dee lifts a palm from my elbow just long enough to shake his in turn, and then places both hands on my arm again. *Right where they should be,* my stupid brain whispers.

"Beta couple?" Dee asks with a tilt of her head.

"That's what I'm calling you now." He presses his lips together. "I've been talking to our marketing team and we've dubbed you two the 'beta couple'. The first of hopefully many successful couples that come together because of RightMatch."

Dee beams and I'm happy to see her this happy, even despite the heaviness and confusion that have clouded the last couple days. I pull out her chair for her and she lets go of my arm to take a seat. I sit in my own chair, but I don't miss the way she instinctively angles her body towards me. Does she know that she's doing this?

I certainly noticed. I can barely tear my eyes off her tonight.

When she appeared at her door earlier, I had to work to keep my jaw from dropping. Dee in a hoodie and leggings is my favorite look simply because that's how she seems most relaxed. I've never seen Dee wear a dress, or a skirt, or even shorts, and look totally at ease. Even on our hottest days playing volleyball, she'll usually wear capris at the very least.

But this dress... I'm a sucker for a good sundress, but this is something else entirely. From a purely objective stand-point, Dee looks *hot*. Sexy in this glamorous, classy, effortless way that aligns more with Grace Kelly than Scarlett Johansson. The fabric hugs close at her waist, and then floats out, emphasizing the soft curves of her body that she usually keeps hidden. Her silver eyes glow against the blue of the dress, and her caramel hair is gathered in an elegant bun—courtesy of Daisy, I bet. And with the straps that fall off her shoulders, I'm blown away by what I'm seeing: her long, graceful neck, the spatter of freckles along her delicate collarbones, her bare, toned upper back.

There's nothing revealing about this dress, and yet, it's a tease. A taste. Leaves maybe too much to the imagination.

I'm not the only one who's noticed. From the moment we stepped into the Brookrose, people were looking. Noticing. I could swear that even Lachlan's gaze rested on her for a beat too long, taking her in.

Because it's not just that she looks gorgeous, it's that she's carrying herself that way. She feels *good* in this dress, and that just makes her even sexier.

Not that I should be having any of these thoughts. But hey, I'm a man in love with my best friend, and I've resigned myself to it. And now that we've kissed, I've also resigned myself to the fact that I can't go back. I can't just be her friend anymore. We've passed the point of no return, and I have no idea what comes next, but we have to move forward. One way or another.

"This is quite the table we got tonight," I say, glancing

all around the classy, wood-paneled dining room of The Brookrose Inn. Because from here, we really can see everything and everyone. We're tucked away in a quiet, intimate corner with a flickering candle at the middle of the table, whose one side is flush against the wall.

This feels to me like that incognito table that restaurant workers go to when they're going over the books or having a meeting or something. It's not like it's overly busy here tonight so I can't imagine why the hostess placed us here.

"Seriously." Dee chuckles. "You'd think that knowing the Inn's owner would help grease the palms a bit."

"I chose this table actually," Lachlan says as he studies at the menu. "Figured we should try and keep this conversation on a strictly need-to-know basis."

Dee and I exchange a look. It's not like we're trading diplomatic secrets or anything. Although this situation has a secret agent vibe that I'm kinda digging.

I'm happy that Dee's meeting my eyes. I was a little worried how things would be between us after the kiss on Sunday. I've actually been thankful over the past couple days that she's been busy at work because I've been preoccupied myself. I spoke with the volleyball boys and with my brother Sam, and tonight, I'm going to tell Dee. Finally tell her how I feel. I've been crazy nervous, but seeing her reaction when I picked her up for dinner has filled me with a low buzz of anticipation.

This time, I *know* I didn't imagine her checking me out.

The waiter comes around and takes our drink order, and as soon as he walks off, Lachlan clasps his hands on top of the table. "So, Diandra, I'm feeling somewhat optimistic about where we're at with RightMatch. If we can hit this properly, present this to the board just right, we could have a successful app on our hands." He then gives me a pressed-lip smile. "Sorry for keeping your fiancée so late the past couple days."

I rest one arm around the back of Dee's chair. She keeps her gaze forward, but her spine stiffens at my touch slightly before she relaxes into my arm. I swear goosebumps rise on her skin where I'm touching her. "No problem. Just happy to hear that things are looking good."

"Yes, better than I expected, which is a surprise," Lachlan says soberly. "A pleasant surprise."

Dee gives an eager nod. "I actually wanted to bring this up with you earlier, Lachlan, but..."

The two then break into a very detailed discussion about coding that goes completely over my head. It's interesting to see the way they talk so easily, the conversation flying back and forth. Lachlan is clearly a match for Dee in terms of intelligence, and I'm intensely proud to see the way Dee steps up. She knows so much, and has confidence in her knowledge. She's shining right now, and I couldn't be happier for her. After all, her passion and blunt intelligence —which, granted, might intimidate some people—are two of the things I love most about her.

"It's all very promising," Lachlan finishes with a satisfied look on his face. "Which is why I've come to a decision..."

Dee's muscles tense, and my own fingers tighten around her shoulder.

"Yes?" she rasps, reaching for her water glass with slightly shaky hands.

"I've decided to extend my stay here in Mirror Valley."

Of course, Dee happens to be taking a sip of her water at that exact moment...

While she hacks and coughs, I pat her back a few times. More than a few people look over, craning their necks but offering no help past their nosy, mildly sympathetic/scandalized expressions.

"Excuse me?" she chokes out.

"Given how things are looking so far, I want to give RightMatch its best chance at success. The rest of the week isn't going to be enough to compile everything we need to present to the board." Lachlan leans forward in his chair, his intense blue eyes flitting between Dee and me. "The next big board meeting is in two weeks, and I'd love to present our case then. If we can sell RightMatch then and there, we'll be set, you'll keep your job, and my company will have another successful app in its portfolio. Sound good?"

"So you're extending your stay," I confirm, not daring to look at Dee.

Because if Lachlan's staying longer, it means that Dee will have to continue working her butt off. That Lachlan will continue popping up randomly around our small town...

It means that Dee and I will have to keep up our fake engagement.

"Two beers and a scotch?"

The familiar voice cuts through our silence, and we all turn to Ivy Brooks, the owner and manager of the Brookrose. She's beaming at us with a tray of drinks perched on her forearm, clearly unaware of the bomb Lachlan just dropped in the middle of our table.

Dee jumps into action first, clearing some space. "Thanks so much."

Ivy places the drinks on the table—beers for Dee and me, scotch for Lachlan—then she puts a hand on her hip. "So what brings y'all in today? The happy couple are looking happy as can be, hm?"

My jaw sets and my gaze returns to Dee's face. I know how *I* feel and what *I* want to do right now—AKA lean into this "happy couple" shtick as much as I possibly can—but I need to figure out where her head's at. Need to see how comfortable she is after our kiss the other day... and with Lachlan's extended stay announcement.

Dee's expression remains neutral, but I see the twitch in the corner of her mouth, the way her spine stiffens again and her hands clench under the table.

Yup. She feels awkward.

And now, I feel awkward. I remove my arm from behind her and try to give Ivy a smile.

Ivy, too, looks awkward.

And now we're all smiling at each other like awkward turtles around the table.

Except for Lachlan, who has his nose in his menu and is oblivious as can be.

"How's the salmon carpaccio?" he asks suddenly, barely giving Ivy a glance. "We're in the mountains in a land-locked state. Bit of an odd place to find salmon, isn't it?"

Lachlan's question—paired with that same pinched-lip, dark-brow glare that kicked off this whole engagement thing in the first place—would intimidate anyone else. But Ivy Brooks is not just anyone. The girl is known for being completely prepared (some might say aggressively over-prepared, but that's just me) for every single question, doubt, statement, or concern that comes her way. She's basically a walking, talking Google search of anything related to the Brookrose or Mirror Valley.

Or salmon, apparently.

"Our Coho salmon is frozen at sea and then flown into Denver before being transported up here, so you can rest assured that the carpaccio is fresh. And totally delicious, if you ask me." She gives Lachlan a winning grin. "In fact, in the fall, you can catch Kokanee salmon right here in Colorado..."

Ivy then goes on to tell Lachlan *way* too much information about salmon. She talks about the salmon runs in Colorado, and fisheries and their environmental impacts, and the differences between farmed and wild caught. Lachlan, surprisingly, lets her go on and almost looks vaguely interested at times.

While Ivy monologues, I catch Dee's eye. Her careful expression breaks and she smiles, and that makes me smile, too. The awkward tension from before disappears and I lay my arm back behind her chair. She leans against me comfortably, and I'm suddenly very grateful for Ivy's fish knowledge and its tension-busting abilities.

"Speaking of," Ivy says excitedly, turning to Dee and me. "Did you see that Mountainview Diner got one of those LED changeable letter signs?"

I furrow my brow. I zoned out, so I have absolutely no clue how she got to talking about signs from salmon, but okay. "I was only there a couple days ago, must be brand new."

"Yeah, Alice was looking into new options for marketing and advertising, and instead of, you know, trying Instagram or TikTok or something, she decided that a brand new sign was the way to go." Ivy rolls her eyes, tutting. "The best part, though, is that her sign is directly across from Pete's Garage."

Dee frowns. "What does Pete's have to do with anything?"

"Well, Pete has his own sign. So..." She pauses dramatically. "It looks like we have a sign war on our hands."

I snort. "A sign war?"

Ivy's eyes widen. "Yup. It all started when Pete changed his sign to read 'Want new tires with that shake?' Alice jumped on the bandwagon and made the diner sign say 'Want a shake with your new car?' And then Pete wrote back 'Ice cream in my new car? Truck no!' And it's gone on from there." She's laughing now, shoulders shaking. "I heard from James that Mirror Grocery updated *their* sign this afternoon to join in, but I haven't been by to see it yet."

I have to laugh. "This is great."

Dee's swiping the corners of her eyes. "I heard about something like this in Missouri! What I wouldn't do to get my own sign and throw my hat in the ring..."

The three of us are cracking up so hard it takes us a full minute to register that Lachlan's just sitting there, staring at us in wonder. He shakes his head and mutters, "What in the small town is this place..."

That only makes me laugh harder.

When we've calmed down, Ivy takes our food orders and heads to the kitchen. Dee and I are sitting comfortably again, and I register Lachlan's eyes traveling across the two of us. I have a feeling he's going to ask us something about our engagement, and so I angle myself towards Dee. She responds in kind, placing a hand over mine.

"Looks like you finally got a ring," Lachlan says as he reaches for a piece of warm bread and tears it in half.

Dee holds up her hand with the ridiculous volleyball trinket ring for a moment. It sure doesn't look expensive. I have to wonder if Lachlan might catch on based on the ring alone. I bite my lip, feeling once again that it's not enough. "Yeah, about that—"

I'm about to launch into some explanation about getting Dee a new, sparkling, gorgeous diamond ring when she cuts me off. "That's right. It's *exactly* what I wanted. Has real sentimental value."

Her words make my chest warm and I smile at her.

Lachlan, meanwhile, looks like he couldn't care less. "Good. So you haven't told me about your upcoming nuptials. Is it all planned and... secured and everything?"

He trails off, seeming disgruntled with his own question. I'm assuming that this is his attempt at small talk. He quickly tacks on, "And don't feel you need to go into detail. I'm not a big wedding guy."

Now, Dee looks at me with some urgency. We did *not* prepare for this question.

I give her a little nod to say that I'll follow her lead. She clears her throat and also takes a piece of bread from the basket. Breaks off a small chunk and dips it in the oil and vinegar mixture, swirling it around and around...

And around.

Like she's buying time. Like she doesn't know what to say.

Does Dee know what kind of wedding she wants? Has she ever even thought about it?

The pause goes on for too long. Dee is absolutely soaking her piece of bread so that it's dark brown and sopping with vinegar. She pops the bread into her mouth and winces.

That answers that question.

Beneath the table, I place a hand on her leg to reassure her, and then, I turn to Lachlan. "We thought about having the wedding here, actually," I start. "The Brookrose is a great venue, especially the gardens out back. Ivy and her husband James had their wedding out there. But Dee and I want something more in keeping with our relationship. So we've planned to have our wedding at a small picnic area outside of town, right in the mountains."

Dee's looking at me, but I keep my gaze on Lachlan. Try not to notice the heat rising from my collar.

"We're getting married near an open field, so we can make a day of it: play ball games after the ceremony, do some dancing, whatever we want. The weather should still be good in the fall, and if not, Ivy's got some tents we can use. We'll have it catered, but also encourage friends and family to bring dishes of their own if they want. Our friend Ethan owns Morning Bell cafe and is a fantastic baker so he'll need to bring some treats. His wife Val is working the front desk at the Brookrose tonight, actually."

I have no idea where the words are coming from, but they won't stop coming. I realize I'm smiling.

"The ceremony will happen earlier in the day, and we're going all out: a big, fancy altar, rows of chairs with flowers, a white carpet down the aisle... Some friends of ours are in a band and they're pretty good, so they'll be playing before the DJ starts up later in the afternoon."

Dee's gone very, very still. I wrap it up quickly. "We just want to celebrate our love and our future with the people closest to us in a way that we can all enjoy. Nothing too serious or formal. Just fun, easy and light, because that's how things are with Dee and me."

Now, partly for the sake of this last sentence, I have to look at her. Her mouth is pinched (no big surprise there) but it's her steel-gray eyes that catch me off guard. They glisten and shine, like she's tearing up. A beautiful pink flush colors her cheeks and her brow is wrinkled in such a way that I'm worried I said the wrong thing.

But how can it be wrong when everything I just described seems *so right*?

I've never really thought about what my wedding would be like, or what getting married would look like. I can't identify within myself where these details came from—that's just the wedding I would want to have with Dee.

"Wow," Lachlan says flatly, and Dee and I both jolt a little. "I mean, you could've just said 'a wedding in a field' and that would've been more than enough."

His phone vibrates on the table. He checks the screen,

wipes his mouth, and puts down his napkin abruptly. "Sorry. Have to take this."

Before Dee and I can react, he's striding out of the restaurant with his head bowed, answering the call with a brisk "Yeah?"

We watch him go, as do several of the other patrons, some of whom are squinting or frowning at him. Which doesn't surprise me at all given how tall he is. It's probably why he chose this weird private table in the first place.

Now that he's gone, I try to read Dee's expression. Try to figure out what she's thinking.

Luckily, I don't have to wonder for long.

"Ohmygosh, Noah," she says quietly. "That was beautiful."

I chuckle. "Thanks. In another life, I was a wedding planner."

"Could do it in this life too, you know."

"True. But I don't think I have much more in me."

Now, Dee's face twists a little. "So that's the wedding you see for yourself someday, huh?"

"Yup. That's the one."

"For whenever you find the right girl."

I pause, wishing I could tell her the truth. Wishing I could say, right here, right now, that *she's* the right girl. What I wouldn't do to be alone with her, in a place where we aren't surrounded by a ton of nosy people, and we aren't waiting for her boss to wrap up a phone call. Instead, I simply say, "Yup."

Dee wrings her hands, staring at the tablecloth and her half-eaten vinegar bread. "Noah, we should stop this."

"Do you want to go home? We can make an excuse. I can take you back."

"No, no," she says urgently. "This engagement thing.

163

We should tell Lachlan the truth, tell him that this is made up. I don't want to be a burden to you anymore."

I blink in confusion. "You're not a burden."

"But you have plans. Plans for your future and for what you want. I can't be in the way..."

Dee goes on, but I spot Lachlan coming back our way at that fast, clipped pace of his. "Dee," I warn.

But she continues, not listening. Not hearing. "I just can't do this to you. You've been so generous, letting me even propose this—"

"Dee, stop talking." My voice is slightly louder. Lachlan's getting closer.

"—and I can't imagine holding you back any longer—"

"He's coming."

"—but the thing is, I can't keep pretending like this, and I just—"

Lachlan's literally steps away. I wouldn't be surprised if he can hear Dee's words right now. She's about to blow our cover, and I'm not convinced that that's what she really wants. What I really want.

I need to get her to stop talking. Need her to pause and take a breath for a minute.

So I do the only thing I can possibly think to do:

I place my hand on the back of Dee's neck to turn her head my way. And I kiss her.

17

NOAH

The first thing that comes to mind during this kiss is that Dee smells different.

She doesn't smell like cinnamon but like something else. Something sharper, sweeter and yet sultry. I hadn't noticed it earlier in the evening, but I'm noticing it now.

Perfume. Dee's wearing perfume. Not too much, just a light spray.

It's... nice.

The second thing I think is that Dee hasn't jerked back. Nope. She's holding herself here, her lips pressed against mine. In fact, she softens against me, letting out a quiet little sigh that makes my blood race.

And the third thing that comes to mind is that...

Once again, I am kissing Dee for the sake of *this freaking other guy!*

Before I let myself get carried away again, I pull back and lock eyes with her. She gazes at me for a moment, a little dazed, a little starry-eyed. And my heart picks up even more speed to see her like this. Almost stunned.

Almost like she might like kissing me.

At that moment, there's a very loud throat clearing.

Dee and I leap apart to see that Lachlan is back in his seat, tapping his fingers on the table impatiently. I run a hand through my hair sheepishly as Dee brushes down the front of her dress.

"Sorry about that." Her voice is impressively even. "Didn't see you there, Lachlan."

"Evidently." He purses his lips. "Shall we get down to business?"

The rest of the dinner goes by surprisingly quickly. Lachlan peppers Dee and I with so many questions that there's no time for me to think about our second surprise kiss. My arm remains draped on the back of Dee's chair, and she places a hand on mine intermittently. I'd say we make a pretty convincing couple, but hey, that's just me.

In turn, we tell Lachlan all the details of "our" story—how "Dee" accidentally invited 20 men on a date on the same night and never imagined that "I" might be the one man she was actually interested in talking to. Lachlan seemed pretty interested in that detail—the app glitch that led to our first meeting in person. He also seemed interested in the short-lived and Mirror Valley-exclusive community board that Dee built into the app after the glitch, and how "we" used that board to advertize local singles events.

By the time dinner's over, we're one of the last tables in the restaurant. Ivy's already come and gone, saying her goodbyes and promising that she'll let us know what's written on the sign at Mirror Valley Grocery.

"Well that was a productive evening," Lachlan says as he leans back in his chair.

Dee nods in agreement while I say, "sure was."

Truth is, I'm exhausted after all the delicious food and the talking and the relentless desire to be closer to Dee while having to restrain myself.

Baby steps, right? And if I want to tell her the truth tonight, I can't get ahead of myself.

"Your friend was correct," Lachlan goes on. "That salmon carpaccio was extremely good."

"Ivy's the best of the best."

He raises a brow. "Maybe we can find her a position at RightMatch as well."

I feel more than see Dee's reaction to this. Sense the glow of happiness and excitement at the fact that Lachlan could even joke about hiring someone new for RightMatch. Clearly, she's feeling a lot more confident about the future of the app, and her own future as well. I give her shoulder a little squeeze.

"About time we get going." Lachlan stands. "Got another big day ahead of us tomorrow."

"Did you need a ride back?" I ask. "I've got my truck here."

He gives this satisfied little smirk. "No need. I rented a Range Rover SUV the second I got to Denver. Been driving it on empty country roads when I've found some time."

Dee's eyes go huge. "*When* have you found time?" she croaks.

We see Lachlan to his car—a beautiful, charcoal gray luxury SUV with literally all the bells and whistles. I have to take a few minutes to admire it alongside him.

As soon as he takes off, wheels spinning in the gravel, Dee and I walk towards my truck. The nerves that I've managed to keep mostly at bay all evening spill into my stomach as I consider what to say. Should we talk about how the dinner went? How she's feeling about the second kiss?

Is it too soon to jump straight to "hey, I know we're best friends and fake engaged but I really am crazy about you"?

"I have an idea," Dee interrupts my thoughts. "Are you up for an adventure?"

"I can't believe you're even asking that question."

"It was a courtesy more than anything else. And a warning." She stops walking and steps out of her adorable little flats. We're on the grass now and she bounces from foot to foot a few times, almost like she's warming up.

I frown at her. "Warning for what?"

She takes a deep inhale in... Then bounds past me.

"Race you to the river!"

Dee cackles as she races through the grass behind the Brookrose. There are no lights back here, but we know this path by heart, have walked it and jogged it many times. The stream that runs past the Brookrose gardens flows from a river, which widens upstream to create the perfect place for a swim. The swimming hole is about a fifteen minute walk from the inn, but in the past, Dee and I have made it there in five minutes running.

Which means that I don't have much time to catch up. The girl's a sprinter.

I rush forward, cursing my stupid loafers. Also wishing I had a ball cap as my newly cut hair still isn't short enough to stay out of my eyes.

I'm about to round the final tree before the swimming hole when I hear a triumphant, "BEAT YOU!"

I spot Dee at the river's edge, hands in the air as she cheers and celebrates.

"You had a head start." I laugh, walking the rest of the way up to her.

"I gave you a warning."

"That was so *not* a warning."

Dee tips her head cheekily. "Come now, Noah, don't be a sore loser."

I shake my head. "Speak for yourself, Dee-bug."

She gestures towards the water. "How's this: because I gave myself a head start, I'll go for a swim first."

I put my hands in my pockets, smiling at her. "You want to swim. At this hour. In THAT water. In our clothes."

"Okay, Mr. Skeptipants—"

"I think that's what Lachlan goes by, actually."

She snorts, then purses her lips, turning serious. "I should take a page from Ivy's book. Be prepared for *all* scenarios, not just the worst-case ones."

"You mean carry a swimsuit around in your tiny purse?"

"Possibly." She grimaces, assessing the small—and I mean *small*—white bag. "Probably not."

She stares wistfully at the water, clearly wishing that she could go in. My exhaustion from earlier has tapered thanks to the run, and I think a dip in the river could do us both some good after the tension of the evening. It'll definitely be refreshing... Aside from the cold alpine water factor, the nighttime temperatures in Mirror Valley still dip pretty low in the summer.

"We could go in with our clothes on." I shrug. "I don't know about you, but I have no plans to wear this suit again anytime soon."

Dee looks down at her dress. "I would, I really would. But Daisy got this dress specially for me. I'd feel bad if I ruined it."

Ruining that dress *would* be a shame. "Looks like we're at an impasse."

Dee doesn't respond. She's just staring at me.

Staring at my torso, actually.

I tilt my head. "What? What's turning those smart little gears of yours?"

"Well... you're always shirtless."

Where's she going with this? "Yeah..."

"And I just need a top. And you just need bottoms."

Now, I catch on. I let out a quick laugh. "So you're suggesting..."

169

"Give me your shirt, wear your pants, and we can go for a swim."

I'm fully laughing now. "You're insane."

"Why not?" Dee whines. "You were going to swim with them on anyway. Why not just lend me your shirt? I'm sure it's big enough to fit me like a big overgrown bathing suit dress thing. All your hoodies do."

I glower at her, one brow raised as I think about it. She smiles back at me, all sweet innocence and gleaming eyes. Finally, I sigh. "Alright, you win." I unbutton my shirt and take it off, handing the garment over to her. "This is one of the weirdest things we've ever done."

"Not even by half." Dee takes the shirt. "Remember that time in school that you lost a bet and had to wear ladies' underwear to swim practice, and I lent you my ones with the Valentine's hearts all over the butt? *That* was the weirdest thing we've ever done." She twirls her finger. "Now, turn around. I have to get changed."

Oh.

Obviously, I took off my shirt and gave it to Dee. Obviously, she'll have to change out of her dress to put on the shirt. Obviously, in a few minutes, all she'll be wearing is my work shirt.

These are all objective facts, but the thought of it all happening *right here, right now* lights a fire in my veins that spreads through my entire body, filling me with heat. I can't just stand here. Not with this energy flowing through me. Not with Dee mere steps away getting undressed. It isn't exactly new or unusual for us—Dee frequently uses my truck as her personal changing room—but now, after our kisses and with everything that I *think* is happening between us, it feels... different.

"I'll do you one better," I say.

And then, I run to the river and jump in.

170

The alpine water hits me so hard that I stay frozen beneath the surface for a moment. My muscles scream for movement and I push myself up to find air, taking a big gulp in. The shock to my system is the perfect distraction from what might be happening on shore, and I tread water, looking towards the moon. It's a perfect crescent tonight, heading towards a new moon.

I'm still thinking stupid moon thoughts when there's a splash behind me, quickly followed by a "GARRRR!"

I turn to see Dee bobbing at the surface, spluttering and choking. "It's freaking freezing!" she shouts.

"Why are you yelling?" I yell back.

"Because this was the stupidest idea I've ever had!"

"Disagree!" My voice returns to a normal volume. "You've had many other, much more stupid ideas."

Dee sticks her tongue out at me and we start laughing. We swim around the river for awhile, circling each other. I keep my eyes respectfully above the surface of the water, and stay a fair distance away from her even though part of me really wants to move closer...

Soon enough, we're both shivering, teeth clattering. Dee pulls herself onto the shore first, and when I exit the water, I join her on the riverbank. She grabs her classy little sundress dress and drapes it over our shoulders.

And so, we sit on the grass beneath the stars. Dee lets out a happy sigh and I know that this is it. This is the moment for me to spill my guts and tell her how I feel. How that kiss (now, kisses) have changed me. Maybe changed us.

My insides are in knots, because of both nerves and anticipation, when Dee stops me.

"So about that kiss tonight..."

Her voice is light, but there's an undercurrent beneath it that I can't read. My own sentence dies in my throat. After a beat, I grimace. "Yeah. Sorry, I know that was a surprise."

"No... well, yeah, I mean, it was a surprise. But you don't have to be sorry."

I look over at her. "No?"

"I *did* surprise kiss you first."

"Yeah. Guess you did."

"I appreciate you going along with it. You really made it convincing," she says slowly.

"What're fake fiancés for?"

I said the exact same words to her when I was fixing her fence the other day. And I had the exact same squeeze in my chest wishing that I could remove "fake" from the equation. But this time, instead of having a disappointed certainty that Dee doesn't feel the same, I'm... well, I'm not so sure anymore. I don't think I was imagining the way she leaned into the kiss tonight, her heavy-lidded, starry-eyed expression when I pulled away.

When Dee speaks again, her voice is quiet. "I don't know if fake fiancés are meant for kissing, but you're... well, you're good at it."

My chest feels tight. So she *did* enjoy the kiss. "You're good at it, too."

Dee's silent and I can almost imagine her blush.

"If you want to lip kiss me again sometime, I think I'd be okay with it."

Now, I tilt my face up so I can grin at the stars like a fricking fool. "I'd be okay with it, too."

Dee and I don't look at each other, and it's probably for the best. I have no idea what my expression might show right now, but I have a feeling it would be too much, too soon.

Because as much as I want to tell Dee how I feel—tell her how much I care about her—I'm realizing that this is enough. This is good, for now. Telling her how I feel at this moment would be a selfish move on my part... Born from a desire to get my feelings off my chest only to place them all on her in one big reveal.

The boys and I agreed that I needed to take things slow with Dee, focus on *showing* her. And I know that's the right call. She likes to take her time, move slowly. It's how she feels most comfortable.

I can appreciate that our relationship changing, in any way, is a big deal for her. I've been ready for it for years, but Dee is only just getting there. The girl compartmentalizes in every area of her life, has done so since we were seven years old. And I understand why she lives her life that way, though it doesn't make the waiting that much easier...

I've been in the friend zone for a long time, but this is a start. A movement towards another compartment. And I'll take it, for now. Just knowing that she's starting to see what I see is enough.

She leans her head against my shoulder and I press a soft kiss to her hair.

"Hey, Noah?"

"Yeah?"

"I think your shirt might be ruined."

I chuckle. "Meh. Haven't worn it since I worked at Luke's firm."

"Yeah... that was a weird move for you, wasn't it?"

"An accountant, I am not."

Dee giggles, wrapping an arm casually around mine. "Stop. You know you could be whatever you wanted to be."

She shifts on my shoulder, bringing herself closer, and we sit like that, huddled together beneath the stars until time loses all meaning. That heart-feeling I only get around Dee is stoking a fire in my chest. At some point, I close my eyes, resting my head on hers and basking in this special, quiet moment with my girl.

It might be the sheer and utter—and slightly cold—bliss

of the moment that keeps us from hearing the steps running up behind us...

"HEY! You two!"

The man's bark shocks us both and I twist around to a flashlight shining straight into my face.

I squint, trying to block my eyes. Trying to see who's yelling at us.

"You're trespassing on Brookrose property! I'm gonna have to ask you to come with me."

18

DEE

There are many ways I thought this evening might go.

After all, I like to be prepared for all worst-case scenarios, right?

But I'll admit that I never expected to almost swoon on my doorstep, have my scary boss break the news that he's extending his stay, choke on vinegar-soaked bread, surprise kiss my best friend (*again*), basically skinny dip in a freezing cold river at midnight, and then get dragged back to our town's fanciest hotel by a very uptight security guard.

Nope. Past Dee could never have anticipated this.

"Don't know what you kids were thinking, swimming in the river at this hour," Hank the security guard grumbles yet again as he marches us through the Brookrose Inn reception. I count my lucky stars that no midnight lurkers are hanging around the lobby. At least our little trespassing walk of shame doesn't have an audience. "Thought you could get away with it, didn't you? Well, I had my eye on ya the whole time."

Noah and I share a look and he winks at me. "You're right, Hank. Dunno what we were thinking making basically zero noise in a quiet, wooded area that isn't anywhere near sleeping guests."

Hank must miss Noah's sarcasm because he steadfastly replies with, "Exactly my point. And just so's you know, the owners of the Brookrose are *not* going to be happy about this."

Now, I look at Hank in full alarm. "You called Ivy?!"

"Here they are, Valentina!" Hank announces gruffly, gesturing to Noah and me before crossing his thick arms across his chest. He's got a real man stance happening right now—legs spread, chin tilted up, lower lip jutted out. "Found the two hooligans who were trespassing in the gardens. Do your worst."

Valentina—who is really Val, a good friend of mine and the Brookrose's front desk manager—simply blinks at Noah and me in confusion. Her eyes are wide behind the maroon cat eye glasses she only ever wears on her night shifts. "Huh?"

"The two kids I saw sneaking out back of the inn," Hank reminds her helpfully. There's a strained pause before he steps towards her, dropping his voice. "The ones I told you about before I ran out of here? Saw them on the monitor?"

"Oh!" Val blinks in a big way, her lips twitching as she looks from me, to Noah, to me again. "Right. The rule-breakers."

"What'd I tell ya? I caught them, didn't I?"

"That you did. Well done, Hank."

He smiles proudly, chest puffing out all the more. With his thick gray mustache, he looks every bit like the cat that got the cream. And right on cue, he trots away happily. Probably off to check his monitors for any other "hooligans" roaming around.

"Swimming in the river at this hour? You guys have a

death wish," Val says with a chuckle, reaching for a box perched high on a cupboard behind the desk. "It must've been *freezing.*"

"I've been warmer," Noah says between clenched teeth.

Meanwhile, I have a full case of the shivers. I'm still wearing Noah's dark blue work shirt and it is soaking wet, sticking to my body in severely unflattering ways. I'm clutching my dress to my chest, hoping against hope that it isn't ruined after being partially dragged through the grass while we were being escorted back here. "P-please don't say the word fr-eezing."

Noah tugs me against him, wrapping himself around me and rubbing his hands up and down my arms in an effort to warm me up. Hank didn't give us time to dry off or anything and the cool night air lingers on my skin from our brisk walk back.

Val has grabbed her office chair and is standing on it, feeling around the tall cupboard. "Ugh. Where's Ethan when I need him?"

"Want help?" Noah asks. His chest vibrates against me with the deep timbre of his voice.

"Don't even think about letting me go," I growl.

"Heard that. And luckily, I got what I was looking for." Val hops down from the chair holding a box with a big piece of red tape that says "Lost and Found". She brings the box to the desk and starts rifling through it. "Let's see what we have here..."

"Is Hank for real? Did he actually call Ivy and James?" Noah's tone has gone quite serious.

Val pauses her searching to check her phone. Her mouth tilts sideways. "Well, I've got good news and bad news."

"Start with the good news," Noah says.

"Good news is, Ivy was already up with Mags when Hank called."

I swallow thickly, remorse flooding my veins. Baby Maggie is only ten months old, I'm sure the last thing Ivy and James want to be doing tonight is losing valuable shut-eye to come all the way down here. "I'm so sorry, Val, I—"

She holds up a hand. "Save your breath. Use it to keep warm." She smirks devilishly. "Though I do have something here that might do the trick also…"

Before Val can produce whatever she's currently holding onto that's making her smile like that, Hank's back. He appears out of nowhere, riding comfortably on that high horse of his. "I almost forgot. I need to escort you to get your cars."

"N-now?" I ask through a shiver. Noah hugs me tighter.

"Soon as the Brooks are done with you."

"Why don't you take Noah to get his truck now, Hank?" Val asks in a tone of voice I barely recognize. I realize it's her managerial "work voice".

"But that's not protocol—"

Val's lips twist in a grin. "Well, it's also not protocol to have freezing cold, half-naked people in my lobby. I'm assuming Noah has a change of clothes in his truck?" Noah nods in response. "Why doesn't he get changed and then he'll be all set for the butt-kicking punishment warranted by his…uh… rule breaking. Sound good?"

Noah's arms stay locked around me. "What about Dee? I'm sure I have something she can wear, too."

"Oh, don't you worry your pretty little head about Dee," Val replies sweetly. "I have the *perfect* thing for her."

Okay, that's vaguely threatening.

Noah meets my eyes but it's very clear that we're not getting out of this. "Be right back," he promises me before reluctantly letting go.

"Sounds go-od," I say, pasting on a wide grin that's meant to be encouraging but likely looks more manic than anything else.

Noah heads off, practically jogging out the door in his soaking wet suit pants that, yes, highlight a particular asset of his to even more asset-y perfection. My shivers briefly subside as I stare after him.

Until Hank follows at a quick pace, hollering to "slow the heck down!"

"H-Hank's a bit eager, isn't he?"

"You know Mirror Valley... there's not much going on around here to keep a security guard busy. He was so excited when he saw you and Noah on the monitors earlier. Like a bloodhound who picked up a scent. Though I'd say he's more of a basset at heart."

I smile after Hank's retreating back as another shiver wracks my body. "Brr!'

When I turn to face Val, I find her *right there* in front of me. Her eyes are wide and excited and slightly terrifying behind her glasses. "I have something to keep you warm, but you have to keep an open mind."

She then holds out a large, nondescript piece of dark brown fabric.

"What is *that*?"

"*That* is the thing you are about to fall totally in love with."

"Right..." I say as she hands it to me. It's a cozy fabric, soft and plush to the touch. I hold it up, shake it out, and snort. "A snuggie?"

"But not just any snuggie," Val says with an unnecessary flourish. "The *hoodie* kind."

The brown fleece blanket thing does indeed have arms, a hood, and a huge pocket featuring a suspicious stain. It's also clearly a size extra-large—the fabric goes all the way to my feet.

Val smiles smugly. "You're welcome." At my mildly pained expression, she adds, "Don't worry, it's been washed. I've used it myself a couple times on a night shift when it's really cold and I've forgotten my favorite sweater. You're totally fine to use it."

"And the stain?"

"Spaghetti. Probably." Val shrugs.

I grimace.

I assess the snuggie again, not sure exactly what to say: that while it looks warm and cozy, I doubt Ivy and James will want to see me remotely comfortable after being dragged out of their home at midnight? That I've done so many stupid things this evening I should probably try and maintain some shred of dignity, which will be completely defeated if I'm wearing this... *thing*?

But let's be honest, I'm totally wearing it. I can't think clearly when I'm this cold. And Val is looking at me with those intent brown eyes just daring me to say no.

So, instead of all the other things I should probably say, I just utter a quick "Thank you" and race off to the bathroom.

By the time I emerge, snuggied up and cradling Noah's work shirt to my chest, James and Ivy are standing at the front desk with Val. Neither Noah nor Hank are anywhere in sight. I stop for a second, my stomach tightening into a knot. But I give myself a little internal pep talk, amping up to apologize.

What I wouldn't do for my whale sounds right about now. Instead, I'm facing James and Ivy while wearing enough fleece to cover the entire state of Colorado.

I step forward in full apology mode. "Guys, I'm so sorry you had to come in so late. I—"

It takes me a moment to realize that their red faces have nothing to do with anger.

Nope. Not at all.

"What?" I asked, totally thrown.

Pandemonium ensues. James and Ivy keel over, hands on their knees, laughing so hard, I'm a little worried one of them might pull something. Meanwhile Val's collapsed in her office chair, head thrown back as she cackles.

"It's the snuggie, isn't it?" I say, lips fully pursed as I tug the brown fabric away from my body.

"No, no, you look great," Ivy chokes out, wiping a tear from her eye. "The way Hank made it sound, I thought James and I were coming in to deal with two ex-cons who rob banks for sport and steal candy from children."

"I thought I might have to call the cops." James laughs. "Did *not* expect it to be you and Noah."

I blink. "So you're not mad?"

"*Mad*?" Ivy's shaking her head. "Not at all."

"So long as you didn't trample the rhododendrons I'm growing by the river, you're all good," James adds.

"'Fraid to say the ship's already sailed there." Ivy wraps an arm around James's waist before leaning towards me and dropping her voice to a stage whisper. "There's a rogue raccoon skulking around the Brookrose these days, getting up to no good."

"Freaking Randy," Val says on a sigh, propping her chin on her hand at the desk.

My mouth is wide open. I'm sure I'm doing a fantastic impression of Ivy's beloved salmon right now, actually. "So the whole trespassing thing...?"

Ivy snorts. "Girl, if you think I'm going to be upset with you for braving a midnight dip in an alpine river... hey, I wouldn't, but you should absolutely be my guest. What's mine is Daisy's. And yours, by extension." She pauses. "And

181

really, what's mine is all of Mirror Valley's. Because that's what this town is."

I chuckle, a little surprised and relieved by this turn of events.

"I'm just glad you didn't get hypothermia or something," Ivy continues. "Could you imagine what Dais would say if something happened to you here at the Brookrose? She would *murder* me. And speaking of, if you need a ride, I can call her to pick you up—"

"NO!"

My shout may or may not have awoken the entire Inn, but Ivy doesn't seem the least bit concerned about her guests right now. She chuckles lightly, one brow raised all the way up her forehead. "Alright, alright. We won't call Daisy."

"Thank you," I say on a quick exhale. "Noah's giving me a ride, he should be here at any second. I just don't know what she'll say about this whole thing. I need some time to get my story together."

"So… you're gonna lie to her?"

"No, absolutely not. I just… want to make sure… I'm giving her all the details in a straightforward, direct kind of manner so she doesn't panic or obsess over anything."

Like the fact that I told Noah I liked kissing him.

And he said he liked kissing me, too.

Now that I'm somewhat thawed and wrapped up in a blanket burrito with arms, I'm having a *lot* of thoughts and feelings. If I speak to Daisy right now, I don't know what I might say. How I might frame it. I'm still processing everything myself, still trying to wrap my head around all the events of the evening. If we talk now, there are things I might be… accountable for. Explanations and details she'll want that I'm not ready to give.

Like the fact that I really do think I'm falling for Noah. And it seems, at times, like he might be falling for me, too.

If I need to talk to anyone right now, it's him, not Daisy. I don't want to give her false hope. Don't want to give *myself* false hope.

After all, this attraction I'm feeling towards him is new, but that doesn't mean we're a viable relationship option. That doesn't mean that we have a future together, or that we could function as a *real* couple... right?

Ohmygosh. I'm already a zillion steps ahead of myself.

At that moment, the door of the Brookrose bursts open and what I see completely stuns me.

Because while it isn't Noah (or even Daisy, at this point, wouldn't surprise me), the couple that tumble through the door, laughing and flirting and *clearly* infatuated, are the last people I would've expected to see together.

"Fran?" My voice is incredulous. "Ray??"

Fran looks over and her face erupts into a wide, beaming smile. She grabs her best friend Raymond's hand, interlacing her fingers with his. "Ohmygoodness, what is this little party we're having?! Ivy and James, you're back so soon? And Dee, my dear... that is not the most flattering cut I've seen on you."

I'm stiff as a board with shock. "You two...?"

"Yup." Raymond places their clasped hands at his chest and gazes at Fran with clear love in his eyes. "We're together."

"Since when?"

"We've been exploring this for about a month, I'd say." Fran looks at Raymond and he nods. "Little dates here and there, you know. Though of course, we never called them dates. And then, at the butterfly convention—"

"Oh, no." Raymond chuckles, shaking his head. "It was when your tire blew out."

"That's right! We were talking to that really very nice biker gang and telling them about ourselves, and they helped us see the light. Helped us see that life is too short to deny true love. Real romantics, the lot of them. So we decided to give this a proper try."

"And things are going well," Raymond murmurs.

"Yes. Ray booked us to stay here overnight so we can take advantage of the spa in the morning." Fran chortles. "A little weekend stay-cation. Just like the kids are doing on that ticky-tocky website."

"I know how much you love the margarita-lime body treatment, my love." Raymond doesn't even look my way. "I've had a crush on Franny for years, but never imagined that she'd feel the same."

She giggles sweetly pushes his shoulder. They look (and are acting) like a pair of lovesick teenagers. "Ray's my rock. My best friend and confidant. I want us to live the rest of our days together." Then, she turns to me with a wink. "And, he's a *fantastic* kisser."

"I'm so happy for you two," I say a little breathlessly, though I mean every word.

Fran looks at Raymond again. "I might've been married before. But this man? He's my soulmate."

She giggles again as they go off towards the rooms, arms linked and her head on his shoulder.

"Wow..." I say, watching them go. "I can't believe it."

When I turn back to Ivy, she's staring at me carefully, almost like she's trying to work something out.

"What?" I ask.

"It *is* pretty unbelievable. But you know, best friends can become something more." She looks towards James. "Just like enemies can sometimes become something more."

I clear my throat. "Not sure what you're getting at."

Ivy gives me another mysterious little smile and shakes

her head. I feel uncomfortable with this whole area of conversation, so I change the subject. "Anyway, uh, let me know what Noah and I can do to make it up to you."

"Don't worry about it. I know how it is when you're young and in..."

She trails off. I pretend I didn't hear her. "Okay, thank you."

"But I don't think I'll be able to keep this from Dais for very long, so you might want to tell her this whole trespassing story sooner rather than later."

"Will do."

Ivy then glances over her shoulder towards James and Val, who are chatting together by the front desk. "By the way, that boss of yours is crazy hot. It's almost a shame you're fake engaged. Otherwise you could date him."

I could swear there's some sort of a challenge beneath her words, but I can't be sure. And honestly, it's not surprising that Ivy's bringing up Lachlan. I should've known that if Daisy didn't harp on about this, Ivy would. The two basically share a brain. At least, the part of the brain that loves noseying into other peoples' relationships.

I laugh it off. "Probably a bad idea to date my boss. Especially because it turns out that he's staying here for awhile. Don't want to blur any lines."

Excuses, excuses. The truth is I would never go for Lachlan because I'm currently falling for someone else.

Which brings me to the one thing I've not let myself truly consider all evening, the one thing I'm worried I'd confess to Daisy if we speak too soon:

Is it bad that I'm *excited* for Lachlan to stay longer because it means more time being fake engaged to Noah?

The door of the Brookrose opens again, and this time, Noah walks in wearing a pair of gray sweats and a hoodie. And while I've been expecting him, it's a pleasant surprise all the same. My heart does a little twitch and hop in my chest.

Yeah. It literally skips a beat.

Noah's eyes lock on mine, and he smiles that special smile reserved just for me. And now, I can't and don't want to move. Now, like so many women before me, I'm the one ensnared and I'm totally fine with it. He walks towards me with such purpose, almost like he's not seeing anyone else in the room.

Almost like I've ensnared him, too.

When he reaches me, his smile only widens. And that feeling, that desire for him to wrap his arms around me and tug me close, is so strong, I'm almost breathless. Noah's proximity, his gaze locked on mine, feels like warm honey and sunshine.

"Hey, Dee-bug," he says softly and I think I might melt into a puddle right here and now.

"Hi," is all I can manage.

His eyes leave mine for a moment, just a second, to drop down my body. He tilts his chin slightly. "I think this is my favorite outfit of the night."

And with that, I suddenly remember that I am basically a beanbag incarnate. My cheeks flush as I break eye contact to look down at myself. The offensive stain is splattered across the center pocket (seriously hoping it's spaghetti) and the fabric pools at my feet.

I must look like a very large five-year-old wearing a fleece nightgown.

No wonder Noah's smiling.

At least I'm comfortable.

I give him a small grin. "Sexy, right?"

But is it just me, or are Noah's eyes actually smoldering? His gaze drops to my lips for a second in a way that makes heat rush through my face. "Very sexy."

I giggle. It's an actual, real giggle that sounds flirty and completely love struck to my own ears. A giggle that sounds a whole lot like Fran's.

What on earth is happening to me?

"Uhm." I clear my throat. "Where's Hank?"

Noah smirks and the intensity between us breaks. Probably for the best seeing as we're standing in the Brookrose reception area surrounded by people who know my sister and therefore might tell her about said intensity.

"He noticed a suspiciously toppled-over haybale near my truck so he's off investigating." He looks a little *too* innocent while making that statement. Then, he glances towards James and Ivy and a flash of worry passes through his eyes. "I'm really sorry, guys. It was totally my bad tonight—"

Ivy cuts him off with a "psh" sound. "Please stop. Both of you. You have nothing to apologize for. I'm just glad it was you two out there. Together."

I choose to ignore Ivy's tone as she says this. Instead, I look up at Noah, "Ready to go?"

"Absolutely. A hot shower is calling my name."

Also choosing to ignore that statement. And any mental images it might invoke.

Noah and I say our goodbyes and head out, but as we leave, the three behind the front desk wear matching smug smiles on their faces. Like they know something we don't.

It's a pretty low-key drive home. Noah and I talk easily with no references to the surprise kisses, or the fact that we want to kiss each other again, or the weird new intensity that appears to be a *thing* between us. But when Noah parks the truck in front of my house, I start to feel nervous. Fidgety and awkward.

What now?

It seems that Noah isn't sure either because we sit in silence for a long moment. I should probably make a move to exit the truck, but I can't bring myself to do it. There needs to be a way to finish off this evening, some acknowledgement of what happened between us. Maybe I can just say, "Hey, so I don't know what's happening between us or what it means, but I think I might be falling for you and maybe like you as more than a friend."

Something along those lines. Brilliant.

Luckily, before I can word vomit something stupid, Noah speaks. "What're you doing tomorrow?"

"Well, you heard Lachlan. I'll be working my butt off."

"If you get some time, I'd love for you to come by the shop. There's something I want to show you."

My chest fills with something light and airy—almost like the pesky butterflies that have taken up residence in my abdomen have decided to move northwards. And is it just me, or is the world feeling sparkly even now, with just this question? "Sure," I reply softly. "I'll come by in the evening."

"Good." Then, Noah does this slow, sexy, charming smile thing that makes my breath catch. "I can't wait."

Me neither, I say internally because I don't trust my voice not to squeak or crack or something. I unlock the door, step out, and give Noah a peace sign as he drives away, sure that I won't be forgetting that smile—or this entire evening—anytime soon.

19

DEE

"YOU GOT ARRESTED?!"

This time, I'm thankful I'm not in my car. This time, Daisy's voice would probably break the speakers.

I wince, holding my phone away from my ear. I can still hear her screeching away tinnily on the other end. I wait until she stops to take a breath, and then, I very calmly say, "No."

"What do you mean, 'no'?!" Daisy's voice is an intriguing mix of snarling and worried and... maybe something else. Maybe something like...

Laughter?

"Are you laughing right now?"

"No!" she wheezes, but then does this weird little cough that I swear is hiding something else. "I mean... maybe! You know how I get when I feel too many things too quickly. My emotions go haywire!"

I do know this about her. I specifically remember the pure mortification and desperation in her eyes while she smiled her way through our great-aunt's funeral. Our parents weren't impressed, but I'll admit it lifted my spirits a little to see a smile. Everyone else's faces, including Daisy's actually, were tear-stained.

"Dais. I did *not* get arrested," I say very reasonably.

"That's not what Ivy said. Or Val, or James, or Hank."

"When were you talking to Hank?"

"You hear things!" Daisy is still screeching. I'm still holding my phone inches away from my ear. I jangle my keys in my left hand, waiting for another tirade about my impending jail time to come to an end. I'm standing just outside my car, but I won't get in and risk subjecting my speakers to Daisy's squawks just yet.

"Give her a break," Luke says in the background. "Everyone's allowed one tiny little criminal misdemeanor."

"Thanks, Luke," I mutter, to which he very clearly says, "You're welcome."

"Am I on speaker?!"

"'Course you are." Daisy finally returns to a normal pitch. "Luke and I are making dinner." There's a very loud throat clearing and Daisy giggles. "Well, Luke is making dinner and I'm lounging and talking to my criminal baby sister who might as well be in the mafia."

I give a very tired sigh. "I'm not in the mafia."

"That's just what you would say if you were in the mafia."

"It's also what you say when you're *not* in the mafia."

But Daisy's giggling away, no longer listening. "Did you hear that, Luke? Imagine, Dee being in the mafia. Like a tech developer mafia. Ohmygosh, Dee's clearly the head of Anonymous." She continues snickering like the entire notion of me being a mafioso—mafiosa?—is so ridiculous, it doesn't bear a moment's consideration.

Which, I mean, I'm really not. But it's the thought that counts, you know?

And now, Luke is joining in. The man never laughs

(except around Daisy) so I'll give him a pass seeing as this is a rare exception for him. And an even rarer occasion that I would be anything close to "arrested".

"Can I assume Ivy told you about the river mishap, then?" I ask when the two of them have settled down.

"Nope. Heard it from Fran."

"Fran…"

Ohmygoodness.

I was so worried about Ivy telling Daisy the truth that I completely forgot that our town's star gossip fiend was *right there with us*. Clearly, my midnight swim with Noah has wiped all logical thinking straight out of my brain. Is this what happens when you start falling for someone? Your mind gets all fuzzy and easily distracted and caught up in thoughts of your alleged crush?

Ugh.

I was a complete wreck at work today. I couldn't stop thinking about the swim, about wanting to kiss Noah and knowing that he wants to kiss me, too. Can friends ever just casually kiss one another once in awhile while keeping everything else totally normal?

Do I *want* us to be totally normal?!

In any case, I don't think Lachlan was very happy with me. But he took it easy on me. Said he noticed how hard I'd been working, including through last weekend. And it might've just been me, but he seemed a tad distracted today, too. He checked his phone more often than usual, had this additional wrinkle in his brow.

When I answered Daisy's call this evening, I thought it would be a quick little catch-up that would take all of ten minutes, which was the perfect length of time for me to drive from my office to the carpentry shop. I thought hearing her voice would calm the nerves that keep threatening to hijack my stomach, would slow my heart that's been relentlessly skipping over itself ever since last night.

But by the time I'm parking the car, a good twenty-five minutes later (Daisy was finally quiet enough to be on handsfree), I'm not feeling that much calmer.

"So I was talking to Ivy and she mentioned something to me." Daisy says this lightly, casually, and I'm abruptly aware of the lack of background noise where it had previously been quite aggressive (seriously, I don't know what Luke was making, but it apparently involved running five blenders at once). "She said that you and Noah seemed different last night."

I clear my throat. "Aaaand it's time I get going—"

"No, please! Just stay on for a minute more?"

I inhale through my nose. "Fine." Then, because a very annoying part of me is kind of curious, I ask, "Different how?"

"She said that you guys seemed more, like, absorbed in each other than normal. That your body language was different, and the way you behaved towards each other. 'Romantic' was the term she used."

"Well, we were pretending to be engaged all through dinner. That's probably why."

Daisy must hear the defensive note in my voice. "Yeah. You're right, that must be it. Sorry for bringing it up."

"No prob. But I really do need to—"

"Although," she cuts me off. "She was referring to something that happened after the dinner and the river thing. Said you guys had a *moment* in the lobby."

I press my lips together, wondering how to play this. How to react to this. I haven't had time to think through how to frame this for Daisy. Or maybe I just haven't taken the time... I think a part of me isn't ready to imagine that whatever happened last night hadn't happened. Part of me doesn't want to dissuade myself from something that felt so potent and precious at the time.

And now, I'm out of time. I go into panic mode. "Right. A moment." I cough out a laugh. "Noah and I had, like, a *moment.*"

"Yeah." Daisy's voice is entirely serious. "She said it was like he couldn't keep his eyes off you, and you couldn't keep your eyes off him. Like the second he walked in the room, you two were drawn to each other. It was magnetic."

Oh. So that intensity *was* noticeable.

And more importantly... Ivy also felt that Noah couldn't keep his eyes off me?

My mouth is dry. "Okay. Uhm. I'm going now," I say not at all awkwardly.

"One last thing. I wanted to ask you how the weather is over there?"

I frown in confusion. "Where?"

"In Egypt." She pauses for a long moment. "Because you're clearly in Dee-nial."

She honks out a laugh whose power and force is directly equivalent to my own cringe. In the background, I hear Luke cackling away too. *Good grief.* "Okay, byeeee!"

I'm fully holding my phone away, ready to end the call, when I hear her squawk anew. "No, I'm sorry! Wait!"

I pause, then gingerly bring the phone back to my ear. "Yes?"

"I just want to give you some final big sister advice from someone who's been there, if you'll let me." I don't say anything, so Daisy goes on. "Look, while you might not be ready to talk about it or even acknowledge it to yourself, if something *feels* right to you, don't let it get away. Don't shrug it off or discount it. Don't assume it happens every day, because it doesn't. I can attest, as a past dating app guinea pig—when something clicks, it's special. Just keep that in mind, okay?"

"Okay, Dais, I will," I reply. "Love you."

"Love you, too."

It isn't until I step out of the car that I realize I don't usually hang up the phone with that particular sign-off. I love my sister, of course, and I tell her often enough, but I never use those words in parting.

I am clearly on a whacked-out emotional roller coaster rivaling the one and only time I went on the California Screamin' ride at Disneyland with Noah (and yes, I was very sick afterwards. Which probably explains why being tipped upside down still makes me nauseous).

I take a few deep breaths before I walk up the path towards the carpentry shop. The office at the front of the building is locked up for the night, the windows dark, but that's not exactly surprising given the time. Raymond's probably out with Fran now anyway...

Ohmygoodness. Ray and Fran!

I smile wide, way too excited to tell Noah the news about our favorite senior non-couple becoming coupled. I hope he hasn't heard the news already.

I also hope he's still out back. He assured me that he'd be working late and he'd wait for me, but it's definitely later than I expected...

I quicken my pace, walking the small path around the side of the workshop. I'm about to come around the corner into the garage when I hear voices.

"So you didn't tell her?"

That's Jarrod. What's he doing here?

"No, I didn't," Noah replies. "It just didn't feel right."

"Really?" And there's Parker. "After an entire evening being all couple-y together, it still 'didn't feel right'?"

I pause mid-step. They're talking about me. That *her* has to be me, right?

"We talked about this, boys," Finn chimes in. "Baby steps."

Now, I'm dying to know what on earth is happening. Why are the volleyball boys here right now, and what are they talking about? My curiosity gets the best of me and I step around the corner into the back of the workshop.

"Baby steps to what?" I ask.

The reactions are almost comical. Finn and Parker are both about to take sips of their beers and they pause, bottles held mid-way to their mouths and the whites of their eyes glowing as they stare at me like frozen meerkats. Jarrod's off to the side with his arms crossed, and his jaw drops wide open when he sees me. And Amir and Noah are standing at the center of it all, clearly awestruck and holding a...

Deflated volleyball?

"What're you guys doing?" I frown, nodding at the ball. "Practice isn't until tomorrow."

"We're, ah..." Jarrod flounders.

"We're just fixing..." Amir tries.

"We're fixing Parker's prize volleyball," Noah says smoothly. "You know, the one signed by Kerri Walsh and Misty May-Treanor?"

He holds the sad looking ball right in my face as if to say, *see?!*

I swat it away. Parker looks at the ground. "I brought it to a match in Longhaven yesterday to impress this girl I like, okay? Long story short, I was showing off and it got punctured and... well, I didn't get her number."

I cover a snort, then turn serious again. Back to business. "What were you guys talking about?"

"When?" Finn asks sweetly. He's blinking his already big eyes in a very big way.

"Just now. Before I came around. It sounds like Noah was meant to tell someone something?" I prod. "A *her*?"

There's another long beat of silence. I can't bring myself to look at Noah for some reason, so I end up staring at the sad volleyball.

And then, "YANICA!"

I jerk my head up to look at Parker. "Sorry?"

"We were talking about Yanica." He nods proudly.

"And what are we not telling Yanica? Baby steps to what?"

Jarrod shuffles on his feet. Finn sniffs and takes another swig of his beer. Noah presses his lips together. Only Amir answers my question, and he does so in a loud shouty voice that isn't unlike a foghorn in its pitch and volume. "Noah hasn't told her he's fake engaged!"

I blink, color rising to my cheeks. "I thought you two broke up?" I say to Noah, my voice uneven.

Noah's too busy shooting Amir a glare to meet my eyes. "We did. We definitely did," he replies firmly. "Yanica and I aren't and were never a thing."

"Okay..." I trail off, feeling uneasy. I believe Noah, believe that he wouldn't string someone along. He might date a lot and have a reputation for it, but he would never intentionally hurt anyone, would never deceive or lead them on.

No. I'm uneasy because there's a very potent, very present air of discomfort in the room right now. It's like someone cleared the area for a stink bomb.

Then, Jarrod slaps his palms to his knees. "Welp! Best we head off, wouldn't you say, boys? Leave these two faux-lovebirds to it?"

There's a loud communal agreement followed by an even louder shuffle and scuffle as the guys gather their things and leave the garage, promising to see us tomorrow for practice. Soon enough, the clinking of bottles being thrown in recycling, the guys' mutters about stopping for pizza, and the sad volleyball are all gone. It's just Noah and me, standing face to face under the glow of the garage lights, surrounded by the sounds of crickets and a nighttime breeze that would probably make me shiver if I wasn't singularly focused on the fact that I'm standing here, you know... *alone* with Noah for the first time since *the swim.*

I'm also not completely or even partly sold on the claim that they were talking about Yanica. But I'll have to bug Noah more on that later.

"Want to take a seat?" he asks. "Probably time I shut the garage door and lock up the back of the shop."

I settle onto a stool by one of the worktables and Noah offers me a beer (which I decline). After he finishes locking up, he pulls up a stool across from me. I have a weird deja vu to sitting here in this shop, on stools like these, when I proposed our fake engagement a week ago.

It feels like longer. Feels like a much more significant period of time has passed given the significant changes in my feelings.

Noah grabs his canteen and takes a big gulp of water. And I watch his Adam's apple bob like I'm hypnotized, my eyes finally coming to rest on the hollow spot between his collar bones. I restrain an urge to run my fingers along the skin there.

"So. You wanted to show me something?"

"Oh, yeah!" Noah leaps up from his stool and jogs around one of the tables. He lifts something—something heavy, judging by the bulge of his biceps and the strain along his upper back, but of course, he doesn't even grunt—and he comes back towards me.

When I see what he's holding, my brows draw together. "And those are...?"

"Kitchen cupboards." Noah places the large wooden structure of a light almond color on the ground in front of me. As soon as he says the words, I notice the intricate carved detail on the four doors, the cute handles that perfectly match the ones that I have at the bungalow...

My eyes widen. "Cupboards?" I repeat stupidly.

"Yeah. I made them for you," he explains, though he doesn't need to. "The ones at your house are a disaster and I finished Rosie's table—she loved it, by the way—so this was my project for the week." He smirks a little, winks. "I had more downtime than usual."

I feel breathless and more than a little shaken by his thoughtfulness. "So this is what you can accomplish without me distracting you, huh?" I joke through a tight throat.

His expression turns soft. "This is what I can accomplish *because* of you, Dee."

My heart might just break open. What could I have done to deserve to know someone so sweet and perfect and incredible? What could I have done to deserve having him as my *friend*? In a past life, I must've been Florence Nightingale or a person who voluntarily picks up trash off highways (seriously, I hope they get paid). No man should ever be this perfect. It's simply not fair for the rest of us regular people.

I feel a twinge deep within my gut at the thought. It's not a bad feeling... but it isn't exactly pleasant either. I file it away for later.

"Noah, I..." I have so much to say and yet I can't say anything at all. Words have never been my strong suit, and once again, I'm coming up short. I finally gesture around the shop. "You're so good at this."

It's lame. Very, very lame. But it's truly all I can manage right now.

But Noah gives me that smile again. Like that actually meant something to him. "I like this, Dee. I like working here with Raymond. It might sound stupid or small, but I feel like I'm making a difference, you know?"

Suddenly, I'm rushing forward, placing both hands on Noah's arms. "It's not stupid. And it's not small." I point at the really very large rectangular object in front of me. "*You* did this, Noah. All by yourself, and it's beautiful and perfect."

I smile up at him and he shines a smile right back. And my knees start to go weak again, so I step away to admire the cupboards. "I'm really happy for you. You've found something you love and you're so good at it."

"Thanks, Dee," I hear the swell of pride in his voice and it makes me even more proud for him. "Want to see some of my moves?"

My head jerks up. "What?"

Noah's grinning at me mischievously. "I can show you how it's done. If you want."

And though I know he's *most definitely* not talking about the *it* that I think he's talking about (AKA, giving me another front row seat to the "Kissing Noah" experience), I nod. So he takes my hand and guides me to one of the worktables. He grabs a couple of safety goggles, some gloves, and a couple aprons, and he shows me how to get ready for this little demonstration he's about to give me. While he's running through a safety briefing (one that I know I should be paying attention to, but ohmygosh his voice and the Noah smell and his overall presence are distracting), it occurs to me that this is just like any other day. Things with us feel so normal and yet so... not.

I'm reminded of what Daisy said—that our friendship might be *enhanced*.

It does feel like that, actually. The spark and intensity

between us does feel like an enhancement.

Which is actually kind of terrifying. Because my friendship with Noah already feels too precious sometimes.

Noah grabs a couple of wood boards and places them flat on the worktable. Then he stands behind me, placing an arm on either side of mine, and we use the saw to cut through them. We might as well be freaking Demi and Patrick in *Ghost*.

Except with a handsaw instead of clay.

Sawing through the boards is no joke, though. I can't tell if it hurts or helps to feel Noah's arms tighten around me as he holds most of the saw's weight. When we cut the first board, I let out a shout of triumph and Noah and I share a high-five. It's just one small move, but it feels like a huge win all the same.

Eventually, Noah puts down the handsaw and we sit on the worktable, side by side. Noah, as expected, looks like he could grace every single page of a calendar featuring sizzling hot carpenters, whereas I probably look more like one of the minions from *Despicable Me*.

"I can see why you like this," I say, leaning back on my hands. The surface of the worktable is solid, peppered with grooves and nicks. "Sawing things is a good way to let off steam."

"Oh, yeah. Anytime I'm upset or angry or sad or just... feeling too much, I come here."

"Like you're ever sad."

He chuckles. "I have my range of emotions, don't you worry."

I look at him then, because of course I know that Noah feels things deeply. He might joke about pretty much anything and everything, but he takes certain things very seriously. Normally, he'd play my comment off, but right now, he seems thoughtful.

He sits forward on the table, staring at our legs dangling above the ground. He clears his throat. "I meant what I said earlier. Yanica and I aren't a thing. At all."

I nod. "Okay... good." *Oh goodness. Why am I so bad at this?!* "I mean, not good. Not if you wanted to be, you know, with her. I..."

I trail off uselessly, is what I do.

Noah shoots me a funny little smile, but then his brow crinkles and he turns to face me fully, eyes on my forehead. "Hey, you might have a problem there."

I frown. "What?"

He reaches up and touches my goggles. Specifically, touches the place where my goggles have wrapped my hair into a big knot. I reach up, feeling the wad of hair tangled around the rubber.

Great. I bet Yanica never gets her stupid hair caught in stupid goggles.

I paw at my forehead for a moment, floundering, before Noah chuckles. "May I?"

I give a frustrated, strangled noise that Noah correctly assumes is permission granted, and he hops off the table. His Noah smell mixed with salt and sawdust takes over my senses and I hope he doesn't notice my subtle inhale. He's standing just ahead of my knees, but I shift closer on the table so he can reach my hair properly.

His lips are slightly pursed as he gets to work on my goggle-nest, his fingers moving slowly and carefully. Tugging, but not hard. Meanwhile, I am powerless to do anything but watch his face. See the wrinkle in his brow as he concentrates, his full lower lip protruding slightly. Notice his deep brown eyes locked on my hair. Even when laser-focused on something mundane, the guy is heart-achingly beautiful. He's not even trying to be.

Finally, something loosens above my forehead, and

Noah slowly removes the goggles from my hair and places them on the table behind me. "Better?" he asks.

I manage a smile. "Much."

My voice gives me away. It's low and uneven in a way that I've never heard it.

Noah's eyes lower to meet mine, and something shifts between us. That intensity—that *moment*—is back, turning the world sparkly again. My fingers claw a little on the surface of the table, my arms going stiff to hold me up. My gaze travels his face. Lingers on his lips, this time.

Noah's pupils darken and I'm suddenly very aware of the way he's placed his big hands on the table on either side of my hips so that his thumbs press against my sides. The veins in his forearms pop as he leans his body close.

It occurs to me that all I'd have to do is sit up a little. Tilt my chin. And our lips would meet again.

Suddenly, my apron feels too heavy, too warm. Too *obstructing*.

And the space between Noah and me feels like altogether too much.

I'm barely aware that my lips have parted until I swallow thickly, my eyes still stuck on that beautiful mouth of his.

"Hey, Dee," he whispers. The husky sound of my name sends my blood racing.

"Yeah?" I whisper back.

"I want to kiss you again."

My heart rate spikes. "Okay."

"But this time..." Now, his voice turns firm. Resolved. His eyes are doing a careful, slow journey across my face, almost like he's memorizing me. Almost like he wishes his fingers could follow. But his hands don't touch me. I wish they would. "This time, I'm going to kiss you without anyone else around. Especially not Lachlan. I'm going to kiss you because I want to kiss you and I know you want to kiss me, too."

My breath catches.

"And before I kiss you," he goes on slowly. "I want to do something with you. Just us. A real first date. None of this fake stuff." He pauses for a breath. "Is that okay with you?"

I'm hypnotized. Totally mesmerized. I'm under Noah Jackson's spell, and I would give my left arm to stay in this moment forever—lingering seconds, breaths, away from his perfect lips, with him looking at me like I'm something precious. Something to be treasured and loved. Something and someone he *sees* in a way that I've never been seen.

He wants to go on a date with *me*? A real date? Of all the women he's dated—the beautiful ones, the smart ones, the kind and good-hearted ones—women who would be out of anyone's league... he's picking, at this moment, me.

And I suddenly understand the twinge in my gut earlier. I suddenly know why Noah and I feel so impossible: *he* is Noah Jackson, and I'm just... me. Ordinary, regular Dee. I'm not putting myself down; I'd say I'm quite pretty, and I know I'm smart and kind.

But I'm not an extreme, and Noah is *all* extremes.

Yet, through the crash of disbelief that threatens to take over my body, I hear a voice. Daisy's voice. Because I know, *I know*, that I am different for Noah. I am different from all those other *extreme*-ly perfect women that he's dated. And he's different for me too.

I might have no words for what's going on between us right now, and I might not be able to wrap my head around it, and the speed of it all is giving me whiplash, but I also know that I would one hundred percent describe this as "special".

So, with Daisy's advice in my ear, I say, "Yes."

20

NOAH

Wise men probably have all kinds of advice for this sort of thing.

You know, the whole "planning a first date with your best friend who you've been in love with for years and is finally starting to feel the sparks between you two" thing.

Yeah, that. Super common.

I imagine they'd say that I should do everything I can to make her feel special. Go above and beyond. Blow her out of the water with a top-notch, totally unforgettable date. Plan something so flawless, so exciting and mind-bending that she'll have no choice but to label it the "best first date—no, best *date*—ever". They might tell me to watch a few romcoms, analyze the grand gestures, and do something just like that.

But in the end, no matter what I planned, no matter what I organized, none of it felt *right*.

It wasn't until I stopped, took a breath, and thought of everything *Dee* that I realized I already had my answer. Dee might love romcoms, but she doesn't love big, showy grand gestures. She might love to feel loved, but she doesn't love having it thrown in her face. Dee is a woman of care, consideration, and patience. She lies in the glorious space between the extremes. She *savors*.

So instead of planning something big, I plan something small. And while I know this is closer to what she'd want, I'm hoping that I got it right.

Dee steps out the door of her bungalow as soon as I pull up in my truck. And as she walks down the sidewalk, I notice her fingers twisted together, the way she's biting her lip. She's nervous, but luckily, I've already thought of a way to take care of that...

I come around the front of my truck and open the passenger door for her.

The second Dee sees me, she bursts into laughter.

"What is *that*?!"

"This old thing?" I blink innocently, pointing down at myself. "Found it in the back of my truck. Thought it looked cozy."

Dee's bent over laughing. "How on earth does it actually look *good* on you?! That much fleece shouldn't be attractive on anybody."

I run my hands down the front of the dark brown snuggie from the night of our second kiss. "You know what they say—the bigger the snuggie, the hotter the man."

"Literally no one has ever strung those words together. Ever."

"Until now." I nod at the truck. "Hop in."

And she does. She settles into the passenger seat, and before I can close the door, she pops open the glovebox. "Score! You still have the Easter candy corn."

I roll my eyes at her. "Give me some credit here, Dee."

She beams at me and I shut the door. But as I'm walking around to the driver's side of the truck, my legs get wrapped up in the snuggie and I tumble forward. I manage to catch myself at the last second and only narrowly avoid falling face first on the pavement (seriously, who on earth needed a snuggie *this* big?)

When I straighten again, Dee's cackling away in the front seat like I didn't just almost die. And the weird thing is, I feel totally at ease despite my near-death experience. It just feels right to be here with her. Making her laugh.

When I come around to my door, I whip off the snuggie and place it in the back seat, grabbing my ball cap instead. And yes, I do notice Dee's eyes drop to my exposed midsection as I pull the snuggie over my head.

That *also* feels right.

"Much better. That thing is *way* too warm."

Dee chuckles around a mouthful of pink and blue sugar. "I expect to get that thing back, by the way."

"You'll get it back when you return every one of my hoodies."

She doesn't reply, doesn't even seem to register the words. It's almost like I'll never be seeing those hoodies again.

"Is this okay, by the way?" she asks, gesturing down at herself. "I didn't know what to wear and I got changed about eleven times. Wait, am I supposed to tell you that on a date? Or am I supposed to be all mysterious and seductive and quiet? Ohmygosh, maybe I shouldn't be saying any of this at all—"

"You look beautiful," I cut her off. I honestly love when Dee tells me her inner thoughts like this, when the words spill from her mouth like she has no control over them. "You're not supposed to be anything but yourself."

She beams a smile my way, finally relaxing into the seat.

She really does look beautiful. Her caramel hair is down around her shoulders, slightly wavy and smelling of cinnamon. She's wearing blue jeans—the nice ones with the funky patch sewn onto one of the butt pockets (which I probably shouldn't know, but obviously, I do)—and a black t-shirt. A frilly one that's delicate, sweet-but-not-too-sweet, and totally Dee.

"So what's the plan?" she asks, popping another candy corn into her mouth.

"It's a surprise, but I think you'll like it." My smile drops a little, suddenly vulnerable. "I *hope* you like it."

She places a small hand on my elbow, and my skin warms beneath her touch, electric currents shooting up my arm. "I'm sure I will."

We fall into easy conversation. Dee tells me about the last couple days working with Lachlan, and the preparations they've been doing for a call he's having with the board of directors tomorrow morning in prep for the big meeting. I give her the highlights of our volleyball practice last night that she missed once again.

Of course, this meant that the boys and I spent the entire hour standing around the court talking about this very date, but I don't mention that part.

And we talk about Raymond and Fran and the fact that our town's token senior best friends are now in a full-fledged, teenage dream level relationship. I have to keep myself from looking at her too much, from telling her how much I hope we can do something similar.

Assuming this date goes well. Assuming Dee wants that for us, too.

I'm keeping with my baby steps, keeping things slow for now, and it seems to be working. Sure, in the garage the other night, I wanted nothing more than to place my hands on her hips, slide her forward on the worktable until our bodies were flush together, and kiss the living daylights out of her. But that will have to wait. I'm happy to wait, if that's where we'll eventually end up—wrapped up in each other, cheeks red, and totally happy.

This is a practice of patience for me, which is something I don't usually excel at. But for Dee, I'm giving it my all.

That night was also a good reminder of *why* I'm giving it my all. The joy in her eyes when I shared with her how much I like working as a carpenter... well, it made my own happiness all the better. So much sweeter. Sharing things with Dee always has this effect for me—like the world is muted until she brings the color, the sound, the *real*-ness of it all.

"How's Bruce doing?" I ask as I take a left turn to leave town. "It's been a few days since I saw him. Does he miss me?"

"He's playing hard to get. You know, acting like he's forgotten you exist."

"Sounds about right."

"But you love him."

"I do." I give a smirk. "And he loves me too. He just doesn't know it."

Dee's silent, and I glance over to see a small wrinkle above her left brow—a sign that she's lost in thought. She's holding a yellow candy halfway to her face, like she's forgotten all about it. I open my mouth. "Corn me."

She blinks, coming out of wherever she went to. She aims and throws the candy corn my way, and I catch it on my tongue. "Did you know that the yellow and green ones don't taste any different to the pink and blue?"

I crinkle my nose. "Nope. No way. The blue ones are *nasty*."

"Are not!" She laughs. "You're thinking of Skittles."

"Blue Skittles are delicious, I don't know what planet you're living on."

"Well that would explain why this bag is almost entirely blues and pinks."

I give her a side glance. "It's partly that. And partly that I know *you* like the blue and pink ones."

Dee blinks at me. "You saved them because they're my favorite colors?"

"Why wouldn't I?" I shrug. "It's such a small thing."

"Small things can make a big difference," she says quietly, and when I look at her, she's peering into the bag. After a moment, she closes it, places the bag almost reverently in the glove box, and leans back in her seat. "Seriously though, where the heck are you taking us?"

"That is for me to know and for you to find out."

Dee raises an eyebrow. "Okayyyy... well, the sun's just set, there are no other cars on the road, and you're driving us far, far outside town. So, really, I have to assume that you're about to serial killer me." She slaps her hands to both cheeks. "All these years, I thought we were best friends but you were just biding your time. Gaining my trust." She tuts. "Should've invited my protective detail *tonight*. Done another protecto-date."

I give a long, slow smirk. "You got me. It all started when we were kids and you beat me to the top of the jungle gym. Even then, I knew that this day would come."

Dee breaks into giggles, punching my arm lightly. "I bet I could take you."

I look at her with both brows raised. "You think?"

"Are you sure you want to challenge me? You remember what happened that same day I beat you to the top."

"Do I ever. You're the reason I chipped my tooth."

Dee's eyes go wide and suddenly serious. "No! I wasn't, was I?"

She was. But not directly.

Because when Shawn Mahon, a known bully—who was two years older than us, by the way—stomped up to me while Dee was getting another juice box and started talking trash about her, he was kinda asking to be taken down a peg or two. I put up a good fight given that he was about three times my size. My older brother Justin broke up the fight, holding us each at arm's length. But the damage had been done—I'd done a defensive move, throwing myself on the ground so that I accidentally hit face first and chipped my tooth.

I never told Dee the real reason Shawn and I got into a fight. Far as she knows, I was sticking up for us younger kids (true), and wanted to put Shawn in his place (mostly true).

Shawn and I later ended up on the same football team in high school. He apologized and explained that he'd had a crush on Dee at the time.

Boy, was he preaching to the choir at that point.

I don't answer Dee's question though, because I'm pulling the truck into a lot just off the road. "We're here," I say cheerily.

Dee looks at the empty lot, then at me. The lot, then at me. Her lips purse. "Wow," she says flatly. "An empty parking lot at night? Girls must be *really* into you if this is what your first dates look like."

"Nope. Just this one."

"Gee... thanks?"

I get out of the truck and open the trunk. Take out a large wicker basket and grab the snuggie, then open the passenger door for her. "Coming?"

"Where?"

"You're making it *very* hard to surprise you, Dee."

"I'm an inquisitive person."

"You'll want to be surprised for this. Trust me."

After a couple seconds, she sighs and gets out of the truck, and I'm minorly touched that she trusts me enough to be in a parking lot at night with me after talking about serial killers.

But the sky is darkening by the minute. I have to set this up fast.

I open the wicker basket and take out a blanket, which I lay over the hood and windshield of my truck to protect the paint and glass. Dee watches me with her brow furrowed, but crosses to the other side of the truck and helps me lay the blanket flat.

I place the basket on the hood, then pat the blanket. "Sit," I command.

And she does. Climbing up the front tire and settling herself on the truck.

I hop up next to her, nerves coiling in my stomach as I'm suddenly second-guessing everything about this. What if things don't go as planned or Dee is disappointed? What if she expected more from this?

It's been a long time since I felt nervous going on a date, so the feeling is pretty jarring. I really do care if she likes this as much I do. As much as I think she will.

We're parked on a hill right outside of town that has a great viewpoint over the mountains and valley during the day. It's dusk now, and the sky is all shades of purple and blue with the mountain peaks in the distance cutting jaggedly through the color in sharp angles. The valley is calm and quiet. Slumbering. Birds chirp in the trees just below us, but they'll settle down for the night soon. From here, I can almost make out the shadowy figures strolling down Main Street.

"I've never been here at sunset before," Dee says. "I take back what I said about bringing your dates here. This is pretty cool."

I look at her as she's looking over the valley. In the fading light of day, she looks ethereal, her silver eyes glowing gold. "Well, I meant what *I* said. I've never brought anyone here but you."

Dee faces me now so half her face is in the shadow and half is in the light. "I guess I'm pretty lucky."

"I was just thinking the same thing."

She grins at me and it's everything I can do not to reach for her and kiss her right here and now. But the best part of the night is yet to come, and I have a feeling that if I kiss her now, we won't be stopping anytime soon.

So, I use the best and most effective blocker I have at my disposal: the picnic basket.

Which I plop unceremoniously on the blanket right between us.

"Food time?" I say in a very sexy and not at all awkward way. Because yes, at heart, I really am that fourteen-year-old kid on a date with his crush.

Luckily, said crush is incredibly food motivated and Dee's entire face lights up. "Why didn't you say so?!"

Together, we lay out a whole smorgasbord of food I packed for us—candy corn and Skittles, popcorn and chips, cheese and ham, and pickles and fresh bread. Basically, all of Dee's favorites. We make up plates of food, each grab a bottle of cherry cola, and sit back against the windshield, upper arms touching as we look over the darkening valley.

"You did good, Noah," she says, a shy smile in her voice. "Not too shabby. In fact, I'd rate this date an 8/10."

"8? You're sticking me with an 8?!"

She blinks at me angelically. "Everything's absolutely perfect but sadly two points were docked because you're currently suspiciously lacking in snuggie wearing. Snuggies are a must on *all* my dates, you know."

I laugh. "Noted."

She watches me for a moment, then shakes her head. "No, but seriously, this is incredible. I can't..."

She doesn't finish her thought.

Because at that very moment, the lights in Mirror Valley turn on, all at once.

The street lamps, the lights outside the heritage buildings, the funky new fountain in the center of town... everything is illuminated. Mirror Valley sparkles like a jewel in the midst of the falling darkness. From this vantage point on this dark road, it makes me think of El Dorado or something —some faraway dream spot that needs to be seen to be believed. Thought so when I drove by here a couple months ago one evening.

And then, finally...

"The signs!" Dee squeals, bouncing up and down.

Yeah, from here, we can see *all* of the town signs. And we are still very clearly in a sign war.

Pete's now reads "Joking. Don't get your tires in a twist," and the diner's says, "Be nice or we'll flip you like our tasty burgers", and Mirror Valley Grocery has, "Someone say tasty? We've got it all in store."

It's out of hand.

"Ohmygosh, the town hall's got a sign, too!" Dee points excitedly. "And the community center! Those must be Daisy's doing."

"I told her we were doing this tonight in case she wanted to join in."

Dee laughs that light, carefree, gleeful sound that's so rare but so incredible, and snuggles up against my side. She's crossed her arms, like she's cold, and I put one arm around her, pulling her even closer.

"I'm changing my rating. This is very clearly an 11/10." She smiles up at me. "Thank you, Noah." Her eyes travel across my features and her expression turns almost shy. "I'm glad we did this alone."

I lift a finger and trace it down her chin towards her ear. She closes her eyes and leans into my palm as I lay my hand flat against her cheek, fingers in her hair. She lets out the most beautiful little sigh, and I can't hold myself back any longer. Can't deny what feels right in this moment.

So, I bend my head, and I kiss her.

For real, this time. No holds barred. For me and her, *alone*.

She tastes just as sweet as the kisses from before, but even better somehow. Because now, we have time. Her hands travel behind my neck, locking into my hair, and I tighten my grip on her waist. She tilts her head slightly to deepen the kiss, and I respond, kissing her just as I wanted to for so long, but couldn't. It feels almost forbidden. Like a release after a lifetime of restraint.

She straightens a little, turning to face me fully. I keep one hand behind her head, and the other at her waist. I let Dee dictate the pace, and so this kiss is slow and meaningful. So full of *savoring*.

Time slows and I'm aware of every single place we're touching, the journey of her fingers across my skin and into my hair.

And I realize something important then. I've lived so much of my life on the surface, skated by without taking anything to heart. For years, I held back from telling Dee how I felt. I made enough money that I never had to work at anything. "Serious" was never my strong suit, and I kept taking the easy way out.

Dee isn't like that. Dee faces hardship and takes risks all the time. She does everything with so much intention, so much heart. And maybe that's why I'm so freaking into her. For her bravery and courage, for being everything I'm not. This past week that we've been fake engaged, I've been able to lean into my feelings for her. I've allowed myself to start seeing a future and a career for myself. I've *wanted* to take those risks.

She really does make me better.

So I kiss her to tell her this. Kiss her in a way that I've never kissed anyone else. With so much love and care that she knows *exactly* how I feel about her. This isn't physical, it isn't surface level. It's serious to me.

I don't hear the car pulling into the lot behind us until the headlights flash over us.

We leap back so fast, I have to grab Dee's arm to keep her from toppling off the truck.

"Oh, hey there. Didn't see you." Then, just as quickly. "Wait... Diandra?!"

You've got to be kidding.

"Hi, Lachlan," Dee says feebly. "You remember Noah?"

I sit up so I can look at him. "Hey, man. What're you doing here?"

To my surprise, Lachlan actually looks embarrassed. He's shuffling on his feet and staring everywhere but at us. "I was, uh, I was out for a drive. And I saw this lot, but I didn't see you, and, uh..." he trails off awkwardly, pushing a hand through his hair. "Sorry for the interruption."

"Is everything okay?" Dee hops off the truck and I follow suit.

"Fine," he says gruffly. "Just doing some thinking."

Dee takes a step forward. "Is it about work? Do you need help with something before the call tomorrow?"

"No, no. It isn't work related." Lachlan shakes his head. "But, ah, glad to see you two are prioritizing dates before your wedding."

I wince a little. Of course he thinks this is just another date in the course of our engagement. It kind of sullies the evening somehow, puts a bad taste in my mouth.

When I look at Dee, she's staring back at me. She takes my hand. "Yup. It's a *real* date."

Lachlan looks understandably unfazed and he goes to get back in his car. "I'll leave you to it."

As he turns away, I can't help but notice the way his mouth twists, the concerned wrinkles in his brow. His hair's all messed up, like he's been running his fingers through it over and over again. He seems distracted, upset, and now I feel bad. Judging by the expression on Dee's face, she sees it, too.

"That's, uh, that's okay," I say. "You should stay. We were going to head out soon anyway, it's getting late."

"Yeah." Dee offers him a smile. "The spot's all yours."

Lachlan presses his lips together, looks like he might argue, but he huffs out a sigh. "Okay. If you insist."

"We do." Dee looks up at me and I beam back at her. "We'll leave you to it."

I love the "we" that she uses, the intimacy behind the suggestion that we made this decision as a team. As a couple. Together.

21

DEE

The next morning, Lachlan calls in sick.

And by that, I mean that he messages me at a crazy early hour to say that he's not well and will be taking the call with the board from home, but will still be "very much hard at work".

With the relatively little I know about him, that checks out.

And while part of me is curious to know if something other than work is troubling my Skeptipants boss—who is definitely sporting a few new frown lines these days and seemed deeply distracted when we spoke to him last night—a bigger part of me is lost on cloud nine.

Honestly. Picture big, fluffy, white clouds filled with candy corn and World Series wins and kisses with Noah.

Because ohmygosh... kissing Noah. I could do it over and over again forever.

I've never felt like this. Beer Breath doesn't hold a candle—a single shadow of a flame—to absolutely perfect, incredible Noah. In fact, our kiss last night shouldn't even be classified as a kiss. A "kiss" isn't a good enough descriptor.

Whatever it was, it was… everything.

I went into the date yesterday absolutely sick with nerves. I spent literal hours on the phone with Daisy trying to figure myself out (she wanted to come over, I insisted she shouldn't. Clothes were strewn about my room in a way that was totally shameful and indicative of just how much of a wreck I was. Bruce, appropriately, was cowering in the corner).

I didn't know what to expect, didn't know whether Noah would want me to doll up like a beautiful woman like Yanica would, with designer clothes and even more designer makeup and hair. And was I supposed to bring anything? Did people offer, like, boxes of chocolates to their dates? (Daisy snorted at that and assured me that this was only a thing on cheesy Valentine's Day episodes in teen dramas).

To top it all off, I had no clue where Noah was taking me or what we were doing. I dreaded the thought of a big, extravagant dinner like in *Some Kind of Wonderful* (grossly underrated John Hughes movie, by the way), but I would've grinned and bore it.

Finally, I chose an outfit that wasn't really anything special—just *me*, but with a bit of makeup and a nicer shirt than usual.

And Noah looked at me like I took his breath away.

We were so comfortable with each other, I almost forgot it was a date. The only tip-off to the fact that things were any different was the buzz of energy between us. The very air felt magnetized, electric. The urge I felt to reach over and touch him, run my fingers along his skin, play with his hair… I found myself wondering whether it had always been there, and if it had, how I'd never noticed it before.

Noah parked in that dark lot on top of the hill, and he asked me to trust him, and of course I do. I'm glad I do. I swear, the man knows me better than I know myself. Because a picnic on top of his truck, overlooking the sparkling lights of the town I love?

It was the date I never knew I wanted.

The ridiculous sign war only added to the magic.

I keep getting sucked back into glimpses of it all. The feeling of his big hand splayed across my back, holding me against him firmly. The way my head felt light when he kissed me, like I'd inhaled too much helium and would never come back down to earth. The brush of his fingertips on the skin of my waist...

When I snap myself back to the present (again), I'm staring at my computer screen blankly (also again).

There's only one solution to this kind of a problem...

"Coffee," I grumble, rising to a stand.

Because yes, I'm essentially a caffeine troll today.

I message Lachlan to let him know that I'm taking a short break, and then I head down the stairs of my office and over to Morning Bell cafe. It's just before noon, which means that the lunch rush is probably underway, but when I walk in the door, only Val and Ethan are in the cafe. They're standing behind the counter with their heads bowed close together.

"Oh!" Val exclaims when she sees me. "Hey, Dee!"

"This a bad time?"

"Goodness, no. I just came to say hi to Ethan and grab a brownie."

She pops open the display case and takes out a peanut butter brownie, biting right into it. Ethan chuckles, wrapping his arms around her and drawing her closer. His face is a little red. In fact, both of them look a bit starry-eyed. "You never get sick of those, huh?" he asks her.

"Nope," she answers, licking her fingers.

Ethan lets go of his wife to walk up to the register. "Coffee, Dee? Your boss coming as well?"

"He's working from home this morning. And yes, *please.*"

Ethan moves to the espresso machine. As he grinds the beans, brow furrowed in concentration and lips pursed behind his beard, I decide that I must've imagined the starry-eyed thing. Both he and Val look totally normal now. The buzz of the grinder is quickly followed by the nutty, roasted smell of coffee and my caffeine troll returns to her cave for the moment.

I'm looking out the window of Morning Bell, so I don't realize that Val is staring at me until she says, "Penny for your thoughts?"

I grin at her. "What makes you think my thoughts are worth a penny?"

Her eyes dance as she points at me. "Because you're blushing."

"Blushing? No, I'm... sunburnt."

"The flush literally rising from your neck *right now* would say otherwise."

I glare at her. She smiles. Val is probably my best girl-friend after Daisy, and she's also one of my oldest friends. We've known each other since elementary school, and while we haven't always been that close, I appreciate her friendship.

Though she and Ethan have been friends even longer than we've been friends...

"Can I ask you something?"

"Shoot," Val replies.

"When you and Ethan got together... Was it a bit weird?"

"Weird?"

"Yeah. Like did you ever feel nervous or anxious about stuff?"

"Which time?" Her lips quirk a little. "Ethan and I technically got together twice."

"Uhm, the first time. Weren't you worried about, like, ruining your friendship?"

Val's expression, which before had been light and teasing, now turns pensive. "Well, Ethan and I first got together in high school. We'd been friends before that, of course, so we had that solid base, and then all the love and, you know, chemistry and physical stuff just added on. Deepened our connection."

I swallow thickly, recognizing these same thoughts and feelings within myself about Noah. "But weren't you scared of losing him?"

Val pauses, glances over her shoulder at her husband. When she turns back to me, she's wearing a small, vulnerable smile. "I *did* lose him. We lost each other for a few years, as you know. But looking back, I would do it all again. I would lose him again if that's what it takes for us to get to the point we're at now."

My eyebrows rise. "You'd be okay to lose him again?"

"Well, I wouldn't want to lose him *now*. But back then, the fear of losing him felt worth the risk. I loved him. He loved me. To this day, I'll always believe that our connection is special, perfectly made for both of us. We were going to end up together. And sure, it took the passing of his amazing grandpa and a crazy road trip to finally push us together for good, but I'd do it all over again to end up right back here."

Ethan appears behind her and puts an arm around her waist, drawing her in for a kiss. They're really sweet, the two of them.

But I can't wrap my head around the risk factor—Val

did lose Ethan for a few years, and I know how hard that was on her. Can I really risk that with Noah? I'm not sure I'm brave enough.

I pay for my coffee and say my goodbyes to Val and Ethan before walking back to my office, lost on an entirely new train of thought.

Everything I felt last night was so new, so *intense*. It at once thrills and terrifies me. Like I'm standing on the edge of a cliff not knowing whether I have a parachute but desperately hoping something will catch me if I fall.

It already feels like I'm falling. Already feels like things are moving so quickly, I can't catch up.

Because those doubts I had a few days ago have been swirling in my head today, too. For a minute, I could pretend that I was enough for Noah, but I have this deep fear inside of me that I'm not. Or I *won't* be, forever. And if we were to do this thing, it would have to be a forever thing for me. I don't think I can return to being "just friends" with Noah. Not after kissing him, not after being on a date with him, not after starting to open the door to those feelings.

I always assumed, if I ever was to get married, that I'd fall for someone sweet and mild. Not someone like Noah. Not someone who should live his life big and wild and *extreme...*

"What took you so long?"

The voice booms from up the stairs in my office and I yelp in surprise, almost spilling my coffee all over myself. "Wha—*Noah*!"

He pops his head over the railing at the top of the stairs, resting his forearms on the wood beams. He smirks down at me, all mischievous innocence and sparkling brown eyes. "Hey, Dee-bug."

Despite my anxiety, my stomach does about thirteen

flips at the sound of his voice. "What're you doing here?" I ask, coming up the stairs.

"Wanted to see you." He falls back onto the red sofa. A sofa which does *not* match my office decor and which he mysteriously placed here a couple years ago with no notice or warning. I'll admit I kinda love it now, though. "Hope you don't mind that I let myself in."

I put down my coffee and place my hands on my hips. "I can see that."

"Where's Lachlan?"

"Called in sick."

Noah shivers. "Would hate to catch the cold that brought that dude down."

I smirk despite myself. "I don't think he's actually sick. Besides, he's got that call with the board this morning."

Noah pats the sofa cushion next to him. And being the totally hopeless person with an even more hopeless crush, I collapse down by his side.

It's weird... Noah is both my best friend, and the person I'm most scared of right now. The one who gives me the most comfort, but also the one I can't help but worry over. He wraps an arm around my shoulders, bringing me in close. He doesn't try to kiss me. Instead, he pushes a lock of hair out of my eyes. "What's on your mind?"

"How'd you know something is on my mind?"

"Because of this." He presses the warm, calloused pad of his thumb between my eyebrows. "This crinkle right here."

I let out a short chuckle. "You think you know me so well."

"Well, I do, don't I?"

I give him a look, but I don't answer. Because he's right. Clearly, he knows me better than I know myself sometimes.

"So, talk to me. What's on your mind? How're you

feeling about our date last night? How're you feeling about work?"

I hate how much I love how much he wants to hear me talk. Hear me vent. All of my ridiculous thoughts that I would never dare inflict on anyone else, Noah just listens. If I was someone else, a different girl, I might be able to organize my thoughts in a logical, concise sentence. But like I said, words and emotions aren't my strong suit. And Noah's always filling the blanks for me. "I feel…" I reach for a word. "I feel nervous."

"Nervous about what?"

"About the kissing." I shift a little against his side, not able to look at him. "Do you think it's possible for two friends to kiss without anything else changing in their friendship?" He goes very still and I wonder whether these words bothered him. Once again, I'm tripping over myself. "Because I really like kissing you, don't get me wrong. But I'm scared about everything else."

"What everything else?" Noah asks and I'm relieved to hear a touch of humor in his voice.

"Like… whether we'll always stay friends, what the future holds for us, how…" I trail off, hearing my words come back to me. "This is dumb. I sound dumb."

Noah's quick to respond to that. "You don't sound dumb, Dee, please don't say that. This… it's anything but dumb. I love how considerate you're being, how aware you are of the *everything else* I tend to forget. That's why we make such a good team."

"You think?"

"I know." He peers down at me, seeming suddenly curious. "Do you *want* certain things to change?"

I look away, pursing my lips. "Maybe I do. I really *do* like kissing you."

He laughs at that, and I'm happy to hear it.

See? I can do this. Open and honest conversations about my feelings don't feel that scary with him. "I'm just worried about what we might lose."

Noah's quiet for a long moment. Then, with his arm still around me, he reaches for the threads on his left wrist. "Do you know why I've never taken off this bracelet?"

"The color makes your eyes pop?" I quip.

He chuckles, turning me slightly so I'm propped against his chest. "It's because it's a reminder of the things I value most in the world. My family, my childhood, and you. Every time I see this bracelet on my wrist, I smile because you make me smile. For all the things I've felt unsure about in my life, all the moments I felt lost or uncertain, I only need to come back to you. You're my only constant, Dee. Have been since before you gave me this bracelet; this is just a physical reminder." His chest rises and falls with another soft chuckle. "So no, I'm not afraid of losing anything, because I already have everything with you."

His words melt me from the inside out. And they surprise me, too. Because I hear the subtext now. I think I finally get what everyone else has been urging me to see...

Noah loves me.

Ohmygosh.

I sit up straight and before Noah can say or do anything else, I throw my arms around him and press my lips to his. He responds immediately, pulling me close. My heart is racing, chest almost aching as I tug him closer.

"Oh, for the love... *Again?!*"

Of course.

Because why wouldn't Lachlan choose this *exact* moment to show up at the office?

I leap off of Noah—who also looks appropriately pissed off—and face Lachlan. He's standing at the top of the stairs, mouth pinched and face flushed. "Diandra. I'm very glad that you've found the love of your life on our dating app. But can you please, *please* keep it out of the office and off the clock? This is inappropriate."

My cheeks have reached new levels of tomato red. "I'm sorry, Lachlan. I swear, this is not... I never... We wouldn't..." I clear my throat. "I haven't signed back on or anything; Noah just stopped by quickly."

"And this is my cue to go." Noah looks at his watchless wrist like he's checking the time and holds up his bare arm to Lachlan. It's a stupid inside joke of ours that started years ago and I can't actually remember where it came from, but the unimpressed eyebrow raise Lachlan gives Noah speaks volumes. Noah then gives a casual shrug. "You know how it is when you're about to get married, man. It's like the honeymoon phase starts up all over again."

Lachlan's mouth gets even pinch-ier. "I don't know, and I don't care to know."

Noah heads to the top of the stairs, raising his fingers in a peace sign. And when Lachlan turns away to set up his laptop, Noah gives me that special, amazing smile of his and a wink.

There aren't enough cages in the world to trap the butterflies that go crazy in my ribcage.

Because now, I know. Noah's kept that old, fraying, ratty friendship bracelet for *me*. And I want to make absolutely sure I'm taking this as seriously as he is.

22

NOAH

The following Sunday, we have another volleyball match. This time, we're playing against a team out of Denver and they happen to be our most serious rivals. We've been tied time and time again. They win one week, we win the next.

As captain of our team, I like to put in some time strategizing before we play them. It's all in good fun obviously, but I take it as a personal challenge. Parker and Amir are good at strategy too, so we often work together to come up with potential plays.

Although, usually we have all six of us playing...

Today, we're having to use an alternate because Dee's stuck at home working. Again. She messaged last night to say that Lachlan's call with the board the other morning did *not* go well. They've been tasked with a ton of deliverables before Lachlan goes back to LA for the board meeting, so she's going to work through today.

She sent about thirteen crying emojis with her message. I know how much Dee loves the competitive and fiery energy with this team from Denver. Not to mention the opportunity to trash talk the players.

The first couple sets go pretty well for our team, but

when we hit the third set, the other team starts pulling ahead. And by the fourth set, it's pretty clear where we're standing.

After the match ends, we all shake hands with the Denver players. The guys grab their waters and Gatorades as I wipe a towel down my face and check my phone for the first time all game.

Dee: Please, please play hard for me today. Wish I could be there *crying emoji*

Dee: Who's winning? Did Denver Jason do that stupid dive thing he always does at the end of a set? Tell him he looks like an idiot for me, wouldja?

Dee: I hope the sub's pulling off some hitter magic.

Dee: Also, and most importantly, is this a Noah shirt on or shirt off kinda game? If I'm picturing you guys winning, I want to be picturing it accurately.

I chuckle as I read through her messages, eyebrows raising at her last one. Dee and I always have teasing, light-hearted banter, but this is straight-up flirting and I love it.

Noah: We just wrapped up. And I guess you'll have to wait to find out ;)

Noah: *gif of Hulk ripping his shirt off*

I rub my knuckles along my jawline, putting my phone down on the bench and slipping my t-shirt over my head. My phone vibrates within seconds.

Dee: Wow. Hot.

I snort, poised to reply, when a large hand slaps my back. "Dude, we played good."

Jarrod's smiling as he tugs his t-shirt over his head, and I gesture to the rest of the team to join me by the bench. "That was awesome, guys. We worked hard today. And even though we lost, I'm really impressed with how everyone played." I nod at Dee's replacement, who's shifting from foot to foot. "Hank, thanks for joining us."

Hank the security guard smiles wide, looking almost as proud as he did the night he caught Dee and me by the river. "Thanks. Felt good to get out of the house. You know how it is with teenagers." He laughs boisterously, his upper body tilting back with the force of it.

Hank was a pretty decent player, it turns out. He happened to mention the other night while walking me back to my truck that he used to captain the school's volley-ball team when he was younger, so I figured I'd call him up for our game. With two teenage daughters at home, he seemed all too eager to "escape the adolescent, rule-breaking hormones."

Which checks out, honestly.

After Hank heads out, the boys and I have a quick debrief on the match, running over our plays. We all agree that we missed Dee, and wished she could have joined us... though I'm sure the guys missed her for a different reason than I did.

"How're things going with you two?" Amir asks as we make our way out of the courts.

"Good. Really good. Aside from the fact that her boss Lachlan keeps showing up at... inopportune moments."

I say this delicately, but Parker's smirk indicates that he's taking my words and running with them. "Sounds like you've got a Loch Block on your hands."

The guys' groan is almost as powerful as my wince, and Parker just smirks on like he's told the world's funniest joke (hint: he has not).

"Anyway," I say, blowing past it. "I've started to forget that we're even doing this fake engaged thing."

"How's that possible?" Parker asks. "You're, like, pretending to be *committed* to someone."

"So?"

"Well, that's not exactly your thing. Your track record is short-term only."

I shove my hands in my pockets, shaking my head with a short laugh. "Yeah, it's been my *thing* with everyone but Dee. She's technically my one and only long-term relationship, even if that is just friendship."

My friends nod their heads in turn.

"I'm crazy about her," I confess. Man, it feels good to say it out loud. Allow myself to hope.

Amir punches my arm lightly. "See? Moving her hair out of her eyes, being gentlemanly... what did we tell you?"

I have to laugh at that. "That's definitely what did it."

"So what're you saying?" Jarrod waggles his eyebrows. "You want to be *real* engaged to Dee?"

"I mean, that's like a thousand steps ahead of where we are now. Sure, I can see being engaged to her someday, but *no way* am I going there now. Patience, going slow, that's what Dee needs, and that's what I'll give her. I've never been so sure in my life that we belong together, and I think she knows it, too."

Amir pats my back. "So when are you seeing her next?"

At that very moment, my phone vibrates my pocket. It's another message from Dee, asking for more details on the match.

"Consider my question answered." Amir laughs.

I look up from my phone with a smirk and give the guys a peace sign. "Later."

When I pull up outside of Dee's house, she's sitting on the front steps with Bruce curled up on her lap. Her hair's in a messy bun again, and she's frowning at the ground darkly.

"Problem, Dee?" I ask, slamming the door of my truck.

She looks over at me, startled, and then shifts like she

wants to stand up but can't because of the ball of gray fur currently occupying her lap. "You're here!" she exclaims, and then bites her lip almost shyly, like she's embarrassed.

I come through the gate and toss something her way. She catches it deftly and when she sees what it is, she squeals so loudly that Bruce's eyes shoot wide open and he launches himself off her legs at breakneck speed. She leaps up and throws herself at me. "Candy corn!"

I catch her in my arms and hold her close. How many times have we stood like this? It all feels so different now. "Thought you could use some provisions. Looks like you're hard at work."

Dee leans back a little to look at me. "You caught me on a break. I came downstairs to feed Bruce while thinking through a problem, and followed him outside where he ended up falling asleep on my lap. I wouldn't dare *move* the guy. You know how crabby he gets when he's woken up abruptly."

Right on cue, Bruce stalks past, shooting us a dirty, nose-crinkled, green-eyed glare.

Dee turns back to me so quickly, her bun almost falls out of her scrunchie. "So how'd the match go? Did we win? How was Hank? Give me the highlights."

We walk into her bungalow together and I catch her up while Dee putters around the kitchen, grabbing me a glass of orange juice. She doesn't drink the stuff, says it's far too sweet for her sensitive tastes (which is B.S. because hello, candy corn), but she always keeps some on hand for me. It's the kind of thoughtful thing I love about her. It might also be part of the reason I spend more time here than at my own place in town.

By the time I finish telling her about the match—and break the news that we lost, to which she lets out a dramatic wail that startles Bruce yet again—we're sprawled on the couch, her limbs on top of mine. I've got an arm wrapped around her lazily, and she's settled against me.

"How's work going?" I ask, fiddling with a few strands of her hair. "Are you coding the crap out of RightMatch?"

She laughs at that. Yeah, my knowledge of coding is minimal, but I'd like to learn, if only to be able to talk to her about it. "I am coding all the crap." She gives her head a shake. "It's been tough. The board's wanting a whole bunch of new features by the time Lachlan goes back to LA for their meeting. We're working like crazy, but I'm not sure we'll get it done in time." She sighs, clearly troubled. "By the way, if you thought Lachlan was scary, these board member guys sound straight-up terrifying. Lachlan's like a kindly old ladybug compared to them."

My eyebrows shoot up. "Can't even begin to picture that."

"It's intimidating." She sighs again. "I'm just glad that Lachlan can actually do some coding. He's not just a big boss guy."

We sit in silence for a moment, my hands tangled in Dee's hair, and her fingers drawing light, lazy circles along my arms. I love moments like this, love doing nothing with her.

"Can I ask you something?" Dee asks.

"I wish you would."

"Does it worry you that I haven't really dated anyone?"

I pause my fiddling for a moment. "Does it worry *you*?"

She gives a sigh, rolling onto her front so we're face to face. She peers at me, her gray eyes inquisitive. "Maybe. I just think about you and all your... experience. You've dated so much, been with so many women."

"That makes me sound great."

"You know what I mean. I guess I'm worried that

there'll be a point that I won't be enough. That you might want to date someone else."

My eyebrows shoot up in surprise. I never in my life would've considered such a thing, *could* never consider such a thing after all these years pining after her. It's baffling to me that Dee would even go there, but it just proves what I said the other night—she thinks about the things I'd never even consider.

And this very thing makes my heart pick up speed all over again. Because if she's asking this question, she's taking this seriously, too. Is picturing a potential future where I might potentially want to date someone else (FYI, I won't).

This is a huge step. Dee is breaking down her walls, starting to play with the boundaries we had set in stone for so long.

"Dee," I say, my voice low. I cup her chin in my palm and meet her eyes. "When I find what I'm looking for, I stop searching."

Her breath catches on my words, but the worried crinkle is still there, right between her eyebrows.

"I want you to feel safe and secure in what we're doing. To feel as sure as I do. I've known my own feelings for years, and I think I know how you feel, too, but if you're unsure..."

I monitor her face carefully. Her expression remains neutral.

"Look. I'll respect what you need to do to get to that point. Maybe *you* want a chance to see what else is out there."

A hot, uncomfortable fire races through my body at the thought of Dee dating someone else. And yet... I also have this strange, firm certainty in my gut that she *won't* go there. Maybe I'm just being foolish. Arrogant.

She crinkles her nose. "I don't want to date anyone else, though. Don't really feel any interest in anyone else."

"Have you tried with Lachlan?" I ask. Foolishly. Arrogantly. *What am I doing?* I just have a feeling that Dee needs this. "You two have tons in common, he's clearly an intellectual match for you. And the guy's hot." Because yeah, I'm secure enough in my masculinity to admit that.

Dee bites her lower lip. I wish I could instead. But we're having this frankly very odd discussion and now is probably not the time to kiss her. "I mean... I don't know." She's blushing again, sitting up and fiddling with her hair. "I just don't know."

I nod, still feeling that weird certainty. Still have that gut feeling. "Well, let me know what you decide." I give her a soft kiss on the forehead. "In the meantime, I'm gonna let you get back to work."

"Okay..." she says in a small voice. Her right leg is tucked up under her and she's staring at me with this confused look on her face, as though wondering herself how we got here. I kinda get it.

But I fight my instincts to wrap her in my arms and protect her from anything that dares create that little wrinkle between her brows. I switch my ball cap to face the front and head back to my truck. My stomach is in a knot, but my heart feels right. What's that old expression—if you love someone, set them free, and if they come back to you, it's your destiny?

Which sounds a little like what Fran said to us in her fortune teller tent last year—that we were destined to be married. I just have to hope that both my gut and Fran's mystical magic powers are correct. That all these years spent knowing and loving Dee actually count for something.

Because if Dee *does* decide that she wants someone else, I don't know what I'll do.

23

___

DEE

"And that's why you should always keep your expenses organized in *this* folder. For situations just like this." Luke shakes his head and I can practically feel the radiating disappointment. "I can't believe your company was using this software, Dee. It's aimed at tiny, mom-and-pop businesses. Not corporations or tech startups."

"Sorry, Luke," I say.

"Well, it shouldn't be an issue for long. A big company acquired RightMatch, right? I imagine they'll put you on their system soon enough." He tuts. Literally tuts. "They really should have done this earlier."

Yes. I am currently being lectured by my big sister's husband about *accounting software*.

Ever since his phone call with the board, Lachlan's kicked into some kind of manic high gear. He's reviewing *everything* about RightMatch. All of our processes, all of our reports, all of our meeting notes. The guy is a machine. I don't understand how he finds so many hours in a day. I'm still shocked that he finds a spare second to use the bathroom, let alone drive his fancy SUV on our country roads.

Most recently, Lachlan's been on a rampage to find an

accountant to review RightMatch's financials over the last fiscal year. He was going to ask the accounting team in LA, but I suggested Luke Brooks. The guy might have the approachability of a pissed off possum, but he knows what he's doing. Luke and his firm, Argent Accounting, are the ones who uncovered an entire embezzlement scheme on Mirror Valley's town council last year. And besides, he works quickly—which I think was the selling point for Lachlan.

Though it is odd that, after all that, Lachlan's missing the meeting with Luke this morning. He messaged at the crack of dawn to say that he wouldn't be able to make it, but that I should go ahead with Luke and give him the highlights later. I typed out a whole message about using his Time-Turner, then decided that Lachlan probably has no clue about the *Harry Potter* movies and their intricate magical details.

Or maybe he knows them so well that he's personally met Daniel, Emma and Rupert. I still can't get a read on the guy.

"My bad?" I say in response to Luke's disappointed stare.

"It's fine. Actually, Noah probably could've told you this. The guy was surprisingly adept at accounting."

"He's good at many things," I say, pinching my mouth to hold back the abrupt desire to shout "LIKE KISSING".

I can't see Luke liking that revelation very much.

He begins to pack up his things. "It's a shame I won't get a chance to meet your boss face-to-face. Dais said he's a bear of a person."

A cool thread of ice travels down my spine at the thought of my sister speaking with Lachlan. Daisy's a chatterbox at the best of times; I can only imagine what she would say to him. Did the truth come out that I stole her love story with Luke? "I didn't know they'd met."

"They haven't." He smirks. "Don't worry."

I let out a laugh, not even trying to hide my relief. Luke and I get each other, in a way. We're similar in that we don't like engaging with people more than we have to. Some call Luke a grump, I say he uses plain common sense and doesn't bother with fluff. Might be why he's with Daisy—she softens his rough edges, brings light and sunshine to his practicality and grounding.

Kind of like how Noah does for me.

I never made that connection before.

Luke and I don't say much as he packs away his things to head back to his office down the street. Professional as ever, he's wearing a full suit and tie and he brought a presentation dossier with him, even though he was only meeting with me in my tiny office today.

Right as he's about to walk down the stairs, he pauses for a moment. "I should probably ask how you're doing," he says. "Dais and I haven't seen you around in awhile. So... you good?"

I have to smile at his awkward, forced small talk. I know he's only asking on Daisy's behalf, but I appreciate it all the same. "I'm good," I say. "Busy."

"And you and Noah are good." This time, it's not a question. He's basically just waiting for me to confirm his statement.

But I find myself hesitating, catching my breath. Compartmentalizing is my game, and I'd compartmentalized the crap out of my conversation with Noah on my couch yesterday. Now that Luke's asking me this question, it's all coming back.

Noah suggested that I try and see if I feel any interest in anyone else. Whether I might want to date anyone else.

I don't exactly understand how we reached that point in our conversation. I was talking to him about my fears that he might want to eventually date again in the future, and we ended up talking about whether *I* have any interest in dating around. In all honesty, I'd never considered it. Was thinking so much about him that I never considered my own experience.

Do *I* want to see what else is out there?

The blaring answer in my head is a resounding "no!" coupled with vivid flashbacks to all of our incredible kisses.

But there's something beneath that, too: my inner data scientist wanting to test out every possible solution to a question. The question being whether what I'm feeling for Noah is so strong because it's the *first* time. The first time I've fallen for someone, felt something for someone, wanted to kiss someone like I want to kiss him...

I'm a head over heart girl, and so if I take my heart out of it, could there be someone who's a better match for me? Someone more on my level. Someone who feels real, versus too good to be real. I don't have the answer to that.

I really shouldn't be surprised that Noah figured this out. That he somehow knows about my freaking inner scientist.

Luke's brow is slowly raising, becoming more and more concerned. I realize I've been staring at him blankly for several minutes, so I utter a "Yeah, fine."

He visibly relaxes. "Glad to hear it."

He waves goodbye and makes to walk down the stairs when the door at the bottom opens. Luke pauses mid-step. "Oh. You must be Lachlan."

There's a beat of silence before the familiar, steely voice speaks. "Yes. And you're the accountant?"

Lachlan climbs the stairs in a few brisk steps, meeting Luke at the top. They share one of those intense bro-y handshakes with matching somber expressions. All I can do is watch from my chair, somewhat captivated to see two powerhouses like Luke and Lachlan in the same room together.

"Sorry for missing the meeting," Lachlan says, a hand in his pocket and his chest puffed out. He seems different today. He doesn't make eye contact with Luke before coming to the desk next to mine and setting up his laptop.

"No problem," Luke replies. "I think Dee got a good sense of everything."

"Sure did," I mutter dryly.

But Luke's staring at Lachlan with his brow furrowed. "You know, you look really familiar. Have we met before?"

Lachlan doesn't even glance over his shoulder. "Don't think so. I live in LA."

"Right..."

Luke's still frowning at Lachlan's back and I begin to get a little worried what might happen if these two strong and silent types start glaring at each other from across the room (imagine the crushing silent treatment). So I stand and rush Luke towards the stairs. "Thanks again, Lukey. Say hi to Dais for me."

"Will do," he mutters, obviously stuck in his thoughts as he walks down the stairs.

As soon as the door at the bottom shuts, I swear Lachlan's shoulders relax a little. I narrow my eyes at him, suspicious but unsure. Did Lachlan recognize Luke, too? Is there a story here?

"So the meeting went well, did it?" Lachlan asks before I can say anything.

I hold my breath for a second. "Yup. It was... enlightening."

"Good."

"Why'd you miss it?"

Lachlan shifts a little in his chair and I realize that this question might be considered intrusive. But can you blame me? The guy lumbers around all mysterious and scowly all the time. I can't help being curious.

Something deep inside me hops to attention, and my inner scientist grabs her notebook and pen. *Why* am I so curious about him? Could this be a hint of romantic interest?

I keep my gaze on Lachlan's profile for a long moment, trying to figure out what I'm feeling.

Nope. I think it's just general interest. If Luke or Ethan or Raymond were walking around all grumbly and shifty, I'd probably want to know what their deal was as well...

Lachlan emits a quick sigh. "Can I help you with something, Diandra?""

I snap out of scientist mode and hustle back to my computer. "Nope. No, all good!"

"Good. And I am sorry I missed the meeting. I had a... personal matter to attend to."

A personal matter?

Dang it. Now, I'm even more curious.

He grabs his phone and turns my way. "Catch me up on the accounting meeting."

So I do. And I'm honestly kind of proud of how much I remember. Sure, a lot of the words go over my head—finances are *not* my thing—but Lachlan seems to be following what I'm saying pretty well.

As our conversation turns back to the upcoming board meeting, I summon my scientist once again. My eyes travel the distance from Lachlan's nicely groomed dark brown hair, to his intense blue gaze. I notice the firm angles of his nose and jawline, even the slight puckers beneath his cheekbones. I register his overpowering presence, his broad shoulders and chest, and the way he sits with his feet firmly planted on the ground and minimal manspreading.

He's the picture of a hot businessman on the covers of romance novels, complete with the way he rolls his shirt-sleeves up to his elbows.

And it *is* easy to talk to him. We both obviously have a passion for all things tech. I have a feeling we could go on for hours, our conversations dipping into philosophy and psychology. He's well-read and intelligent and clearly very creative. These are all traits I deeply admire and respect.

But... that's it.

That's all I can feel for him. He's an attractive and intelligent man, who actually seems like a good person beneath the grumbles, and the skeptical glares, and the cement voice. In another world, maybe Lachlan and I *would* make a good match. We could date and get married and have technologically gifted children.

But that sparkly feeling? That deep, in-my-gut attraction to more than just his sharp lines and beautiful edges? It doesn't exist. I can't feel it, no matter how much I will it to.

I've only in my life ever had that sparkly feeling with one person...

And I suddenly realize that Daisy was right in our conversation all those nights ago. But she wasn't right in the way she thought she was.

My inner scientist puts down her pen. I've come to my final conclusion.

"Hey, Lachlan?" I ask, my voice a little raspy, when he finally turns in his chair to get to work. "Can I take a fifteen minute break?"

He purses his lips, but nods.

Ten minutes later, whale sounds blaring, I'm pulling up in front of the carpentry shop. As I hastily get out of the car and lock the door, I spot Raymond in the front window, puttering around with a huge smile on his face. A moment later, Fran appears and she throws her arms around him, pressing a sweet kiss to his lips.

So much for no hanky-panky, I think to myself, remembering what Raymond said the day Noah and I agreed on the fake engagement.

Feels like ages ago. Feels like I've forgotten that we're meant to be pretending.

I race around to the back of the workshop and spot him immediately.

Holy...

Noah's standing at the worktable outside, turned away from me as he focuses on his work. He's wearing an apron but his shirt's off so the sun caresses his tanned skin. I watch his arms for a moment, mesmerized. Watch the muscles of his back ripple and move as he lifts whatever he's working on. He's covered with a light sheen of sweat so he glows beneath the midmorning sun. His ball cap is sitting backwards on his head, and I see the protruding bone at the top of his spine as he looks down. The way his chinos sit low on his hips to reveal the two little dimples above his waistband.

I swallow so loudly that I'm surprised he doesn't hear.

Because the world has gone sparkly again. Fuzzy around the edges. My heart is pounding, and my blood's racing, and my stomach is packed full of butterflies.

It's all the confirmation my inner data scientist could ever need.

Before I can think about what I'm doing, I'm running forward. Sprinting towards him.

I crash into Noah, my arms circling his waist. He lets out a yelp. "What the—!"

He trails off when he sees that it's only me... suctioned like a freaking barnacle to his back.

"Hi!" I exclaim breathlessly.

He chuckles, and the movement ripples through his abs beneath my fingers. I can't let go. So he awkwardly shifts within my arms to face me, locking his hands behind my back. "Hi, Dee. Whatcha doin'?"

Now, my face is pressed to his chest. Truly, I am only part-human and mostly barnacle at this point. "I wanted to see you."

"Always a pleasure. But you know this probably isn't the best place to scare a person?"

"I know."

He chuckles again, but doesn't let go. Which is good. Very good. And very nice. We stand for a moment, wrapped and tangled around each other. His heartbeat's next to my ear, steady and strong and sure, and I close my eyes against it.

"Lachlan's hot," I blurt.

Noah snorts. "I know."

But his heartbeat's raised just a bit. I lean back to look him in the eyes. "No. He's hot, but he's not like... you."

"Okay."

"I did what you said. I tried to see if I'm interested in him."

His face becomes a mask. Forehead uncreased, eyes guarded, mouth in a small smirk. "Oh?"

I shake my head adamantly. "I wasn't. I have every reason to be, and I probably *could* be in another world where he isn't my boss. But I wasn't. At all." I take a deep inhale and release it. "It's you, Noah. It's only ever been you."

He blinks. "What do you mean?"

"I mean, I think I've been into you for a very, very long time. I just..." A dry smile hits my lips. "I was in denial about it."

Now, Noah's face softens. I urge myself to press on.

"Remember back in high school when you thought I was into Sam?" I wait a beat for Noah to nod. "It all started that day you and Sam came back from volleyball camp and you gave me this ring." I hold up my hand with the silver volleyball ring. "I was so touched that you thought of me that summer of all summers, and then you gave me a hug, and well... I had a sparkly feeling."

His lips twitch. "Sparkly feeling?"

"Yeah. You know, like, in a movie when—"

Noah holds up a hand and nods. "I get it."

Of course he does. I go on, encouraged. "It was the first time I felt anything like it. Butterflies and heart racing and blushing and all the rest. But I didn't know what to do about it, so when Sam hugged me afterwards and you thought I was blushing for him, I just... went along with it."

Noah stares at me. "I thought I was so clever and observant."

I just shake my head and poke him lightly in his very firm stomach.

"So, wait." He frowns. "When Sam asked you out and you turned him down, you didn't do it because you weren't interested in dating?"

"Well it *was* kinda for that reason. I knew I couldn't date him—date *anyone*, for that matter— when I was feeling a certain way for you. But then, I also knew that I had no business feeling that way in the first place. We were such good friends, and you were dating so much. It felt impossible that anything could come of those feelings, and it was easier to shut them down. Compartmentalize them and put you fully in the friend zone. Exactly where you had me." I pause for a moment. "Or so I thought...?"

"So we friend zoned each other." Noah smiles this goofy smile. "Even though we were both into each other. Because

Dee, the only reason I was dating that much was to get over *you*."

"What?" I ask breathlessly.

"Yeah. I was so into you, it wasn't even funny. My brothers, my friends back then... everyone used to rag on me all the time."

Ho-ly.

And then something bizarre happens: I let out this weird, high-pitched, drunken giggle thing. It's the most foreign noise I've ever heard.

Noah laughs (understandably) and then raises one hand to my face, tracing his fingers down my cheek, along my jawline. His eyes are so deep and soulful, I fall right into them. And I'm not giggling anymore.

"I guess..." I hesitate, wondering how to vocalize this. "I wanted you to be my all, but never my nothing. Does that make sense?"

Noah nods, eyes boring into mine.

Then, he moves his face closer, but right before our lips meet, he tilts his head a little. Presses kisses down the side of my neck, one by one, all the way to my collarbone. A shiver moves through me even as my skin heats beneath his touch. I tip my head back instinctively.

"Is your boss anywhere close by?" he asks in a growl against my throat.

"No," I whisper.

"Good."

In a second, he spins us both around and places his hands on my waist, lifting me onto the worktable. His palms land on the table just behind me, and his lips finally meet mine. Over and over again. Hungry, ravenous, passionate kisses like we haven't had before. There's no holding back now, on either side. I lock my arms behind his neck, pulling him closer, and yank his cap off so I can tangle my fingers in his hair. He leans his body towards me, and I wrap my legs around his waist, now less barnacle and more baby monkey.

He releases my lips for a second, kissing down my neck again and nuzzling at my earlobe. All I can do is close my eyes as he whispers, "You have no idea how long I've been waiting to do this."

I find his lips again. "I really do," I reply.

And I mean it. I am intensely, incredibly, startlingly aware of just how long I've wanted to do this. It's like a veil has been pulled from my eyes and I'm finally seeing the world clearly. I'm seeing how much I've lied—lied to everyone around me, lied to *myself*—about my feelings, for years. I pushed them down, convinced myself my actions had a different motivation at every turn...

A collection of memories flash before my eyes. I remember when I went off to college and Noah stayed in Mirror Valley, and we would call or text each other every night before bed. I remember when I moved back here and he was away, but I didn't feel like I was truly *home* until he was here, too.

I remember when he broke up with Lauren last year and went to a singles event, and for a minute, I wanted to make him jealous so I went with Luke (of all people) as my fake date. I didn't know why I felt the need to do it, couldn't explain my own actions past wanting to see what Noah would do if I appeared to be dating someone else.

He didn't seem to care. And I ignored the way my heart splintered. The way the shards were further destroyed when Fran pronounced us *destined to be married*. Because I knew that it was all a joke. Taunting me.

We were impossible.

Now, the world's cracked open and the possibilities feel endless.

But the only one I really care about is right here, right

now, with Noah kissing me so well and thoroughly and *necessarily* that I might be flying. Everything about this feels so right, my body aches with relief.

This time, gloriously, no one interrupts us. But the kisses slow, become sweet and meaningful. Noah's hands are cradling my face, his thumbs stroking along my cheeks. My hands are behind his neck after traveling the length of his biceps and back. I'm playing with his curls, wrapping them between my fingers. Savoring every second of this.

Finally, I press my forehead to his, just as he did when I hurt my knee. "I need to get back," I whisper. "Lachlan's going to be *mad*."

Noah chuckles, his hands resting on my waist. "What's a little makeout for an engaged couple?"

I laugh at that, leaning back to look into his eyes. "Oh, Daisy..."

"Name's Noah, but okay."

I whack him in the arm. "No. I just hate it when she's right."

"Wise old bird, that one."

I roll my eyes and Noah helps me off the table. He holds out a hand and I take it, and we walk back around the shop and to my car. He kisses me once more before I drive back to the office, the whale sounds not needed over the gleeful, ecstatic pounding of my heart.

24

DEE

You would think that the days after you and your best friend finally admit that you're into each other—have always been into each other—would be a mess of chaotic happiness and constant interactions and head-spinning kisses. Right?

Wrong.

Well, mostly wrong. But also kinda correct. We *have* done a lot of those things—even to the extent that Daisy, of all people, called us out on being "annoyingly cute" one evening at dinner—but it hasn't been nearly enough in my books.

Because while my love life might be finally coming to some sort of reality (who knew pigs could fly?), my work life has gone to crap.

To the extent that RightMatch should now probably be renamed RightCrap. Complete with the little poop emoji instead of the heart adorning the "i".

If I thought things were hard last week, this week is even rougher. My brain is constantly in overdrive as I work through potential solutions to the problems and tasks that

Lachlan collected on his call with the board, while simultaneously fighting bouts of anxiety and what-ifs.

What if all this work comes to nothing?

What if everything falls apart right at this last hurdle?

Spoiler alert: I hate living with this level of uncertainty.

I've planned my life around reducing them. It's part of the reason I've worked at RightMatch for so long, part of the reason I've stayed in Mirror Valley. My home base is *everything* to me. Some people—perhaps a therapist or two—would say that it's because of what happened when I was seven. They'd say that trying to control every outcome became my coping mechanism, a way to calm my nervous system.

I call it survival instinct. But that's just me.

Needless to say, the past week has been both the best and the worst I've had in a very long time.

And if it's possible, I'm falling even more for Noah. Or maybe I've simply been discovering the layers upon layers of love I already had for him. I love him when he drops off coffee to my office on his way to the carpentry shop. I love him when he makes me dinner in the evenings, or else eats whatever disgusting thing I put together when I attempt to cook as a way to unwind. I even love him when he teases me mercilessly about missing more volleyball matches and practices.

The funny thing is that he would have done all these things in the Before Time. But seeing them now, with this lens of knowing my real feelings for him—and his feelings for me—everything is amplified, magnified.

Enhanced.

Noah is my *partner*—has always been my partner. I just never noticed it before.

The day before Lachlan is set to return to LA is a long, thankless slog of a day. We're both running on fumes, at this point. Lachlan has even started wearing his funky glasses to the office instead of lenses, and his shirts aren't ironed anymore.

Despite my own body-breaking levels of exhaustion, I've come to admire him more and more over the past days: the effort he puts into everything, the long hours he's pulled alongside me. The guy is a good boss and has a good heart, and I respect the heck out of that.

Sometime around 3pm, Lachlan leans back in his chair with a long sigh, which echoes my sentiments exactly. We've been sitting in silence for most of the day, trying to get what we could get done on the coding. The list of things we have to do seems endless as ever, and there's been this heaviness weighing on the room that maybe, just maybe, we won't be able to finish everything in time...

"What're you doing tonight, Diandra?" Lachlan asks, his voice less grumbly and more resigned. I think I'd prefer the cement-voice right now.

"You mean after work?" Lachlan doesn't respond, so I go on. "I'll probably just see Noah."

"Hm," he replies. Then, a moment later. "Any chance you two would want to grab a beer?"

My eyebrows raise and I half-turn to face him. He's got an elbow on the desk, propping his chin up. He looks about as inspired as I feel, and that might be the most terrifying thing I've ever seen in him. "You want to grab a beer with Noah and me," I repeat.

"I think we could use a break after the past couple weeks."

I stare at him blankly for a moment, then give a short nod.

He nods back. "Where should we go?"

"McGarry's is fun. That's our go-to after volleyball."

"Good, let's go there. Give us a chance to let off some

steam before I head back home tomorrow. It's been... nice working with you."

There's a note of finality in his voice that makes my stomach clench. I try to bite it down. "You too, Lachlan."

He gives a small, pressed-lip smile, then stands. "Listen, I'm going to take the rest of the day off, and I think you should, too. You did good work."

Through the fog in my brain, I know what this means. I know what this *has* to mean. But I can't quite grasp it right now. So, I just say, "Thank you."

He grabs his bag and heads for the stairs. "See you tonight."

I don't follow him. Instead, I sit and stare at my computer screen for awhile. Part of me wants to trudge forward, keep working, keep *trying*...

But I have the sense that I just witnessed Lachlan giving up. And now, my body, mind, everything within me is begging to do the same. Take the afternoon off, take a break and step away, resign myself to whatever future is in store for RightMatch and for me.

I'm not stupid. When Lachlan showed me the board's list of demands, I knew we were running on borrowed time. I knew that it would take nothing short of a miracle to get through every single thing they asked of us before this upcoming Monday.

Sometimes you win, sometimes you lose.

This time, we lost.

And I, like Noah, am a sore loser.

On autopilot, I finally turn off my computer, shut off the lights in the office, and grab my things. I head out the door, locking up behind me, and then I drive home in complete silence—not even whale sounds will soothe me right now.

When I park the car in front of my bungalow, I spot Noah's truck and come back to myself a little. I head into the house and find him in the kitchen wearing his carpenter's apron and clutching a pencil between his teeth.

"What're you doing?"

Noah startles, and when he sees me, his face breaks into that warm smile of his. "You're home early."

"Yeah." I drop my bag on the counter, not wanting to get into just *why* I'm home so early. "What's happening here?"

Noah gestures towards my sad, broken cupboards. A couple of them don't even have doors anymore. "I'm working out how to replace these. The new ones are in the shop, ready to go." He places his big hands on his hips, shakes his head. "How you've been living like this is a mystery to me, Dee-bug."

A wave of something powerful washes through my body. So strong that I feel breathless and I hiccup. I don't realize I'm crying until Noah drops the pencil and rushes forward to place his hands on my cheeks, running his thumbs beneath my eyes. "Hey, hey. Dee? Everything okay?"

"I..." I gasp. "I..."

I am a wreck is what I am. I don't know what's happened since I discovered my feelings for Noah, but it's like *all* of my emotions have taken this small opening of the Feelings Door and come breaking right through. I'm feeling everything so much more these days. Am so much more aware than I've ever been. Falling for Noah seems to have broken a dam to every emotion I've never allowed myself to experience. Good and bad.

"I'm so *tired*," I finally wail, collapsing into his chest.

He wraps his arms around me and hugs me close, just as he's done basically every night this week. He presses a soft kiss to the top of my head. "That makes sense to me."

"Everything feels really hard right now."

"You've always been a hard worker, Dee-bug. But this week has been something else."

I shake my head against his chest, gripping his shirt in my fists. "It's all for nothing..."

Noah freezes. "What do you mean?"

My eyes are clenched shut. "Lachlan's going back to LA tomorrow. We didn't finish everything we needed to get done. I think it's just... over." I brave opening one eye, spot the cupboards, and my stomach dips horribly again. "And now, you're fixing my stupid broken cupboards and being an absolute dream, and I don't know what happens next. If I have to move or find another job or start all over again..."

Noah squeezes me even tighter to his chest, letting me break down, letting me cry and feel horrible, and just... being there. When I calm down a little, he whispers, "I do. I know what happens next."

"What?"

"You pick yourself up. Dust yourself off. Dee, you are *so* much stronger than you give yourself credit for. You think you need these things and this job and these people, but you've got everything you need at your disposal. You sell yourself short."

I let his words infiltrate my mind, caressing and soothing the places that are afraid. "I wish I could believe in myself like you believe in me," I whisper against his shirt.

"We'll figure this out, just as we've always done. Even if you have to, like, move to California, we'll figure it out."

I chuckle a little. "I have always liked the sunny California weather."

"I do, too. I'd go with you."

I lean back to look at him. "You would?"

"Of course." His smile becomes vulnerable. "You're the main reason I stayed here in the first place. I mean, yeah, I love Mirror Valley and I'd miss it if I left, but you come first, Dee. *We* come first."

I blink.

Hang on.

Noah stayed in Mirror Valley because of... me?

This man, who has so much potential, who could do literally anything with his life, anywhere. This man, who loves his family and might reasonably want to live closer to them. This man, who I always thought should live his life big, wild and extreme, but never did, because of... me.

My heart skips over itself a few times. Tripping and falling and getting back up.

I squeeze my eyes shut again, returning to my position pressed up against him. I'm shocked, and touched, and floored that he stuck around. Obviously. I've needed him, needed my best friend. At times, it felt like I couldn't do this life without him. But at what cost?

I grind my teeth together, clenching my jaw against the questions. Noah has made it clear that he has continually chosen, and is still choosing, me. He's the best man I've ever known, and he makes me want to be better, too.

So I hug him tighter, knowing with full confidence amidst this cloud of uncertainty that I hit some sort of jackpot when Noah Jackson chose to love me.

25

NOAH

Dee goes upstairs to take a nap and I stay in the kitchen a little while longer, measuring the cupboards and working out the best way to secure the new ones onto the wall. Bruce makes an appearance, twisting between my legs and stretching up against the fridge while doing some slow blinks at me. Such a flirt, that one.

Eventually, I give up and head up to Dee's room. As I might've expected, she's not napping but sitting on her bed, reading a paperback. Which *is* surprising. Dee is more of a Kindle girl.

"How's it going?" I ask, leaning against the door frame.

She puts the book aside. "I couldn't sleep. Too much to think about."

Without a word, I place one arm beneath her knees, one behind her back, and scooch her over. I hop onto the bed next to her, and soon, we're lying on top of the blankets, facing each other. Dee takes my hand, interlaces her fingers with mine. "Lachlan wants to have a drink with us tonight."

"Yeah?" I screw up my face. "How come?"

Dee shrugs, eyes on our interlocked hands. "I don't think the man needs a reason to do anything he does."

"True."

"Tell me about you. What's going on? This whole week, I've been going on and on and *on* about my stupid work. I want to hear about you."

I roll onto my back and put a hand behind my head. Dee nuzzles a little closer into my side. "This week's been good. I told you about baseball practice—last I heard, Dylan's pinky finger is on the mend. Other than that and volleyball, I've mostly been at the shop with Raymond. He's passing more projects onto me. I think he's starting to trust me and my judgment."

"Really?" I hear the smile in her voice. "That's amazing, Noah."

I grin at her ceiling, at the three glow-in-the-dark stars that we accidentally super-glued up there when we were ten. "Ray's been talking about how things are going with Fran. They might take a cruise come the winter, and he'd want to leave me in charge of the shop."

"Wow! For how long?"

"Six weeks."

"You'd be running the business for six whole weeks?!"

"Yup."

"You'll be great, Noah." Dee stifles a yawn. "You're great at so many things, could do anything you want to do."

Her words warm me from the inside out. In the past, the thought of running Ray's carpentry shop would've been overwhelming, a bit too much commitment. I would've taken the easy way out. But now, I kinda love the idea of taking on the business for a few weeks. Helping people. Providing a service to the community.

And it means the world that Raymond trusts me. He believes that I can run the business that he started from scratch and has been working at alone for decades. Obviously, there's a ton of training I'll have to do before he leaves, but I'm motivated. More motivated than I've ever felt about anything.

"I think it'll be a great opportunity. And besides." I poke Dee lightly in the arm. "Maybe I can invest in a sign for the shop and join the sign war."

Dee hiccups with laughter, her breath warm against my upper arm. "You should definitely do that."

"We'll do it together. There's no way I'm joining the sign war without my prank partner."

Dee doesn't answer. I wonder if she's thinking about the conversation we had earlier about her moving to California. Dee loves Mirror Valley and I know she doesn't want to leave—her ability to live and work here is one of the reasons she stayed at RightMatch for so long. But things this week have clearly not been good, and I'm not sure how the board meeting this coming Monday is going to go.

Dee takes so much pride in what she does. I can't even imagine how much it must bother her to know that Right-Match might be out of the game...

Her breathing is slow and steady, and I assume she's fallen asleep until she whispers, "Are you awake?"

"Yup," I whisper back.

"Thank you for being here. For doing this. For just... being you."

I kiss the top of her head. I know what she's saying, what the subtext is behind her words. She loves me. I love her. Plain and simple. We're a team, and we'll tackle any problems together. We always have. "I've had twenty-seven years of practice."

"Well, you've had barely two weeks of engagement practice, but you're also the best fake fiancé a girl could ask for." Her tone is joking and light, but my insides twists a little and I look back up at the ceiling. Dee must notice something because she asks, "Is everything okay?"

"Yeah, fine."

"Noah. Talk to me."

I swallow. "It just cheapens it, you know?"

"Cheapens what?" Dee rises up on her elbow to look at me.

I lock both hands behind my head, feeling weirdly vulnerable. "Us being together. Dee, come on. I'm *really* crazy about you. You're *really* crazy about me." I take a deep breath and hold it. "It was never really fake for me."

Dee's beautiful gray eyes go extra wide and earnest for a moment. Then, she shakes her head. "It isn't fake for me either."

I cup her cheek to kiss her lightly, just once, before we lie back down on her bed. "Now, get some rest. We have beers with Skeptipants later and I need you to bring your A-game."

Dee settles down next to me and I close my eyes, listening to our breaths sync up until I fall asleep with her.

26

DEE

You know that expression, "fake it 'til you make it?"

Yeah, I never realized to what extent the line between fake and real could be blurred.

Because when Noah and I agreed to pretend to be engaged, I never could have imagined that things would go this way. That everything between us would start to feel so *real*. I mean, we're not actually engaged, and I do not *intend* for us to be engaged anytime soon. But the "togetherness" of it all?

That part is very real.

Which is wild because it means that one of the most real things I've ever experienced in my life came from what started off as a massive lie.

"What can I get you guys?" Noah asks, placing his big hands on the back of a chair while Lachlan clears space on the table he chose. A table which sits in the far back corner of McGarry's and comes complete with a burnt-out light-bulb hanging above it, so it's not only isolated but also dark and mysterious.

I don't completely understand why he would choose the

most incognito, sketchy table in the place, but hey, to each their own. And this guy *owns* his weird quirks, I'll tell you.

"I'll have a glass of red," Lachlan replies, and then wrinkles his nose slightly. "The most expensive on the wine list."

Noah and I exchange a glance—should we break the news that the closest McGarry's has to a wine list is a sticky laminated menu with bar snacks and meaty dinners on one side, and alcoholic drinks, mocktails, and desserts on the other?

Lachlan literally "harrumphs" as he pats at his pockets willy-nilly.

Okay, maybe we won't tell him.

Noah holds up a hand quickly, apparently catching on to Lachlan's angry pocket patdown. "No, please, it's on me." My boss opens his mouth to argue, but Noah cuts him off. "Let me get this one. You can get the next."

Lachlan seems mildly appeased, his mouth returning to that stern line we all know and vaguely accept at this point. Though I personally would be very surprised if we stayed for more than one drink. Noah confirms my order—a light beer—and he goes off to the bar, leaving Lachlan and me alone. We sit in silence for a few moments, and it occurs to me that Lachlan and I have never really "chit-chatted" about anything that wasn't work related.

Honestly, this arrangement is fine with me. And judging by the way Lachlan is scrolling through his phone, he must feel the same.

After my nap with Noah this afternoon, I feel better. Not a *lot* better, but somewhat better. I have a hard time letting go of things, and while there is a line to what I'd do to save my job—AKA I would never *actually* move to California—saying goodbye to RightMatch feels like a failure. A loss.

Talking to Noah, as always, dulled the ache. Took me

out of my head a bit. The guy is like soothing aloe vera applied to a sunburn. Like ibuprofen to ease a headache. He always somehow knows exactly what to say and do to make me feel better.

Noah is my own personal lifesaver. I simply couldn't do this without him.

I'm watching the bar—mostly because I'm facing that way and this corner's so dark, my gaze is drawn to the light like a flame-hungry moth—so I see the woman approaching Noah before he does.

She's pretty in that effortlessly beautiful kinda way, wearing only a smidge of makeup and absolutely rocking her denim dress, cowboy hat and brown cowboy boots. She's feminine and petite, and her cute little ski-jump nose crinkles up as she smiles and taps him on the shoulder. Noah turns to her, and I can't see his face but I notice the way she lights up as they talk. The way her laugh twinkles and sparkles like glitter raining down across the bar.

She must be an out-of-towner; something about her naturally tanned skin and rich auburn hair and overall *look* screams Arizona or Texas to me. I'd bet she's one of those cross-country road trippers with only her van and a guitar. And a dash of influencer status.

They chat until the drinks arrive at Noah's elbow. He says goodbye to the cute blonde, and then walks back our way with a little smile on his face and his cheeks the slightest bit pink. I wonder what they were talking about. Was she flirting with him?

I have sudden flashbacks to the countless times that I've watched Noah get approached over the years. At McGarry's, at the cafe, on the street... He was even approached by the public toilets in the park once. The guy is a total chick magnet.

"I just met this girl by the bar who's spending a few

months touring around the country in her campervan. How awesome is that? What an adventure." Noah places the glass of red wine in front of Lachlan, the beer in front of me, and then takes a sip of his own beer before sitting down, his eyes on me and smiling.

Meanwhile, all I can think is that leaving my bungalow and Bruce and my plants for a few months to go live in a van would probably give me a meltdown of Dee-spair proportions (another term Noah once coined after a rough day at RightMatch followed by a distinct lack of consolation candy corn).

And so, while any other girl might feel jealous of her fake-not-fake fiancé/boyfriend/whatever chatting with a pretty, adventurous girl at the bar, I just feel... remorseful.

Because this only reminds me that Noah stayed in Mirror Valley for me.

How many opportunities has he missed out on? In terms of dating and van travels, sure, but also in terms of jobs and general *fun*. Mirror Valley is a small town; there's just not a ton happening here compared to a big city like Los Angeles or New York or even Denver. Does he ever regret staying in our hometown?

I look up at Noah and his eyes meet mine, and he gives me that smile reserved just for me. I appreciate the way he's looking at me like we're sharing this moment together, like we're in this together. The wave of remorse subsides as he loops his arm around the back of my chair.

"Oh, and I got the nachos for us as well." He directs this to me, off-hand in that way of his. And of course he would get nachos. Of course he loves nacho sandwiches as much as I do. He takes another sip of beer before turning to my boss. "So Lachlan, what's next for you?"

Lachlan puts his phone to the side, screen up. "You mean at work?"

"Sure. Or with travel or whatever. Any van adventures in *your* future?"

Lachlan looks horrified, his scowl reaching new levels of scowliness. "I like my bed and kitchen and gym and toilet to be separate from my vehicle, thank you very much."

Noah smirks. "So you won't be hitting up any more small towns, I take it."

"No, I'll be in the city for a few months. Don't get me wrong, I've enjoyed your sweet little town and everything... but I'm looking forward to getting back to my penthouse. My own bed." He shifts in his chair. "The one here is too small."

I have a sudden mental image of Lachlan sleeping on a tiny twin bed with his bare feet hanging off the end like some overgrown toddler, and I have to cough to cover an abrupt laugh.

Man, I really need more sleep. I'm going loopy.

The nachos arrive, Lachlan orders a second drink for himself, and without work chat as our buffer, the conversation quickly dries up even despite Noah's best efforts. Lachlan and I just don't have much to say about Right-Match. We both know what to expect when he goes back to LA tomorrow—he'll have Friday and the weekend (to take care of these stressy "personal matters" of his, perhaps?), and then the meeting with the board of directors on Monday that will decide the future of the app.

I can't bring myself to ask if I should start my job search now. Mostly because the thought of starting over again from scratch makes a well of despair open in the center of my chest.

Not to be dramatic or anything.

"Your flight's early tomorrow, isn't it?" Noah eventually asks, wiping cheese grease onto a napkin. The nachos are well and properly picked over by now... mostly by Noah.

Lachlan hasn't touched them (probably exclusively eats fancy oat cheese or something) and I've eaten a couple but don't have much of an appetite.

"6am. Have to get the Range Rover back before that."

"And then back to the office?"

Lachlan nods. "It's actually very lucky that we're an hour ahead here. That's an extra hour I can work tomorrow."

I exchange a glance with Noah while Lachlan sips his wine.

"And there's nothing you can do for RightMatch?" Noah asks, earning himself a kick under the table. He looks at me all wide-eyed and innocent as if to say, *what? There's nothing else to talk about.*

But to my surprise, instead of giving his trademark scowl and changing the subject, Lachlan lets out a sigh. "I've been playing it over and over in my mind the last few days. Trying to figure out how I can convince the board to work *with* us instead of *against* us. But I'm coming up blank. It's like they don't believe this app can work..."

He trails off then, his eyes darting between Noah and me. A weird feeling starts to bubble up.

"You know what convinced *me*?" His gaze finally settles on me, laser-focused. An intense, steely blue that cools my insides immediately. "You two. Your engagement."

"Right, our engagement." I glance at Noah. His arm has stiffened slightly on the back of my chair and he isn't smiling anymore. I think back to our conversation earlier, remember how much the "fake" aspect bothers him.

But I couldn't get a word in edgewise if I wanted to, because suddenly, Lachlan's leaning forward with his elbows on the table and talking so quickly, I can barely keep up. "Maybe that's the angle we need to take. Convince the board of the success story before we can convince them of the app. We have to sell them on *love,* not data. What an idiot I've been—"

"The most dire of idiots," Noah and I both whisper, too quietly for Lachlan to hear.

"This is a *dating app.* At the end of the day, the love is all that matters. The weddings and engagements and the end-game success."

He's frowning, his jaw clenching as he thinks. I can't tell if it's the lack of sleep, or the running in a constant state of stress for days on end, or the very real probability that the thing I've put so much work towards is about to go up in smoke, but my mind is blank. It's just white noise behind a quiet rendition of John Fogerty's "Centerfield" on a loop in there.

So I can't describe my level of surprise when Lachlan makes his next announcement:

"Diandra, you're coming to California."

"Excuse me?" I blurt out when I realize that Lachlan actually said the words and I'm not having some weirdly vivid hallucination. "I'm doing *what?*"

But I've already lost him. Lachlan's picked up his phone and is typing furiously fast, mouth pressed in a line.

I look at Noah and he's staring back at me with eyes that are probably as wide as my own. What just happened? What is Lachlan tap-tapping about now?

When he puts his phone down, all he says is, "There was one business class seat left on my flight."

That exhausted, mildly delirious part of me is momentarily distracted by the "business class seat" statement in an

Ooh, shiny! kinda way before I tune back in. "One seat on your flight..."

"To LA."

I hold up my palms. Shake my head, my hands, everything. "Woah, woah, woah. Just hold on a second—"

"Don't worry. It'll be a quick and easy trip." He waves a hand casually like he's just told me that he's planning on getting a haircut versus telling me that he's booked a spontaneous plane trip for me. Then, he glances at me with a frown. "Wait. You don't have anything going on this weekend, do you? I got you a return flight for Monday night after the board meeting."

I blink a few times, trying to keep up. My brain feels broken. "What're you? Why are you...?"

"You're flying to Los Angeles," Noah says slowly, sounding mystified. "Tomorrow morning at 6am."

Ohmygosh.

I can't keep up with this. And so, as one might expect, I blurt out an entire flow of consciousness freakout with both the speed and volume of a freight train in the night. "I have to go to LA? I haven't packed. Who's going to watch Bruce? What about volleyball? I need to water my plants. I've got a full chair of laundry to do as well, and I lent Daisy my laundry basket last week and I don't think I have *any* clean pants. Or underwear! And—"

Thankfully, before I can continue ranting at my boss about my underwear, Noah closes his arm around me. "It'll be okay, Dee-bug. I'll watch Bruce, water the plants, and tell the volleyball boys you're missing another match."

"Aghhh," I finish off gracefully with a strangled grunt.

Lachlan's staring at me like he's fearful for my sanity (which, honestly, will teach him to surprise me with an early morning, last-minute flight across multiple states). Then he shrugs in a *whatcha gonna do?* kinda way. "I said that I

266

would do everything I could to give RightMatch its best chance, and this is the best thing I can think to do. One final fight, one final push. Are you with me?"

My first instinct is to give another big *agh!* and then have a meltdown in the bathroom where no one can see me. I can't imagine getting on a flight first thing tomorrow morning with no warning. I've taken trips away, don't get me wrong, but I'm a girl who likes to mentally prepare. Marinate with it for a few days, make sure I have a plan in place while I'm gone, and set myself up for when I return.

My home base is everything to me, and I don't leave it easily.

But Noah's big palm on my arm calms me. Grounds me. Reminds me of what's important here. Mirror Valley isn't going anywhere. *He* isn't going anywhere. My home base will still be here when I get back. And in the meantime, don't I owe it to RightMatch—to *myself*, and the years of blood, sweat and tears that I put into this app—to try one last thing?

So drawing comfort from the feel of Noah's hand on my skin and the knowledge that he's got me, I paste on a smile. "Put me in coach."

Noah smiles at me, clearly recognizing the line from "Centerfield", while Lachlan just blinks at me in a big way, looking even more concerned for my sanity. I can't tell if I prefer this look or the Skeptipants look. He gives his pressed-lip grin/grimace. "Well. I did already book you a business class seat."

Noah and I exchange a look.

"But it's settled then, you'll come with me to sell..." He waves his hand. "Well, *you*."

I can almost feel Noah's smile slide off his face, but before I can react, there's a shout across the bar.

"Dee, Noah! Woohoo, guys!"

I look over to see none other than Daisy and Luke tumbling towards us sporting matching bright blue shirts. I've never needed to see my sister more than I do right now, and I stand immediately, wrapping Daisy in a big, mildly desperate hug. Luke gives Noah a nod, then turns to Lachlan. "Good to see you."

"Likewise." Lachlan picks up his phone again. Probably booking us a spontaneous skydiving session, or hot air balloon ride, or spa day or something.

Hmm. Honestly, I wouldn't be opposed to a spa day *at all*. After the last couple weeks of nonstop work and this absolute stress of a day, sitting in a massage chair with cucumber slices on my eyes and a goopy face mask sounds alright.

"I'm Daisy." My big sister throws her hand out towards Lachlan. "Nice to finally meet you!"

Lachlan, in turn, barely looks at her, just gives her outstretched hand a quick shake. "Good to meet you, too."

Daisy continues beaming at him, but then her brows furrow. "Wait. Do I know you?"

He shakes his head, leaning back in his chair so his face is in the shadow. He peers back at her. "Don't think so." Daisy's expression remains the same and he shrugs. "Must have one of those faces."

Daisy and Luke exchange a quick look and he gives her a little nod like he agrees with her assessment.

That's strange. Why would Daisy and Luke *both* think they recognize Lachlan?

"Anyway." Lachlan turns to Noah and me. "What were we talking about? How you two got together?"

Through the white noise and "Centerfield" on loop, alarm bells start going off in my head.

Daisy and Luke can't find out that I stole their love

story. Not here. Not now. Not when Lachlan and I are doing this final push for Rightmatch.

"Nope," I say brightly. "We were talking about my flying out to LA tomorrow!"

Daisy's eyes go wide and excited. "You're going to *LA?* Why didn't you tell me?!"

"Just happened," I say with a shrug, basking a little in the relief of the conversation redirection. "I'm flying out with Lachlan so we can work together over there before the meeting on Monday."

"You'll have to tell me everything about it! And take lots of photos of the city," Daisy gushes before letting out a loud, bubbly laugh. "Though knowing you two, I should probably ask Noah for all my Dee updates." She winks at Lachlan. "Aren't these two just the cutest? They've been the best of friends *forever*. They are our perfect hometown love story."

Daisy then goes on to tell Lachlan a story about baby Noah and me running around naked in his backyard with handfuls of dirt like rogue children in the wild. It's a funny, harmless story—well, harmless as a highly embarrassing and personal story being told to your boss can be—and I start to relax a little.

This is good. I'll bear this humiliation gladly so long as we veer away from Daisy and Luke (and Lachlan) finding out the truth.

"Wow, you two really *have* seen each other through thick and thin," Lachlan says now, smiling. Actually smiling and not grin/grimacing. "We should share some of these stories with the board. Give you two a bit of background to show that you couldn't have progressed to your engagement *without* RightMatch."

Daisy's brow crinkles a little, and a horrible, sinking feeling hits me straight in the gut.

Oh, no. Oh, no...

She faces me. "Dee, tell us again exactly *how* Right-Match brought you two together?"

I feel sick. Abruptly sick. I might as well be back on California Screamin', going upside down and right-side up and topsy-turvy. Daisy and Luke are staring at me curiously, Lachlan seems expectant, and Noah...

Well, Noah's looking at me with something between resignation and pity. He's looking at me as if to say, *the jig's up, Dee-bug.*

I swallow, and the sound seems to echo around the bar. It's time to come clean and tell Lachlan that I lied—and have continued to lie—for the past two weeks. That the story of Noah and me actually belongs to my sister and her husband. Of course, Noah and I *are* together now, and it *was* because of RightMatch... Just not in the actual use of it.

It's either that or continue as is. Continue to act like Daisy and Luke's love story is actually mine and Noah's.

In that workaholic, super driven part of my brain, it's hard to imagine breaking down now when we're so close to the end. The thing is, the lie has a deadline on it—everything will be clear by Monday night, and the truth can come out then. We've worked so hard, and fessing up now will disappoint Lachlan not only because I lied, but also because it will steal the hope for a future for RightMatch.

He said we had to give the app its best chance, right?

Before I can talk myself out of what is probably some very flawed, tired-brain reasoning, I'm speaking. Parroting Luke and Daisy's love story back at them. It only takes a moment for their expressions to dawn with understanding, and then another for Daisy's face to scrunch up in shock. Luke, meanwhile, shakes his head lightly, back and forth. Back and forth.

Of course, they know the details of their story even better than I do, so I wrap it up quickly.

As soon as I'm done, Daisy gives me the world's most frightening smile. "That's all very nice, you two. Very romantic."

I press my lips together and nod, praying that she doesn't give me away. My eyes plead with hers. "Very much so."

Her smile becomes somehow even more frightening. Has a touch of a nightmarish ventriloquist dummy to it. "Dee, can I speak with you alone for a sec?"

Uh oh.

"Are you sure you want to pull Dee away right now? We don't want to be rude to Lachlan," Noah interjects smoothly. My freaking hero, this guy.

"It'll only take one teeny, tiny second." Daisy's ocean eyes are boring into mine like two piercing laser beams. "Just having some lady issues. You know how it is."

Lachlan looks thoroughly appalled. Though I can't quite tell whether it's because of Daisy's spot-on ventriloquist dummy impersonation or her casual relaying of supposed lady issues during their first meeting.

But I know I owe her an explanation. So I rise to a stand.

She takes my hand and practically drags me back towards the bar. I lead her around a corner, figuring some privacy might be nice for what's about to unfold. AKA when Daisy unleashes her big sister guilt-trip on me.

As we're out of view of our table, she drops my hand, and with the actual light in this area of the bar, I finally notice that her bright blue t-shirt has a "Hello, my name is" nametag with a scribbled "Mackerel" finishing the sentence.

"Holy mackerel," I quip. Stupidly.

Daisy frowns at me. "What?"

"Your nametag." *What I wouldn't give to be a mackerel myself right about now.*

She looks down at her front, then waves a hand. "We had a marine life field trip at the community center today for the elementary school kiddos. I'm a mackerel. Luke's a grouper."

"Sounds about right."

I say this brightly, but Daisy knows this play and she crosses her arms. "Why are you saying that you and Noah got together because of a miscommunication on RightMatch?"

I swallow. Look down at my toes. "Because I... kind of stole your story with Luke. But made it about me and Noah instead."

Daisy's silent for a long moment. Long enough for me to peek up at her. She has one brown eyebrow raised all the way up her forehead.

"Has anyone told you how nice your brows are looking these days?" I say, hoping I can de-escalate this whole situation with a shower of compliments. "You'll have to—"

"Nope. Don't even try it."

I screw up my mouth, then sigh. "Look, Dais, I didn't mean for it to get this far. I thought I was going to lose my job, and your story just came out. It was a mistake that totally snowballed."

"It's not a mistake, Dee, it's a *lie*. You lied to your boss." She shakes her head, lips fully pursed. "Telling him that you're engaged to Noah is one thing, and obviously I was all for it as it's basically what I've been saying you guys should be doing for years now." I open my mouth to say something, but Daisy continues, "But I had no idea that you told him an entire love story that wasn't yours."

The feeling of regret increases by a factor of a hundred. "I know. I feel awful about it."

Daisy tilts her head, almost like she's trying to understand. "The Dee I know doesn't lie... so why keep lying?

Why are you still going along with it? You and Noah are together now, anyway."

"Like I said, it snowballed. Lachlan ended up staying longer than he was supposed to, and so I just kept going along with it... until it kind of became true." I wring my hands. "You were never supposed to find out. I'm sorry, Dais."

"Whether I found out or not isn't really the issue here. This is a freaking house of cards, Dee. But I'm not even upset for Luke and me. Or Lachlan, for that matter."

"You're not?"

"No. I'm upset for Noah. You should've seen the look on his face when you were telling *our* love story. I've never seen the guy look so sad."

The words are like knives piercing and then twisting into the center of my chest. I stagger a little. "He did?"

"Yeah. I know you didn't intend to cause any harm, but from where I'm standing, you're playing with peoples' feelings at this point. Playing with *Noah*'s feelings." She shakes her head, and her expression is one I'll never, ever forget. "He deserves better than that and you know it."

Daisy gives me one last resigned look, and then turns on her heel to head back to our table. Only then do I see that the back of her bright blue shirt features a shark fin flapping about.

I feel suddenly a bit breathless, the weight of everything I've done sitting heavy on my chest. This all went too far, I've been selfish, and Daisy's right, I'm now sitting upon a massive house of cards that are about to tumble down around me.

What a mess. I'm likely going to lose my job and the app I've worked towards for a decade, I've upset Daisy, and worst of all, I've hurt Noah. The person I love most in the world.

Everything has gotten so far out of control. I can't keep anything straight anymore. All I know is that I need to try and fix it. Now.

I need to make everything better, make everything normal again, like it was two weeks ago. Like it was before I told this stupid lie.

When Dee returns to the table, she's wearing an expression that I've never seen on her before. And that's saying something considering how many of Dee's expressions I've seen over the years. Her eyes are wide and downcast, and her mouth is twisted. Daisy and Luke made excuses to leave soon as Daisy returned to the table, and I have a strong feeling that whatever the sisters talked about is the reason for Dee's mood change.

Lachlan seems to pick up on it (and apparently misunderstands it) because he chugs the rest of his wine while muttering about the "unhealthy obsession with fish" in this town. He then insists that we get on home so Dee can pack for their early morning flight.

I drive her back to her bungalow, and she's quiet the whole way. She doesn't even reach for the candy corn in the glove compartment; just sits in her seat, staring out the windshield blankly. I don't put the radio on.

When I park the truck in front of her house, I take Dee's hand in mine. Her fingers are limp, her palm cold and clammy. My insides twist into an even bigger knot.

Yeah. Something is very, very off.

"You okay?" I venture. "Feeling sick or something?"

"No." The word comes from her throat as a rusty, croaky sound, like she hasn't spoken for years. "I'm fine."

"Wanna tell me what you and Daisy talked about?"

Dee catches a quick breath. Shakes her head. "It was nothing. I mean, it was something, for sure, but nothing you wouldn't expect. Daisy's upset that I lied. That I took her love story and sold it to Lachlan as our own."

I nod slowly. I had a feeling it had something to do with that. "Well, lying probably wasn't the best idea, these things tend to spin out. But I get why you did it."

"You don't have to be so nice to me."

Her words are so quiet that I think I misheard. "What was that?"

"I said," she speaks louder. "You don't have to be so nice. It was a dumb mistake. I know that."

I blink, a little taken aback. "I didn't say that."

"No, but it was. I should never have lied. I should have come clean to Lachlan right away, and instead, I let it drag on."

"Dee, everyone makes mistakes. Everyone lies sometimes. Don't beat yourself up too much. You're still a good person."

"I just regret it so much." Her voice is tight. "I hurt everyone. Hurt Lachlan indirectly, hurt Daisy. And worst of all, I hurt you."

I glance at her. Sure, all these lies about us being engaged haven't felt great lately, and I'll admit it bothered me tonight when she wouldn't fess up about our actual relationship. But it's not so much that I would hold it against her. It's not so much that I would feel as hurt and bothered as she's making it seem. "Where is this coming from?" I ask.

"I just..." She pauses. Squeezes her eyes shut. "Do you ever think that we should go back to how things were?"

I frown, not understanding. "What?"

"Do you think you'd be happier if we were just friends?"

I'm at a loss for words. I'm all in with Dee, have *been* all in with her, and I thought that was pretty clear. So why on earth would she think that I would ever want to "go back" to being just friends?

Unless that's what *she* wants... Which, after the past few days together, doesn't make any sense to me. I can't believe that she might want to take a step back. That she's not here with me.

"Would *you* be happier?"

She doesn't respond, doesn't even look at me. And that speaks volumes.

I shake my head. "I wish you wouldn't do this."

"Do what?"

"Shut me out." I look forward, fiddle with the friendship bracelet on my wrist. "What you said awhile ago about wanting me to be your all? I get that, Dee, but I feel like I only have half *your* heart sometimes."

In the corner of my eye, I see her fingers clenched in her lap. I wish I could take her hand, as I've done so many times before, but there's this weird, unfamiliar chasm between us right now. "I don't want things to be that way," she whispers.

"I know. And I understand why. I get why you compartmentalize your life. After what happened with your parents... well, anyone would." I clench my eyes shut. "The bottom line is that you make me happy. Just as you are. Just as *we* are. So no, I don't think I would be happier if we go back to being just friends. But you need to believe it, too. Because I can't fight for us alone."

As I say the words, I realize how true they are. I love Dee so freaking much, but at some point, she has to decide for herself that she's all in. I can't keep believing we're a team when she keeps shutting away parts of herself.

"I don't know what to say," she finally says. "I want to do what's best for you."

"But that's the thing. I want to do what's best for *us*."

There's a long silence, that final, two-letter word hanging in the air. Then, I swear I hear a whispered, "So do I", but just as soon, there's a metallic creak and I look over to see her opening the passenger door.

"I have to go. Have to be up early tomorrow."

"Right," I say quietly. "Have a good time in LA. Maybe I'll go somewhere, too. Visit my brother."

"That would be good. Sam misses you."

I don't really know how to respond, so I just nod. She hops out of my truck, but before she closes the door, she looks at me. Her eyes are wide and glistening in the light from the street lamps. "I'll miss you, Noah."

Then, she shuts the door and runs into her bungalow. I watch her go, unable to bring myself to follow her this time. Because I know the subtext to those words, I know what she means underneath it all...

I just don't know if that's enough.

28

DEE

There are several things to love about California.

The sun, the beach, the happy, smiling people. Plus, the food's pretty dang incredible, and there's just so much *happening* all the time. Music in the streets, dance-offs in graffiti-streaked skate parks, kids rollerblading past you at a speed that surely can't be legal. There's color and sound everywhere you go.

Of course, I haven't been able to enjoy any of this for two very specific reasons:

One, because Lachlan and I have been locked in the conference room of his big fancy office space in downtown LA all weekend, strategizing and putting together a presentation to state our case on Monday.

And two, because any second that I'm not thinking about work, I'm thinking about Noah.

That night in his truck, all I wanted to do was tell him how much he means to me, how crazy I am about him, but I couldn't. Couldn't find the words, couldn't get them out. Of course I want to do what's best for Noah, but in that moment, all I could think was that I was hurting him.

But that look on his face when I asked if he'd rather we go back to being friends... I don't think I'll ever forget it.

Now, things seem so up in the air between us, I'm not sure what the future holds.

I've taken to channeling all this emotion into this final push for RightMatch. It's basically the only thing keeping me sane right now. Keeping me from breaking down into a big ol' mess of the very, very hot variety.

Since arriving in LA, I've tried to pivot Lachlan *away* from using Noah and me as the sole selling point in our presentation. It was wrong for me to lie in the first place, and I don't want this lie to be the thing we're basing our entire case on. So, I've been busting my butt to find *other* success stories. Combed through all our reviews, good and bad, for nuggets worth sharing. Contacted any and all couples who did, for real, meet on the app or at one of the singles events posted on the community board that I briefly set up last year.

I've tried to add a few of these love stories to our presentation. I've also added some "end-game" data points I painstakingly collected that shows the app's successes and where we can grow next.

Despite this, Lachlan still brings up my own "engagement" often. And all I can think is that I only have to keep this up for three more days.

Two more days.

One more day.

By Sunday evening, I'm still sleep-deprived and generally overwhelmed, but I've reached my fiftieth wind and am feeling fairly optimistic. I think we have a solid case for the company to move forward with RightMatch. I'm just hoping that the board of directors agrees tomorrow.

Lachlan and I are sitting in the conference room again, eating cold pizza that we ordered sometime around lunchtime. Or maybe we ordered it last night? I can't remember, everything's gone blurry. I'm tearing up the crust of my pizza—I don't like the crusts, and Noah usually eats them for me. A pang of sadness hits me square in the chest at the thought of him. I wish he was here right now.

Not to eat my crusts, necessarily. Just to... have him here.

"You miss Noah?" Lachlan asks, apparently able to add "mind reading" to his list of quirks.

Until I realize that I'm staring wistfully at my pizza slice. It might as well be sporting one of Noah's charming smiles. That'd be weird, though.

I give a nod despite my buzzy internal monologue.

Lachlan harrumphs a little. "Look, I'm not good with the... *love* stuff." He glances towards his phone, and despite the heaviness of the moment, my curiosity is swiftly piqued. Are Lachlan's "personal matters" of the... relationship variety? He continues before I can wonder about it any more. "You two seem really happy together, you seem like a good match. I'm sure that your marriage will be, you know, wonderful and happy, and there'll be times that you almost wish you were apart so you *could* miss him."

I let out humorless chuckle. But then something deep inside me cracks. *Our marriage...*

One more day suddenly feels impossible.

I place my palms flat on the cool surface of the table. "I can't do this anymore."

"Hmm?" Lachlan grunts, mid-bite of his cold pizza while he stares at his computer screen.

"Lachlan, I have to tell you something."

Something in my voice must tip him off because he's suddenly looking straight at me, his brick-sized hands clasped on top of the table and his ice blue gaze piercing through my very soul. Seriously, does the guy wear color contacts or do his eyes somehow become more striking when focused directly on you?

I take a seat across the table from him. Level my gaze on his.

"I lied to you."

Lachlan's expression remains the same. He doesn't seem surprised, or shocked, or disappointed. The only hint that he even heard me is the little twitch at the corner of his mouth. "Excuse me?"

"I lied to you." I take a breath. "Repeatedly. Over the past couple weeks."

"Lied about what?"

"About Noah and me."

He stares at me. "How so?"

"Well, we're together now... but we weren't when you first came to town."

His eyes narrow slightly. "I'm not sure I'm following."

So I come clean. Finally.

The jig's up, indeed.

I tell Lachlan that I freaked out when he was asking about RightMatch's "success stories", and so, I essentially stole Daisy and Luke's love story, thinking he wouldn't be satisfied to know that there was even one degree of separation. I tell him that I asked my best friend in the whole world to play along with me. And I tell him that I deeply regret it now. Regret lying to him about the engagement, but also regret what the lie has done to the people around me.

By the time I finish, Lachlan's leaning back in his chair, pizza slice forgotten. He's staring at me with his brows furrowed, like he's thinking something through. I hang my head, ready to accept my fate. Ready for him to yell at me, curse at me, fire me, whatever.

As much grief as I feel at the thought, I also know that I

did the right thing. For Lachlan, for Daisy and Luke, for Noah.

What I'm not ready for is the laughter.

At least, I think it's laughter. There's a low, gruff, sort of deep and surprisingly rich hiccuping sound that I've never heard emerge from this man even once.

When I look up, Lachlan's smiling, his eyes clenched shut, and that *sound* is coming from his mouth. He's leaning back in his chair, his hands clasped behind his head and he looks... decidedly *not skeptical*.

Yup. Lachlan Chase is laughing. At me.

I don't know that I've ever felt this shocked in my life.

All I can do is sit still, feeling at once mesmerized, horrified and strangely relieved.

"Well, I can't say that I was expecting *that*," he says when his laughter calms down. "I'm not easily fooled, but you two... you're very compelling actors."

"I'm really sorry, Lachlan. I should never have let it get this far."

"No, you shouldn't have." He's back to Skeptipants Lachlan in a matter of seconds. "I don't appreciate being lied to. The lack of integrity you've exhibited is pretty staggering."

I deserve that. It hurts all the same.

"And this friend, boyfriend, whatever, of yours, I can imagine he's quite upset by this situation as well. Especially if, like you say, you two actually are together now."

"He was—*is*."

"Rightfully so. I'm afraid I'm not sure how to proceed here. Withholding this information greatly affects our presentation to the board tomorrow, and normally, I'd be forced to hold a disciplinary hearing. You would likely be suspended from work while we review your case."

I bite the inside of my cheek.

"That being said, I know how hard you've worked to get this across the finish line for the meeting..." He presses his lips together in thought. "I believe the most fair solution is to allow you to still come to the meeting and assist in presenting our case, with the knowledge that your job is very, very much in question right now. Even if we cannot manage to save RightMatch, I'm not prepared at this time to move you into another area of our company."

I nod mechanically. "I understand."

"Now." He sighs deeply, turning back to his computer. "This means that we have some *significant* edits to make before tomorrow. I cannot allow our presentation to stand on a lie."

"I've actually flagged all the spots that focus on Noah and me," I reply helpfully. "They should be easy to edit or remove altogether. The other success stories I've collected are pretty convincing, I think."

"Assuming they're real."

I think that was a joke? I can't tell, and I'm certainly not going to choke out a laugh right now. I give him a weak smile instead. "Some of the couples I found were happy to call in and speak with the board, if needed."

"Let's hope it's enough." He rises to a stand. "I've got a couple calls to make. So let's reconvene here in about fifteen minutes."

"Sounds good."

As soon as Lachlan leaves the room, I take out my phone, heart pounding. There's one person I absolutely need to speak to right now.

Luckily, Daisy picks up on the second ring. "Hello?"

"I told him," I rasp. "I told Lachlan the truth."

There's a long silence and I wonder if Daisy hung up.

"You still there?"

"Yup," she replies. "Just processing."

284

"I couldn't hold it in any longer, I had to tell him." The words are tripping over themselves as I stare at the table, head in my hand. "I felt so terrible about what I did to you all with this lie."

Daisy lets out a long breath. "Look. I've been thinking about it. Thinking about you, and Noah, and how you guys ended up together."

"I can't bear to think that I hurt him, Dais."

"So... why'd you do it?"

I'm picking at an old piece of tape on the table. "I told you. I was going to lose my jo—"

"No, not the initial lie. Why did you *keep* lying?"

I go quiet for a moment. Continue picking the tape. "Because..." I take a breath. "Because I *wanted* it to keep going. I wanted to keep pretending with Noah."

"Why?" Daisy says this gently, patiently. I have the uncanny feeling that she's leading me to something.

"Well, because at a certain point, it didn't feel pretend." And it's true. After that first kiss, it was no longer pretend for me. "I guess I just kept him at arm's length for so long. That was what I defined our relationship to be." My voice sounds strangled. "After what happened with mom and dad..."

I trail off.

Daisy and I never talk about our mom and dad past what we need to. We certainly don't talk about what *happened* back then. But I can't keep this in any longer. I take a shaky inhale. "You know that I've always sorted my life into boxes. It's just easier that way. But ever since things started escalating with Noah, it's like those boxes have toppled over. I can't keep hold of anything anymore."

Daisy makes a sympathetic noise in her throat. "I wish I could take on the weight of that day for you, Dee. I wish I could bear the shock and confusion. Seeing our dad..." She gulps loudly. "It makes sense why sorting your life in this way became your coping mechanism."

My fingers are clenched tight under the table. Very few people know what I saw that day when I was seven years old. Only Daisy and Noah know the whole story.

I remember it all so vividly now. Remember coming home early from soccer practice because I had the stomach flu. Mom and Dad were meant to be at work. Instead, I saw Dad going into our house with a woman with frizzy hair and bright red shoes. I didn't know her, had never seen her before. But they were giggling, faces close, his arm around her waist. And right before the door slammed shut, Dad saw me. He rushed over, all smiles, and told me that it was nothing, that the woman was a client at his law firm, and that it was such a tiny, small deal that I shouldn't even bother telling Mom.

I might not have really understood at the time what was happening, but I kept Dad's secret. Did my best to forget that moment had even happened. I convinced myself that it was a dream, some hallucination because of my stomach sickness. I was good at it, too, had more or less forgotten the incident had happened...

"Back then," I say robotically. "It felt like if I could just do the right thing—keep the secret, not tell Mom or you or anyone else—then everything would be okay. And then, when I did bring it up... you remember the fight Mom and Dad had?"

It was *that* summer—the summer after my freshman year of high school. Things in our house had always been on the cooler side (especially relative to Noah's loud and boisterous and overly affectionate family), but in the past few months, our family ties had chilled to downright frosty. So when Mom and Dad sat Daisy and me down one night and said that they were splitting up, it wasn't surprising.

Then, I asked if it was because of the lady with the red shoes.

Both of them wore distinct, horrified expressions before sending Daisy and me to bed at 6:30pm.

I didn't tell Daisy the full story about the lady with the red shoes until years later when we were close again. But Noah? I told him everything that very night. It was that summer that he brought me the silver volleyball ring and I began to realize that *he* was home to me. He was *it* to me. In the midst of my home life imploding, he and his family kept me tethered. Kept me going when all I wanted to do was fall apart.

I relied on that, on *him*, so much.

Still do. Perhaps too much.

"It wasn't your fault, Dee," Daisy says, her voice a careful mix of gentle and fierce. "You couldn't control our dad's—*an adult man's*—behavior. You were just a child."

I clench my eyes shut. Then, on a whisper so quiet I can barely hear it myself, I voice my deepest fear. "But Dais, look what I've done. I've lied so many times. Maybe I'm more like Dad than we know."

"You're not," she says immediately with a firmness that makes me want to believe her. "For one thing, you fessed up. You told the truth. And you apologized. I'm sure it wasn't easy, but the right things—the best things—hardly ever are. It doesn't mean they aren't worth doing."

I'm silent for a long, long moment. "How come we've never talked like this before?"

Daisy lets out this light breath, almost a chuckle. "Well, I process by talking things out, you process by staying silent. Marinating. You had to process this and come around in your own time."

"I'm sorry it took me so long to get here."

"Don't be silly, we all process things differently, and so

287

we all experience things differently. Everyone's on their own journey, but I see what Noah does for you on yours. He opens you up. Since you two have gotten together, I can so clearly see the change in you. We *all* can."

I shake my head. "Everything about us scares me. We're moving too fast, too far. But at the same time, I've never felt safer. It's hard to explain. I think he's healing me." I let out another shaky breath. "And I went and pushed him away. I don't know how to fix this."

"That's the thing, Dee. You can't control that outcome either. You can't dictate whether you two end up together, you can only control your side of it. If you love him, you need to *show* him and *live* it. Do what you can to embody the love you feel for him, and let the pieces fall where they may."

I take a deep inhale in, closing my eyes so this time, I feel the tears fall. "I can't control it."

"You can't."

"I have to let go."

"You should."

And with those words, there's an incredible release in my chest. It's like Bruce has been curled up against my esophagus for the past decade and has only just moved.

Maybe I *don't* have to bear the weight of everything. I *don't* have to draw lines and boundaries to demarcate everything in my life, and then maintain them with a gripping, life-or-death urgency that's as much comforting as it is paralyzing.

The only thing I can do is show up genuinely, authentically, *real*-ly. And let the pieces fall where they may.

And with that release comes something else. I've relied on Noah and Daisy so much through the years. They were my crutches, the people I held onto so tightly for fear of losing them.

But this, too, is not ultimately up to me. And maybe this, too, I don't want to do anymore.

Because I can only control my own actions, my own behaviors, and the choices I make.

It's time that I try standing on my own two feet. Time that I realize that I can be my own support. I can pick myself up, fight for myself, and try for myself. Try for us, because maybe being together *is* what's best for us.

"Thank you, Daisy," I say quietly. I'm looking at this whole situation with entirely new eyes. "I'm back in Mirror Valley in a couple days. Promise me we'll talk about you and only you."

She laughs, the sound tinkling and light. "I can definitely promise that."

"I have to go now, but I love you."

"Love you, too."

And with that, I hang up the phone, take out a sheet of paper, and start making a plan.

29

NOAH

August in Washington is colder than I would've thought.

Or maybe it's just this place. Cascade Point is a tiny town on the coast whose most romantic aspect might be its name. It's breezy as can be, smelling of saltwater and fish and seaweed and other unnameable pungent sea scents. The morning air is cut with the sounds of crashing waves and cawing birds.

Seagulls, specifically.

Yeah, I can't get far enough away from those.

When I booked my flight to Seattle, I didn't put much thought into it. I just knew that I needed to get away and put some space between me and that heavy moment with Dee in my truck. We've been texting sporadically given Dee's hectic, work-filled weekend, but I let her know that Bruce and her plants are taken care of until she returns Monday night. And then, I left Sam a voicemail letting him know that I'd be on the next flight out and would find my way to his place.

By the time I landed in Seattle, I had three missed calls from him and another six from Karina, who I came to find out had driven to the airport to pick me up as soon as her appointment at the nail salon finished.

She drove me to the townhouse that she and Sam bought last year with her fingers splayed out against the steering wheel, ET style, lightly chastising me for thinking for a second that she and/or Sam wouldn't greet me at the airport.

As might be expected during my spontaneous visit, Sam and Karina had other plans. They both took the Monday off from their business, and were intending to drive out to Cascade Point to visit his old friend, Beau Brighton. Funny enough, Beau is also from Mirror Valley. Sam had been meaning to make a trip out to see him, drive along the coast, make a day of it. Until his lovesick big bro (AKA yours truly) crashed his plans.

"You two should totally go," Karina suggested this morning at the ungodly hour of 5am. Because my little brother truly lives up to his early-to-bed, early-to-rise reputation, even on his day off.

"You don't want to come?" I asked her as I stuffed the only hoodie I brought with me into a bag. Sam and I were dressed and mostly ready to go, but she was still wearing her pajamas, her hair a bedhead mess. She had literally only one eye open.

"You two need family time," she replied. Sam pressed a kiss to her temple, and she waited for him to leave the room before leaning towards me. "I'd actually much rather stay here today. Cascade Point is nice and all, but I can do without getting dive-bombed every three minutes."

I frowned in confusion. "Dive-bombed? By who?"

"Oh... you'll see."

And I would see. I really, really would.

She continued, "Don't tell Sam, or he'll get all excited

and preachy and take it as his own personal challenge to get me to go."

She rolled her eyes, let out a big yawn, then padded back to bed.

Which is how Sam and I ended up here in Cascade Point, alone, a couple hours later.

Fighting the seagulls.

"What the—!" I shout, flailing an arm around frantically to deter a particularly dive-bomb-happy gull.

"Cover the top of your Gatorade, and it'll all be fine," Sam says in a calm, even voice.

"These are seagulls. Not freaking bears," I reply as the gull makes another dive attempt. "I don't know what's scarier, honestly."

Sam says that the gulls here are more aggressive than your average bird. There was a failed experiment a few years ago in which the town tried to coexist peacefully with them, leaving out food in an attempt to placate the birds so they'd leave people alone. This only resulted in making the seagulls even *more* demanding. Not to mention chunky. When neighboring towns began to call Cascade Point "Fat Bird Point" (clever, right?), that was pretty much that on the experiment.

Somehow, Sam and I manage to finish the rest of our drinks—no small feat, let me tell you—before setting off at a fast jog through town. Beau's working and won't be available until the afternoon, so Sam and I have planned to spend the morning running along the coast and exploring the bay.

With his and Karina's nutrition company, Sam hits the gym often and is in pretty perfect physical shape. Which is awesome for me because I'm ready to go hard today. If I'm working hard, it means that I won't need to think or talk about what's going on with Dee.

We're rounding a corner and hitting a consistent pace outside of town when Sam speaks through a choppy exhale, "So, how're you doing, man?"

There's a note in his voice that hints he already has an idea.

So much for not talking about it.

"I'm fine," I reply. My heart's beating strong, but I can't tell if it's from our pace or Sam's question.

He glances at me. "Are you?"

Those two little words may seem innocent, but I hear what he's *not* saying loud and clear...

I told you so.

And honestly, I don't know what to say this time. I'm crazy about Dee, and I know, I *know* she's crazy about me too. That's what's so painful about this.

In the past, I knew where I stood with Dee, and that was firmly in the friend zone. But now, I've had a taste of what it could be like to be with her for real. I know what it could be like to be her partner, to support her through difficult times, and have her support me. I'm craving it, wanting it.

"Do you know what you want to do?" Sam asks as we loop around the block, the pads of our shoes hitting dirt as we veer onto a side trail. "I adore Dee, you know that. But you're my brother. You come first to me."

"There's some stuff you don't know. Stuff in Dee's past."

"Not to minimize her experiences or anything, but we all have stuff to deal with. If the girl's stuck in the past, she can't focus on the present, let alone the future. Can't focus on building and growing what comes next. And I can see it, man. You're thinking of the future, you're wanting that next part."

I let Sam's words rest, pushing forward with my quads.

He lets out a quick, "Hey!" but keeps pace, doing a sprint alongside me.

When my muscles burn so much that my thoughts are singularly concentrated on that sensation, I slow down, focusing on the sound of my breath, on our footsteps. I focus on the feel of the cool, humid air against my skin.

"I love her..." I manage to say. "I'll always love her."

Sam's panting alongside me. "I know. These things never go away. When you feel that bond and connection with someone, it's eternal. Whether you stay together or not."

I hear what he's saying but can't accept it.

"I don't want to push you or anything," Sam continues. "But you're more than welcome to stay longer if you need a change of scenery. And actually, one of Karina's friends is married to a carpenter. He could probably help you finish your apprenticeship and find a position in the city. Plus, Seattle's got *all* kinds of hot women... not that I'm looking, of course."

I look over to give him an eye roll and he waggles his eyebrows.

"But seriously, Karina and I would love to have you stick around. If you want to start fresh, you can always stay in Seattle."

Start fresh.

The words are at once so full of hope and despair. Because I know what he's saying: I can stay here if I want to forget about Dee and attempt to start over with someone new.

The thought tastes about as bitter as that time I chugged apple cider vinegar (yes, this was a prank Dee pulled on me, and no, I don't ever care to repeat it). But I know Sam just wants the best for me and I appreciate that.

So I focus on that part of it. Force a half smile as I throw a sweaty arm over his shoulder. "I'd love to be around you too, lil bro."

He shoves me away with a laugh. "Just think about it."

"I will. I really will."

30

NOAH

Sam and I end up running all the way up the bay, looping back around to Cascade Point, and then continuing south for awhile. Our footsteps keep a steady rhythm as we pass from pavement, to dirt trails through lush forest, to stretches of yellow sand on the beach.

As we run, Sam's words knock around inside my head.

When I love something, I don't quit. It's not in my vocabulary, it's not how I was raised, it's just not me. Which is why I've continued to play volleyball and baseball and all these other sports over the years. It's why, now that I've discovered my love for carpentry, I can't imagine doing anything else.

I also can't imagine quitting on Dee. But there's gotta be a breaking point. I can't keep wanting it *all* with her if she can only give me a part of herself. I'm all in, but what if she can't get there?

By the time we're coming back into town, it's just after noon. Sam and I have stripped off our t-shirts and our skin is dewy with a sheen of sweat.

Sam checks the time. "Beau should be off work. Let's go see him."

To my surprise though, Sam doesn't walk down the street but instead ducks into a small, dingy side alley. Making me wonder where on earth this Beau guy could be working.

I stop, frowning after Sam's quickly retreating back. Cascade Point seems like a funny little town, but you never know who might be lurking in alleyways. "Where are we going?" I shout after him.

"Just come!"

I let out a grunt but follow my little brother through the alley, passing pungent garbage bins and dripping drain pipes. The alley does a stern 90 degree angle linking it to another street, and right in the corner, I'm shocked to see a huge, colorful mural of a mountain lion in front of a sunset. I pause for a moment to admire the artist's work. The lion's dark eyes, speckled with an orange that matches the paint of the sunset, seem to pierce right through me.

"Nice, huh?" Sam asks with a little lift in his lips. "Cascade Point has its very own Banksy."

"Mirror Valley *definitely* doesn't have one of those. Unless you count the splotchy graffiti behind the school."

Sam chuckles. "Come on, we're not there yet."

We exit the alley and cross the street, veering right, before Sam ducks in through the side door of a tall, dilapidated brick building with the words "Cascade Point Fire Hall" carved along the front.

I follow him into a very large and very cluttered central room. A row of fire trucks, piles of boxes, bits of old machinery, two worn couches... this fire station is a mess but I kinda like it.

At the center of it all, Sam is fist-bumping a tall man with broad shoulders dressed in a dark blue t-shirt and yellow suspenders. The man also has the most incredible beard I've ever seen in my life. His beard makes legendary goalie Tim Howard's beard look like a sixteen-year-old's five o'clock shadow.

Which makes me think of Dee.

Not because of the beard, though. Dee and I just watched a soccer game together the other night.

Things between us feel messed up right now, but it doesn't stop me missing her. Doesn't stop me craving to be next to her, to talk to her. Doesn't stop me wondering how the board meeting will go this afternoon...

I push Dee to the back of my mind again and walk up to Sam and Beard Man. I'm not small by any means, but this guy is something else. I idly wonder if he might have some help in the supplement department, but judging by the way he speaks and carries himself, I don't think that's the case. He's just a beefy dude.

Sam throws an arm around me. "Noah, this is Beau."

I freeze. "Wait. *You're* Beau Brighton?"

Beard Man smirks at me, not looking the slightest bit like the tall, lanky kid with a bad dye job a few grades below me in school. He's completely unrecognizable now. "Sure am." He gives me a fist-bump. "Another Mirror Valley escapee?"

"I don't know about escapee—"

"We hope so." Sam cuts me off with a wink. "This one's got some girl troubles back home."

I roll my eyes, but Beau smiles, his eyes twinkling. "Girl troubles, huh?"

Seems that Mirror Valley isn't the only place for gossip hungry twenty-something guys. I let out a laugh. "Well, not really. She's my friend... girlfriend..."

"Fiancée?" Sam adds.

I ignore him. "Long story."

Beau chuckles, his entire face lighting up behind that majestic beard. Dee always seems to like when I'm clean-shaven, so I keep my scruff short. But then, I guess... if I was to move here like Sam was saying, I could wear my facial hair however I want to.

"Anyway, doesn't matter," I say quickly. "How you been, man?"

Beau's expression turns all business. "It's been hectic, as you can imagine. It's a bad summer for fires." He shakes his head, and as he does, I get this striking sense of familiarity. Fleeting, but strong. Can't quite put my finger on it, though. Probably left over from when we were kids. "I'd rather be busy than doing nothing."

"Like you could do nothing." Sam scoffs, jerking a thumb towards Beau. "This guy has so much energy, I think he might outpace you."

"No way," I say with a wide smile. "You were on the school basketball team when we were younger, right? We should play a game sometime if you're up for it."

"Sure." He shrugs. "I usually shoot some hoops on the evenings I'm off."

"This guy is so freaking modest." Sam rolls his eyes. "He kicks my butt anytime we play."

Beau laughs, crossing his beefy arms. "Well, Noah, if you stick around Seattle, let me know and we'll organize a game."

"Deal."

"You off work yet?" Sam asks him. "Want to grab a beer?"

"Let me get changed and we can go."

"Great. And I'm gonna use the bathroom," Sam says chirpily. "Karina says I should wash my face after a run. Better for my skin or something."

He rolls his eyes and Beau laughs and the two of them disappear behind the row of fire trucks. In the meantime, I wander around the big room, not that you'd know it with the amount of stuff in here. As I pass by a random hole in the brick wall, I send up a prayer that the building is structurally sound...

Beau soon returns wearing forest green slacks and carrying a duffel bag, which he puts down on a small wood side table.

"Cozy in here," I say as I lean against one of the trucks.

"Has to be." Beau rifles through the duffel bag. "This crew takes care of fires in town but we also help with wildfires in the summer. It's the biggest station in a forty-mile radius." He takes out a ball cap and clenches it between his teeth while he continues searching, so his next words are muffled. "Really want to fix up the station soon."

Finally, he tugs a white t-shirt out of the duffel and lets out a triumphant "A-ha!", catching the ball cap as it falls from his mouth and placing it on top of the bag.

"Town seems nice," I say conversationally. "A little rough around the edges but pretty homey."

Beau shrugs off his work shirt. "It grows on you."

"Talkin' about that fungal infection again, B?"

The woman's voice, so light and teasing and totally at odds with the content of her sentence, comes from somewhere just behind my right shoulder. I whip around and come face to face with a tiny speck of a woman wearing a full firefighter uniform. Truly, she can't be taller than five feet. She has wide, dark eyes, full lips, and a smatter of freckles across her cheeks. But the thing that stands out most about her is her smile. Her front tooth is slightly crooked, but the force with which she smiles puffs up her cheeks and makes her entire face come alive.

Beau lets out a sigh as he tugs the white t-shirt down his torso. "You mean yours, Jordy?"

She lets out a booming laugh, extending a hand towards me. "Jordana, but you can call me Jordy. I take it that you're friends with this pest?" She gestures towards Beau, who rolls his eyes as he comes to stand next to her.

"He's Sam's brother," Beau explains.

"Noah," I introduce myself with a laugh, shaking her hand.

"Yes." Beau smirks as he looks down at her. "And Noah, meet Mini-me."

Jordana puts her hands on her hips, puffs out her chest, and wrinkles her nose at Beau. "Who you calling Mini-me? Seems to me that my height comes in *very* handy sometimes, thank you very much. A forest isn't made entirely of tall trees."

She shoots a wink my way and Beau purses his lips. "Excuse Jordy and her manners."

"Hey. Anyone who shamelessly roasts me on first meeting is usually good people in my books."

Jordy smiles wide. "I like this one, Beau."

"He's taken, Jordy."

"Oh." Her eyes meet mine again and she smiles sweetly. "Shame."

Then, she skips off, disappearing behind the fire trucks. I turn back to Beau and he just rolls his eyes. "Aaaand that's Jordy."

A loud "Oh, Hi!" comes from behind the trucks, followed by a muffled conversation, and then, Sam emerges, pushing a hand through his hair. He smiles at Beau and the two chat easily while we leave the station.

Meanwhile, I'm lost in thought. It's not like I'm interested in Jordy or anything, but it's hard not to notice the striking differences between her and Dee. On first meeting, Jordy screams sunshine and laughter and happiness, where Dee is more serious. Dee could barely tell me how she felt, but Jordy seems the type to wear her heart on her sleeve.

Maybe, in another world, I would go for a girl like Jordy.

Maybe, in that world, we'd have a good life together. I could picture laughing for hours on a porch swing somewhere, picture that smile brightening my mornings. I would stay here in Washington and be a carpenter and live close to my brother.

It would be so easy...

But if I'm honest, that's not the life I want. It's *never* been the life I wanted.

"You guys survived the seagulls, I see?" Beau asks, pulling me from my thoughts as we shuffle into this funky-looking, nautical-themed bar, which is already packed at 3pm.

"Barely." Sam shudders. "They're worse than the last time I was out here."

"The town keeps trying to come up with solutions, but clearly, nothing's working. When I moved out here originally, they were just regular birds and not these chunky flying raccoons, believe it or not."

We're settled into a booth now—one that features an old-timey gaslamp at the center of the table and a fishing net over our heads full of sea stars.

"Why did you move all the way out here?" I ask. I've been trying to remember Beau's story, but the details are fuzzy. I believe there were three Brighton kids: Beau, the younger brother Marcus, and a half-brother who was a few years older. The boys all grew up in Mirror Valley, but took off basically the minute they all turned eighteen.

"My grandparents live here, and I used to stay here every summer when I was younger. I originally came back just to visit, but ended up staying. This place kinda draws you in and won't let go."

"Are your parents here, too?" Alan and Darla Brighton used to have a coffee shop in Mirror Valley—the Valley Roast. They sold it a few years back, and then moved away.

"Nope. They've been on cruises around the world for the last couple years, but their new base is in Florida. I keep telling them to come visit but it never happens. So it's just me and my grandparents here. My brothers and I aren't in touch. Last I heard, Marcus was off gallivanting in Central America, and Lockie was based in LA."

"Lockie's your older brother?"

"Yup." Beau shrugs. "Haven't heard from him in years. I think he's some bigshot executive or something now. Works for an online dating website."

A weird, tingly shiver travels the length of my spine.

It couldn't be. There's no way. It's too much of a coincidence.

"This is probably dumb, but is Lockie's full name Lachlan?"

"Yup." Beau nods with a crooked smile, then very grandly says, "Lachlan Chase Brighton."

My eyes go so wide, I think they might pop out of my head. "Lachlan Chase..." I repeat slowly, turning the familiar name over in my mouth.

It can't be possible. And yet...

Is this why Daisy recognized him that time? Why Lachlan always wore a weird incognito outfit or sat in a quiet place whenever we were out in public?

I clear my throat. "There's a chance your brother just spent the last couple weeks in Mirror Valley working with my best friend. Without telling anyone who he really is."

"Sounds like him." Beau shrugs. "The guy plays everything close to the chest, it's impossible to know his real agenda. Which is part of the reason we'll never be close; he's just too cagey and untrusting of everything and everyone around him."

I nod, trying to process this information. Why would

Lachlan come back to Mirror Valley without telling anyone who he really is?

I want to call Dee, tell her about this weird little twist. She's always the first one I talk to when I learn something this crazy. But I hold back. It's almost 4pm, which means that her big meeting with the board of directors will be starting at any minute. She'll be going up in front of all of these important people and telling them that we're engaged. As much as I want to talk to her, it'll probably only throw her off...

So I decide to wait.

By the time we're both home in Mirror Valley, surely we'll have a clearer idea of where to go from here.

I just hope Dee wants the same path as I do.

31

DEE

It wasn't enough.

At the end of it all, after the board people left and the projector was shut down and the glaring fluorescent lights were giving me a headache, Lachlan went on to say that most likely *nothing* would have been enough. The board already had their minds made up when the company acquired RightMatch all those months ago.

Which was a small comfort. Tiny. Because it meant that not everything hinged on my stupid lie about an engagement.

And yet, as I pack away my things in preparation for my flight later this evening, I'm not thinking about RightMatch, or the wasted time, or the wasted potential.

All I can think about is Noah and the words he said to me days ago. That I'm stronger than I give myself credit for. That I rely so much on my job and the things around me for support. I understand what he means now. I've spent years gripping onto these things with a fervor and panic that was unhealthy.

Now, with hindsight, I can see that Lachlan and I put up a good fight. And while it ultimately came to nothing, life will go on. Things will be okay. I wouldn't go so far as to say I'm an *optimist* by any stretch, but it's a relief to relinquish, to believe that things will work out, one way or another.

That being said, I also know that I have a lot of work to do when I get back to Mirror Valley. Have some amends to make. I want to do what I can, the best that I can, for the people that I love.

"Are you about ready?"

Lachlan's voice startles me. He's been in his office for the past half hour, pacing a hole in the floor and speaking on the phone. I give him a short smile, waving around a folder. "Almost."

He looks worn out, his shirt sleeves pushed to his elbows. I could never pinpoint the guy's age—always assumed he was a couple years older than me—but right now, he looks closer to fifty. I can tell this loss is affecting him too, and I appreciate that about him. Appreciate how hard he works for the things he believes in. Weirdly, I feel a bond with him. Not a romantic bond at all, but I feel like I understand him. Like we could've been friends in another life.

Another life where I hadn't spent our entire acquaintance lying to him. You know... that one little glaring issue.

"Hey, Lachlan?" I say before he leaves the room. I'm still not used to the whole expressing emotions thing, but I want to be better at it. "I just want to say thank you. It means a lot that you worked so hard with me these last couple weeks. That you believed in me and in the app, and that you fought for it even after I told you the truth. You're a good guy. A good boss."

I feel a bit shaky. Lachlan looks stunned.

Man. I might actually miss this guy and his unexpected show of emotions.

"Thank you, Diandra." A tiny smile presses onto his lips. "Sorry... *Dee*."

I give him a small smile back. "I don't expect you to find another place for me in the company or anything, but I did enjoy working with you. And I genuinely wish you the best with everything moving forward."

I expect Lachlan to give a nod and then hightail it back to his office or something.

Instead, his expression crumbles. Truly crumbles.

He drops his eyes to the floor, tossing a hand through his hair.

"Dee, I might've been a little unfair earlier," he says, sounding different. Sounding... guilty?

"What do you mean?"

"What you did was wrong. Lying was wrong. But I lied to you, too."

I lick my lips. "About what?"

"I had an ulterior motive when I came to Mirror Valley."

Lachlan then goes on to completely blow my mind with the revelation that he's originally *from* Mirror Valley. He tells me that his last name is actually "Brighton" but he dropped the name when his career started taking off. He's been living in LA ever since he left our small town and has never looked back, but when he learned that I was working and living in Mirror Valley, he felt this pull to visit.

"I love the big city, don't get me wrong," he says gruffly, his blue eyes wide and unblinking and, for once, not totally frosty. "But I needed to get away. There was some stuff going on here in LA and..."

He trails off, shaking his head. My inner gossy-gossip is fully tuned in now, and I'm mere moments away from asking, "Was it *love* stuff?" when he speaks again.

"Needless to say, it was a good time to go back and visit

the old haunts. My parents left Mirror Valley a couple years ago, and I've been away for so long, it almost felt like a made-up place. But when I got there, no one seemed to recognize me and I realized that I didn't want them to... Which is why I didn't tell anyone who I really was."

I'm reaching back in my memories, trying to work this out. I only vaguely remember the Brighton brothers growing up.

"Hang on." I frown. "Luke and Daisy recognized you."

He nods, looking sheepish. *Sheepish!* "That surprised me, too. Luke was a couple years below me in school and I would help him out with soccer sometimes. And I used to see Daisy at the community center. I never imagined those two would be the only ones to see it, but here we are."

"Wow..."

Lachlan shrugs. "I wanted to share this with you now that everything's done and dusted."

"I appreciate that. Obviously, I know how awful it feels to lie and how hard it can be to fess up. So, thank you."

Lachlan gives that tiny nod. "How about we make a pact to be honest going forward."

"I've made that pact with myself, don't you worry." I give a little smile. "And... going forward?"

He presses his lips together. "There are a few things I have to work out, obviously, but you're very bright and a good worker, Dee. I'd love if you would stay on with us. If you want. Without RightMatch."

There's a little squeeze in my chest, but I can't tell if it's good or bad. "Maybe. I'd be curious to hear what kinds of opportunities you have available. *Remote* opportunities."

I tilt my chin up cheekily and Lachlan's little genuine smile makes an appearance before his eyes drop to my bag. "Come get me in my office when you're ready, and I'll call a car to take you to the airport."

32

DEE

I think about Lachlan's offer the entire flight back to Denver. I'm still thinking about it when Daisy picks me up at the airport and I run over to give her a big, big hug.

But as soon as I get in the car with her and Luke, I stick with my promise to focus completely on them.

I lean in from the back seat, listening to them talk about work, the house, whatever Ivy's been up to, and all the craziness on the town council. Daisy's pregnancy test all those days ago was negative, but they're feeling hopeful. And they give me updates on the sign war, which, indeed, has escalated so much that a reporter from Denver came out to do a segment on it.

"So, basically, we're famous now," Daisy says with a flick of her wrist. In the rearview mirror, I see Luke give her the side eye with a small smirk on his lips. On the center console, he traces a thumb lightly over her hand which is clasped in his.

I love these two together.

"Gone for one weekend and Mirror Valley is suddenly on the map," I say with a laugh. "I shouldn't be surprised. Fran is a celebrity just waiting to be discovered."

"Real Housewives of Mirror Valley, here we come," Daisy replies. "Ivy says she's had a ton of new bookings at the Brookrose since the segment aired. Who'd have thought a sign war would become such a *thing*?"

I bite my lip as I remember my date with Noah at the viewpoint overlooking the signs. We passed that same spot on the way from the airport, but I didn't want to say anything. Didn't want to distract from Luke and Daisy. Noah's definitely on my mind, though.

We're about to pull up to my bungalow when Daisy turns in her seat to face me. "Okay, you've showered us with enough attention for one day. How'd things go in LA?!"

I breathe in. Breathe out. "RightMatch is done."

Daisy's eyes go huge. "No. No way..."

I nod. "We even had some of our successful matches call in and give their endorsement, but the board wasn't interested. Lachlan thinks the company mostly acquired RightMatch for a piece of our code, and they always planned to dismantle the rest of the app."

Her jaw drops further. Luke's eyes in the rearview mirror are concerned. I can understand why these two would be taking this to heart given that RightMatch really *did* bring them together. Not in the traditional sense, but still.

Daisy's eyes glisten a little as she places a palm on my knee. "I'm so sorry, Dee. You should've called me. Called us. I would've said something. Would've convinced them."

I give a small smile. "If anyone could do it, it would be you, Dais. But it's actually... it's okay." I say this tentatively. Testing my newfound feelings and finding no resistance. "I'll be okay."

Her eyes scan my face, intent on finding a hint of a lie, evidence of me hiding my feelings. I keep my expression open and honest. No more lying here.

I place a reassuring hand on top of hers on my knee. "I've done a lot of thinking since we talked. I relied so much on RightMatch for so long. I put years of my life into that app. It was my baby. But there's more to life than just jobs and the things we use as crutches."

"So what're you gonna do?"

I shrug, almost shocked at how nonchalant I'm being. How nonchalant I'm *feeling*. It's like the world is clear to me now. I'm seeing things so differently. "I'm not sure yet. Even after I spilled my guts about the fake engagement, Lachlan offered to find me a position in his company. I have some crazy news about him, by the way, but more on that later. I think I'm going to take a break for awhile. Not work, just think about what I actually *want* instead of grasping and holding on too tight to what I can get. I have savings, I can afford to take some time to figure myself out."

Now, both Daisy and Luke are staring at me with matching shocked expressions. I have to laugh.

"This is me relinquishing control, guys. Letting the pieces fall where they may. I want to keep working, of course, and I want to keep trying, but I have to figure out what's worth fighting for."

"That makes sense." Daisy nods. "I'm proud of you, Dee."

I reach up to hug Daisy, and then Luke. "Love you guys. Can I take you out for dinner tomorrow?"

"Sure thing. I heard there's a new pop-up taco truck on Main Street."

Luke looks at her, horrified. "Tacos from a... *truck*?!"

"You'll love it, Luke. Trust me on this one."

Luke gives that gruff chuckle of his, shaking his head, and it occurs to me, once again, that he'd only do it for Daisy.

When I walk into my bungalow, the first thing I see is

that Bruce has made the house his kingdom. His toys are scattered throughout the living room, bits of biscuits surround his mostly-full food bowls, and he's currently perched atop a high shelf, his green-eyed stare focused on me in a very "who goes there" kinda manner.

As I drop my bags, he leaps down from his perch, stretches languidly, then rubs up against my leg. Apparently agreeing to share his kingdom with me.

I give him a little pet and he purrs loudly.

The second thing I notice is Noah's absence. I may have no idea what to do with my future and my career, but I know without a doubt that I want to give my all when it comes to Noah. I want to show him how much he means to me, how much I truly, honestly, really love him.

I don't want to put him into any more compartments. Don't want him in only one area, one zone, of my life. I want him everywhere, involved in everything.

All of him, for all of me.

That motivation, that clear-cut intention, is only multiplied when I push open the door to my bedroom and see something on my bed.

A body pillow.

Noah left me a body pillow with a print-out of his face pinned to it. Wearing his t-shirt.

I let out a sound that's part laughter, part shriek as I collapse onto my bed and wrap myself around it. With everything that happened in LA—the highs and lows and revelations and disappointments and new hope—all I want right now is Noah. I want to share everything with him, tell him all about my trip, and hear about his visit to Washington.

Far as I know, he's coming back in three days. And I've got a plan.

Noah always seems to just *know* what I need, and he

gives it to me time and time again. Reliably. Selflessly. Generously. Even when I was pulling away, he somehow still managed to move towards me in the perfect way. So much so that this plan of mine feels like a tiny drop in a massive ocean of good deeds that he's done for me.

But I know Noah. I know that, in a romcom, he's the guy who would love a grand gesture.

I just hope he accepts mine.

I mean to get up, unpack my bags and organize myself. Instead, bone-tired and heavy with all of the stress and exhaustion of the past couple weeks, I fall into a deep, dreamless, coma-like sleep, nuggets of hope gathering like flecks of gold inside my heart.

33

NOAH

"Got everything?"

I look up to where Sam is propped up in the doorway of the guest room. Zip up my duffel. "Ready."

"Karina's starting the car. She made you some snacks for the plane."

I give a lopsided grin. "It's only an hour flight."

Sam shrugs. "She probably assumed you get random bouts of hunger as often as I do."

"That's really sweet of her."

"Ah, she's likely doing it for your seat-mate more than for you." Sam winks. "It's her way of keeping me quiet on flights so I'll leave her alone to read."

Sam and I laugh as we troop down the stairs of his town-house. There was a point last year when Sam was thinking of moving back to Mirror Valley, but now that he's settled here with Karina, I can see why he chose to stay. The two seem really happy, and I'm hopeful their new business takes off with the Seattle market. Won't stop me missing him, though.

The past few days have gone by so fast. I can't believe I'm already headed back to Mirror Valley. Dee and I haven't spoken on the phone or anything, but it's not like we've been without contact—we've been exchanging regular GIFs. No context, no words. Just stupid moving pictures, but it works for us.

Honestly, I miss her a ton, and I'm excited to see her. Even though I still don't know what our future holds.

Daisy texted me about Dee's board meeting the day after it happened. Let me know that RightMatch was done and Dee was now officially out of a job. I felt awful for her, and how scared and hopeless she must be feeling. I was about to throw out all my reservations and call her, but then I wondered if this was another thing she preferred to keep to herself.

Either way, we'll both be home soon, and we can talk then.

The thing is, you can't just *stop* loving someone. Can't suddenly stop caring about what happens to them. It's actually kind of beautiful the amount of energy you can put out into the world towards another person. Love is this deeply selfless, wonderfully selfish thing.

I've known for years that Dee Griffiths was my soulmate. But what happens when your soulmate can only give a part of themselves?

When we get to the car, Sam hops into the driver's seat and I grasp for the handle to the backseat. And just like when we were younger, Sam inches the car forward, bit by bit, keeping me from opening the door.

"Hey, cut it out!"

Sam chuckles away, watching me gleefully in his side mirror as he presses the gas, the brakes, the gas, the brakes.

"You're making me nauseous!" Karina bellows. "Let him in, Sammy."

Sam is still snickering when I get the door open and hop into the backseat. "You're a turd," I tell him.

"What're brothers for?"

"No, he's right, babe," Karina says with a resigned shrug. "You're a turd."

Sam laughs, and from where I'm sitting, I see the glow in Karina's face to watch him. When Sam announced that they were getting married last year after only a few months of dating, I think my family were all a bit skeptical. But the moment we saw them together, we knew. Sam and Karina are meant to be. Soulmates, through and through.

I soak up every moment with my brother and his wife on the drive to the Seattle airport, and when we pull up to the drop-off lane at the domestic terminal, Sam cuts the engine. Turns in his seat to face me. "You sure about this?" he asks.

I swallow thickly, but nod. "I'm sure. If I stay any longer, I'll be leaving Ray in a bind. Not to mention our volleyball team's probably gone to crap with both Dee and me gone."

The last part is meant to be a joke, but the reality hits me all too hard that I will, indeed, have to face the volleyball boys. Tell them that Dee and I have hit a rough patch. I can already imagine their expressions—they were almost as invested in this as I was.

"Fair enough. But I meant what I said when we went to Cascade Point. You always have a place to stay here."

Karina shifts her entire body to look at me with wide, green eyes. "It'd be great to have you stay longer. Goodness knows I could use more of your help managing this one." She rolls her eyes, ruffling Sam's hair.

I have to laugh at that. Laugh at the sweet way they tease each other.

"Appreciate it, guys," I say, meaning every word. "Seattle's a cool city, I could see myself living here. But no matter what, I'll be back to visit soon. I'm sorry it's been so long since I came to see you. I want to be better about that going forward."

"Same here." Sam nods. "If you decide to stay in Mirror Valley, I'll make more of an effort to come see you, too. After all, if I can make it to Cascade Point, I can definitely come see my big bro."

I smile wide, slapping his shoulder.

Sam, Karina and I say our goodbyes in a mess of hugs and well wishes, and then I'm off to catch my flight. Karina did, in fact, pack me a little Ziploc bag of cheese, organic crackers, almonds and apple slices. It reminds me of the date Dee and I had with the charcuterie board of food on the hood of my truck. I had so much hope then, felt like everything was finally falling into place...

I land in Denver at nightfall, and after picking up my truck at the airport parking and slinging my duffel into the backseat next to the brown snuggie (yes, I still have it), I hit the road towards Mirror Valley.

I'm of two minds and two hearts right now. I want to go to Dee's place right away, can feel a tug and pull towards her that's so intense, it's almost blinding. I want to see her. I missed her so much.

But that other part of me is still uncertain. Unsure whether I should just head home and see her tomorrow with (hopefully) a clearer head and heart, ready for a discussion about what comes next.

The battle is still raging deep in my ribcage as I crest the last hill before Mirror Valley.

And then, something catches my eye.

NOAH in bright lights.

I do a double take, squinting out the windshield towards the sparkling gem in the darkness that is Mirror Valley.

Yup.

My name is written in big, glaring, LED lights on the changeable-letter sign for Pete's garage.

And if I'm seeing things right, the other signs have words on them too...

I frown, wanting to make them out, but also realizing that I'm driving down a winding road at night and now is not the time to be distracted. I spot the turn-off to that same parking lot that Dee and I went to on our date and I pull in, stopping the truck.

As I squint out towards town, my jaw drops.

Because it's not only my name. It's not only one sign.

Pete's Garage: *NOAH I WAS THE MOST DIRE OF*

Mountainview Diner: *IDIOTS. AND I LOVE YO*

Mirror Grocery: *U. FOR REAL. ENTIRELY. TOGETHER*

Mirror Valley Central Bank: *IS WHAT'S BEST FOR US AND I WILL FIGHT*

Town Hall: *FOR US TOO. I AM, HAVE ALWAYS BEEN, AND*

Community Center: *ALWAYS WILL BE ALL YOURS. DEE*

My heart is racing. So cheesy, so extreme.

So amazing.

Dee knows I'm a sucker for those stupid grand gestures at the end of the romcoms she watches. I've seen more than enough of them lounging next to her on her couch after another date of mine that went nowhere, and could never go anywhere.

I stand in front of my truck for a long time, leaning against the cool metal as my eyes dance across the signs, over and over.

Finally, I get back in the driver's seat. I know exactly where I'm going.

34

DEE

Noah's flight landed at 8:40pm.

Unless it was delayed.

Which it wasn't. Because I checked.

Because apparently love makes you into an anxious semi-stalker. Who'd have thought?

Why isn't he here yet?

Maybe there's traffic. Late on a Thursday night. Or, maybe he got caught up at the airport for some reason. Maybe he passed a bear on the side of the road and stopped to take photos. The guy *loves* a bear sighting. Especially a mama and her cubs. It would be strange to see a family of bears wandering around at nighttime, but it's not impossible.

Look at me. Conjuring up a whole fictional bear family like I'm freaking Goldilocks to explain why Noah isn't here.

The more plausible explanation is that he saw the signs... and ignored them. After everything I put him through, I guess I wouldn't blame him. He doesn't deserve to be treated the way that I treated him. Shutting him out. Pretending we were just pretending.

What I wouldn't do to take it all back.

This whole sign confession hoopla is the first of many ways that I intend to make it up to him. Show him that I'm fighting for him, and I want him involved in every part of my life. You know, my grand gesture.

Although, given that he arrived by plane, a more traditional, classic gesture would've been for me to show up at the airport and surprise him like Rachel did in *Friends*... Maybe that's what I should've done.

Maybe Noah found his own Seattle-based Julie.

Nope. No spiraling, Dee.

Noah's probably gone straight to his apartment. We've been messaging GIFs to each other since we've been away, but maybe those didn't mean anything for him. Because for me, those GIFs were saying, *I'm thinking of you, I miss you, I wish you were here, I can't wait until you're home.*

I curl up around my Noah body pillow. I've been sitting in this exact spot on my couch for the past hour, waiting for his truck lights to appear. I'm not ready to give up yet. I want to lay all my cards on the table, speak my truth, and show him how much he means to me.

After another fifteen minutes with no truck lights, I stand up. Time to regroup, reassess. Maybe it's not that Noah saw a family of bears, or that his flight was delayed, or that he's given up on us. Perhaps he simply didn't see the signs while he was driving. The grand gesture was perhaps *too* grand.

I return to the couch with a glass of water and lemon. Take the body pillow and circle it around myself like it's a cozy, Noah-scented python. And then, I grab my phone from the coffee table and type out a text.

I've barely sent the message when my front door blasts open on its hinges so powerfully that I think it must be broken.

Suddenly, my living room is packed full of men. The

volleyball boys are standing in my house, completely unannounced, mere moments after I messaged them.

Jarrod collapses onto the couch next to me so heavily that I ricochet in a bounce. "What's up, Dee?"

"We saw your text," Amir says from my kitchen, where he's opening the fridge and my gorgeous new cupboards—because yes, during my time in LA, superhero Noah also replaced my freaking cupboards.

"How'd you guys get here so fast?" I ask, mildly mystified.

Finn and Parker both splay out on the floor in front of my couch, long legs spread in front of them. "We were parked outside in Jarrod's car," Finn replies with a cheeky grin. "Just doing some light stalking."

These are men after my own heart, I tell you.

"So, nothing?" Parker pries. "We never saw Noah pull up, but we figured he might've messaged you."

I shake my head with a frown. "Nope. Maybe he didn't see the signs, guys. Or maybe he saw them and ignored them."

Yes, I involved the volleyball boys in my stupid, cheesy grand gesture for Noah. When I got to work on my plan, I started by asking Pete's Garage about his sign. And Pete being Jarrod's dad, news spread about my idea pretty quickly.

Funny enough, the boys didn't seem *at all* surprised to learn that Noah and I had really fallen for each other during our fake engagement. They also didn't seem shocked to learn that I'm crazy about him and want to show him how much he means to me. The boys were all in, asking other businesses in town if we could take charge of their signs.

My protective detail, it turns out, are more along the lines of romantic softies.

They also told me about some of the conversations

they'd had with Noah. They told me how bothered he was when I started dating and how he wanted to *show* me, through his actions and our (apparently obvious) chemistry, that there was something more than friendship between us. And that I was, in fact, the *her* they were speaking about at the workshop that time.

All of this made shivers run across my entire body. And it made me more motivated than ever to *show* Noah back. To answer all of those questions that he'd asked through the things he'd done for me.

Because I really do feel sparks. I really do love him back. I really do intend to give him all of my heart.

"I doubt he missed them," Jarrod replies. "Have you seen those signs? They're freaking bright."

"Not to mention the guy wouldn't be so stupid as to ignore you saying you love him." Amir's lips twitch. "I mean, he might end up *rejecting* it, but he wouldn't ignore it..."

Finn punches him in the shoulder. "He won't reject it. Or ignore it. We've been waiting for this moment for ages."

"Seriously," Parker mutters. "Took you guys long enough."

I purse my lips. "Guys, I treated Noah so badly at the end there. Made it sound like I wanted to go back to being friends. I *don't* want to be just friends. I don't want to be 'just' anything with him. I want him as my partner, my everything. I want us to be on the same team—"

"You do?"

The low, honeyed, wonderfully familiar voice speaks from the front door, which is still ajar. I emerge out of my Noah python pillow and spring towards him before I can even think about what I'm doing.

I slam into him so hard that he takes a couple steps

backwards. "Woah!" He exhales quickly, like I knocked the wind out of him. "Hey, Dee. Like the pillow, then?"

"Shut up." I say against his chest. "It's a poor man's Noah, that's for sure."

To my immense delight, Noah chuckles. His chest rises and falls against my cheek, and I feel his heartbeat, so firm and steady, beneath my ear. I close my eyes, not wanting to let go.

But Noah grasps the tops of my arms, prying me off him gently. He peers at me, his brown eyes so soft and rich and beautiful, they take my breath away. *He* takes my breath away. I was an idiot for ignoring this for years.

His gaze is curious, guarded. His lips are pursed, like he's trying to work something out. Meanwhile, I have nothing to hide. I let my pure adoration for him show on my face just as clearly as I'm feeling it right now. I probably look as lovestruck as Fran did at the Brookrose with Raymond.

I *hope* I look that lovestruck.

"Uh... we should probably go." Amir's voice is like a distant whisper on the breeze. "Leave you two to it."

The four of them hustle out the door, disappearing into the night like a pack of vandals.

"Come inside?" I ask Noah a little breathlessly. "I have some stuff I want to say."

He nods, that guarded expression still on his face.

We sit on the couch in silence, not touching. I've been full to bursting with all the things that I've wanted to say to him, but now that we're here, I don't know how to start. Instead, I take a moment and drink him in. Notice the five o'clock shadow across his firm jawline and strong chin, the way his eyes crinkle at the sides like he's tired. He smells different, still has the Noah smell, but more... salty or something. Like he carried some of the seabreeze back from Seattle.

"How was Washington?" I ask, my voice almost grating with emotion.

Noah takes a breath in, like my question surprised him. "Good. Sam and Karina were great hosts."

"I bet." I smile. "They're sweet together."

"I heard about RightMatch."

Noah's comment doesn't surprise me. As much as I wanted to share the news with him when it all happened, I held back. I needed to figure out how to stand up on my own. Just as he knew I could.

"I'm sorry, Dee," he says as his eyes scan my face. "I'm sure that's been hard."

My hand itches to reach forward and land on his. The way he's placed his big hands on his thighs, I'm wondering if he has the same urge I do. Not anything romantic, but just because that mindless touch between us has always come so easily.

"I'm okay," I say with a smile, trying to meet his eyes. "Really, I am. Obviously, it's a blow in that I worked on that app from scratch, but it doesn't feel as devastating as I thought it would. As devastating as it would be to lose... you."

Now, Noah meets my eyes. Now, the words are coming quickly.

"I know I already said it in a sign, but I also have to tell you in person. I wish I'd told you that night before I went to LA, because of course it's true. Of course I've always loved you. And I hope it isn't too late. I hope you'll give me one more chance..."

I trail off, unable to say more around the squeeze in my throat. But I press forward.

"I've relied on you so much over the years, Noah. Too

much."

He's shaking his head. "That's what friends and family are for, Dee."

"No, but it *was* too much. To the point that I felt paralyzed at the thought of you even leaving Mirror Valley. Or marrying someone else. I didn't know if I could go on without you, and that's the problem. It made it impossible for me to consider taking a risk because the thought of losing you was way too scary. I let that fear, crippling as it was, cloud what I really wanted and my real feelings for you. And I'm sorry, because I never should've put that on you." I squeeze my eyes shut. "I never tried leaning on myself, and it was because of *you* that I realized that I should. That I *could*. I can't thank you enough for that."

When I open my eyes, Noah's hand is on my knee. I can't remember him putting it there, but it feels just right.

Warm, firm, sturdy.

"I want to be there for you, Dee," Noah says quietly. "I want to support you and be the one you lean on. But you can't keep shutting me out or taking steps backwards."

"I know." I swallow. "And you should know that I told Lachlan the truth."

This is apparently news to Noah. He looks taken aback, and I feel ashamed that he does. I was so short-sighted in trying to save my job. "You did?"

"You were right. I couldn't go on pretending. It was wrong on so many levels, but mostly wrong because it was hurting you, hurting... us." I meet his eyes and am happy to see the light of recognition from the conversation in his truck. "If I'm going to fight for us, I need to fight fair. And that means being honest and telling the truth."

"But do you think that cost you guys RightMatch?"

"I don't know. Probably not, but maybe? It doesn't matter, though. I just knew that I wanted to be true to myself and true to our relationship. Wanted to be true to our future. If we still have one?"

I force myself to keep my eyes on Noah's. My heart is beating so loud, and the ensuing silence is so complete, I can almost hear it echo around the living room. Noah's face gives me nothing. He just stares back, his expression is one of stone—not unlike Lachlan's, actually.

"Look, Dee," Noah says on a long sigh. He takes off his ball cap and tosses his fingers through his hair as he stares at his lap. "I'll be honest with you, it's been tough. There's a difference between giving something a good try, and quitting before you start for fear of losing."

"Well, we all know I'm a sore loser," I quip feebly.

"I'm a sore loser, too." Noah smirks. "Which is why I don't believe we really have anything to be afraid of. I'm always saying I'll do anything for you, Dee, and I will. Well, within reason. I will *not* be going anywhere with seagulls anytime soon." Noah shudders and I blink at him in confusion. "But that being said... I would try this again. So long as you actually want to be all in this time."

"I do," I say immediately.

"Even if things don't work out and we eventually break up."

"I still do." I give a half-smile. "And we won't." Now, I reach out and take his hand. "We're a team. Any problems, we'll work them out together. You and me."

Noah smirks. "Where have I heard that before?"

"I heard it from some old, wise person once."

"He sounds brilliant."

"He's alright."

Noah chuckles and then I don't know who makes the first move, but suddenly his arms are wrapped around me, and mine are locked around him, and we're tangled together on the couch in a mess of limbs.

Goodness. The real thing is so, *so* much better than the body pillow.

"Love you, Dee," Noah whispers against my shoulder.

I hug him even tighter, relishing every point of contact, relishing having him so close to me. "Love you, too. Always have. Always will."

Noah leans up on his elbows to look me in the eyes. Pushes a strand of hair back behind my ear. His gaze travels around my face, resting on my eyes, my lips, my chin. I do my own exploration, my fingers following the trace of his nose, along his sharp cheekbones. I touch the scar next to his eye created by a baseball bat when we were in high school and he had his arms around me, showing me the proper technique, and I accidentally swung a little too hard and hit him in the face.

I press my lips to that scar, just as I know I've always wanted to do, and Noah's lips meet mine next. He kisses me for one long, heart-stopping minute. Everything feels at peace right now. I feel cherished, I feel vulnerable, and I feel open in the best way possible.

And I know so strongly that I'll never, ever take this for granted. I'll never run from this man, or shut him out of my life again.

With him, I have everything. He's my all and could never be my nothing.

6 Months Later

"DEE-AH!!"

The high-pitched, nonsensical squawk is followed by a rush of footsteps and an arm wrapping around my shoulder, knocking me towards Dee.

"Watch it!" I shout, laughing, as I regain a hold on the basket I'm carrying. A basket which is full of precious hot food and drinks.

Daisy giggles, keeping her arms firmly in place on mine and Dee's shoulders. The three of us continue walking like some weird three-legged caterpillar thing, our footfalls kicking up dirt on the trail through the garden.

"That's your couple name, by the way," Daisy sings.

Dee frowns. "Dee-ah?"

"It sounds like a short form of diarrhea," I chime in helpfully.

Dee snorts with laughter and Daisy gives me a tired glare. "That is entirely untrue. But on an unrelated note, have you ever considered changing your name, Noah? You guys would make a cute 'Dee-Vote' or 'Dee-Light'"

"You know, you're right. I *have* thought about changing my name to 'Vote', but 'Light' sounds great too. Light Jackson. Got a nice ring to it, huh?"

"Call yourself 'Light Jackson' and you'll be out a girlfriend," Dee says cheerfully, then purses her lips. "Although, it's a good name for an athlete. Could be a cute nickname for a baby."

Both Daisy and I stop walking and stare at Dee with our mouths open. She stares back at us in confusion, as though *we* were the ones who had just said something completely out of character.

"What? I think about those things sometimes, don't you?" she asks, her cheeks taking on this sweet pink flush that has nothing to do with the cool, fall air. A flash of something resembling mortification steals across her features. "Oh, gosh, I said too much. No pressure obviously, I know we haven't talked about kids and have only technically been dating six months…"

She trails off. I want to drop the basket and kiss her. Kiss that blush right off her face.

"Dais, don't disturb the love bugs." Luke's firm voice is cut with a note of laughter as he catches us on the trail. Daisy drops her arms from our shoulders and skips back to her husband, looping her arm through his. Luke gives her a sweet, all-too-rare smile, the kind that lights up his face. "Where are we going anyway?"

"I don't know," Daisy replies. "Ivy said to meet us by the river out back of the Brookrose."

"I think I know," Dee says, meeting my gaze. I smile back at her, like I don't *actually* know.

After the midnight swim Dee and I took last spring, Ivy and James decided to create a *Secret Garden* style picnic area by the swim spot for locals only. A local secret. They've been working on it all summer and early fall, and today's the big unveiling. Right before winter hits. Which is spectacular timing, but hey, nothing can stop Ivy when she sets her mind to something.

Or at least, that's what she's been telling people.

I shift the weight of the basket, holding it under one arm so I can take Dee's gloved hand in mine. It's been a pretty pleasant fall, but there's a breeze blowing through the Brookrose gardens that sends a wave of sound through the drying leaves. A fresh, crisp smell fills the air, a hint of the snow to come, and I'm looking forward to it. Looking forward to celebrating every season with Dee. We did the pumpkin patch stuff, watched the World Series, and celebrated Thanksgiving together. Next, we'll kiss under the mistletoe, and watch the Superbowl together, have Valentine's Day as a couple, and then enjoy MLB spring training wearing matching jerseys.

I can't wait for any of it. All of it.

We reach the clearing next to the swimming hole and I have to stop walking.

The clearing is transformed. The trees and bushes have been pared back and the weeds have been cleared. There are benches and chairs set up in sunny patches around the perimeter, and at the center of it all is a small paved area with a fountain. And while it might be early winter, it's clear that a ton of flowers and plants will be blooming here come spring.

It really does feel like a serene secret garden, right on the riverbank.

It's hard to believe that, just six months ago, Dee and I were swimming here. That we crossed the line of our friendship when we spoke about wanting to kiss each other. It feels at once like it happened just last night, and also years ago.

Time has gone elastic since I've been with Dee. And

after six blissful, incredible months together, all I want is to do this forever. Be with her, season after season.

"You made it!" Ivy squeals, coming out of nowhere to hug us. James follows moments later, carrying their little girl in one arm.

"Hey, Mags," Dee says sweetly, booping the little girl on the nose so she giggles.

Ivy and James aren't the only ones waiting in the clearing. Hank the security guard is standing by a table piled high with food, and I give him a fist-bump after I set down our basket. The volleyball boys are standing to the side, and they greet Dee very loudly even though we saw them just last night for practice.

A very pregnant Val and Ethan (they're expecting twins, it turns out) are here too, and they walk over to join Dee, Daisy and Luke by the water. Ivy and Luke's grandparents are seated on a bench with James's parents. Even Grumpy Tony is here, along with Mrs. Perez and Mr. Wilhelm, who are still friends despite their disagreements over Shakespeare.

"Hey, bro."

I turn to see my little brother Sam and Karina. Their business has totally taken off, and they flew in a couple days ago from Seattle to spend some time in Mirror Valley before full winter hits.

"How're you feeling?" Sam asks quietly, rocking forward on his toes.

I glance around. "I feel good. Everything's good."

"Alright. Well, I got you." He gives me a wink, and then he and Karina head off towards the food.

"Hello!" a booming, familiar voice cheers at the entry of the clearing. "So good to see you!"

Fran and Raymond are making their entrance, hands clasped together so their matching wedding rings shine in the sunlight. The two tied the knot last month after a whirl-wind engagement, and they'll be leaving on their honeymoon soon.

I walk over to greet them with a smile, extending a hand for a shake. "You two excited for the cruise?"

"Absolutely." Fran smiles wide. "Bahamas, here we come. Ray thinks that thirteen bathing suits is too many. What do you think, Noah?"

"My love, I didn't say 'too many', I would never say 'too many,'" Raymond replies. "I simply said that the cruise will be air conditioned, so bring a sweater or two."

"I don't know where you'll be, my dear, but I plan to spend most of my time by the pool."

"I'll be wherever you are."

The two share a kiss and I couldn't be happier for them. They still act like a pair of teenagers, even all these months later.

"Speaking of which…" Raymond turns to me. "How're you feeling, son? Any last minute questions about running the shop while I'm gone?"

I shake my head. "None at all. Don't worry about it for a minute."

"I'm leaving the shop in good hands, I know that." He lets out a laugh. "You're basically running it yourself now anyway."

"And doing a fantastic job," Fran adds. "Thanks again for taking on more of the business side of things so that Raymond could semi-retire. You've given us more time to spend together."

I duck my head with gratitude. Raymond announced that he was semi-retiring during the summer and asked if I would be interested in stepping up a little more. I immediately said yes. I've never felt so sure in my life that carpentry is exactly what I was meant to do, and being more involved with the business has been an unexpected pleasure.

Not to mention, I know how anxious Raymond was feeling about the future of the shop. He doesn't have children of his own to take over the business, and has been more than happy to teach me everything he knows. I've loved working with him and learning from him.

He's even gone and changed the name of the shop from "Ray's" to "Ray's and Noah's".

And yes, I did invest in an LED changeable-letter sign with that same name on it.

As Fran and Ray walk off, I turn back towards the river where my incredible girlfriend is standing with Ivy and Daisy, cooing over baby Maggie. Dee has never really been one for kids, but she and Mags have developed a surprising bond. Maybe because, at eighteen months old, Mags is already showing her smarts.

Dee *would* bond with a baby genius.

Dee spots me and smiles. I walk over to her, reaching for her hand. "Come with me?"

She nods, letting me lead her to the edge of the water.

"Remember what happened here?" I ask.

"Which time?" Dee chuckles. "There were all those times that I beat you running."

"Woah, woah, woah. You beat me *twice*."

"Three times if you count the time that I found this place."

I roll my eyes. "In your dreams, honeypants."

Dee knocks her side gently into mine. My arm is around her shoulder, and I love the way her body feels pressed up against me. Like two pieces of Lego fit perfectly together.

"I think the best time was the time you said you wanted to kiss me." Dee stares at the surface of the water, looking at me in the rippling reflection.

I see the beaming smile break across my own face. "That was my favorite time, too."

Dee looks away from the water now, turning to face me and looping her arms behind my neck. Her eyes pore into mine, searching, loving, promising something eternal. "These past six months have been incredible, Noah. I keep falling more and more in love with you. It doesn't even feel real."

Her words send my blood racing. I clasp my hands at the small of her back, wondering if she can sense how nervous I am. No, not nervous... I'm full of anticipation. "You're right." I shake my head. "It doesn't feel real. I've wanted this for so long that sometimes I'm afraid it'll all disappear. But I know it won't."

"It won't." Dee shakes her head firmly. "I'm all in with you, Noah. I feel even more sure now than I did the day I made that promise. Our life together is what I want."

This is it. "I'm so glad to hear you say that because..."

I turn to where Sam and Karina are lingering nearby, keeping a not-so-subtle eye on us. I motion for Sam to step forward, and he does, presenting a little black box. When I turn back to Dee, she's frowning like she's confused, and her expression makes me want to laugh. Even more so when her face suddenly drops with realization.

A pink flush rises from her chest, up her neck, to her cheeks. "Oh my..."

I get down on one knee, reciting the words I've been practicing for weeks. But they don't feel memorized. They feel real. "Dee Griffiths, I am totally in love with you. Will you do me the honor of being my wife—"

A gasp.

"—to have and to hold, forever and always—"

A squeak.

"—during which time I will do everything in my power

to make you feel as happy, loved and cared for as you've made me feel every single day that we've been together?"

Dee's mouth is wide open. Which is good, because I'm not done.

"We've been everything to each other. You're my oldest and best friend, my confidante, my partner, my teammate, my crush. You're the one I want to do life with—the highs, the lows, the best of times and the worst. I've never been able to imagine my life without you, and now, I don't want to. You're my soulmate..." A small smile touches my lips. "And now, I want you to be my real fiancée."

My heart is slamming against my ribcage in uneven beats. Dee's eyes are wide and shining, her face at once red and white, and her lips are twitching, twisted in a smile. She looks divine.

It only takes a moment before she drops down to her knees, just like I did at the carpentry shop all those months ago during her fake proposal.

"YES!!" she screeches and throws herself forward, arms looping around me as she glues herself to me in that unique barnacle-Dee way that I absolutely love.

Unfortunately, I'm not on super stable ground and I lose my balance...

Topple sideways...

I barely manage to throw the ring back onto the riverbank before Dee and I tumble into the water.

But when I go under, I'm not thinking about how cold the water is, or the fact that I'm now soaking wet. All I can think, all I can feel, is... *she said yes!*

I break the surface, laughing, and hear Dee's laughs too. I reach for her waist beneath the water, and she grasps for my shoulders, pulling herself to me. My lips meet her cold ones and she tastes like a dream. Like the Dee I've known and loved my entire life.

It takes a second to register that everyone has come to the riverbank and they're cheering for us. Dee and I come out of the river, holding hands and shivering, and Ivy—over-prepared as ever—hands us the brown snuggie and a blanket. I look at Ivy questioningly and she shrugs. "Figured I'd bring them, just in case."

I want to hug her, but also don't think she'd appreciate having a freezing cold man wrapped around her.

I give Dee the snuggie and keep the blanket for myself. Dee slides it on, looking like the cutest little wet burrito I've ever seen.

Congratulations ring out as all of the people Dee and I know and love group around us. When we reach Sam and Karina, Sam gives me the little black box again—he rescued it from the riverbank—and Dee removes the silver trinket ring so that I can finally place the real thing onto her finger. It's a gorgeous, sparkling diamond, one that I envisioned giving to her during our fake engagement.

When we get to Daisy and Luke, Daisy sweeps us into a long hug. "Congrats, you two," she says tearfully. And then, she punches me in the shoulder. "I didn't know you were doing this *today*!"

I smile at her. "I wanted it to be a surprise. Only Ivy knew the truth so we could get everyone here under the guise of the secret garden unveiling, and I swore her to secrecy. I know you love a surprise too, Dais."

"I do," she says, swiping a tear away.

Luke smiles a big, beaming smile that kind of takes me by surprise. No less because it looks so natural on him. Is it just me, or is he a little flushed? "Any chance you might need a flower girl for your wedding?"

Daisy elbows him in the stomach. Hard.

Dee and I both frown. "What?"

Now, Luke looks sheepish. "I take it back. Ignore me."

336

Daisy's face has gone beet red and Dee is staring at her, eyes wide and unblinking. "Dais...?"

I glance between Luke and Daisy, who both look more than a little shifty. "What's going on?"

Then, Daisy blows out a breath and her voice drops to a whisper as she grasps Dee's forearms. "I'm pregnant! We got a call from the doctor this morning!"

Dee jumps forward, throwing her arms around her older sister. "I'm so happy for you!"

"I'm so happy for *you*!"

Luke and I share a glance. We've got our hands full with these two, but I couldn't imagine anything better, honestly. I shake his hand, then draw him in for a quick hug. "Congrats, man."

"You, too."

Eventually, things in the garden calm down. Someone lights a fire in the small firepit nearby, the food gets laid out, and people take seats around the clearing. Soon, the smell of hot food and campfire smoke fills the air. I sit on one of the vacant benches, and Dee takes her spot on my lap. My arms clasp around her waist and we sit silently, basking in the happy sounds of laughter and conversation, the feeling of being surrounded by people we love.

"Well, fiancée, what did you think?" I finally ask in a low voice.

"It was perfect. I'd rate this proposal an 11/10. Better than mine for sure."

"Don't sell yourself short. Yours was pretty romantic."

"I attacked you afterwards and we fell into a pile of wood shavings."

"If that isn't romcom material, I don't know what it is."

She holds me tighter. I kiss her shoulder.

"Excited to see Lachlan again?" I ask quietly, monitoring Dee's face.

True to her word, Dee took the last few months off work. She took classes online, read *a ton* of books, worked with me to start renovations on her bungalow (it looks incredible, if I do say so myself, has that "cozy modern-ish" aspect that Dee was craving), tried new hobbies, and just generally shifted herself out of that panic mindset she used to have.

At the end of it all, she discovered that she really *does* love coding. She loves being a developer and building something from scratch. Which I can relate to.

Dee contemplated starting her own app, but she realized that she didn't particularly like management and had no interest in running a business. She looked at different companies, considered a few offers...

But then, Lachlan reached out about a new app his company was interested in developing. The two parted on good terms after his whole "I'm from Mirror Valley" revelation, but what surprised Dee was that she was actually... interested. The app concept sounded like a fun challenge. And Dee felt there was already an established trust between them (I mean, they made pacts not to lie). He has full faith and belief in her, and she trusts the way he works.

Dee took a month to consider his offer. Called him whenever she had any questions or concerns, and he answered every one with confidence. Or at least with a reassurance that they would figure things out together. And so, Dee said yes. Lachlan's flying to Mirror Valley tomorrow to give her a debrief on what to expect, and this time, he promised, he wouldn't keep his identity hidden.

But now, she's pressing her lips together and looking at me like she's really thinking through my question. And then, she smiles. "I really am. I think we'll keep each other honest. Might even be friends."

I laugh at that, and Dee shakes her head.

"Seriously, I could never go through all that ever again. Having you pretend to be my fiancé? What was I thinking?"

"It wasn't all bad." I kiss her shoulder again. "I could get away with a lot more, really sweep you off your feet."

"What on earth is Lachlan going to say when he finds out that we're engaged... again. For real, this time."

"We'll tell him you're my real fake fiancée."

She lets out a laugh, shaking her head. "Let's go with that." Dee presses her forehead to mine. I tighten my grip around her waist. "Love you, Noah, forever and always."

"Love you, too."

With our foreheads joined, our limbs tangled together, and surrounded by our favorite people, my body's buzzing with the anticipation of starting our life together. Me and Dee and everyone we love most in the world. Because that's what life's about, right?

And that's what life's like in Mirror Valley. It's just a small town in the middle of the mountains with the most ridiculous people, absurd sign wars, delicious baked potatoes, a well-meaning town council, a gorgeous alpine inn, and the best people you could ever meet.

Thank you so much for reading!

If you enjoyed this book, please leave me a review. As a new author, reviews mean everything to me. I appreciate each and every one of them.

THANK YOU FROM SJ!

Ohmygoodness, y'all.

Here we are, at the end of Love in Mirror Valley... And all I want to do is say THANK YOU!!

Thank you for picking up a copy of Dee and Noah's story. Thank you for joining me on this adventure featuring a fake engagement between best friends.

Dee and Noah's story is simultaneously one of the hardest books I've written and one of the most meaningful. I put a lot of myself into these two characters, and several characters you see here are based on real people/cats that I know.

If you've read the other Mirror Valley books, you are the real MVP and thank you for joining me along the way. I hope Dee and Noah's story bookended the series for you and were everything you dreamed of! I can't thank you enough for sticking with me <3

To my incredible, wonderful ARC readers, I couldn't do this without you! A few of you have been with me from the beginning and you make this author journey so rewarding. I value each and every one of you so much. Your feedback and encouragement make me stronger as a writer and make me want to create better and better stories for you. Thank you for picking up an early copy <3

Finally, I have to say thank you to KB for being my biggest cheerleader and supporter. You rock, and I've LOVED seeing this through with you. Thanks as always for being such a guiding light and shining star when I'm spiralling hahah.

Finally, if you have ANYTHING you'd like to say—thoughts, concerns, questions, whatever—I would love to hear it. My inbox can be quite boring sometimes so getting messages from readers (no matter the content) is honestly a highlight haha!

Now, I'm off to craft the next series (two guesses who it'll feature from this book), do some happy dancing, and gorge myself on candy corn.

Sending all the love your way.

Sara Jane

ALSO BY SARA JANE WOODLEY

Brighton Brothers

The Lying Game

Love in Mirror Valley

The Last Chance Road Trip - *prequel novella*

The Next Worst Thing

The Right Wrong Match

The Real Fake Fiancé

Aston Falls (sweet contemporary romance)

More Than Second Chances

More Than Just Friends

More Than Meets the Eye

Legacy Inn (sweet YA romance)

The Summer I Fell for My Best Friend

The Summer I Fell for My Fake Boyfriend

The Summer I Fell for a Billionaire

The Summer I Fell for My Enemy

Printed in Great Britain
by Amazon